THE
PR

D0000754

THE ANTHRAX PROTOCOL

JAMES THOMPSON

PINNACLE BOOKS
Kensington Publishing Corp.
www.kensingtonbooks.com

To my soul mate of thirty-three years.
The bravest, most courageous person I know,

Terri Ann Thompson.

PINNACLE BOOKS are published by

Kensington Publishing Corp.
119 West 40th Street
New York, NY 10018

All Kensington titles, imprints, and distributed lines are available at special quantity discounts for bulk purchases for sales promotions, premiums, fund-raising, educational, or institutional use. Special book excerpts or customized printings can also be created to fit specific needs. For details, write or phone the office of the Kensington sales manager: Kensington Publishing Corp., 119 West 40th Street, New York, NY 10018, attn: Sales Department; phone 1-800-221-2647.

This book is a work of fiction. Names, characters, businesses, organizations, places, events, and incidents either are the product of the author's imagination or are used fictitiously. Any resemblance to actual persons, living or dead, events, or locales is entirely coincidental.

PINNACLE BOOKS and the Pinnacle logo are Reg. U.S. Pat. & TM Off.

ISBN-13: 978-0-7860-3730-8
ISBN-10: 0-7860-3730-X

First printing: March 2016

10 9 8 7 6 5 4 3 2 1

Printed in the United States of America

First electronic edition: March 2016

ISBN-13: 978-0-7860-3731-5
ISBN-10: 0-7860-3731-8

Prologue

Tlateloco, Mexico, July 5, 1520

Bernal Díaz del Castillo stumbles over some unseen object and falls. He lands on his hands and knees, his face mere inches from the pustule-covered body of one of his soldiers. "Aiyeee," he cries, pushing the ghastly corpse away, scrambling over dusty soil to escape the stench of putrefying flesh.

The effort causes him to begin to cough again. He crawls on hands and knees in the dirt. A boiling tropical sun bakes his back while he coughs and retches, vomiting blood until he collapses, exhausted.

Scarlet tears, tinged with blood, fill his eyes and run down his cheeks, forming slender rivulets until they begin to clot in his coarse beard. Raising his head, he peers across a clearing surrounding the temple. The place is littered with bodies, lying where they fell. Indian workers lying next to and, in some cases, upon his soldiers like rotting flotsam on a grassy sea of heat, humidity, and death.

He rolls over on his back, momentarily blinded by the sun, and shakes his fist at a muggy blue sky. Muttering incoherently, he curses God for allowing this plague to decimate their command.

As he squeezes his eyes shut to block out a fiery furnace from above, his thoughts return to the preceding week when the terrible sickness began.

Hernán Cortés, supreme commander of Spanish forces in Mexico, had badly miscalculated the gentle nature of natives here. Upon their arrival in Tenochtitlan, the Aztec capital city, Chief Montezuma welcomed them, believing them to be representatives of his pagan god, Quetzalcoatl. Hernán, too arrogant to use guile, took the Aztec chief prisoner. He thought to use Montezuma as a hostage to ensure the Indians' good behavior. Hernán was supremely confident in his military judgment, and he ignored his lieutenants' suggestions to go easy on the natives.

For a time it looked as if he was correct. Initially, the Indians were docile, almost friendly. Then his overconfidence betrayed him. Hernán left on a tour of surrounding villages looking for more gold and jewels to send back to Spain as proof of their expedition's success. When he returned, thousands of Aztec tribesmen, stirred into action by shouting priests, accosted his soldiers and began rioting.

Hernán and Bernal had gone to Montezuma's cell, finding him seriously ill. He was being guarded in a small stone room with a few of his favorite pets. When Hernán arrived, he found the chief slumped in a corner, near death. Montezuma could only be revived by pouring cold water on him, which also served to wash dried blood off his face and robes.

Again seeking to intimidate the Indians, Hernán dragged a chained, weakened Montezuma to a stone platform in front of the largest temple overlooking the city. He had one of the missionaries who had taken time to learn the Aztec language, Father Bernardino Sahagún, explain that he would have their chieftain killed if they did not disperse at once.

His threat, and Montezuma's obvious illness, infuriated the Aztecs even more. They responded by hurling stones and pieces of wood at soldiers on the platform, wounding Chief Montezuma severely in the process when misguided rocks went astray. Everyplace on the chief's body where he was struck by stones and sticks began to bleed copiously, inciting the villagers even further into a furor bordering on madness.

Finally, with the crowd out of control, Hernán withdrew, taking Montezuma back to his cell. The Indian leader looked as if he might not survive the night. He had a raging fever and blood was seeping from his eyes, nose, and mouth. He was coughing and vomiting blood and had dark, purple bruises on his skin. Hernán summoned Bernal and a squad of soldiers, instructing them to take the Aztec chieftain and his shrieking pet monkeys to a neighboring city, Tlateloco, and if Montezuma died, to have his corpse and his monkeys prepared for burial in the traditional Aztec way. He pulled Bernal aside and ordered him to entomb the emperor and his pets where none of his followers would find the bodies. Hernán knew he would be unable to control a full-scale revolt if the Indians discovered their leader was dead. He was already making plans to try to bribe the priests to convince the natives to follow his orders and to bring him more gold and jewels as an offering to the new gods from Spain.

* * *

Díaz struggles back to his hands and knees, thinking, Hernán has sentenced me to die in this pit of hell. He has gone back to Spain with boatloads of riches for the king, leaving the rest of us to perish from this hellish pestilence.

Too weak now to stand, he crawls a circuitous route, weaving among bodies rotting slowly in the tropical heat, toward the temple at the edge of the clearing. Sweat runs from his pores and drips on barren ground beneath him, even as fever chills cause him to shake and quiver in the jungle's oppressive humidity. He must find shade, a cool place of refuge to await his inevitable death.

His journey seems to take hours, although it is only a distance of forty yards. Finally, his strength waning, he manages to push aside a reeking corpse blocking the entrance to Montezuma's tomb and crawls into a tunnel carved through heavy blocks of stone. Laboriously, overwhelmed by increasing pains in his chest, he makes his way deeper into the shadows. The air grows noticeably cooler as he enters the shaft.

At the end of the passageway, when he reaches the entrance into the inner burial chamber, he stops and sits with his back propped against the rocks. He takes a journal from his waistband and rests, panting, with the diary in his lap. For a moment he wonders if he has time to complete his writings before death claims him as it has all the others.

The leather covering of the journal shakes and becomes slick with sweat from his trembling hands. Cooler air in the tunnel has exacerbated his chills and he spasms and quivers, muscles jerking in a continuous ague.

Leaning to one side, he empties his stomach in a gout of blood, scarlet liquid appearing black in the darkness.

He chokes and begins to cough again, knifelike pain coursing through his lungs, making him dizzy.

After a moment the spasm passes and he is able to withdraw a sharpened piece of charcoal from his trousers to begin what he knows will be his final entries. He gave up on quill and ink two days earlier when constant tremors made his writing all but indecipherable.

As he opens his journal, he rests his head against the cool stones of the tunnel, letting them take the fever from his body.

He wonders how he, Hernán Cortés's scribe, can be so cursed by God. He always says his prayers and gives his tithe to Mother Church—he doesn't deserve to end his life in this miserable, stinking jungle.

Another sudden, hacking cough brings him upright and bends him over, pain exploding in his head and blinding him momentarily. He knows with certainty his time is very short. He must finish this final duty to his commander. A warning of the terrible curse Montezuma and his heathen gods have cast upon this place must be given to the others who will return from Spain. With a mighty effort, he wills his arm to obey him and he begins to write:

> *They are all dead. I am the last left alive.*
> *Hundreds of bodies lie where they fell, covered with*
> *sores, the hungry earth drinking their blood. At the*
> *end, they were too sick and weak to bury others,*
> *dying in agony from the plague our intervention has*
> *wrought.*
> *The illness we first observed in Emperor*
> *Montezuma has now claimed every life in this village.*
> *It begins as a simple cough, with fever and chills.*
> *After a day or two it somehow passes, and the victim*

*is thought to have recovered. This Black Plague
seems to wait in the body to reappear, gathering or
rebuilding its evil strength for a final assault to bring
death to the sufferer. The illness returns rapidly.
Victims become fevered and weak and begin to cough
up blood. Even the mouth and eyes bleed until the
sick are too weak to move, and they die in an agony
too terrible to contemplate.*

*There is no one left here alive, no one. Even the
animals are not spared, but are also succumbing to
the curse. Our horses are dying as we are, bleeding
through their muzzles until they grow too weak to
carry us.*

As he writes, Díaz's nose and eyes begin to drip blood on the parchment pages of his journal, partially obscuring some of his words. He is too ill to care. He glances down the tunnel leading to the inner tomb. At least, he thinks, the workers had managed to seal off the grave before they became too weakened by illness to move heavy stones blocking the entrance. He writes, again with a trembling hand:

*Montezuma was correct in his prophecy. He
foretold that all who desecrated the honor and
sacred places of the Aztecs would face the wrath
of his gods and die in horrible pain.*

Díaz looks up from his writing. A large jaguar is dragging a villager's body into the jungle, while a smaller animal, a panther, is eating another corpse where it lies. Soon there will be little evidence this plague ever existed.

He grows dizzy for a moment, darkness invading his vision, pulling him into unconsciousness. When he awakens, blood has caked on his eyelids and he must pry them open with his fingers, causing fresh tears to flow.

He knows his time is at hand and manages to scribble a few last words:

> *Montezuma has had his vengeance. Heed this warning and leave this land of strange gods to the jungle, lest all who come here are doomed. . . .*

The charcoal falls from his fingers as his muscles contract and his back arches. With a mighty spasm, he coughs out his life onto the dusty floor of the tunnel.

The ground begins to tremble. Trees sway back and forth, while jungle animals screech and howl across a tropical forest. Dead bodies in the clearing move as if they had been resurrected for one last mad dance. A small earthquake ripples through the region. In a final frenzy of geologic activity, as if nature is not yet through with Cortés and his Spanish soldiers, the earth heaves and tilts. Large cracks appear in the ground, swallowing corpses the scavengers have not yet carried off, a quake filling the air with dust-like smoke from hell's fires.

Blocks of stone in the small temple collapse, tumbling down to cover the lifeless body of Bernal Díaz del Castillo and seal the tunnel leading to the emperor's tomb.

It will not see the light of day again for almost five hundred years.

Chapter 1

Tlateloco, 2014

Charles Adams groaned, his patrician features drawn into a grimace, his teeth bared against pain, as he squinted into a boiling tropical sun. His wavy, silver hair lay plastered against his skull; his safari shirt was wrinkled, stained with blood and vomit, clinging to him like a second skin.

Adams clutched his chest, doubling over as pain blazed between his shoulder blades like a hot knife. A cough started deep in his thorax and exploded from his mouth, wracking his body with spasms. Blood, mucus, and bits of lung tissue sprayed onto the cracked leather cover of an ancient journal lying in his lap.

His colleagues and all his associates were dead. Some were lying in a tunnel leading to a deep inner chamber beneath the ancient Aztec village known as Tlateloco, struck down where they stood by a mysterious illness. Others died more slowly, suffering in makeshift tent hospitals his staff erected or in campsites near the dig. Many died so suddenly there hadn't been time to summon medical help, literally bleeding to death in a matter of hours— hemorrhaging through their noses and mouths and ears, bleeding internally, dying so quickly they rarely uttered a coherent word before a vacant stare dulled their eyes.

A number were graduate students whose young lives had just begun, an elite group of the best candidates in the University of Texas's archaeological doctoral program. And now they were dead, all dead, and he knew in a short while he would join them.

Sweat poured off his face, soaking his khaki shirt as he was shaken by an almost continuous chill, his teeth chattering and muscles twitching beyond his control. He leaned back against the cool, rough stones of the tomb and shut red-rimmed, bloodshot eyes. He knew he was dying and there was nothing he could do to stop it.

Strangely, thoughts of his death did not terrify him as they once would have. In spite of his physical agony he felt an inner peace, an almost mystical rightness about his dying here in this place where the body of the chief of the Aztecs lay.

He chuckled around a wrenching, hacking cough. It was true, he thought. Nothing focuses the mind like the knowledge of imminent death.

He used his sweat-drenched sleeve to wipe blood and gore off the journal and opened it with weakened, trembling hands.

It was all here in the diary, he thought, resting against a tunnel wall near the outer door to the tomb. Warnings had been given, yet he and the others ignored them in their haste to solve an historical mystery. It read like sixteenth-century superstition, those writings by Díaz. Rambling notes in archaic Spanish about ancient curses and what Díaz called the Black Plague. Cortés's men and the Aztecs were dying from unknown causes, their skin turning black as they bled out, choking on their own blood. A curse, Díaz wrote, cast by Aztec gods who were angry over the looting by Hernán Cortés and by his disrespectful treatment of Emperor Montezuma.

But that was in the year 1521, when no one understood infectious diseases or how germs were spread. It would have been nonsense to heed some vague warning written more than four centuries ago and overlook the possibility of making a discovery like this, the burial chamber of fabled Aztec Chief Montezuma—a tomb that was filled with priceless artifacts and implements and perhaps much more that could reveal so many of the Aztecs' undecipherable secrets.

Now, as Dr. Charles Adams lay dying at the door of a cleared passageway into Montezuma's tomb, he knew he should have heeded Díaz's warning. Some ancient disease, some fungus or a germ of unknown origin, had lain dormant in this burial chamber for hundreds of years only to awaken and kill all of the interlopers to this sacred tomb.

He chuckled again, delirious, thinking an ancient curse could not have been more deadly than whatever hellish disease had felled him and his students.

Adams's head lolled to the side, peering in the semidarkness down a long passage to the dig outside the emperor's tomb. Through an opening in the tunnel, he could see several of his friends' and colleagues' bodies lying where they fell, baking in a blistering tropical sun. A small jungle cat of some sort was pulling on a bloated corpse's leg, attempting to drag the body into the forest where it could be consumed in safety.

He glanced down at Díaz's tattered diary, remarkably

preserved in its leather bindings, protected from time and the elements in a sealed tunnel. An incredible find in itself, a record of Cortés's expedition to the New World and its first contacts with the Aztec Empire. Scribbled notations near the end of his diary had seemed out of character for a meticulous chronicler like Díaz was known to be.

His rambling, almost senseless descriptions of curses and Black Death and his repeated warnings not to enter Montezuma's tomb almost read like the ravings of a madman. Then the written record ended suddenly, a few final pages spattered with faded bloodstains. Too late, Adams now believed he understood the significance of the blood. He glanced down and saw similar blood spatter on his trousers and shirt.

Too late, he realized he had solved not only the mystery of Díaz's death but also the mystery of what had caused the Aztec civilization to vanish completely without a trace.

He shook his head, trying to clear it of a fog creeping into his vision, numbing his mind, making him incoherent. Another cough coursed through his lungs, digging its razor-like claws into his brain. He blacked out for a moment, his vision narrowing to a fine point of light surrounded by darkness.

When he awakened, skies were darkening outside. Tropical dusk was rapidly descending, elongating shadows and blurring most details of the forest. Adams knew with a certainty chilling him to the bone that he would never see the dawn. His halogen work light grew dim. He followed its beam with his eyes into the chamber, to Montezuma's mummified corpse reposed on a stone slab.

The mummy was flanked by the bodies of two monkeys, decayed flesh pulling away from flinty white bone, curled in fetal positions. One wore a jeweled collar, a wrinkled deerskin band decorated with rows of emeralds and bits of hammered gold. The other monkey's collar was missing—it had been around the shriveled creature's neck when Adams first opened the tomb. A local workman had surely stolen it before everyone started to get sick.

In the beginning, team members entering the tomb experienced flu-like symptoms and a quick recovery lasting two or three days. Then the bleeding began—and later, sudden agonizing death.

He knew his mind was wandering, damaged by the unknown illness coursing through his bloodstream, yet he couldn't take his gaze from Montezuma's corpse. Perhaps the best-known Mexican ruler in the West, he lay mummified inside a twenty-foot chamber a few yards away, his final resting place a mystery until almost a week ago.

At the young emperor's feet were clay urns and tablets and ornaments so valuable to the field of archaeology they were literally priceless—a find that would make worldwide news. But with the unearthing of Chief Montezuma's mummy, another event loomed larger than the discovery's contribution to the study of archaeology or the baffling mysteries of ancient Aztec civilization. Some dark force had been released . . . Díaz called it a curse, a Black Death so potent it survived five hundred years to awaken and strike everyone at the dig site.

Some form of disease had surfaced by the simple removal of a huge stone blocking the entrance to Montezuma's tomb. In a daze, not quite lucid, Adams now blamed himself for the deaths.

He forced his mind to concentrate, knowing what he had

to do. No one without extensive experience in medicine would understand the gravity of what happened here. Medical specialists were needed immediately and Dr. Lauren Sullivan, his associate and trusted colleague at the University of Texas, would know what to do . . . who to call, where to begin.

He coughed and spat blood. With a supreme effort he pulled the cell phone out of a scabbard on his belt and hit the auto-dial button. Maybe by now the damned Mexican phone company would have a cell available and his call to the United States could go through . . .

He felt his lungs burn and sleeved more blood from his upper lip. "Please answer," he croaked in a phlegmy voice thickened by blood as a series of electronic beeps initiated his telephone call across a continent.

He heard a ring and was silently thankful a connection had finally been made. Coughing again, he almost lost consciousness when a wave of dizziness swept through him. A third ring, then a fourth, without an answer. "Damn it," he said in a hoarse whisper. "Answer the phone, Lauren."

On the sixth ring a sleepy voice said, "Hello."

"Charles," he gasped, blinking furiously, trying to clear a tangled maze of cobwebs from his vision. "Trouble. Big trouble. Listen very closely. What I'm about to tell you will sound ludicrous. Insane. Just please listen to me."

"Dr. Adams . . . Charlie? What's wrong?"

He cleared his throat. "I'm dying. Everyone at the site is dead. There's a sickness of some kind. We got sick as soon as we opened the tomb . . . right afterward. It was like the flu. Then it went away. A few days later everyone started bleeding from the nose and mouth. Within hours they were dying. Robert and Bonnie and Kelly died first.

I sent someone for a doctor, but Jules died behind the wheel of our Jeep before he could reach help. A farmer found him slumped behind the wheel with blood all over his body. I can't understand it. We tested for gases and cinnabar the way we always do. Everything was okay. The farmer who found Jules is also dead."

He retched violently, gritting his teeth against pain so intense it almost rendered him unconscious. Again, he focused his thoughts on warning her of the danger. "You must contact the Mexican authorities. Call Professor Eduardo Matos at INAH. He's an old friend. Tell him what's happened. Warn him not to enter the tomb. Don't come here. Don't let anyone else disturb this place."

He took a ragged breath, air whistling into his lungs. "Everything must be burned . . . destroyed completely . . ."

Lauren's voice was suddenly clear of sleepiness. "Charlie, you're not making any sense. What are you talking about?"

"There isn't time." Charles choked, fighting back another spasm of coughing. "It's in journal translation I sent you." He was interrupted by another bout of coughing and vomiting. "Read it . . . but don't come here! Promise me . . ."

"Okay, Charlie, I promise. Just tell me what's happening!" Adams could hear Lauren's voice rising in panic.

"Hang up. Make that call. It's too late for me . . . for all of us." He put a shaky finger on the End button, his head falling back against the stones. His fingers relaxed on the telephone. It fell to the floor of the tunnel.

"Charles!" Lauren screamed into the phone, "Charles, are you there?" There was no answer, only the static of the long-distance carrier signal.

Austin, Texas

Lauren's chest was heaving and she felt sick. She knew in her heart her friend was dying, or worse, perhaps he was already dead.

The thought caused her to rush into the bathroom to splash water on her face. She remained there, looking at herself in the mirror with tears coursing down her cheeks.

Shaking her head, she threw off her nightgown and stepped into the shower. "Enough feeling sorry for yourself, Lauren," she muttered sleepily. "Get in the shower, get your head clear, and then get on the telephone." She knew if there was any possibility some of the students and faculty were alive, she must act quickly. She took a fast shower, the water as cold as she could stand it. While toweling her hair dry she hurried to her bedroom phone.

She sat on the side of her bed and switched on a table lamp. After digging in the drawer of her nightstand for a few moments, she found a registry of members of the International Archaeological Society. Thumbing through the pages, she located Dr. Eduardo Matos's name and home phone number.

She glanced at the clock, almost midnight. Too tired to calculate the difference in time between Austin and Mexico City, she realized it didn't matter. This was no time to worry about waking someone up. She dialed as fast as her finger could move.

A deep masculine voice answered, speaking in rapid Spanish through faint static on the line, *"Hola, soy Dr. Matos."*

"Hello, Dr. Matos. This is Lauren Sullivan from the University of Texas . . . Dr. Charles Adams's associate."

Matos switched to clear, unaccented English. "Of course,

Dr. Sullivan. I remember you from the international conference last year. How are you?"

Lauren took a moment to arrange her thoughts. She needed to present her story in a logical manner. "Professor . . ."

Matos interrupted her. "Please, call me Eduardo. There is no need for such formality among friends."

"Thank you. Tonight I received an emergency call from Dr. Adams."

"Charles? But I thought he was at the dig site at Tlateloco."

"He is. He called me on his cell phone. He said his entire team was dead and that he was dying." Her voice broke as she remembered what Charlie told her over the phone. As best she could she recited symptoms of the illness he described and that now every other member of Charlie's student excavation team was no longer alive.

"Dios mío!" Matos cried, reverting for a moment into his native language.

As her eyes filled, Lauren struggled to keep from sobbing as she spoke. "Charles said it was some illness, something from the tomb they were excavating and that it had killed all his students and workers. He called it a plague."

"What kind of plague?"

"He didn't say . . . I don't think he knew." Her voice tightened again, and she was on the verge of losing control. "He told me the entire site should be quarantined until someone can identify what the illness is, and no one should come there. He was afraid the disease would spread if the site were disturbed." She hesitated, "He also said the entire place should be burned."

"Did he say anything else? Did he give any further details of the symptoms?"

"No, he was very ill. He was coughing almost continually, although I could hear him saying something about bleeding, that everyone was bleeding."

Matos said, "Lauren, try to calm down. I know you and Charles are close, but we must proceed very carefully. This can be a delicate situation." He paused a moment, static crackling over a weak phone connection. After a few seconds, he spoke again. "The disease must act quickly. Charles has only been in Tlateloco a little over three weeks."

"Professor, what should I do? I've got to try to help them. In spite of what Charles said, some of the students may still be alive. He wasn't thinking clearly."

"Let me think." A moment later he said, "The problem is our medical facilities here in Mexico are still somewhat primitive, especially in regards to infectious diseases. Thankfully, the site, though close to Mexico City, is relatively isolated, accessible only by primitive jungle paths. It is unlikely to be visited by anyone not directly involved in the excavation . . . unless grave robbers discover it."

"Do you think we could get some doctors from the States to fly in and . . . ?"

Matos interrupted, "We are in a precarious political situation. Our government here is very proud, and more than a little resentful about incursions into our territory by the so-called colossus to the north."

His next words were drowned out by a burst of static and crackling as a solar flare disrupted transmission.

Lauren said, "Excuse me, Eduardo, could you repeat that? I didn't hear you."

"I said, even getting Charles permission to excavate the tomb took months of delicate negotiations at very high levels." He was silent a moment, then he added, "However, there may be a way. Let me make some calls and I'll get back to you." His voice changed and became more forceful. "Until then, Lauren, you must promise me not to tell anyone else of this! No one, do you understand me?"

"No, Eduardo, I don't. We must get help to Dr. Adams as soon as possible."

Once again his voice became soft, reassuring. "That is what I am going to do, Lauren, but you must allow me to do it my way. All right?"

Lauren sighed, tears running down her cheeks. "Okay, Eduardo. Just please call me back as soon as you can."

"I will, Lauren. Just be patient and I will take care of everything."

Mexico City

Matos sat staring at the phone in his hand for a moment, cursing under his breath. He knew this could be a dangerous catastrophe, not only for the country, but more importantly for him personally. He was the one who'd convinced the government officials to allow the *Americanos* to come into their country and do the dig in the jungle, arguing that only they had the expensive equipment and expertise to do the job adequately. Now his arguments were going to come back and bite him on the ass unless he acted very quickly and handled this exactly right.

He glanced at his watch and sighed as he dialed his phone to call Dr. Julio Cardenez, director of the Mexican Public Health Service.

The phone was answered after only a few rings. *"Hola."*

Matos licked dry lips and started right in. "Julio, this is Eduardo Matos. We have an emergency that I need to discuss with you."

After a brief pause, "What sort of emergency?"

Matos explained about Adams's call to Dr. Sullivan and the emergence of some sort of infectious organism from the tomb and how it had killed over thirty workers at the dig site in just a matter of days.

"Dammit, Matos," Cardenez almost shouted. "I told you we should have sent our own people down there. Now we are looking at an international incident! How am I going to explain the deaths of so many American college students and professors?" He paused, "I must get a team of medical experts together at once and get them down there to see what they can do. Perhaps it is not too late to save some of the workers."

"Julio," Matos said, trying to calm the man down. "You are not thinking clearly."

"What?" Cardenez shouted into the phone.

"We have much more to be worried about than the deaths of a few American students, no matter how famous or influential they might be."

"What are you babbling about, Matos?"

"Calm down and think for a moment, Julio. What if this infection or plague or whatever it is escapes and somehow travels to Mexico City? We might be looking at thousands, or God forbid, even millions of deaths."

Matos could hear Cardenez gasp over the phone as the implication sank in.

"And you and I were directly responsible for inviting the Americans here to do the excavation," he continued. "That means, if you send local doctors down there and the infection spreads and kills more people, you and I are going to be blamed for not containing this plague. We will be ruined professionally. Hell, we might even end up in jail for malfeasance of duty."

"Goddammit, Matos, this was all your doing. I only . . ."

Matos laughed grimly. "That's not going to work, Julio. I may have given you the recommendation, but it is your name on the permit for the dig, not mine."

"But . . ."

"No, Julio, we must stand together on this or we are doomed."

"What do you have in mind, Eduardo?" Cardenez asked, his voice milder and less panicked as his mind searched frantically for a way out of this mess.

"I have an idea that may just get us out of this no matter what happens with the infection."

"Tell me."

"The *Americanos* unleashed this terrible plague, so I say let the Americans deal with it. You could arrange for a team of American doctors to come and investigate the dig site, and that way if the infection escapes the jungle and causes many more deaths, you would be able to lay blame for it on the Americans . . . say it was their fault the infection was released in the first place, and it was then their fault it was not contained before it could do further damage."

There was silence on the phone as Cardenez thought this proposal through. "Eduardo, I think you may have a point. I will call the Centers for Disease Control in Atlanta, Georgia. They are America's foremost experts on infection. I will see if I can have them get a team down to the dig site. We will give them full cooperation and if they fail to contain the plague, we will shrug and say they should have done more. Hell, we might even be able to get the American government to pay reparations for all of the damages to our country by the plague they caused to be released."

Matos chuckled. "Julio, you are even more devious than I imagined."

"Well, don't thank me yet, Eduardo. This is still your mess you've gotten us into, so I want you to go to the dig site with the American doctors and oversee their intervention."

Matos sobered immediately. "But, Julio, I am not a physician. I am an archaeologist. How can I be of any assistance to the Americans?"

"It was archaeologists you picked that opened up this tomb and started all of this, so I think it is perfectly reasonable for me to send an archaeologist down to the site with the Americans to assist them if further excavation is necessary."

"But, the infection . . ." Matos said.

"I am sure the Americans will take all necessary precautions to protect you from harm, Eduardo. Now, you call Dr. Sullivan back and suggest to her that perhaps she should accompany you and the doctors from the CDC down to the site."

"What reason should I give her?" Matos asked.

"Oh, tell her she will need to identify the bodies so that we may be sure all of the American archaeologists died on-site. After all, the bodies will have to be destroyed there and not returned to America for burial in order to contain the infection."

"All right, but call me back with the arrangements for

transport of the Americans to the site. It will have to be by helicopter as the site is very remote."

"I will call you back as soon as I've discussed the matter with the CDC."

After he hung up, Matos sat thinking for a moment and then he cursed. *"Bastardo!"* He knew Cardenez had just set him up. If he somehow succumbed to the plague, then Cardenez would be able to blame the entire fiasco on him, and he would be dead and unable to refute any of the charges. Cardenez was a devious bastard, but Matos still had a few tricks up his sleeve. He would make sure that no matter what happened to him, Cardenez would not escape without his share of the blame.

Chapter 2

Atlanta, Georgia

Dr. Mason Williams jerked awake at the shrill tone of his phone ringing on his bedside table. He cursed under his breath when he glanced at the clock and saw that it was two o'clock in the morning.

He rolled over and fumbled with the receiver for a moment before finally bringing it to his ear. "Yeah?" he rasped.

"Dr. Williams?" a heavily accented voice asked.

"Uh-huh," Mason mumbled through a yawn.

"This is Dr. Julio Cardenez, Director of Public Health Services of Mexico."

Mason knew Julio reasonably well. As Director of Public Health Services in Mexico, Julio had worked with him on the huge earthquake in Mexico City a few years ago, trying to prevent an outbreak of cholera after the area's sewer system had been destroyed. The man was a self-important martinet, but Williams had managed to work with him reasonably well, as long as he'd been willing to give Cardenez all of the credit for the lives saved.

He sat up on the side of his bed and slipped his feet

into his house shoes. Cardenez wouldn't be calling a CDC doc unless it was a genuine emergency. Williams hoped there hadn't been another earthquake.

"I'm sorry, Julio," Mason said as he walked toward the kitchen to make a quick cup of coffee. "It's early here and I'm not fully awake yet."

"No need to apologize, Señor Williams. I'm sorry for calling at such an ungracious hour, but we have an extreme situation that I fear may need the expertise of you and your excellent group of physicians."

Mason placed a K-cup of Green Mountain Dark Magic coffee in his Keurig machine and punched the brew button. He had a feeling he was going to need every bit of the mega-caffeine in the extra-bold blend.

In seconds he was gulping the coffee while simultaneously readying a pad and pen for notes. "Go on, Julio."

In his stilted English, Cardenez began spelling out the problem. "A few months ago, one of our archaeologists recommended I approve an expedition from the archaeology department of the University of Texas to a dig in a remote area west and south of Mexico City. After the usual bureaucratic delays, the expedition finally embarked about three weeks ago."

Mason sighed, hoping he wasn't being called in to deal with an outbreak of food or water poisoning so common in tourists who traveled to the interior of Mexico. "Excuse me, Julio, but just how does this involve the CDC?"

Cardenez bristled. Who does this Americano think he is to interrupt a man of my importance? he thought. "I would think, Dr. Williams," Cardenez spit out with more than a little sarcasm, "that your CDC would appreciate being consulted when over thirty American students and professors have contracted some mysterious illness, which, if the reports I just received are to be believed, has killed them all in a matter of days."

"What?" Mason gasped, almost choking on his coffee. "What kind of illness . . . ?"

"Let me save us both some time, Dr. Williams," Cardenez said. "Here are the names and phone numbers of the two people who reported this incident to me just moments ago. Perhaps you should get the details of the illness and the location of the outbreak from them."

Mason belatedly realized his mistake in antagonizing this man. Mexico and its health officials were sensitive to the point of paranoia about having to ask for American assistance in the best of circumstances, and this had all the earmarks of being a real clusterfuck, he thought, wondering just what the Americans had gotten themselves into. "I apologize if I seemed rude, Dr. Cardenez," Mason said, laying it on thick. "As I said, I've just woken up and I'm not at my best until after at least two cups of coffee."

Cardenez's voice softened a bit. "I understand, Doctor." He recited Dr. Matos's and Dr. Sullivan's names and phone numbers and then added, "While you are consulting with them, I will begin to make arrangements for you and your team to obtain the necessary permits and transportation to proceed to the area in question as soon as you are ready."

"Thank you again, Dr. Cardenez. I'll call them both right away."

Mason stuck another K-cup in the coffee machine and dialed Eduardo Matos's phone number while his cup filled with the aromatic brew.

After Matos told him briefly what Lauren Sullivan had said and then described the location of the dig as being in a dense jungle setting near an ancient village named Tlateloco, Mason began to question him more closely about what he'd been told.

"They were bleeding from the nose and mouth?" he asked, all trace of sleepiness gone from his voice.

"Hemorrhaging, according to what was reported to me by the archaeologist's associate who talked to him on the site by telephone as he was dying."

Dr. Matos hesitated, "Dr. Williams, I am not a man who is easily alarmed, but according to what I've just been told by Dr. Sullivan, there may be as many as thirty deaths in Tlateloco, all with a very sudden onset of fever, vomiting, and hemorrhage. They are all American archaeologists or students working at an Aztec village in the jungle, a new discovery thought to be the tomb of Montezuma."

Matos hesitated, cleared his throat, and said, "Lauren Sullivan said that Dr. Charles Adams, the leader of the dig, called her as he was dying and asked her to make the call to me and to tell me of the tragedy."

"Why did he ask her to call you, instead of medical personnel?"

"I believe he told her the situation was too dire and it was too late for medical intervention . . . in fact, he made it rather clear that he did not want anyone else to come to the site but that he thought that it should simply be burned to prevent further spread of the illness and further loss of life."

Matos mentally crossed his fingers, hoping this American doctor would follow Adams's advice and he would not have to risk his life flying into the hellhole Tlateloco had become.

Mason said, "I'm afraid that's impossible, Dr. Matos. The site will have to be visited, any possible survivors found and treated, and the illness identified before we can even think of destroying the site."

Damn, Matos thought. It looked like he was going after all. Well, he'd better do as Cardenez said and at least get the Sullivan girl to join him on the trip.

"Perhaps, if it is possible, Dr. Sullivan would be willing to join us—to direct us to the site, and if necessary, identify the bodies. I'm told she knows the area well from previous digs nearby."

"What do you mean 'us,' Dr. Matos? Are you telling me you intend to travel to the site with my team?"

"I'm afraid so, Dr. Williams. Dr. Cardenez says that the Mexican government must be represented and that as an archaeologist I am to be that representative. I promise you I will try my best not to get underfoot or to hinder your examination in any fashion."

Mason sighed. He knew it wasn't going to be easy to get his team into the Mexican interior and clean up this mess, even without having to babysit amateurs.

"Is this Lauren Sullivan a medical doctor?" he asked, fearing he already knew the answer.

"Uh, no, I do not believe so. As she is an associate of the archaeologist on-site, I suspect she is also an archaeologist."

"Well, since the site is an archaeological dig, you and she might be of some use to us if we have to do any digging."

"Well, since I am head of our Institute of Archaeology and am representing the Mexican government, it will be up to me to see to the proper disposition of any historical relics that may be discovered."

"I don't know anything about Central American history or historical relics, so it probably makes sense for both you and Sullivan to come along," Mason said, draining the last of his coffee. "If you believe the report is accurate, I can have my team in Mexico City by tomorrow afternoon. I'll need a pilot who knows the terrain and a helicopter, one big enough to bring in our equipment." He stifled a yawn. "The symptoms sound like hemorrhagic shock to me, but it's anybody's guess as to the cause. I'll have a mobile lab on standby that can also be transported in by helicopter, just in case this is real."

"Well," Matos said, "Dr. Sullivan certainly thought it was real since she said Dr. Adams died while talking to her on the phone." He hesitated and then continued, "If it is all right with Dr. Cardenez, I believe I can have one of our army's helicopters waiting for you at Mexico City International Airport with an experienced pilot by tomorrow afternoon."

Mason glanced at the clock on his kitchen wall. "We'll be in Mexico City sometime after noon to meet you. I'll start making phone calls to my team now. But Dr. Matos, we need to both hope this is not hemorrhagic fever, 'cause anything that causes that is not something we want to be dealing with."

"I understand, Dr. Williams, and I share your trepidation. Even though I am not a medical doctor, I have heard of hemorrhagic fever and like you I want nothing to do with it."

"Uh, Dr. Matos, one more thing, if you don't mind."

"Anything, Dr. Williams."

"I'm going to be extremely busy the rest of the night setting up this trip for my team, so would you mind calling Dr. Sullivan for me? Since you've already talked to her and sort of know her, I feel it'd be best if you relay our schedule to Dr. Sullivan so she can join us for the trip . . . if she's willing."

Matos chuckled. "So, you don't want to get hung up talking to a hysterical female, huh?"

Mason laughed. Matos was more intelligent than most of the Mexican bureaucrats he usually dealt with. "You got it, Doctor."

He hung up and pushed the first button on his auto-dialer, talking into a speakerphone as he dressed hurriedly, awakening a night supervisor at CDC in order to prepare equipment packs for his team of specialists. As head of the CDC's Special Pathogens Group, nicknamed "Wildfire Team," he was about to launch what was called a Wildfire Emergency Intervention. In spite of the hour and the gravity of the situation, he felt his pulse begin to race—this was what he lived for.

Austin

Lauren was still sitting on the edge of her bed, her body numb and her mind racing with thoughts of Charles Adams and what her life and career would be like without him in it to give her support and advice as he'd been doing as long as she could remember.

She jumped as the phone rang and fumbled with the receiver for a moment before lifting it to her ear.

"Hello," she said, her voice rough with emotion.

"Hello, Lauren. This is Eduardo Matos."

"Yes, Eduardo."

"I've just finished speaking with Dr. Julio Cardenez, the head of our public health service."

"Is he going to send a team of doctors down to the dig site?"

"He is going to do better than that," Matos replied, forcing his voice to seem hopeful. "He has a close relationship with your American CDC."

"CDC? I've heard of them but I'm afraid I don't know exactly who they are or what they do."

"CDC stands for Centers for Disease Control and Prevention. They are based in Atlanta, Georgia, I believe, and they have an infectious disease group that can be dispatched anywhere in the world very rapidly to identify and control epidemics. They were here a few years ago after the earthquake in Mexico City killed thousands of our people. Dr. Cardenez was quoted as giving them credit for stopping the outbreak of cholera after the city's water system was contaminated." This was a bit of a stretch as Matos knew Cardenez had himself taken most of the credit.

"Do you think we might be able to get permission for the CDC to fly to Tlateloco in time for them to help?"

"That is what Dr. Cardenez is working on right now. And I've already talked to a doctor at the CDC and he has agreed to intervene. They have an additional interest since the victims are all Americans."

"So, this is really going to happen?"

"Lauren, the doctor in charge of the infectious disease team at the CDC is Mason Williams. I am told he is relatively young; however, he is head of the international team that investigates potential outbreaks in foreign countries. Dr. Cardenez said that since Dr. Williams agreed to come, he would clear the red tape and make it happen."

"That's good news."

Matos cleared his throat. "Lauren, I want more than that. I am directly responsible for Charles being at that dig, and I feel a responsibility for what has happened. In addition, as Director of INAH, our National Institute of Anthropology, it is my responsibility to control activity at any archaeological dig. Therefore, I intend to travel with the CDC to the site, and I would like for you to come, too."

"But . . ."

"We need you, Lauren, and more than that, Charles and the other students need you. The CDC doctors are specialists in infectious disease, but they know nothing of archaeology or dig sites. They will need our expertise in case they have to excavate at the site, or precious relics may be lost." He hesitated, "And there is the problem of identification of the . . . uh . . . bodies."

Lauren stifled a sob at the thought of what she would be asked to do . . . to identify the bodies of students she'd taught and become friends with was almost too much to contemplate.

She took a deep breath. "All right, Eduardo. I'll get an early morning flight to Atlanta and join the CDC on the flight to Mexico City. I have some questions I want to ask Dr. Williams and the flight will give me time to do that."

"Good. Pack light and bring some nausea pills and perhaps some Cipro to prevent food poisoning. We will have to change planes to a helicopter at the Mexico City airport. Tlateloco is inaccessible by airplane, and the helicopter ride over the mountains can get quite rough."

Lauren agreed and hung up. She sat on the edge of her bed, her mind racing, trying to think of all the things she had to do to get ready for an international trip. She dialed Continental Airlines to arrange for the earliest possible morning flight to Atlanta. She got a flight leaving at six a.m.

She called her teaching assistant and after apologizing for calling so late, told her what was going on. The young girl was devastated at the terrible news but agreed to cover Lauren's classes and to explain to the dean why she was leaving for the next couple of weeks. For a time she merely sat there staring at the floor of her apartment, feeling helpless, until she finally forced herself to get up. She had a lot to do before her plane left for Atlanta at six a.m. She took a suitcase from her closet and began filling it with clothes, letting the activity take her mind off Mexico and the horrors there.

After she snapped the suitcase shut, she went to her briefcase and thumbed through a stack of papers inside until she found copies of a translation of Díaz's journal that arrived in yesterday's mail.

Too keyed up to go back to sleep, she propped a couple of pillows against the headboard, put on her reading glasses, and turned to the first page. Perhaps the journal would offer some clues to the fate that had befallen her friends and colleagues at the Tlateloco dig. At the very least, she reasoned, it might help keep her mind off the agony she'd heard in Charles Adams's voice.

Though her Spanish was tolerable, she was grateful for the translation Charlie had included with the copies of the original document. In spite of her vow to try to put Charlie's phone call out of her thoughts, she found it hard to concentrate. Her mind filled with images of all the kindnesses and special moments she and Charlie had shared in her years at the university.

Finally, she pushed all maudlin thoughts aside, vowing to grieve for her mentor later. Now it was more important for her to read and try to understand as much as she could about the mysterious illness Díaz had named the

Black Plague. As she read, she wondered if this Dr. Williams and his team of experts would be able to solve a mystery that had its beginnings almost five hundred years ago. She hoped so, for she simply had to know what happened to Charlie and all the others.

Two hours later, physically and emotionally spent, she set her alarm, turned off her light, and drifted into a fitful sleep, tormented by dreams of dying men and animals in the jungle. In the morning she would be on her way to Atlanta to join a doctor by the name of Williams and his team on a journey into the face of a death so horrible that it could barely be contemplated.

Chapter 3

Mason Williams unlocked and entered the conference room at CDC headquarters his Wildfire Team used whenever they had a thorny problem to discuss. Stifling a yawn, he threw his "go-bag" packed with the clothes and toiletries he'd need for two weeks in the jungle in the corner and proceeded immediately to the rear table holding the most important equipment in the room, a coffeepot.

Minutes later he was sitting at the head of the long burl wood conference table and drinking the wake-up juice while he went over the notes he'd taken while on the phone with Dr. Matos. From the doctor's description of the sickness, he felt sure it was some form of hemorrhagic fever, but he was damned if he could think of anything endemic to Mexico that would produce those symptoms.

He finished his coffee and was just getting up to pour another cup when he saw two of his team members entering the door.

Lionel Johnson and Shirley Cole walked in side by side, looking like Mutt and Jeff as they tossed their go-bags into the corner with Mason's.

Lionel Johnson, MD, PhD, was six feet four inches in height, tipped the scales at 250 pounds, and was an easy-going African American who was the world's foremost authority on fungi and mycobacteria. Although he'd gone to Duke on a football scholarship and had been a fierce competitor on the field, he was very shy and gentle in everyday life and spoke so softly that he often had to repeat himself in meetings. His features were, like the rest of him, large and coarse. His most prominent attribute were his ears, which stuck out like Clark Gable's and were often the subject of fond teasing by the other members of the team.

In contrast, Shirley Cole had a PhD in Microbiology, was only five feet two inches tall, and was almost that wide. At forty-four years of age she was the oldest member of the team and was slightly matronly. She had been extensively involved in army biological and chemical warfare secret laboratories prior to coming to work at the CDC. She was the unofficial den mother of the team and spent most of her off time baking cookies and muffins, which she brought to all of their meetings. Usually calm and centered, she could still get quite testy if her conclusions were questioned but then usually felt guilty and baked even more goodies to make up for her temper.

They smiled when they saw Mason standing next to the coffee machine as Shirley approached, handing him a platter of banana nut muffins. "Try these, boss," she said. "They'll get that bleary look out of your eyes."

Lionel nodded, smiling around the crumbs on his lips. "Yep," he mumbled. "Mighty tasty all right."

Mason grabbed one and motioned to the coffee machine. "Better drink up, guys. I have a feeling we're gonna need all the coffee we can get to handle this case."

Before he could continue, the other three members of the team came hurrying through the door, all jabbering about what could be so important to yank them out of their beds at this ungodly hour.

Mason stepped back so Sam Jakes, Suzanne Elliot, and Joel Schumacher could gather around the coffeepot and get their fair share of caffeine and muffins. As he sipped his coffee and watched them mingle and tease back and forth he thought back to the amazing changes each of them had undergone since joining the Wildfire Team. Once highly independent loners who were all at the pinnacle of their fields, they were now members of a team that required the most intimate cooperation imaginable . . . not only their very lives depended on it, but the lives of thousands of others, also.

It had been just a few years before when he had been tasked with finding and recruiting the best medical and scientific talent available. He was told to form a rapid response group that could be ready to mobilize at a moment's notice to travel anywhere in the world to attack and defeat any disease threats to the country and the world.

Mason remembered the first to join his team was Sam Jakes, who had an MD and PhD in virology and had been doing cutting-edge research at Columbia University. When Mason first approached the irascible gnomelike man, he found his personality was perfectly suited to New York City—he was brusque, rude, and totally convinced of the unassailability of his giant intellect.

About five feet five inches tall and weighing over two hundred pounds, Jakes was sensitive about both his short stature and his pudgy profile and was quick to take offense at the mention of either. The fact that he was balding with flyaway frizzy hair and bushy caterpillar eyebrows and an ugly blot of a nose didn't help his self-esteem issues regarding his appearance.

In spite of that, he was also supremely arrogant about his abilities and rarely respected anyone else's feelings or intellect and was both condescending and argumentative on almost every subject.

However, since he knew as much about virology as anyone on earth, Mason ignored the fact that he wasn't a team player and overlooked his faults and convinced him to join the team by promising him the chance to see and treat firsthand diseases most doctors only read about.

Mason had then traveled to New Orleans and recruited Lionel Johnson from Tulane University, where Johnson was doing research on resistant strains of tuberculosis that had showed up following the recent AIDS epidemic. Unlike Jakes, who tested Mason's patience daily, Johnson's shy manner and sly, understated sense of humor made him a joy to be around.

His next trip was to Maryland and Fort Detrick, the home of USAMRIID, the United States Army Medical Research Institute of Infectious Diseases. He'd heard of Dr. Shirley Cole, who had a PhD in Microbiology and whose research on disease-causing bacteria was the talk of the CDC. He was initially concerned about taking on a middle-aged woman who was not in the best physical condition, but in time he'd found his fears to be unjustified. She'd fit right in with the group from the very first day. Her acceptance by the group was helped along by her wizardry with baked goods.

Shirley had told Mason he had to see if he could recruit Suzanne Elliot, an RN with a master's degree in epidemiology who'd traveled all over the world tracking a number of elusive causative factors in the spread of disease in a dozen different countries. Shirley and Suzanne had crossed paths on a joint army and United Nations task force fighting a cholera outbreak in Haiti, and Shirley had been very impressed with the nurse.

When Mason approached her, he found a medium height, about five-foot-five-inch-tall woman who was slim and strong but not masculine. Suzanne was in fact entirely average, neither pretty nor ugly, and dressed rather blandly, as if not wanting to draw attention to herself. When Mason explained the reason for his visit, she was more than happy to join the team and work once again with her old friend, Shirley Cole.

The last member of the team to be recruited was Joel Schumacher, a computer specialist who was in charge of the CDC's Special Pathogens database, which contained information on all previous outbreaks of infectious diseases and plagues, as well as the locations of all "hot zones" where dangerous organisms were known to be endemic. He was a top man in computer science analysis in medical applications and had developed several of his own programs so highly specialized that no one else could understand them, but he could make them sing. He was of average height and slightly dumpy, the picture of a typical geeky nerd, and very Jewish, wearing a yarmulke at all times. He liked to joke that he would gladly join the team since the frequent travel would enable him to escape the women his mother was continually trying to set him up with, who were usually daughters of friends of hers. Early on the other team members began to tease him about still being a virgin, which made his ears and cheeks blaze crimson, but he maintained he was saving his virtue for just the right woman.

Mason felt a welling of pride in his chest as he observed his team getting ready to deploy, knowing he had the best and brightest in the world who could face whatever horrors the jungles of Mexico were about to throw at them.

As the group took their chairs around the conference table, all of the muffins and most of the coffee having been consumed, Mason stood at the head of the table with his arms crossed on his chest as he addressed them.

"I know you're all wondering just what I'm about to get us into with this middle-of-the-night expedition, but I have to admit, I don't know just yet."

When they all started to protest at one time, he held up his hands. "Wait a minute, and I'll tell you what I know and maybe together we can figure out what we're going to be going up against."

Sam Jakes raised his hand and asked irritably, "Why don't you first tell us where this latest hot zone is located?"

"In the jungle just south and west of Mexico City," Mason answered.

"Oh shit!" Jakes exclaimed. "Don't tell me we're gonna be traveling all the way to Mexico to treat some travelers who've developed Montezuma's revenge and need the experts from the CDC to come cure their diarrhea?"

Mason laughed. "You may be closer to the truth than you think, Sam. This may in fact be Montezuma's revenge, but the disease we're gonna be facing is a little bit more serious than diarrhea."

Shirley piped up, "Diarrhea can be pretty serious, Mason, especially if it's caused by cholera or bacterial dysentery."

Mason again held up his hands for quiet. "Okay, guys, why don't you listen while I tell you a story?" He paused until he had everyone's attention. "There once was a group of thirty professors and students from the University of Texas who traveled down to Mexico to find and excavate the ancient tomb of Emperor Montezuma in a tiny, remote village named Tlateloco."

Jakes smirked, spread his arms, and glanced around at the group. "See, I told you . . ."

Mason's face became serious. "Now, according to what I've been told, all thirty of the group and an unknown number of Mexican laborers are dead."

The team became quiet, all eyes on Mason. "How'd they die, Mason?" Suzanne asked.

"The symptoms sound like hemorrhagic fever and shock, exact cause unknown."

"Bullshit!" Jakes said, slapping his hand down on the table. "It can't be hemorrhagic fever 'cause there are no known human pathogens that cause this particular constellation of symptoms extant in the Western Hemisphere."

Suzanne Elliot frowned and glared at Jakes. "Why don't you just shut the fuck up, Sam, and let Mason tell the story before you get your panties all in a twist?"

"Why . . . you . . ." Jakes sputtered, his face flaming red.

"That's a good idea, Suzanne," Mason intervened before the argument could get out of hand. He sat down at the table and leaned back in his chair. "Here is what I've been told . . ."

He went on to relate the early morning phone call from

Julio Cardenez and his subsequent discussion with Eduardo Matos, head of the Mexican Archaeology Society. He explained how Professor Charles Adams had called one of his colleagues in Texas and told her about the deaths and how he had described the symptoms exhibited prior to dying.

Lionel shook his head, his eyes worried. "So, all of this information, including the descriptions of the symptoms, is not only thirdhand information, but it is coming from nonmedical personnel . . . archaeologists?" he asked in his soft voice.

Mason nodded. "That's right, Lionel. But even though the symptoms are described by nondocs, they are spot on for hemorrhagic fever and shock, and in follow-up phone calls none of the students or teachers are answering their cells."

"Well," Suzanne said, looking around the table. "Regardless of the possible cause, if there are thirty deaths, then we are certainly looking at a hot zone of some sort."

"Mason," Shirley Cole said. "I've been thinking about what Sam said. There is a pathogen extant in Mexico that could cause symptoms similar to those of hemorrhagic fever—anthrax."

"Oh Jesus," Jakes said. "Even a virologist knows that woolsorter's disease, which is the only form of anthrax that is airborne, has never been shown to be transmitted from person to person." He shook his head at her. "In addition, hemorrhagic shock is only caused by viruses, not bacteria. So unless you think that thirty different people could somehow have simultaneously inhaled enough anthrax spores to all go into shock at the same time and each and every one die from the disease when the normal death rate is only four or five percent, then I doubt that our pathogen can be anthrax."

Now it was Shirley's face that turned red. "I didn't say that, you arrogant asshole," she stated firmly. "I know anthrax doesn't cause hemorrhagic shock, but it does cause extensive internal hemorrhage and major bleeding into lymph nodes of the lungs and stomach, so the hemorrhagic symptoms could simply be caused by coughing and vomiting up blood. Nonmedical observers would be hard-pressed to tell the difference."

Jakes snorted. "What about the abnormally high mortality rate of this hot-bug?"

She shrugged. "That I can't explain."

To make peace, Mason asked, "How about one of the Ebola or Marburg viruses, perhaps imported to the site by one of the local workers?"

Jakes shook his head irritably. "No, no, that is just not possible!" He then launched into a pedantic discourse on the origins of Ebola, reminding them that the Ebola virus is named for the Ebola River, which is the headstream of the Mongala River, a tributary of the Congo, or Zaire River, and its endemic area is ten thousand miles from Mexico City and would therefore be a highly unlikely explanation for the deaths described in Tlateloco. "Hell," he said smiling, "even if someone contracted Ebola in Africa and then traveled directly to Mexico City, by the time he could get from there down to Tlateloco, he would already be dead from the virus and unable to infect anyone else, let alone thirty additional people."

Suzanne was staring at Jakes. Finally, she asked, "Sam, are you forgetting about the hantavirus and hantavirus pulmonary syndrome? It can certainly cause hemorrhagic shock, and the rodents that carry the virus are known to live all over North and South America."

Jakes raised his eyebrows and smiled. "Very good, Suzanne. Of course, you are right, the symptoms could be from HPS, except that the virus is primarily found in dry, arid areas such as Arizona and New Mexico in the United States, and in Mexico it's usually found in desert areas." He scratched his chin, "I seriously doubt the virus could survive in a humid, jungle environment, but I will keep your excellent suggestion in mind."

Further discussions among the group considered other possible pathogens such as dengue fever, bubonic or pneumonic plague, and other rare causes of the symptoms Matos had described to Mason.

Each and every one was eventually shot down as the possible culprit for one reason or another.

Finally, as dawn was breaking, Mason concluded the meeting. "As we have been given no empirical evidence that would enable us to come to a definitive diagnosis of the cause of these deaths, I feel an on-site intervention is justified. As team leader, I am declaring this a 'Wildfire Emergency.'" He stood up. "I will contact the Mexican government for permission to mount a full-scale incursion into the area as soon as travel arrangements can be made. I suggest the rest of you get together and make a list of the equipment each of you will need to do a full diagnostic workup on the bodies of the victims, including full Biohazard Level Four precautions."

"Shit," Jakes mumbled as he got up from the table. "I hate those fucking Racal suits."

Joel Schumacher said, "While you guys are figuring out what lab equipment you'll be needing, I'll run a database search on all entities that can cause the symptoms we're looking at. That way we'll have a list to work against when we start doing diagnostics."

Mason grinned and patted his shoulder. "Great idea, Joel."

He looked around at the group. "Now, get a move on. We're burnin' daylight."

Chapter 4

Lauren entered the Arlen Specter Headquarters and Emergency Operations Center at the CDC headquarters in Atlanta just after nine a.m. A helpful young man at the front desk directed her to the suite of offices occupied by Dr. Mason Williams and his Wildfire Emergency Response Team.

She entered the door into a sort of controlled chaos, with men and women moving around, talking urgently on cell phones, waving their hands in the air and shouting at each other across the room as they tried to organize the resources and equipment they would need for their upcoming excursion into the jungles of Mexico.

Finally, she spied the man in charge and raised her eyebrows. He was younger than she expected him to be to have such a position of power, appearing to be in his early thirties. He was tall, a little over six feet, and looked to be both lean and muscular in the way of an avid outdoorsman, not a weight lifter. He had dark unruly hair and seemed to run his hands through it when he was thinking or perhaps in frustration at his orders not being carried out quickly enough.

He was good-looking without being classically hand-some, and he had a quiet air of authority that belied his young age.

After a few moments, he spotted her standing just inside the door with a rolling duffle bag on the floor next to her.

He rushed over and held out his hand. "Dr. Sullivan, I suppose?"

"Lauren, please, Dr. Williams," she said, noticing his eyes were a deep blue in color and red-rimmed from being up all night.

"Then it's Mason, Lauren." He glanced back over his shoulder. "Please excuse the madness, but it's always like this just before we head out to a hot zone—we never quite know just what we'll need in the field."

"Hot zone?" she asked.

"Oh, excuse the jargon. . . ." He smiled and she realized suddenly it was a very nice smile. "You'll probably be hearing a lot of unfamiliar terms during the trip. Hot zone is any area with an infectious agent capable of spreading rapidly and creating an epidemic, especially if it's highly fatal."

She frowned. "So you think whatever caused all these deaths is still . . . active . . . still a threat?"

He stepped back and looked at her appraisingly. He took her arm and said, "Come with me into my office, Lauren. Let's talk."

She followed him into his office, and he sat next to her on a couch against the wall. "I was told you talked to Dr. Adams and he explained to you that all thirty members of his expedition and all of the Mexican laborers in the camp had died . . . and died rather horribly?"

"Yes," she answered in a low voice.

He put his hand on her arm. "Lauren, I'm not going to lie to you or try to sugarcoat this situation. If I'm right, then we are about to travel into a real hot zone, one that at the very least is extremely dangerous. And what's more, we have no idea of just what the agent is that has caused all of these deaths, so we'll have to take extremely broad precautions against any of us catching the same bug."

She nodded slowly. "And you're wondering if I know just what I'm getting myself into by going with you, is that right?"

He leaned back, nodding slowly while he gazed into her eyes. "Yes."

"Dr. Williams . . . Mason," she said, squaring her shoulders. "What I know is that over thirty people have possibly died, most of whom were friends of mine. I also know that there just might be one or two that are still alive out there in that jungle. I would never forgive myself if I didn't do all that I could to see to it that the dead—and even possibly the still living—were properly identified so that their families would be able to get some closure and would know what had happened to their loved ones."

She took a deep breath. "I also know that there is some danger in going into this hot zone, as you call it. Well, Mason, I have been on over twenty field archaeology expeditions in some of the most remote areas of the earth, all of which had some danger to them." She relaxed and smiled grimly. "In short, while I am no hero rushing blindly into danger without a thought, I am ready if you are."

Mason, watching her speak, had the rather irrational thought that this lady has some balls. He also noticed that her emerald-green eyes darkened in anger at his suggestion she might not be up to the trip. He smiled to himself. Interesting . . .

"Okay then," he said, slapping his thighs and jumping to his feet. "You've been warned, so let's get your gear ready to be loaded."

Fort Detrick, Maryland

Colonel Woodrow "Blackie" Blackman leaned over to pluck a cigar from the mahogany humidor perched on the corner of his desk. It was just after nine a.m., time to enjoy his first cigar of the day along with a cup of his specially brewed Colombian Suprema coffee. He paused, frowning, instantly alerted when a light flashed on a control panel announcing an incoming scrambled call.

He stuck the unlit cigar in his mouth and flipped a switch on the console. An LCD began passing a decoded message across the screen in front of him and he was both surprised and alarmed by the message from one of his "moles" coming in during office hours—his spies usually reported late at night when they were most likely to be unobserved.

At the U.S. Army Medical Research Institute of Infectious Diseases Research Laboratory in Fort Detrick, Maryland, known as USAMRIID, the army's secret facility for the study of biological and chemical weapons, it was business hours and there were dozens of officers and office personnel hanging around that weren't in the loop about his spy network or the research he conducted in secret. It would be a disaster if any of them suspected what he was doing.

The message read:

Janus. Hot-bug in jungles of Mexico near Tlateloco looks very promising. Human-to-human transmission

strong possibility. Over thirty dead. Signs of hemorrhagic
shock in all victims. Reported three-to-seven-day incubation period. Will send samples when isolated. Watch how
you handle this one—it sounds like it's a definite
Biohazard Level Four bug.

Blackman read the sign-off for Janus, drumming his
fingers on a desk top. CDC's Wildfire crew was heading
to some remote part of Mexico with a hot zone and a bug
his informant thought had strong possibilities. The colonel
knew Mason Williams was no beginner despite his age
and he wouldn't have called for an intervention without
definite cause.

This could be it, Blackman whispered to himself, his
heart rate soaring in excitement. Thirty-plus victims probably meant an almost one hundred percent mortality rate,
and a three-to-seven-days incubation period was more than
promising, unless its host turned out to be some form of
rare jungle beetle or mosquito, which would limit wartime
usage.

The most promising news from Janus was the possibility of person-to-person transmission, which might make
this bug as devastating as a nuclear bomb. Now, all he
could do was wait for samples of the hot-bug and hope it
had a real potential for biological weaponry.

Blackie, as he was called by his associates at Fort Detrick, sighed and turned to a computer screen to call up
map files of Mexico to find Tlateloco. Coded coordinates
had come with the message from Janus. None of this secrecy would be necessary if there were any cooperation
between USAMRIID and the CDC. There couldn't be, of
course, simply because the research that Colonel Black-

man was conducting at Fort Detrick violated an executive order from 1969, when President Nixon declared the United States would not conduct any additional studies of biological or chemical offensive weapons.

What was going on here could end careers if it were discovered, not the least of which would be ruining the career of Colonel Woodrow Blackman, with an almost certain court-martial and probably a lengthy prison sentence for defying a presidential edict.

He'd just have to make sure Janus was not discovered, at least not until he had his hands on this latest hot-bug if it was even half as deadly as Janus suspected. After all, Janus had just months earlier tipped him to the suspected morbillivirus infecting horses and handlers in Australia and New Zealand—a hot-bug his biological research team was still evaluating as the next great top secret offensive agent for the U.S. biological weapons arsenal.

Just a few miles from USAMRIID headquarters in Maryland, U.S. Congressman Michael O'Donnell was both frustrated and worried. He had real concerns about what was going on at Fort Detrick, having heard whispers in the Congressional cloakroom about ongoing germ warfare studies there, which might be in violation of a presidential order signed in 1969 forbidding just such research. As a freshman member of the House National Security Committee, Military Research and Development Subcommittee, he had been secretly looking into USAMRIID activities, fearing what might happen in his home state should a deadly biological agent escape Fort Detrick. The area surrounding the army base was densely populated and any kind of contagion could quickly spread from there across the entire United States with disastrous results.

But what really worried him was the chance that Colonel Blackman would find out about his interest in his activities, for Blackman had the reputation of being a very, very dangerous opponent. Blackman was known on the Hill as a blood-and-guts soldier, a patriot from the "old school" who still believed in the big Communist threat and a world takeover by some lunatic dictator like Hitler or Stalin or Mussolini or even some "towel-head" named Achmed.

Blackman lived in a world of his own, shrouded in secrecy, which he believed was necessary due to some poorly defined threat he insisted would come from Russia or Europe or China or the Middle East. He justified everything he did as a necessary part of patriotism, and as such was entirely unpredictable.

In fact, O'Donnell knew men who'd shown too much interest in Blackman's career or activities who had been known to suddenly disappear—a fact that had O'Donnell looking over his shoulder more often than not.

He also knew that not even his status as a United States congressman would protect him if Colonel Blackman deemed him to be a threat. The man's egomaniacal personality and hair-trigger temper coupled with the ability to "disappear" an enemy made him as dangerous as a cobra.

O'Donnell realized he was going to have to tread very carefully if he was to survive his quest to find out just what Blackman was up to. It's not paranoia if they really are shooting at you, he reasoned.

Chapter 5

The hammering staccato of helicopter blades slicing through air was a constant drone in Dr. Mason Williams's ears, annoying him and making his head throb in tune to the beat of the blades. The sound was magnified inside the cavernous Huey because the cargo doors were open so members of the team could lean out, hanging on for dear life, staring at the jungle tableau flashing below them.

But it was what Mason saw below the chopper that kept him from further irritation over the noise as their Mexican Army pilot hovered above an ancient vine-covered stone temple. Lauren had told him it had been built by the Aztecs in a small jungle opening over four hundred years ago and had been the site of hundreds or thousands of blood sacrifices to their sun god. But now after so many years sitting abandoned and forgotten in the wilderness, jungle foliage had reclaimed the area until its pyramid-like shape was now almost completely cloaked in cloying green vines, and bushes and trees were growing from cracks between the boulders making up its sides.

Mason turned from the temple and began counting bodies, the ones he could see from two hundred feet above the dig site at Tlateloco. Most of the crumpled shapes were in a cleared area surrounding the temple, though some could be seen partially obscured underneath nearby coppices of trees.

The corpses seemed to lie everywhere, some bloated by jungle heat, others partially eaten by scavengers. Tall grass and leafy vines made it difficult to be sure of the count—hurricane-force downdraft from the helicopter's blades caused too much movement, turning jungle greenery into a swirling morass of wind-blown vegetation revealing a leg or an arm or a torso here and there. The constant agitation of the greenery made it impossible to tell if body parts were still connected to a corpse or to get any kind of accurate count of people who'd died here.

Jesus, Mason thought. The area below looks like a god-damned war zone. The way the dead bodies are splayed in contorted positions makes it look like they've been machine-gunned by some rampaging army. He shook his head at the horror, thinking that in a way they had been killed by a rampaging army—an army of viruses or bacteria intent on nothing less than massive death.

He squeezed his eyes shut, trying to clear them of the grisly images of young people cut down in the prime of life by some microscopic killer, a killer that was going to be his job to face and, he hoped, conquer.

He'd come to the CDC early in his career hoping to encounter just such challenges—knowing he could save far more lives by defeating and stopping plagues in their tracks than he ever could by doing research at some med school or by treating infectious diseases in private practice. And as trite as it sounded, saving lives was what he was all about.

In fact, while some in his med school class had laughed at the archaic Hippocratic Oath they'd all taken upon graduation, he'd taken the words to heart, believing they represented all that he'd sacrificed and worked so hard to obtain.

"I counted eleven so far!" Shirley Cole shouted above the pounding of the Huey's turbine, peering out of the chopper's door with a fierce grip on a lifeline.

"There's no way to tell from here!" Sam Jakes cried, holding his own length of rope affixed to the Huey's parachute rod while he gazed down at the jungle floor. He turned to Lauren Sullivan and nodded once, his eyes fierce as if he were going into combat with whatever had caused the massacre below.

"It would appear your information was correct, Dr. Sullivan! I see absolutely no signs of life. The entire expedition must have perished, along with a goodly number of Mexican laborers." He took a deep breath and placed a comforting hand on her shoulder. "Now we have to find out what killed them!"

A knot was forming in Mason's stomach. If this archaeological team had truly died the way Lauren described their deaths, he and his Wildfire Team were about to step into a time warp from the 1920s, when Dr. Howard Carter's expedition to Egypt unearthed King Tut's tomb and his workmen and fellow archaeologists began to die mysteriously.

But that was ninety years ago and the cause of death had been found later to be an encapsulated fungus preserved for thousands of years, which no one in the sciences or medicine knew anything about back then.

There was a far more potentially deadly threat await-ing them here if the symptoms described were genuine. These people had reportedly died from some form of he-morrhagic shock or at least a massive infection mimicking such, not a fungal infection; and their copious bleeding spelled any number of dangerous possibilities.

What didn't make sense to him was the apparent human-to-human transmission pointing toward a virus of unknown origin, an Ebola-like epidemic in the wrong place on the planet, ten thousand miles from any known outbreaks, as their virology specialist, Sam Jakes, had pointed out with his typical arrogance when Mason first called the team together for input.

He sighed, knowing in his gut that this was going to be a bad one, one that would require all of his focus if it was going to be defeated before it wreaked havoc on the rest of the world. He was just going to have to shut out the im-ages of the dead and do what he and his team did best—identify the killer and find out how to kill it before it spread from its jungle location.

He pushed his microphone close to his lips and spoke to the pilot. "Put on your breathing mask and set us down as far away from the bodies as you can after we're suited up. I'll tap you on the shoulder when we're ready."

Mason took off his seat belt and got out of the copi-lot's seat. "It looks like we have a hot zone, ladies and gentlemen!" he shouted into the belly of the craft, strug-gling to make himself heard over the roar of the engine.

"One of you help Dr. Sullivan put on her Racal suit and make sure it's fully pressurized! We are going down!"

He glanced at Joel Schumacher and made a telephone sign with his hand next to his ear. "Radio our backup group at Mexico City airport to be on standby with the

Cytotec BL Four mobile lab! From the looks of things up here, we're sure as hell gonna need it and sooner rather than later!"

Mason forced the cargo door shut to keep out the wind, and he and the rest of the team began to unpack the large crate in the hold that held their Racal suits and breathing apparatus.

As he pulled the suit up over his feet and turned so Jakes could pull up the rear zipper and make sure it was airtight, he realized how dependent they all were on each other. Even a simple act of suiting up in the Racal was a two-man job, impossible by oneself.

Once he was zipped up and Jakes had secured duct tape over all the seams and the zipper, Mason turned to do the same for him.

As the helicopter bumped to a jarring landing on the grassy turf of the far edge of the clearing, the hiss of the metallic-tasting air from the tank on Mason's back cleared the fog on his faceplate and made his nose pucker at the smell.

He moved his arms and took a couple of tentative steps, making sure everything worked correctly; after all, his life depended on the integrity of the suit. Finally satisfied, he climbed down out of the copter and waited for the rest of his team to disembark.

Mason was accustomed to the odd feeling of detachment inside a Racal space suit after so many years, and so were the other members of the team, but when Lauren showed signs of panic after climbing down from the chopper he understood and spoke to her through his headset in a gentle voice.

"Relax, Dr. Sullivan. It's a strange feeling being enclosed in a Racal the first time, but it will pass. Breathe normally, and it isn't necessary to hold your arms out like that or walk with stiff knees. These suits are very flexible, even if they are a bit clumsy."

She tried for a smile, her face distorted behind the Plexiglas faceplate of her hood. "This is weird, like being in some kind of bubble. I feel dizzy and sick to my stomach."

"You're hyperventilating. Breathe slowly. Whatever you do, don't take off your headgear if you do vomit. It won't be very pleasant, but we can't take any chances. If this is a hot-bug like we think it is, removing any part of your suit could kill you."

He moved over to stand directly in front of her and put his face up close to her faceplate and his hands on her shoulders to reassure her that he was there for her if she needed him.

Seeing her face, he was reminded again how pretty she was. Tall, about five and a half feet, with long auburn hair, brilliant green eyes, and finely chiseled features; she wasn't classically beautiful, but she was definitely not hard on the eyes. He smiled to himself, thinking the dusting of faint freckles across her nose and cheeks was like icing on a delicious cake.

He guessed her age at thirty and he'd liked her athletic build the moment he saw her at CDC headquarters early this morning, although her eyes were puffy and it was easy to see she had been crying. After hearing the story firsthand of her mentor's late-night telephone call, her grief was easy to understand.

"I don't know if I can do this, Dr. Williams," she said as the Huey rose noisily above their heads, buffeting them with its downdraft. "It's very hard to look at them, especially in the decomposed condition they're in. In almost every case, they are my friends."

"Someone *has* to identify them," Mason replied shortly, watching Sam Jakes and Shirley Cole lift metal suitcases full of gear and move them over to the shade of some trees and out of the blazing tropical sun. The equipment in the cases was delicate and wouldn't take well to overheating.

Suzanne Elliot and Lionel Johnson carried boxes away from the prop wash of the helicopter while Joel Schumacher hoisted his computer equipment, carrying it as if the cases were full of eggs.

Mason glanced at a few of the nearby bodies and realized Lauren was right . . . this was not going to be easy for any of them, and especially not for someone who'd known the victims personally. The hot, humid climate had accelerated decay and decomposition to the point where the bodies would be difficult if not impossible to identify. He hoped they would all have passports or other identification on their bodies. That would take some of the pressure off Lauren.

He turned back to Lauren to apologize for the tone of his voice. "Sorry. I know how very difficult this is going to be, especially since you knew all of them personally. Just take one quick look at their faces and give me their names if you can. If you can't tell by looking, they may have some identification in their clothes that will help. A voice-activated recorder on our com-link will store the names and someone at CDC will notify relatives after Joel links up with Comsat later."

"Okay," she said hesitantly, "I'll do my best."

He looked at her and wondered if he'd made a mistake bringing a newbie on a trip this dangerous. If she screwed up, it could cost her her life, as well as potentially put all of them at risk.

Well, he thought, there's nothing that can be done now. She's just going to have to suck it up and do what's necessary. I just hope she's tougher than she looks or we're all in trouble.

He knew wearing a Racal suit was an unpleasant experience but that was what she'd signed on for. The claustrophobic feeling of being shut off from all external stimuli, the metallic taste of recycled air, and the constant buzzing of the air recirculator fan all combined to make even experienced investigators uncomfortable, and for first-timers it could be extremely frightening.

He took a deep breath and decided to try to be more sympathetic, but before he could say anything else, he was interrupted by Sam's voice booming through his headset.

"It's some sort of hemorrhagic illness all right. This boy died of apparent hemorrhagic shock. There isn't any doubt whatsoever." Dr. Jakes was kneeling in a clump of tall grass thirty yards away with Suzanne leaning over his shoulder.

Mason could see a pair of blue jean–clad legs protruding from the brush.

"I agree," Suzanne added, bending over the same body.

Mason nodded. He knew that if any member of the team could immediately recognize symptoms of known epidemic disease it would be Suzanne Elliot, the team epidemiologist.

Shirley Cole, esteemed microbiologist, walked over to stand looking down at the body between Suzanne and Jakes.

"The copies of Díaz's journal we read on the way down

here mentioned the disease among the Spaniards and Aztecs started in animals and livestock. If it's the same organism, it might be a form of woolsorter's disease . . . respiratory anthrax, or something similar," she stated.

"Bullshit!" Sam snapped, angrily shaking his head within his Racal helmet as if the statement was patently ridiculous. "It's much more likely viral—in fact, I'd go so far as to say it's certainly viral."

He hesitated a moment, his eyes flicking uncertainly to Shirley as if he knew he'd gone too far. "Of course, we won't know for certain until we see tissue samples under a microscope."

He chuckled, trying to ease the obvious anger on her face and to defuse the situation. "I think you've jumped to an unfounded conclusion in favor of bacteria, Shirley," he offered in a slightly less confrontational tone of voice.

"I only said it might be . . ." she growled through clenched teeth, her eyes flashing, showing she didn't buy his contrite tone for a minute. "In fact, anthrax and a host of other bacterial diseases can cause symptoms almost indistinguishable from hemorrhagic shock or fever, just in case you've forgotten your freshman microbiology, Sam," she added sarcastically.

Though they often argued and bickered like young children over potential etiologies of plagues they worked on together, Mason knew in the end they'd come to an accurate diagnosis and somehow remain the best of friends so he ignored them and looked to other members of his team to see what they had to say.

"Here's another one," Lionel said from a spot north of the others. "A young woman . . . or what's left of her. These ants are all over the place."

Mason heard a slight gasp from Lauren's microphone and made a mental note to tell the others to be a little more careful in their descriptions of the bodies.

Shirley Cole's voice broke through and interrupted him before he could see what effect the graphic descriptions had on Lauren.

"Here's one more," Shirley said over the helmet microphone as she stepped a few feet further into the jungle and away from Jakes and Elliot.

"All visible orifices evidence dried blood—the ears, nose, mouth, and tear ducts." She pulled a knife from a scabbard on her waist and gently sliced open the clothes on the body.

She gently peeled the layers away, baring the nude body. "Hemorrhage also occurred in the anus and penis. It certainly looks like hemorrhagic shock all right. It's hard to believe it could be anything else." She chuckled low in her throat. "Hell, God help us all, but maybe Sam is right this time and the etiology is viral."

She carefully stood up so as not to cut her Racal suit and put her knife away.

She turned to face him, her eyes wide behind the plastic face shield of her helmet.

"You were definitely right, Mason, when you said it looked like we had a hot zone on our hands. I'll get tissue samples under my scope as soon as I can, but we'll need the Cytotec lab for serology and blood chemistries. You may as well notify the guys at the Mexico City airport to head this way in the Sikorsky, and tell them not to drop the damn thing this time. A lousy fifty-dollar cable bolt cost CDC half a million last month when we were in Australia."

Mason's face flamed at the memory of the ass-chewing he'd received from the agency bean counters over that incident and he let go of Lauren's arm, trying to ignore the shocked and frightened look on her face in response to the look on his.

He walked over to Joel Schumacher to give the order to call Mexico City.

Joel was setting up his computer and dish antenna and glanced up. "Should I try the cell, Mason, or wait for satellite uplink?" he asked.

Mason hadn't considered it. A cell call might not be able to get through from Tlateloco since there were no towers within a hundred miles. They were definitely going to need to use the sat-phone or wait an hour for Joel to set up the satellite dish for a satellite uplink.

"Before we send for the lab, does anyone have any doubts?" he asked, moving in a circle to get a better look at his team members.

"None!" Sam Jakes said quickly. "We've got a hot one here and it could be damn near anything," and then, forgetting the helmet mike would pick up even a whisper, muttered under his breath, "Though I know damn well it's a virus."

"I agree with Sam," Shirley Cole said. "It's most probably a virus of some sort causing hemorrhagic fever and shock, though I still maintain that from the written record of Díaz, it could still be anthrax, or some other form of zoonosis, a bacterial infection spread by and from animals." She glared a challenge at Jakes, daring him to disagree. "That'd be my guess if the evidence of widespread hemorrhaging wasn't so prevalent."

"Anthrax is not transmittable from human to human!" Sam Jakes said with heavy sarcasm, his voice harsh with his customary lack of tact. "How the hell can you explain that little fact away, or have you forgotten your own freshman microbiology, Shirley?"

He shook his head as if he were talking to recalcitrant students. "It could just as easily be dengue or breakbone fever, spread by mosquitos, or hemorrhagic rabies from fruit bats, or . . ."

"Hemorrhagic viruses aren't usually spread from animals to humans, Sam," Suzanne said, forcing her voice to be patient. "At least, none that I've ever encountered before, and Díaz's journal clearly states the disease began in the animals around the camp."

"But . . ." Jakes began.

"Send for the lab," Lionel said, cutting him off. "This shit could be damn near anything at this point! I vote we just run all of the tests for both viruses and bacteria and stop all this goddamn guessing and backbiting!"

Everyone gaped, not used to hearing the mild-mannered gentle giant speak so harshly.

He walked over to kneel over a decimated corpse with dried blood all over the face. "The only thing I'm fairly certain of is it's not from a fungus or mycobacteria . . . at least not any that I know of could spread this fast or be fatal in such a short period of time as we see here, nor would they cause this much hemorrhaging."

Mason left Joel to peer down at the corpse where Lionel was kneeling. If he'd needed any further convincing it wasn't necessary now. The body of a young woman lay in a pool of dried blood. A swarm of black ants, so thick they covered her from head to toe, was feeding on her.

All the signs of hemorrhagic shock were in evidence, a profusion of bleeding from every orifice.

"Send for the lab, Joel," he said without looking around. "And notify CDC we've got an emergency hot zone of unknown proportions."

Chapter 6

Mason Williams stood with his hands on his hips as he looked around the clearing, watching his team work. He took a deep breath. He was just about to put in motion events that would have a profound effect on Mexico—events that could not be undone once begun.

"Have them start the ball rolling with the Mexican government to get this area sealed off, and be sure you give this a Biohazard Level Four code. They'll want to know if it's airborne and we can't give them an answer yet, so make certain the Mexican government understands how potentially dangerous this is. They have to give us a maximum perimeter until we give this bug a name and a source. No telling what the host will turn out to be, or even if it's viral or bacterial, but it has to have something to do with unearthing Montezuma's tomb or we'd have seen it here in Mexico before."

"The worst thing they've ever had down here is the food," Sam grumbled, opening his case to take out a scalpel and a pack of glass slides and petri dishes. "I don't see how anybody can eat the spicy shit without developing either cast-iron intestines or colon cancer."

Lauren stepped over to where she could look into Mason's face mask while she talked to him, even though everyone in the team could hear her as well. "Mason, Díaz's journal said the disease started in the animals. If that was true here, how are we going to get wild animals to obey a quarantine perimeter?"

He shook his head and raised his hand as if to run it through his hair, which was impossible in a Racal suit. "We can't, Lauren. That's why we need a really large perimeter and we hope the infected animals, if they are indeed the vector, get sick and die before they travel across it."

"Yeah, and we hope like hell it's not transmitted by birds, like bird flu is," Suzanne said. "If it is, then we're toast and any hope we have of containing this son of a bitch is dead in the water."

"Luckily, I think that possibility is almost nil," Jakes chimed in. "If it were transmitted by birds, I think by now we'd have heard of more deaths spread out all through the jungle from here to Mexico City."

Mason sighed deeply. "I hope you're both correct and we are able to keep the disease within the perimeter."

"Here's two more," Shirley announced, bending over. "It looks like a boy and a girl. They have their arms around each other like they lay down together. I suppose they knew they were dying and tried to comfort each other."

"Are you writing a fucking book or are you going to get us some samples to look at?" Sam asked impatiently while carving slices of decaying flesh from his corpse.

Mason looked toward the Aztec temple, trying to ignore the bickering. He knew it was because of the tremendous stress of finding so many young people dead from a horrible disease of unknown origin. Even though his team members were consummate professionals, finding so many young bodies on the site was going to be very difficult for them and they would all have to deal with it in their own ways.

He wondered what sort of killer had been unleashed when these archaeologists opened Montezuma's hidden burial chamber. Was it viral or bacterial? A virus could not survive more than a few minutes outside a living host, making it harder to consider a viral source when Montezuma's tomb had supposedly been sealed for hundreds of years.

While he was too pragmatic to believe in curses, he pondered the cause of so many unexplained deaths. If it had come from some source in the jungle, someone in medicine should have diagnosed it or reported its symptoms before now, prior to its sudden appearance at Tlateloco.

This was ultimately his Wildfire Team's job, to identify microscopic monsters and to figure out how to stop them before they were able to cause widespread death and destruction.

Howard Carter hadn't lived long enough to see what kind of demon he brought to the surface in Egypt. At the time no one understood invisible dangers, other than to blame "bad air" or "unhealthy humors" or "ancient curses" for unexplained illnesses.

Was the unearthing of Montezuma's tomb the beginning of a far more lethal discovery? According to Dr. Sullivan, as many as thirty-two people may have perished here, if the entire archaeological team was found to have died, and that was not counting several Mexican laborers who were usually used for the heavy lifting and digging according to Lauren.

Mason turned around when he heard a soft groan. Lauren was bending over a body, reaching down to brush some of the ants off the face so she could make an identification.

He walked over and when he looked into her face he noticed a single tear coursing down her cheek.

"Are you okay?"

She looked at him and nodded. "Yes, I'm just saying good-bye to them as I make the IDs." She hesitated and then she added, "When I come to one of the laborers, I'll go through their clothing and see if I can find some sort of ID so we can at least give the Mexican government their names."

He nodded his thanks for her extra effort and patted the arm of her Racal, trying to show her he understood how difficult this was for her, and then he turned and went to see how the other members of his team were making out.

He walked over to where Suzanne was kneeling to take samples from a body. When she finished and stood up he stretched his neck inside his helmet and looked into her eyes. "I've got a bad feeling on this one, Suzanne. I don't rely on hunches or guesswork, but I can't shake the sensation that we're about to find something we hoped we would never see."

"What's that, boss?"

"A bug so hot that it will cause a pandemic that will spread across the North American continent like Grant going through Richmond—and will cause even more destruction than he did in his march across Georgia."

After checking in with the other team members and finding no one needed his assistance, Mason walked over to the entrance to the temple and leaned his head into the stone door.

When he shined his flashlight into the darkness, he saw a four-foot-square tunnel carved into the wall of square stones. He eased in, bent down onto his knees, and crept slowly down into the tunnel opening.

He soon found it led into the bowels of the temple. He swept the walls and floor with his flashlight, making sure he didn't crawl over anything sharp that would violate his suit.

Forty feet into the shaft he discovered a body. This was an older man, almost certainly Dr. Adams since all the other members of the archaeological team had been young students. A flip-top satellite cell phone lay between his legs and a leather-bound book rested on his lap, still held tightly in his hands.

Mason eased it out of his grasp and flashed his light on it, seeing that it was the original copy of Díaz's journal. He gently placed it back in the man's lap. He would leave the honor of taking it to Lauren—it was the least he could do.

The body's facial features were frozen in a rictus of agony. Dried blood covered his cheeks and lips and neck.

"Hemorrhagic shock," Mason whispered. "It got every one of them, whatever the hell this is . . ."

He carefully stepped over Adams's outstretched legs and moved deeper into the stone-walled tunnel. After he'd gone only a few feet, he encountered a giant slab of rock pulled away from the entrance to a dark inner chamber.

Out of simple curiosity, he edged through the opening and noticed the ceiling had receded and the room was a good fifteen feet high and almost twenty feet deep. He stood, relieving the pressure on his aching knees, and moved the beam of his flashlight over a scene taken from the pages of ancient history.

A shriveled corpse lay upon a stone altar, arms folded over its chest, preserved by some primitive mummification method, which along with the airtight seal of the tomb had prevented most decomposition of the skin.

Surrounding the altar were clay urns and piles of deteriorated cloth, possibly robes or garments worn by an Aztec king.

"Montezuma," Mason said softly, mouthing the name rather than actually speaking it aloud.

The remains of two mummified monkeys lay curled in fetal positions near Montezuma's feet. As he leaned down to look at them more closely, he noticed one was wearing a deerskin collar embedded with precious emeralds and rubies with beaten silver bands while the other's neck was bare.

He straightened up and looked around the chamber again. Standing in a burial tomb from the 1500s, Mason felt he understood the excitement Dr. Adams and his team members must have experienced when they entered this room. How could they have known this was also potentially a time bomb, waiting for centuries to explode?

He passed his flashlight over a few more relics and backed away, moving toward a square of daylight at the end of the shaft. More than history had been uncovered here, he told himself as he stepped around the corpse of Dr. Adams to begin the serious work of finding out what caused so many sudden deaths.

In the pit of his stomach he felt more than uneasiness, as though what brought him here would forever change mankind's view of epidemic disease in ways even he, with all his medical training, couldn't begin to comprehend.

When he emerged in the bright sunlight he saw his team members intent upon their specialized tasks and briefly, he felt better. He had some of the best men and women in their respective fields, a crack medical investigative force despite their personal differences.

Mason smiled grimly. If anyone could find out what caused these deaths at Tlateloco, his Wildfire Team stood the best possible chance.

He started back across the clearing with his flashlight to add his own specialty, bacteriology, to the effort. Walking past rotting corpses, he wondered about Lauren Sullivan and the advisability of bringing her along. So far she was showing toughness he hadn't expected her to possess. Hopefully, she would continue to hold up under the extreme pressure of the gory job he'd given her to do.

What he hadn't told her was the primary reason identification of the bodies had to take place in Tlateloco. If this were truly an extremely contagious epidemic, as it appeared to be now, the remains of every student archaeologist and staff member and laborer would have to be burned in place—destroyed completely to keep the germ from spreading, whatever it was. The risks of sending the bodies home for burial were simply too great.

And he didn't want to even consider the potential political and scientific outcry he would have to overcome if he had to advocate fuel bombing the entire site and destroying those precious archaeological relics in the tomb.

He chuckled to himself, thinking about what a shit-storm that would be.

He paused for a moment, glancing around the clearing at bodies lying everywhere, his team covering them with black plastic sheets to prevent further scavenging by predators. He was reminded of old newsreels from the Vietnam War of fire zones containing corpses of young American servicemen lying like stacked cordwood, awaiting transport back to the States.

His lips tightened when he reasoned that these young archaeologists also died in a war, though their killer wasn't foreign soldiers but some microscopic assassin even more deadly.

He pushed the grisly images from his mind and offered a silent prayer, knowing if his team was not successful here they could be looking at a death toll far greater than what America suffered in Southeast Asia or even World War II . . . an epidemic of potentially limitless proportions.

He didn't want to even contemplate what would happen if the hot-bug that had caused one hundred percent mortality in this site were to escape the jungle and travel to civilization without a cure having been found.

As he strode toward a tent roof Lionel and Joel had erected over various pieces of laboratory equipment resting on folding aluminum tables, he was suddenly distracted by a moving shadow in the jungle off to his right.

At first he thought it might be an animal, until a closer look revealed a half-naked boy with pronounced Indian facial features looking over his shoulder at the men in orange space suits while running deeper into the forest.

"Son of a bitch!" Mason cried, pointing to the place where he saw the boy disappear. "Someone just ran into those trees," He yelled, starting to run after him. He knew that if the boy had been exposed to this disease, whatever the hell it is, he could spread it all over this part of Mexico.

The other members of the team turned and looked at Mason, but they were too late to see the fleeing figure as it disappeared into the brush.

Chapter 7

As she identified more and more of her friends' bodies, Lauren became increasingly unsteady on her feet, breathing in short bursts despite Dr. Williams's warnings. Her battery-operated air supply hummed loudly in her ears, buzzing like a swarm of angry bees. The harsh noise combined with the claustrophobic feel of her hood and the rubbery smell of filtered air made her feel queasy, nauseated.

To make matters worse, she was quietly sobbing, caught in the grip of despair so deep, so intense that words could never have described it. At the edge of the jungle forest she leaned against a palm tree, fearing what her next few footsteps would reveal.

In dormitory tents erected where shade offered some escape from central Mexico's furnace-like heat and humidity, she knew she would find the bodies of many of her friends and former students. She could see some of them now, lumpy forms lying on canvas folding cots beneath tent roofs surrounded by mosquito netting. They were partially hidden in patches of mottled shade provided by leafy limbs where the jungle canopy thinned near the clearing's edge.

This was . . . had been Charlie's camp. According to department records, thirty-one graduate students had accompanied Dr. Adams here this summer, students from every level in the archaeology program. She remembered their excitement when Charlie told them his initial expedition to this spot convinced him he'd found the fabled Aztec city of Tlateloco, and a massive stone temple where records found in an overlooked collection of four-hundred-year-old documents in Spanish archives hinted at the location of Montezuma's burial chamber, a find that had eluded archaeologists and treasure seekers since the year 1521.

Jungle growth so dense it was virtually impenetrable had hidden the temple for centuries, until chronicles written by Bernal Díaz del Castillo and sent by carrier ship to the King of Spain recording Cortés's expeditions to the Aztec Empire were recently discovered in Madrid, pointing to Tlateloco as Montezuma's final resting place.

Thus the need for so many eager students this summer: to clear away the jungle, begin establishing grids for excavation, and painstakingly dig beneath the jungle floor looking for signs of streets and avenues and homes in the area around the temple. An uncounted number of local workers, Maya Indians and local fruit farmers who knew this jungle, were also all working from a grant given by a couple of foundations, with enough funding to hire workmen and sustain thirty-two members of the university archaeology team for two months.

And now, after little more than three weeks working the site, they were all dead. Lauren still couldn't quite make herself believe it and yet the evidence was here and undeniable no matter how much she wished it wasn't so.

Rotting corpses covered the entire area—the bodies of friends and associates, which she must identify without breaking down in utter despair, an almost impossible task. Her friends were lying among dead Mexican laborers who would most probably remain forever unnamed as few of them seemed to be carrying any identification on their persons.

As she glanced around at the carnage surrounding her, she realized the fetid, ozone-laden recycled air she was breathing in her helmet was in fact a blessing—the smell of decomposition would have been so much worse, especially since much of it would have come from her friends.

She remembered entries from the translation of Díaz's journal that Charles had sent to her, of the explorer witnessing scores of deaths like these as he himself lay dying in a chamber beneath the temple.

Lauren had only been able to glance quickly at four bodies, tasting bitter bile rising in her throat when she saw Bonnie Evans, half eaten by swarming ants, her gold chain with its tiny golden cross still around her neck. She wondered briefly if Bonnie had prayed for salvation when the first symptoms ravaged her body or if she cursed her fate when she saw her friends dying horrible deaths before her eyes.

Knowing Bonnie as she had, Lauren felt certain her response to the horror would have been prayers, not curses. But her prayers, like everyone else's in the group, had gone unanswered.

Little Robert Conway lay a short distance away; a brilliant boy from Montana with the sweetest disposition, only a semester from graduation. He'd given Lauren flowers on her birthday and gotten a kiss on the cheek as a reward.

Kelly Woods was lying in Robert's arms when they

died, and the sight of them embracing in death had almost been too much for Lauren. She remembered Robert had given Kelly his fraternity pin the week before they left on the expedition. She wondered briefly if it was still pinned to the inside of Kelly's bra, a university tradition.

Lauren had closed her eyes and said the names into her recorder, remembering who they were, how much they meant to her personally as students and as friends.

She glanced over at Mason Williams as he bent over a body, wondering if he and his team were as affected by the stacks of bodies as she was, or were they as doctors used to seeing such sights and just looked upon her friends as interesting mysteries to be solved?

Earlier, after hearing him and his team describe her friends' bodies in graphic terms without the least amount of sympathy in their voices, she'd felt like screwing up all her courage and standing before him and telling him she would do what was necessary, not for him or for his damned team. But she would do her best because her friends deserved the very best she could do and she was damned if she'd let them or Dr. Adams down.

She grinned to herself, wondering what he would've done had she told him that if she were not enclosed in a helmet she'd spit in his eye.

She took a deep breath, trying to calm down. After all, he and his team had not really done anything wrong except to go about their jobs efficiently and professionally, and perhaps they were hurting at what they were seeing as much as she was but were just better at hiding their feelings.

She hoped this was true, for she found she really liked the team, even the irascible Dr. Jakes.

Now Lauren could hear members of Dr. Mason Williams's party talking over their headsets, discussing

blood and brain tissue and what they continued to call hemorrhagic shock. They talked about dead bodies in an almost conversational way, as if they were nothing more
than objects.

But the bodies here were much more than mere objects
to Lauren, and the doctors' apparent detachment was difficult for her to comprehend and made it hard for her to give
them the benefit of the doubt about whether they really
cared about the students.

"These were people," she whispered, gathering her
strength and resolve before going to the tents to identify
more corpses. "Why can't those assholes understand these
were real people . . . ?"

"I suppose we should resent being called assholes," a
voice said through her radio headset. It was Mason who
spoke to her.

"Lauren," he said gently, "please don't mistake our pro-
fessionalism for heartlessness. While we are working, we
must maintain a distance from our patients lest we let our
feelings influence our findings."

He hesitated, and then he added, "Believe me when I
tell you that everyone here will grieve in his or her own
way after we finish our work here today. There is no dis-
respect of the dead here, but we show our respect by finding out what caused their deaths and preventing it from
killing more people across the world."

She glanced in his direction as he spoke, realizing his
good looks had been a distraction. His deep blue eyes
conveyed sympathy his callous demeanor belied when he
talked about body parts and tissue samples like they were
pieces of machinery.

When they'd first met this morning in Atlanta she'd
noted his sloppy manner of dress and only later, while

they were talking, did she notice his angular jaw, muscular neck and arms, and his curious, catlike grace in his movements.

He didn't look like a doctor, at least not like the ones she'd known at the University of Texas. She'd immediately realized he had a strong chin and had smiled, remembering her mother always told her men with weak chins were weak-willed and shouldn't be trusted and that she should endeavor to find a man with a strong masculine chin.

Lauren shook her head, trying to put these thoughts out of her mind, realizing they were highly inappropriate given the circumstances. "I'm sorry," she said. "I forgot everyone could hear me."

"It's okay, Dr. Sullivan. We understand what you are going through," Lionel said. "In fact, I myself am more than a little pissed off! I don't mind quite so much when our work brings us into close contact with middle-aged or older dead people, but these young ones were just getting started living their lives and were cut down in the very beginning of their careers." He took a deep breath. "So, yeah, we may sound and act professional on the outside, but I assure you, Lauren, my heart aches at your loss as much as yours does."

Lauren's eyes teared up at Lionel's confession.

"Are you getting a little more used to wearing the Racal?" Suzanne asked in an obvious attempt to change the subject.

"Not really," she replied, glancing over her shoulder. Mason was standing under a canvas canopy a hundred yards away, setting up some type of apparatus at the end of a table. Seeing Williams and his team now, dressed in bright orange space suits, working diligently over decaying corpses, was like something out of a bad science fiction movie.

"If you get dizzy again, lie down. But be careful not to tear your suit," Mason said without turning to look her way. "A Racal is fairly durable but it won't withstand sharp objects."

"In spite of what you must think about my earlier . . . hyperventilation, Dr. Williams," Lauren spat, "I am not stupid. I remember everything Suzanne told me when she suited me up."

Without waiting for an answer, Lauren turned back to the group of tents and walked a short distance toward them. "Most of the students are over here. It's where Charlie . . . Dr. Adams, set up camp for the students and about twenty-five yards farther on are the ones for the Mexican workmen."

She hesitated. "I haven't had a chance to go inside the tents just yet. I can see them lying on their cots, even from here . . ." She fought back a sob, not wanting the others to hear her.

"One of us can come over to assist you in a moment, Dr. Sullivan. Right now we're all very busy," Mason said, concern evident in his voice.

"It's okay. I can do it alone. I just need a few minutes to work up the nerve. I've never seen so much blood. It's all over everything."

"Take all the time you need," Mason said. "As you may have guessed by now, we expect to be here for a while. One of our portable laboratories is being flown in by chopper. This isn't going to be easy, identifying the bug."

"I wish you'd stop calling it a bug," she whispered, once again forgetting the others could hear her.

"Here's something!" Dr. Jakes exclaimed in his dry,

caustic voice. "Meningorrhagia, hemorrhage into the cerebral meninges. I need another piece of that boy's brain. Open his skull at the suprameatal triangle and I can see if the spinal meninges are affected."

"Dear God," Lauren thought, leaning harder against the tree trunk when she heard Dr. Jakes talk about opening Robert Conway's head, as though he was breaking an egg for an omelet. Lauren wished for a way to turn her headset off. Listening to this grim discussion of her friends' body parts and brain tissue was only making her feel worse.

Taking a moment to collect herself, she summoned all the courage she could muster and strode slowly to the nearest tent, pushing a veil of mosquito netting aside. She promised herself she would not look at the blood or the faces any longer than absolutely necessary.

"Tom Butterfield. Sally Ann Higgins. I'm not quite sure who this one . . . it's David Wong . . . his face is so badly swollen I hardly recognized him. Carla Jenkins. The boy lying on the floor is Timothy Greer, a second-year graduate student with a four-point GPA." She gulped, "He *had* a four-point GPA. I know his mother. All these ants are making it more difficult to see who they are . . ."

Lauren left the first tent to enter another.

She coughed and swallowed stinging acid, grateful again for the filtered air, which smelled only of rubber and not the stench of death that she knew surrounded her like a fog.

"In the tent on the right is Malcolm Collins. He was working on his dissertation this spring in Central American Indian studies. The blond girl beside him is Gertrude Wolf, a German student, a senior in the undergraduate program. The boy beside her is Wayland Burke, a kid from Wyoming who qualified for a Brinkman scholarship. I'm not sure about this one . . . I remember his face, but not his name. If I can, I'll look in his luggage for his passport."

She knelt beside a bloodstained cot and gasped. "Maggots! Oh my God! Maggots are crawling out of his nose!"

"Remain calm, Dr. Sullivan," Mason said quickly from the center of the clearing. "Maggots are simply fly larvae. It's to be expected in this heat. Don't look too closely. All we need are their names."

She took a passport from a duffle bag beneath the cot and opened it. "Richard Willis. He was only twenty years old."

At least, Lauren thought, they were all beyond suffering now. Everything these bright young people had been or ever hoped to be was finished. Their hopes and dreams lay rotting here in the jungle, their bodies food for hungry scavengers and insects.

She stood up and walked to a nearby tent. "I think this tent contains local workers Charlie hired." She glanced inside. "There is a man curled into a ball on one of the cots. He looks to be a local Indian, possibly a Tarrahumarra, by his red hair and light skin coloring."

Her worst experience was saved for last, when Mason told her a body was lying in the tunnel running underneath the temple. "Be careful, Lauren. This one might affect you more than the others," he warned.

Not understanding how anything could be worse than what she'd already seen, she took a flashlight and entered the tunnel. When she reached the corpse she gasped, and then she sat down in the tunnel and cried as quietly as she could.

"It's Charlie. Dr. Charles W. Adams, head of the

Archaeology Department at the University of Texas in Austin. He has two grandchildren and a daughter living in Delaware. Someone must let them know right away."

She couldn't look at Charlie any longer and stumbled past his body to the entrance into a rock-lined tomb. There she saw the mummified remains of Montezuma and his pet monkeys, for he was known to keep a number of animals as household pets.

Several rotted wooden cages held decayed bodies of large lizards and snakes. Piles of hand-woven cloth, clay tablets, urns, and stone carvings were arranged in neat rows around his sepulcher.

Lauren stood there for several minutes, her training as an archaeologist momentarily overriding her deep sorrow for what had happened to Charlie and his students. Suddenly she noticed a distinct feeling of apprehension developing within her despite the importance of such a monumental archaeological find as if some ghostly apparition was in the tomb with her now.

She convinced herself it was merely her imagination and the horrors she witnessed here were working on her overactive mind. In order to take her mind off such superstitious meanderings, she examined Montezuma's face in the beam of her flashlight, his twisted, wrinkled cheeks and distorted expression, the result of losing fluid from facial tissue and skin over time, exposing a row of yellow teeth that had been filed down to sharp points.

It almost looked as if the Aztec ruler was smiling—an evil, wicked smile adding to Lauren's deepening sense of foreboding.

"There are no such things as curses," she said to herself.

* * *

Dusk had begun to darken the sky above the jungle when the rhythm of a helicopter's blades came from the east. Lauren was sitting on a canvas stool as far away from Mason Williams and his team members as she could, unable to watch any more of what was going on beneath their canopy, dulled by what she'd seen today, feeling drained to such a point she couldn't cry any longer.

In truth, she felt strangely removed from what was happening now as if this were all a bad dream, a nightmare from which she would soon awaken. The strain of the previous eighteen hours had taken its toll on her, and she sat as though in a stupor, not listening to any more of what was being said by the doctors simply because it was too horrible to comprehend.

If she could, she would have turned her headset off to be spared the agony of hearing the doctors describe their gruesome dissections of her friends. The bodies of Charles Adams and twenty-six students had been identified, leaving five unaccounted for. She'd also found nine local workmen among the dead. Mason told her they could expect to find the others somewhere in the jungle tomorrow morning, and when the last identifications had been made Joel would radio for a helicopter to take her to Mexico City, and then she could fly home to Austin.

As promised, Mason had notified Dr. Cardenez and Dr. Matos of what they found here, along with an urgent request to have the Mexican Army establish a far-flung perimeter around the ruins at Tlateloco. They'd assured him it would not be too difficult as the few roads that traversed this part of the jungle were small and easily blocked.

To the rest of the team, he continually voiced concerns

about some Indian boy he had seen earlier running through the jungle, although no one else recalled seeing anyone alive here after the helicopter dropped them off.

Now the Mexican Army helicopter hovered above the clearing, appearing as a huge, wingless iron bird with a silver box resembling a railroad car or double-wide modular home suspended below its belly on thick stainless steel cables.

Lauren listened to Joel Schumacher direct the helicopter downward over the radio as the noise from whirling blades grew louder. Prop wash made the jungle grasses and vines dance with a life of their own as Joel called for the chopper's slow descent.

This was the mobile lab Dr. Williams had talked about before, and when Lauren saw it she was reminded of something belonging on a lunar landscape. Downdraft from the circling blades whipped everything in sight, blowing the roof off their temporary canopy, scattering odd bits of assorted gear in every direction on mighty gusts of wind as the lab building was lowered toward a small clearing away from the tents and equipment of the ill-fated expedition.

"Tell them to send down the portable generator," Joel said into his headset to someone aboard the aircraft. "And then lower the containers of gasoline and propane after everything down here is secured."

The lab settled gently onto a carpet of grass and the massive cables were released. Joel left his radio to join the others helping with guiding more crates and containers being sent down on thin steel lines.

After the massive load of equipment was offloaded, the chopper set down briefly and another orange-suited figure emerged, walking clumsily in the suit as if he wasn't used to wearing one.

Lauren heard the name "Dr. Matos" mentioned over her helmet radio as the new arrival was greeted by the other scientists. Dr. Matos had apparently kept his word to join them here at the site.

Lauren noticed another member of the team wearing an orange suit hang back a moment, connecting some sort of instrument to Joel's radio. No one else appeared to be aware of this team member's absence near the portable laboratory, too busy themselves to pay attention to what was going on. Lauren couldn't see who it was and it seemed odd at the time, but then what did she know about Wildfire Team procedures?

Chapter 8

Sweat beaded on his forehead and dripped into the young *Indio*'s eyes as he trudged through jungle humidity darkening rapidly as dusk approached. Even though centuries of evolution had caused his people's perspiration to be unappetizing to the horde of mosquitos and other biting insects of the wilderness, they continued to swarm around his head, filling his eyes and nose and making it difficult to breathe without inhaling the noxious creatures.

Their buzzing irritated and distracted him as he listened for the grunt of a night-feeding jaguar or the squeal of a boar protecting its young, either of which could be fatal if he missed their warning signs. He'd been careless once today already, letting the man in the orange clothes spot him as he watched them work.

He froze when he heard the sound of a jeep engine a few hundred yards ahead. The sound suddenly ceased, and he decided to investigate. Stepping nimbly through dense undergrowth without making a sound, he soon parted the leaves of a jacaranda tree and peered into a small clearing next to the narrow stone and gravel road that meandered through the forest.

He saw a tall, thin Anglo gathering wood in the darkening light, preparing a campfire as he laid out a sleeping bag and cooking utensils. In a few moments, the smell of coffee and soup boiling made the boy's mouth water and his stomach growl. He had eaten nothing other than bananas and berries for two days and was weak with hunger. The sudden sickness and deaths of the Anglos at the camp had made him afraid to eat any more of their food, though they'd been generous with it before the curse came and killed them all.

The tall white man hummed to himself as he prepared his supper, causing the *Indio* to take a chance that the man would be good natured enough to share his food. After all, he knew he could disappear in the jungle in seconds if necessary. No white man could slip through the undergrowth as nimbly and fast as he could, having done it ever since he could walk.

Taking a deep breath, the boy cried softly, "*Hola, señor*," and stepped from his hiding place into the clearing, his hands held out from his body in a nonthreatening manner, his legs quivering, ready to take flight should the man prove unfriendly.

The Anglo was startled, dropping his coffee cup and cursing in surprise. "Goddamn!"

When he saw the small teenage boy, he grinned sheepishly and shook his head. "Shit, boy," he said, bending to pick up his coffee cup. "You scared me half to death sneaking up on me like that."

It was a sign of how surprised he was that he instinctively spoke in English rather than Spanish.

The boy answered in broken English he had learned from priests who visited his village, "I am most sorry, señor." He pointed at the pot bubbling over the fire. "Hungry."

The man waved an arm in a carefree gesture. "Come on in and join me. There's plenty for both of us. My name's Malcolm Fitzhugh. What's yours?"

"I am called Guatemotzi," the boy replied as he took a bowl from the ground next to the fire and ladled rich-smelling soup into it. His mouth watered and his stomach growled again, causing him to blush with embarrassment.

The man, playing the generous host, pretended not to notice. He was used to the extreme poverty and hunger that most of the Indians in this part of Mexico lived with daily.

There was little talk for a while as the two squatted in the firelight and ate, Fitzhugh showing Guatemotzi how to dip chunks of bread into the meaty liquid to sop up every last drop of the tasty brew.

When they were finished, Fitzhugh poured coffee for both of them into tin cups, adding large spoonfuls of sugar and a dollop of condensed milk from a can into the thick liquid. He leaned back against a log, lit a cigarette, and peered at Guatemotzi over the rim of his cup as he drank.

"What are you doing wandering out here all alone in the jungle at night, boy? Is your village nearby?"

Guatemotzi shook his head, blowing on the hot liquid to cool it. "No. Is many kilometers south. I work at *Americano* camp, helping dig until they got sick."

Fitzhugh raised his eyebrows, smoke trailing from his nostrils. "The archaeological site of the American university professors? That's where I was heading."

Guatemotzi shook his head vigorously. "No, señor, you must not go there. All *Americanos* very sick, and most now dead. It is bad place—is cursed."

Fitzhugh smiled uncertainly, firelight reflecting off his teeth in the moonlit darkness. "Are you sure they're dead, not just suffering from dysentery? Those Americans never learn not to drink the local water."

He didn't really believe the boy, for he'd been there only last week making acquaintances with workers who would be willing to sell him artifacts from the dig site they'd stolen. They couldn't all have died in such a short amount of time—the boy must be mistaken.

Guatemotzi lowered his eyes. He knew it was much worse than simple diarrhea. It was the curse of the God Montezuma that had killed the *Americanos*, but this Anglo would never understand that. Still, he had to try. "No, señor, you must not! I tell you they all dead!"

Fitzhugh continued to stare at the boy appraisingly, lighting another cigarette off the butt of his first. "I've got to go there, boy, it's my job. I buy the things the scientists dig up and sell them in the city. You understand?"

Guatemotzi nodded, becoming very excited. Perhaps this Anglo would give him money for what he had found in the emperor's tomb after the *Americanos* got sick.

He reached into the deerskin pouch slung over his shoulder, the one in which he carried his poison arrows for killing game. He pulled out a leather collar with green and red stones and hammered silver embedded in it.

Fitzhugh's eyes bugged and his heart hammered and his mouth became dry as the boy handed him the collar.

"Like this, señor?"

Fitzhugh took the artifact in trembling hands, trying to calculate in his mind what it would be worth in Mexico

City or Houston. "Where did you get this?" he asked, knowing it could only have come from the tomb itself.

"From cave where Emperor Montezuma lay," Guatemotzi answered. "When *Americanos* got too sick to pay me, I took this for work I did. It was around neck of small monkey near emperor's body."

Fitzhugh's eyes narrowed as he stared at the way firelight sparkled in the emeralds and rubies and reflected off the silver strands woven around the deerskin strap. He'd read stories of how Emperor Montezuma kept small jungle animals as pets, so he knew the boy was telling the truth. That this collar had been worn by one of Montezuma's pets made it almost priceless in value.

He pulled a wad of *pesos* from his pocket and handed them to Guatemotzi. "I'll give you twenty thousand *pesos* for it. Is that enough?"

Guatemotzi was astounded. That was more money than he had ever seen. His would be the richest family in the village.

"Si, señor!" he said, placing the bills in his deerskin pouch.

Fitzhugh grinned and scrambled to his feet. He ran to his jeep and placed the collar in his duffle bag before the boy could change his mind. He took a bag of army rations and handed them to the young Indian. "Here is some food for you. I won't be needing it anymore. I'm leaving immediately for Mexico City."

Without another word or a look back, Fitzhugh jumped into his jeep, started the engine, and roared off following his headlights down the dirt road, visions of untold riches flitting through his mind.

As he drove through the darkening evening, Fitzhugh pulled the collar from his bag and held it before his eyes, grinning and watching the moonlight play off the jewels' facets.

With a gleeful laugh, he brought the collar to his lips and kissed it. He had no idea it was a kiss of death, or that he would be dead within a week.

Thousands of microscopic spores drifted off the deer-skin collar where they had lain for four hundred years. They swirled in the moonlight and wind and were inhaled by Fitzhugh as he kissed the collar. They traveled in through his nasal passages and throat and lodged in the mucosa of his trachea and lungs.

The spores, tiny polysaccharide balls, were formed by the plague organisms when they were unable to find suitable hosts in which to multiply. Inhabiting the spores like tiny astronauts in individual spaceships, they were able to hibernate and survive almost indefinitely without food, water, or air, lying in suspended animation awaiting only moisture to reawaken them like some malevolent Rip Van Winkles.

As the spores were moistened by Fitzhugh's mucosa, they split open and poured hundreds of thousands of plague organisms into his bloodstream. There they immediately began to split and multiply again and again, overwhelming the white blood cells his body sent in defense. Soon these organisms would begin to secrete toxins, which would destroy the parts of his blood that allowed it to co-agulate, eventually causing massive hemorrhaging from every orifice.

The process could not be stopped now short of death.

Chapter 9

Lauren felt weak, as if her blood sugar had suddenly dropped. She had been gazing at familiar faces ravaged by decomposition and predators without a break almost since they arrived—identifying corpses while the doctors were setting up equipment, and worst of all, cutting, probing, and otherwise desecrating the bodies of her friends and colleagues.

She was emotionally wrung out, physically exhausted, and feared she was also becoming dehydrated. It was impossible to eat or drink while enclosed in a Racal and she had sweltered inside the space suit all afternoon, sweat running down her face, stinging her eyes, and irritating her skin. She lost count of how many times she swiped at her faceplate with a gloved hand, trying in vain to wipe salty perspiration away.

At least she was no longer crying—both her tear ducts and her grief had suffered overload from the enormity of the tragedy she found in Tlateloco. She felt emotionally numb and sat there on a box staring off into space trying to distance herself from all that was going on around her as if that might assuage her grief at all she had seen. She felt if she could only isolate her feelings of loss and grief and somehow put them outside herself she might just survive this hellish mission.

She was startled when Mason put a hand on her shoulder. The Racal hood prohibits peripheral vision and she hadn't seen him approaching as she sat beside an escoba palm tree in the coming darkness, apart from the others and their grisly experiments on the dead, illuminated by portable halogen lamps.

"Dr. Sullivan, we've finally managed to get the mobile lab set up. If you're ready, I'll walk you and Dr. Matos through the procedure to enter and get out of your suits."

"Is it air-conditioned?" she asked hopefully, watching Eduardo in his orange protective gear standing at the base of the Aztec temple with a flashlight, probing its stones with the beam.

Mason nodded to her inside his hood, and in dim light from the generator lamps she noticed a smile and how it changed his appearance. His temples crinkled when he grinned, softening his ice-blue eyes, making him look like a small boy playing Starship Trooper in his orange space suit.

He was handsome, in a bookish way, she thought. She sighed and struggled to her feet, crediting her feelings to some strange hormone flux, some inner chemical assault brought on by physical stress and exhaustion, not to mention dehydration and extreme hunger.

He led her toward the silver laboratory brought in by the helicopter, sitting at the edge of the clearing a short distance from the tents and cots that contained the bodies. "The procedure is really quite simple," he said casually, "although it can be a bit frightening and . . . embarrassing the first time you experience it."

She tripped over uneven terrain once in the half dark and said, "Just so it's air-conditioned." And then she thought, what does he mean by embarrassing?

"We'll enter through a door at this end of the lab. The first chamber is quite small, only room for two of us at a time. Once inside, stand still with your arms outspread. I'll pull a chain and we'll be showered with three different solutions—phenolic acid, bleach, and water. That should disinfect us and kill any germs clinging to the outside of our suits.

"Once the shower stops, we'll enter a larger inner chamber where we'll help each other out of our Racals, which we'll hang up on special hooks on the wall to your left."

"That sounds simple enough." She said it without really thinking about the procedure he described.

Mason cleared his throat, and his voice changed pitch slightly. She glanced at him and could see his cheeks flaming red.

"Then we have to remove all our clothes and shower again in a mild chlorine solution and then we will change into scrub suits. The clothing we wore under the Racals will be put into sealed plastic bags to be burned later in case of inadvertent contamination."

She hesitated. "You mean ALL of our clothes?"

"Yes. Of course," he added quickly, "I'll turn my back and face the other way."

Lauren heard someone chuckle over her headset and she knew some of the other doctors were listening to their conversation with more than clinical interest.

Mason said, "I apologize for this, but the Cytotec BL Four isn't engineered for privacy, only for safety from infection."

He addressed Dr. Johnson quickly, as though wishing

to change subjects. "Lionel, bring Dr. Matos to the lab and take him through the procedure step-by-step."

Lauren smiled to herself, liking Dr. Williams for having the grace to be apologizing for their situation, to be worried about her dignity even in the face of what was going on around them. In truth, she wasn't too concerned. She was, after all, an adult and he was a doctor. But then why, she wondered, was her pulse suddenly beating faster at the prospect of disrobing in a small room with him?

"I'll bring Dr. Matos," a distant voice replied. "I suppose if you're the boss, you get the best assignments."

Another soft chuckle came from a different member of the group.

The disinfecting shower was a little scary at first, with a spray of chemicals splattering against her face mask. Lauren had fewer concerns about disrobing in front of Mason with both their backs turned. However, when they stepped into a shower that was barely big enough for both of them, all thoughts of modesty were banished. For his part, he tried his best to keep his eyes focused on the wall of the shower and not her naked body.

Once the shower stopped, she put on a pair of green scrub pants and a sleeveless top.

"Ready?" he asked, still with his back turned.

"My word, Doctor, but you've got a cute butt," she said mischievously.

"What?" he exclaimed, pulling a towel tight around his waist.

She laughed, trying to relieve the pressure of what she'd been through all day. "Just kidding, Dr. Williams, just kidding. I kept my gaze averted like a good little girl."

He turned and saw that she was already dressed in her

scrubs. Whirling a finger in a circle, he smiled and said, "Then please turn back around while I dress. I am very shy, you know."

She grinned and dutifully turned her back. "But, I'll bet it is cute, isn't it?"

"I wouldn't know, not being able to see myself from behind," he answered with a chuckle.

Once dressed, he opened a tightly sealed door leading into a room where everything seemed miniaturized: a small table and chairs, a sink, and a refrigerator like the ones found in travel trailers.

She was immediately aware of the wash of cold air against her skin and heard the hum of air-conditioning coming from the roof.

"This is better," Lauren sighed, sinking into a tiny plastic chair at the table, resting her chin in her palms as she watched Mason open the refrigerator. Even as tired as she was she found herself noticing his good looks again, and the ease with which he seemed to accomplish any task. He had, she realized, economy of movement. Everything he did was accomplished without any wasted motion.

Mason prepared a large pot of coffee, "a doctor's life-blood" he called it, and placed a tall bottle of Gatorade on the table. "Try to drink some of this," he said, offering her a paper cup. "The heat and sweating inside a Racal causes you to lose a lot of sodium and potassium. This electrolyte solution will replace it and hopefully keep you from having muscle spasms and cramps later."

"I won't need much encouragement to drink the whole thing," she said, filling the cup to the brim and taking a swig. "By the way, Dr. Williams, what does the name Cytotec BL Four mean?"

"First," he said, turning to look at her over his shoulder

as he fussed with the coffee machine, "I think it should be Mason and Lauren from now on. We don't stand much on formality here in the lab," he added in a matter-of-fact way.

"The quarters are too small and, as you've already seen, personal privacy is almost nonexistent."

Lauren smiled weakly and nodded her agreement. "It's Mason and Lauren, then," she said, gulping more fluid, aware of a slight tremor in her hands, probably from exhaustion and the dehydration he mentioned earlier and not from any excitement to be in such close quarters with a very attractive man.

"As for the name, it comes from the term Cytology Technologies, the company that manufactures the lab and equipment we use to do studies on tissue and blood samples," he continued, interrupting her reverie. "The BL Four stands for Biohazard Level Four, the highest level, meant for study of the most infectious, dangerous organisms in the world."

"And that's what you think you've found here?"

"In a BL Four we can study the filoviruses, like Ebola, Marburg, and Lassa, and also anthrax, dengue, and rabies. All organisms that are lethal and for which there are no effective treatments or vaccines. We don't know what this bug is yet, but it looks to have almost one hundred percent infectivity and one hundred percent mortality, so that makes it right up there with the worst I've ever seen."

As Dr. Johnson and Dr. Matos entered the shower room, Mason asked her, "Would you like a quick tour? The lab is so small it won't take long . . ."

"Why not?" Lauren hadn't wanted to leave the comfort of her chair, but when he asked so gently, with a curious quality to his voice, some inner urge gave her new energy.

Mason took her through various rooms, almost all of which had strange, futuristic equipment with myriad dials, computer screens, and printers attached to the walls.

"Since this is a so-called mobile lab, we try to make use of every nook and cranny to stuff as much diagnostic and communications gear in as we can," he said as he opened a door to a tiny cubicle containing both a commode and a handheld shower hose.

"I guess there'll be no soaking in a luxurious hot bathtub to soothe my aching muscles," Lauren said. She was amused when her remark appeared to embarrass him, as if it were somehow his fault things were so cramped. Or could it have been the mental picture of her soaking in a hot bath that had him flustered, she thought. Hmmm . . . she'd have to think about that.

Mason cleared his throat. "Hopefully, we'll be able to get you out of here and back to Mexico City before too long. Now that you've identified all the . . . all your friends, I'd like to get you out of the danger zone as soon as I can."

Lauren offered no reply. A part of her wanted to stay now until someone provided some answers to what had happened here, but another part wanted to fly away home and leave all the gruesome images of decaying corpses and lost friends far behind her.

The problem, she knew, was she would never be able to get those scenes from her mind—no matter how far she flew or how long she lived.

The last chamber he showed her was adjacent to the shower room. It had a metal door with thick, double-paned glass, and could only be entered from the room where the

Racals hung. She peered through heavy glass at a row of empty orange suits, hanging like discarded carapaces of obscene insects after they had broken free.

"That's the laboratory where all of the tissue and blood samples will be examined and tested. That work has to be done while wearing Racals, since we have to assume the specimens are still infective."

He pointed to the ceiling where she could see several air vents. "The room is kept at negative pressure so that any bugs that escape into the air are sucked up through the vents and bubbled through a chlorine solution to kill them."

She could see several cot-like beds surrounded by monitoring equipment similar to what she'd seen in a hospital intensive care unit when her father died.

"What are those for?"

Mason seemed uncomfortable answering her question. "Those are for treatment and study of any hot zone survivors or for us in case one of us becomes infected by a hot-bug we're investigating. We have almost everything we need to treat someone medically, short of doing major surgery."

"Have they ever been used?"

"Yes." He hesitated. "Just last year in Australia we had to take care of the wife and daughter of a horse trainer who had contracted a mutant strain of equine morbillivirus, a disease similar to measles in humans, but much more deadly."

"What happened to them?"

"They died. The entire family."

"How do you deal with . . ." she pointed through the glass at glass slides and vials of blood arranged neatly on a counter, "all this death?"

He stared at her a moment before he spoke, and his

eyes looked haunted. "In the only way any of us can. By focusing on all the possible deaths we may be preventing by what we do." He thought for a moment, and then he added, "And on good days, we save more than we lose."

He ran his hands through his hair, though it did nothing to ease the unruliness. "Look, Lauren, I know you must think us doctors are unfeeling robots from the way we dispassionately discussed your friends out there, but it is simply not true."

He hesitated as if trying to find some way to explain it to her. "It's kinda like surgeons who play rock and roll or classical music while they are doing intricate operations," he said, his eyes serious, "or why cops make dark jokes when confronted with horrible traffic accidents. Some things are just too terrible to confront head-on and must be accommodated in individual ways so the horror doesn't make us incapable of action."

"I know I'm not explaining this very well, but sometimes to cope with terrible things we must focus on mundane parts of our job in order not to be paralyzed with thoughts of what we are dealing with."

She glanced through the window in the wall at the test tubes and petri dishes containing specimens his team had collected earlier that day.

"I think I understand, Mason," she said. "It's like when I'm unearthing ancient bones from a dig site, I don't dwell on what those bones represent but only on the job I've got to do to make some sense of their current condition."

His gaze followed hers to the specimens in the next room. "We may be too late for Dr. Adams and his students, but there are fifteen million people in Mexico City a few miles away, and the only thing right now standing between them and what you've seen here today, is us."

"It must take a terrible toll on you."

"Sure. Dr. Jakes has been married three times, and Lionel has an ulcer the size of the Grand Canyon, and I'm so grouchy my secretary holds up a silver cross every time I enter the office." He gave a dry chuckle. "I'm afraid it just goes with the territory."

Lauren felt too tired to laugh appropriately. "Charlie and these kids could have used a few silver crosses."

Mason nodded, "But even if they'd had them, it wouldn't have helped. I'm afraid the only thing that is going to defeat this hot-bug is modern science, not ancient superstitions."

After a moment, he grinned, trying to lighten her mood. "Now, Doctor Lady, unless you want to miss our sumptuous dinner feast, we need to get back to the dining room."

"What are we having?" she asked, putting her hand to her stomach, which growled at the mention of food.

He made a show of sniffing air. "Unless I miss my guess, Chef Lionel Johnson will soon be preparing his *specialite du jour*, MREs sautéed lightly in a microwave."

"MREs?"

"Meals Ready to Eat, courtesy of the U.S. Army. Guaranteed to be slightly less than thirty years old. We should hurry. We won't get dessert if we're late."

"Dessert?"

"Oreos with powdered milk."

They found Dr. Matos and Dr. Johnson in the kitchen, and Lauren thought she saw fear in Eduardo's eyes. Although he was close to sixty he looked remarkably fit, graying slightly around his temples without any other pronounced signs of aging.

"I have never seen anything like this in my entire life," he said, speaking to Lauren. "I started to feel dizzy. Dr. Johnson said I had to come inside to drink electrolytes before we go back to the temple."

Suiting action to words, he took a drink from the paper cup in his hands.

He glanced at her over the rim of the cup. "I must see Montezuma's tomb, Lauren. I do not feel I can wait another day. Will you go with me?"

She looked to Mason for approval.

"After you've both eaten and consumed enough fluids," he told them quietly. "We'll be up all night working the specimens, so no one will be getting much sleep around here anyway, and the jungle can get quite cold at night so you won't be bothered by the heat like you were earlier today."

As the team gathered around the table in the main room of the lab, Mason excused himself, saying he wasn't hungry and wanted to get some of the cultures set up and cooking.

Lauren dug into her MRE as if it were a thirty-dollar steak, finding, to her surprise in spite of what she'd seen, she was famished.

She glanced at Suzanne, who was sitting next to her. "Suzanne," she began.

"Yeah?"

"What's the story on Dr. Williams?"

Suzanne's lips curled up in a half-smile. "Well, let's see . . . he's thirty-three years old, mountain bikes five miles a day unless we're in the field, and he's ex-military—did two years as a doc in the Navy." She thought for a minute, and then she added, "I believe he likes to fish and bird hunt in his spare time, of which he has none."

Lauren raised her eyebrows. "You seem to know a lot about him."

Suzanne's eyes turned wistful. "Yeah, seems I had a bit of a crush on him when I first came to work at CDC, but he's married to his work and never gave me a second look."

She stared at Lauren. "Maybe you'll have more luck than I did."

Lauren blushed fiercely. "But . . . I don't . . . Hey, listen, Suzanne," Lauren said, "Mason may be a handsome man, but I've just lost over thirty friends and a man I looked upon as a father and I've absolutely no interest in romance at this point in my life!"

Suzanne sobered and waved her hand in the air. "That's okay, I'm just kidding."

"What about you?" Lauren asked, as her breathing slowed to normal. "How did you come to work for the CDC?"

"Well, I'm kind of a natural fit. I'm an army brat; my father was an army doc in Vietnam until Agent Orange ate all the flesh off of his body, and my brother was also an army doc until Saddam's germ warfare in the Gulf War messed up his system so much he had to take a medical retirement."

"Saddam used germ warfare in the Gulf War?" Lauren asked around a mouthful of ham and beans.

Suzanne smirked. "Oh, the army denies it, but I know what I saw when my brother came home—his body as broken as his spirit."

"I'm sorry," Lauren said.

Suzanne smiled grimly. "That's the chance you take when you work for Uncle Sam, Lauren."

"What about Sam Jakes?" Lauren asked quietly to change the subject. "Do he and Shirley Cole really hate each other as much as it sounds like?"

Suzanne chuckled. "Hell no. In fact, the old boy's kinda sweet on her if you ask me . . . especially her baked goods. All that jawing back and forth is just for show. They're really quite close."

Lauren was about to ask more when Mason stuck his head in from the lab and said, "Come on, troops, we don't have all night. Eat your Oreos and get a move on; we've got bugs to grow and tissue to stain and lots of other fun stuff to do before we turn in tonight."

Chapter 10

Guatemotzi was very afraid. Terrified. Watching these men wearing odd warriors' costumes the color of *naranja*, the orange, was enough to frighten him by itself. But the curious rituals they had performed over the dead *Americanos* made him wonder if these men in orange might be *Los Oráculos*, messengers from the ancient gods sent from beyond the sun to see for themselves death had come to everyone who violated the Aztec temple, Chief Montezuma's sacred place of eternal sleep.

Perhaps these were not men at all, but creatures from the Spirit World his grandfather told him about so long ago—evil spirits with the shapes of men who walked among the living seeking out those who departed from the pathway sought by true believers. They had even arrived in the belly of a strange metal bird like the winged god of his ancestors, Quetzalcoatl, the plumed serpent.

Every *Americano* is dead, Guatemotzi thought. Everyone who went in the sacred temple died in agony, writhing on the ground, bleeding, gasping for breath. Everyone . . . but me. I did not get sick like the others. I am alive and they are dead. I do not understand. Why would *Los Dios* spare me from the curse?

Watching these warriors in orange suits from the trunk of a palm tree, Guatemotzi knew one of them had seen him. Would they come after him in the dark and hunt him down? If they were truly *Los Oráculos* they could see in the dark as if it were daylight and no place would be safe for him to hide.

And what had they been doing to the bodies of the *Americanos*? Cutting them to pieces with small knives, opening their skulls and taking pieces of their brains! Did they intend to consume the body parts, as he had been told the priests of his ancestors did, or would they use them in some other ritual only the gods and priests knew about?

And what of the giant silver box carried from the sky by the metal bird? It had windows. Were *Los Oráculos* planning to live inside this box? Or was it a huge coffin for the dead *Americanos*? How could he know such things, being only a boy from a small village in the mountains to the south?

In early spring his father had warned him not to go to the North, not to leave their hidden village in Michoacán, for he said it was very dangerous in *El Norte* and a poor *Indio* boy like Guatemotzi would not belong in a world filled with automobiles and tall buildings and foreign gods and strange rituals of which he had no knowledge.

The black-robed priests of a new god had come to his small village, teaching the children *Español* and telling them of the one true god, Jesus, who preached kindness and love. Strange teachings for a god, and much different from the gods his grandfather spoke of, who conquered enemies and took their wives and children for slaves and who ripped the beating hearts from their enemies and ate them to steal their strength and courage.

This one true god seemed weak to Guatemotzi, who had been named for the last and strongest emperor of the Aztecs. His father had told him his name meant "one who has descended like an eagle when he folds his wings and drops like lightning onto his prey," and symbolized aggressiveness and fierceness. This foreign god seemed no match for the ferocious gods of his ancestors.

For this reason Guatemotzi had avoided the cities of the new god, keeping to the mountains and jungles, hoping to learn more about the world outside Michoacán without losing his life to its many dangers. He knew this timidity was not living up to his name, but he figured he'd have plenty of time to be fierce when he grew larger.

He'd tried to explain to his father that he was only curious to see what other places were like, that he was not turning his back on his *Indio* heritage or his people by going away.

He wanted only to visit the burial place of his ancestors' emperor, Montezuma, whose daughter was the wife to the original Guatemotzi, and to pray and perhaps to see if the ancient gods were still alive, to see for himself if they had been driven off by this new god, Jesus.

He was, after all, a full fourteen *años*, and his namesake had been the emperor who succeeded Montezuma and it was he who was killed when he wouldn't reveal the location of the Aztecs' gold treasury.

With such a powerful and important heritage he was surely brave enough to be traveling on his own, even across the dangerous North. By avoiding the cities there was little risk, and when he met the *jefe* of the *Americanos* and the others digging in these ancient ruins, he'd been offered a job using a machete helping to clear away vines and carrying brush.

The *jefe* had been a kind man, not like he expected from someone who came from the North, and the others were very gentle people who only wanted to dig for pieces of old pottery belonging to the Aztecs.

The *jefe* was very interested to find that Guatemotzi was a descendant of *Los Aztecas* and to discover that he spoke the ancient tongue, Nahuatl. The *jefe* often took time to sit with Guatemotzi and ask him questions about the tales of the ancient days his people had told him. *Jefe* even knew about his ancestor and namesake, the original Guatemotzi, and told him many people thought he was even greater than Emperor Montezuma.

Thus, Guatemotzi thought it fitting, to be able to help these kind Americans discover more about his people and their history . . . and they paid him so well! Six hundred *pesos* a day only to cut vines and carry limbs to brush piles!

It had seemed like a miracle to find such a wonderful job while wandering through the jungle, a gift from *Dios* Himself. When he came back to his village he would be a rich man who could be generous with his mother and father and sisters and brothers. But those were dreams he had before everyone started to die. . . . Before he stole part of the treasure.

The bleeding was unlike anything Guatemotzi had ever seen. The sickness began all at once, striking everyone. And within hours many were dying. They needed doctors, *curanderos*, and when the *jefe* sent Julio—they called him Jules—in an automobile with no roof to find a doctor, Julio died on a jungle road to the city before he reached a *curandero*. A farmer brought him back to the camp in his burro cart and three days later, the farmer was dead from the same strange illness, the bleeding.

What Guatemotzi still did not understand was why the sickness had spared him. He did not bleed now, nor had he bled when all of the others did. Were the gods of *Los Aztecas* saving him for some reason he could not comprehend?

He watched the orange-clad warriors until it grew dark and then he left for a hidden spot near a mountain spring where he kept food the *Americano* named Fitzhugh had given him, stored in green pouches and metal cans that had to be opened with a special tool.

While the food was tasteless and faintly unpleasant to smell, it was an alternative to hunting small game and Guatemotzi had few darts left for his blowgun, and he was unable to find the poisonous tree frogs from which he made the killing potion that would drop a deer in its tracks within only a few steps after the dart entered its flesh.

He resolved to eat the strange-smelling food and conserve his darts for later, when he would eventually undertake the long journey south to his home village.

A sound from the warriors' camp startled him, the noise made by a small motor. Suddenly, lights were burning in the clearing and he could see lighted windows in the big silver box brought by the noisy flying machines. *Los Oráculos* meant to continue their rituals into the night.

Silently, as Guatemotzi trotted along a narrow jungle trail to the secret spring, he prayed the warriors in orange would not come to kill him tonight for what he'd done with the dead monkey's collar he took from the sacred temple. It had seemed a small thing at the time, to take the collar from the dead monkey, hoping later to sell it for a few *pesos* to buy food with. The little collar was very old and it held only a few of the pretty green and red stones and some hammered silver.

What harm was done? The monkey would surely not miss it and the money the traveler in the jungle had given him would be put to good use in his village, making sure there was plenty of food for all of his people.

Perhaps, while *Los Oráculos* were busy within the metal box, he could sneak up without being noticed and see for himself what they were doing inside. After all, was he not known to be the best tracker in his village, able to creep up on deer and javelina and move through the jungle without making a sound?

He turned around and started back toward the clearing and its unearthly inhabitants. Moving silently through thick jungle vines and undergrowth, Guatemotzi slipped up to the edge of the forest and then crept to a wall of the iron box to peer carefully through a window.

"Madre de Dios," Guatemotzi whispered, unconsciously mimicking the black-robed priest who taught him Spanish. *Los Oráculos* had shed their orange skins and had taken the form of ordinary humans, both men and women. Perhaps they were like *el coyote*, known as the trickster among his people, and could shape-shift at will. If so, their magic was indeed strong.

Though he couldn't hear their voices, *Los Oráculos* appeared happy, laughing and joking among themselves much as the people of his village did when the rains came and the crops grew green and thick and food was plentiful.

And they were eating from the same green pouches *Los Americanos* had given to Guatemotzi. Were they saving the trophies and body parts they had taken from the dead bodies to eat later, or had they already consumed the souls and courage of the dead *Americanos*?

As Guatemotzi crouched outside the window, clouds parted and a full moon appeared overhead, bathing the clearing in ghostly white light. One of the females inside, the one with long hair like his mother's (only a red-brown color instead of black) turned to gaze out the glass, her eyes locking on Guatemotzi's. As she opened her mouth and pointed to him, Guatemotzi realized he had been seen.

With hammering heart and a dry mouth, he turned and sprinted through the jungle, thin legs pumping as fast as he had ever run in his life.

Lauren's exclamation of surprise stopped all conversation in the lab as she pointed at an empty window. "There, outside that window! I saw a face staring in at us, a boy! I know I didn't imagine it!"

Mason ran to the window and peered out. All he could see in the moonlight was branches of nearby bushes shaking as if someone had run through them. It had to be the same boy he'd seen earlier in the day.

Who was he, Mason wondered, and how had he escaped the plague? He knew the answer to those questions could very well be just what they needed to defeat this damned bug and possibly prevent many more deaths in the future.

Finding him would have to be a priority once daylight arrived.

Chapter 11

Eduardo's face looked pale behind his Plexiglas face mask in the light from a flashlight he carried and his voice sounded different to Lauren when he spoke to her as they walked toward the temple. There was an animation and excitement in it that was normally absent from the taciturn professor's usual rather formal demeanor. She knew that in spite of the deaths that had resulted, this would be the crowning glory of Matos's career. He would be forever known as the man who'd made possible the discovery of Emperor Montezuma's tomb.

"This does not seem possible," Matos said, looking down and shining the light where he placed his feet so that he wouldn't stumble. "All of them dead, and their blood appears to have left their bodies entirely. I have never seen or heard of such a thing. Of course, I am not a medical doctor; however it would seem logical to have something in the newspapers or on television reporting a disease in which every drop of blood drains from the human body. I wonder if this has ever happened before. I will ask Dr. Williams what it is, and if he has ever encountered so many people dying like this."

Lauren realized he was babbling on because he was still nervous about the cause of so many deaths and was, in spite of his excitement over the archaeological discoveries, terrified that he would somehow become infected. Matos might once have been an intrepid explorer, but he was certainly not a brave man anymore. Perhaps he'd spent too many years behind a desk in the ministry and had forgotten what it was like to be in the field where death and danger were never far away.

Lauren quickly passed her flashlight beam over a body with a black plastic covering. She wanted to cry and couldn't, as if no more tears were possible after what she'd seen today.

"They are calling the disease hemorrhagic shock," she said, answering his earlier question. "I have no idea what that means. I think it's a general term and is a condition caused by many different illnesses. Dr. Williams says they still have no firm knowledge as to what killed Charlie and the students, though they have some suspicions . . . they haven't given the disease any kind of name yet."

She glanced at Matos and tried to put it in terms the archaeologist would understand. "It is reminiscent of Dr. Howard Carter's team after opening Tutankhamen's tomb in Egypt, when so many died from a long-dormant fungus."

"Aspergillus," Eduardo remembered, nodding his head. "Though these symptoms are very different. That disease took many weeks to develop and the victims took even longer to die. Here," he hesitated as if overcome for a moment, "they became ill and died within a matter of a few days."

He paused to collect himself, and then he continued, "My heart is heavy over the loss of my friend, Charles, for it was I who arranged his permit to dig in Tlateloco.

How could I have known I was giving him a death sentence? This was an archaeologist's dream, to find the burial place of Chief Montezuma. I felt I had no choice but to arrange things for him since it was his work leading to the discovery of the chronicles of Díaz in a Madrid cathedral that led him here. And now my dear friend is dead, because I begged the Ministry of Antiquities to grant him special permission to excavate. I have not truly wept in many years, but now my heart weeps for my professional colleague whose death is forever on my conscience."

"You couldn't have known," Lauren replied woodenly. "How could anyone know this was going to happen?" She directed the beam of her flashlight to the tunnel opening. "Charlie's lying in there. I asked Dr. Williams to cover his body so I wouldn't have to look at him. They put him in some sort of plastic bag like the ones outside."

She stepped around a tangle of vines to continue toward the shaft running beneath the temple. "In the morning, as soon as I've identified the others, I'm going back to Austin. I can't stand to be here. There are too many memories of my association with Charlie and these students."

"It must be a terrible thing," Eduardo said, "to be asked to identify the bodies of so many friends. I do understand why you wish to leave."

"There's the tunnel," she said, aiming her light at a dark square near the foot of the temple, still too unaccustomed to the sound of her Racal's breathing apparatus to ignore it completely when she spoke.

"Montezuma's remains are about a hundred feet beyond the opening in a walled chamber. There are mummified bodies of monkeys and snakes and other animals in the tomb with him. Along with some clay tablets covered with hieroglyphs and a few extremely well-preserved garments."

"Be careful where you step," she said, shining her flashlight along the floor of the tunnel to reveal multiple small- to medium-sized stones lying half-buried in the sandy loam. "There appears to have been a minor quake at some time, causing the partial collapse of portions of the roof, especially near the entrance. It may explain why things are so well preserved despite this high humidity. The quake must have sealed the tunnel off completely, making it virtually airtight."

"Charles and the students must have had to work very hard to excavate this tunnel," Matos said, awe in his voice.

"Yes," Lauren answered, "Charles was an excellent field man who knew how to get the most out of his students and the local laborers he hired."

"As I said, due to the dry air of the tunnel and inner chamber, most of the artifacts show very little deterioration . . ."

Matos turned to glance at her. "Yes, but now that the tomb has been opened, the humidity and dampness will quickly work to ruin the specimens in this tomb. We either have to reseal the entrance with plastic or work very quickly to recover the artifacts and put them in plastic bags or otherwise protect them from the environment."

She wondered how they could be talking about artifacts when Charlie and thirty-one students were dead all around her. Was she simply blocking it out or just using the talk of mundane detail of relic recovery to take her mind off the tragedy that had occurred?

She'd loved Charlie in ways few people would understand; he had been a father figure and a listening ear when the world seemed to be caving in around her in graduate school. She experienced a broken relationship of six years, the death of her father unexpectedly during her second semester of the doctoral program, and an overriding depression afterward lasting almost a year. Tears filled her eyes again, as she remembered Charlie.

"I just hope we are able to contain whatever this plague is," Lauren said. "It would be a catastrophe beyond comprehension if whatever killed Charlie and the others were to escape and be unleashed on civilization."

"The army has begun setting up perimeters around the site as Dr. Williams requested," Eduardo said. "No one will be allowed in or out. Dr. Cardenez is also fearful of a widespread epidemic so close to Mexico City. The death toll could be staggering, but I simply cannot allow a discovery such as this to be destroyed as Dr. Williams believes it must be."

He paused and stared at her. "Perhaps, Dr. Sullivan, you could be of help to me in reasoning with Dr. Williams."

"Oh?"

"Yes, he has been talking of using a fuel bomb to completely burn this entire area in case they cannot find the cause of this terrible plague, or in the event that the cause is found but has no cure. You need to help me explain to him that the burial place of Montezuma is too important to the history of Mexico to be destroyed without first cataloguing all of the wonderful treasures here."

He spread his arms out wide. "There must be some way to decontaminate this area. I know virtually nothing about diseases; however I will not permit something so important to be burned. Many secrets of the Aztec Empire may lie buried underneath this temple, so many unsolved riddles no one has ever been able to decipher. My government will never allow this place to be firebombed without absolute proof there is no other choice." He hesitated, fixing on her with his eyes. "Will you help me?"

Lauren led the way to the tunnel opening and bent down to go inside, thinking about her answer. The wants and needs of science versus the potential deaths of hundreds or many thousands of innocent people was no contest.

"The decision may not be up to your government, Eduardo," she said. "If enough people start dying like this, every country in the Western Hemisphere will demand that something is done to halt its spread."

"It is unthinkable how such a disaster could occur with a simple archaeological discovery . . ."

The fan in Lauren's breathing apparatus seemed louder in the tunnel as they followed the beam of her flashlight. "From what I have seen today, this is no simple archaeological find," she said in a voiced dulled by sorrow. "Charlie may have found an explanation for the Aztecs' sudden decline after Cortés looted their treasuries and in the process lost his life to the same fate as an entire civilization. Dr. Williams said he and several of the other doctors believe this is something that has been buried here for centuries, like what Carter unearthed in Egypt. Finding the burial place of Montezuma may not be the blessing it first seemed to be when Charlie discovered it."

"How can you overlook the importance of it, Lauren? It is perhaps the most significant archaeological find in the history of Mexico, a missing piece to the Aztec puzzle and the collapse of their empire. My government will not allow its destruction, I can assure you."

If enough people start dying in Mexico City they might, she thought, but kept her opinion to herself. She'd heard and seen enough of death in the past twenty-four hours to want to avoid discussing it whenever she could.

Although she was tired she knew she could never sleep . . . not here, not now, not until she left this dreadful place. Even though she found she liked Dr. Williams and other members of his team personally, this place would forever be synonymous with the deaths of her friends and mentor.

"Remember what Dr. Williams said about these suits, Eduardo," she advised when she saw Matos stumbling along the tunnel, "to be very careful not to rip them or remove any part of it for any reason."

Her flashlight beam fell on Dr. Adams's body, the bag he was in. "This is where we found Charlie," she said, with bottomless despair clotting her voice.

She stepped around the body bag and continued along the tunnel, resisting an overwhelming urge to break down and cry again. For some reason, now she thought about the terrible contradiction here. The excitement in Charlie's voice when he came back from his first expedition to these ruins, and how sure he was this was Montezuma's lost burial chamber described in letters he found last fall in Madrid. He had told her then that every sign, every marking on the temple pointed to the correctness of his assumption.

Then the full-scale expedition this summer with the big foundation grants to prove his theory, the discovery of this tunnel and Bernal Díaz del Castillo's skeletal remains with his handwritten journal and its descriptions of what had happened to Montezuma and the Aztecs at Tenochtitlan, the Aztec capital a few miles away.

The journal proved Charlie's assumption, he told her

THE ANTHRAX PROTOCOL 121

breathlessly when a cell call finally made it through the Mexican phone company's maze one night as he labored with a hurried translation, that they would be opening the inner chamber the following morning.

It was the last time Lauren would hear his voice until he called to describe the horrors of what was happening here, what had happened here, what was happening to him. Even Díaz's journal, which he had been so happy to find, had been left lying in his lap within the body bag. Mason feared it was too contaminated to allow out until they'd discovered the cause of the deaths.

Lauren entered the inner chamber and cast her light upon the corpse of Montezuma. Eduardo's flashlight wandered from place to place, from relic to relic, until he halted it on the mummified remains lying atop the sepulcher.

"The Emperor, as Hernán Cortés described him," Eduardo said quietly, almost reverently. "Chief Montezuma, discovered at long last. Charles has been vindicated for his belief in this temple as Montezuma's tomb. So many at the ministry doubted him, calling him a fool, saying Tlateloco could not possibly be the right place for burial of a mighty king . . . there can be no doubt now. The animals, the robes, the tablets, are proof of Montezuma's identity. There, on this clay tablet near his feet, is the royal Aztec symbol used during Montezuma's reign."

Eduardo moved his flashlight beam to a piece of flattened clay covered with etchings. "This is priceless, a discovery beyond measure." He inched forward, approaching the sepulcher, squatting down to read pictographs on the tablet.

Lauren took a deep breath, wondering if Charlie truly

felt vindication now or if it mattered at all. Knowing him as she did, he would have placed a much higher value on the lives of his students and coworkers. No discovery on earth would have been worth the price paid in human lives to Charles Adams.

"What is this?" Eduardo asked, reaching into an urn where, in the illumination of moving light from his flashlight, small green stones glittered on some sort of object fashioned from a piece of bone.

Remembering Charlie, at the moment Lauren truly did not care what it was.

"Look!" Eduardo exclaimed, carefully withdrawing a long flint knife with a jewel-studded bone handle. "A sacrificial dagger, the sacrificial dagger of Montezuma."

He held it before him, examining it closely, and the sparkle of gold filigree encircling bright green emeralds inlaid in a piece of bone reflected off his faceplate. "What a treasure. Just think, Lauren, this very knife was probably used to cut the beating hearts out of Montezuma's enemies so they could be eaten by the high priests to gain their courage and strength. This find alone will occupy archaeological scholars for years to come."

He was turning to Lauren, extending the knife to her, when suddenly his foot slipped off the side of a rock imbedded in the dirt floor of the chamber.

As he started to fall he dropped his flashlight to protect the precious relic he took from the urn.

She heard a cracking sound, then a muffled shriek before she could aim her beam of light downward.

"My mask!" he cried. "The knife has broken my face mask!"

"Eduardo!" Lauren screamed, forgetting that her scream

was being broadcast through every headset worn by the Wildfire Team.

Lauren quickly ripped a spare piece of duct tape off the hip of her Racal where all the team members carried them for just such an emergency. Moving rapidly she slapped it over the gaping crack in Matos's faceplate.

Trying to calm him down and stop his hysterical moaning, she led him out of the chamber and down the tunnel toward the mobile lab where all of the other team members were already gathered, having heard the commotion over the radios.

Dr. Williams frowned, looking around the duct tape on Dr. Matos's mask to examine the cut on his cheek in the light from one of the portable lamps resting on stands outside the mobile lab. Mason and Dr. Jakes had come outside to gather more samples while Lauren and Eduardo were in the tomb.

"I'm afraid we can't let you leave, Dr. Matos," he said gravely. "You've potentially been exposed to the germ now, whether it's airborne or transmitted by contact, and by leaving, you could carry it with you. Until we know what it is, you'll have to be quarantined here."

"But I must get to a hospital immediately," Eduardo said.

"They won't have the slightest idea what to treat you for," Dr. Jakes remarked, after his own examination of Eduardo's face. "We don't know yet what this bug is. We're working on it, but for now you'll have a much better chance here with us."

Eduardo stiffened. "You have no authority in my country

to tell me whether or not I can leave," he said with the crisp air of one who knows his rights. "I want you to radio for a helicopter at once to take me to Mexico City to Sanatorio Medico."

Dr. Williams wagged his head. "And do what? Spread this disease all over your capital city? Until we can identify what this is, there can be no treatment. I'm sorry, Dr. Matos, but you'll have to stay until you've passed the longest possible incubation period, at least ten days, possibly longer. There is no other alternative."

When Matos opened his mouth to object, Mason added, "Of course, we'll immediately start a course of every antibiotic that might possibly be effective against whatever bug this is, and hopefully in a week or so you'll remain uninfected."

Lauren sank to a canvas stool, feeling faint. The noise of a portable generator buzzed faintly through her headset. Had Montezuma's plague claimed yet another victim?

"This is too much," she said, staring at the ground where light from a halogen bulb cast eerie shadows among trimmed vines and stalks of cut brush in the clearing. "I can't stand any more of this. I have to go home."

"We can send you back tomorrow, Lauren, after the last identification is made," Mason promised. "Unfortunately, due to the violation of Dr. Matos's suit and the cut on his face, he can't leave until we identify the causative agent here and figure out how to treat it."

Lauren heard someone sob into a microphone on a headset as Eduardo took a step back from the two doctors.

"Am I going to die?" Eduardo asked, holding out the knife as if he wished he'd never found it.

"No one can say for sure, Dr. Matos." It was Mason Williams who spoke. He glanced at Lauren. "Thanks to Dr. Sullivan's quick action in putting duct tape over the crack in your faceplate, you may not even be infected."

Dr. Jakes turned to Mason. "This may give us an excellent chance to study the symptoms as they develop. We'll have a better fix on the incubation period and an opportunity to perform blood work while the disease progresses if this subject has contracted . . ."

"That's enough, Sam," Mason interrupted harshly, glancing over at Matos, who had surely heard the inconsiderate remark. "We can discuss this later. Now get back to work!"

Eduardo slumped against one side of the mobile lab, looking down at the dagger. "*Madre!* What have I done?"

Lauren's thoughts bordered on total disbelief. This simply could not be happening. First Charlie and every student at the site, and now Charlie's dear friend, Eduardo Matos, had come in contact with something so deadly inside Montezuma's tomb it was apparently unstoppable.

"As I said, we can't say for sure you've contracted it," Mason said to Eduardo. "We're only playing it safe. Some of the top doctors and specialists in infectious diseases in the world are here. If anyone can do anything to help you, it will be a member of this team. Once we identify it. Right now, we haven't the slightest idea what this bug is."

"A bug? You keep calling this monster a bug?" Eduardo asked incredulously, his voice breaking.

"It's a matter of terminology, Doctor. Under a microscope this thing, whatever it is, will be a living organism. We call them bugs. I suppose it's medical slang."

"I must call my wife to explain," Eduardo said, his

voice calmer now, but Mason could see his face was covered with sweat and tears. "She will be worried if I am not home tomorrow."

"We'll ask Joel to arrange it in the morning," Mason assured him.

Lauren sat on her stool remembering the moment when Eduardo found the dagger. While she could never make herself believe in curses, it was as if Montezuma himself had arisen from the grave to bury his jeweled knife into the heart of Charlie's friend, Eduardo Matos. Although she was not a believer in the supernatural, it certainly seemed as if there was a curse surrounding this ancient tomb.

A moment later she stared at the dark jungle, recalling the face of the boy she'd seen through a lab window. She was sure it wasn't her imagination. How could anyone survive here without a space suit? she wondered, if the illness were as dangerous as Mason made it sound.

Funny, she thought, that she was thinking of him as Mason now instead of Dr. Williams.

She glanced over at him as he rapidly gave orders for the isolation and medical treatment of Matos. Yep, he was quite an impressive man.

Chapter 12

Mason felt like a mother hen trying to keep all her chicks in line. Working with a team of brilliant, ego-centric scientists is like trying to herd cats, he thought. Just when you get them all going in one direction, something happens and they scatter.

Mason, Jakes, and Shirley Cole were in their Racals in the Cytotec lab, all trying to process blood serum samples, stain tissue sections with exotic dyes to make different forms of bacteria illuminate under microscopes, and generally getting in each other's way.

To make matters worse, Shirley and Jakes had been sniping at one another all evening. Mason wished the two wouldn't be so competitive, but then he reasoned, if they weren't, they probably wouldn't be as effective as they were at ferreting out secrets of the microscopic world.

Shirley said, "Why don't you quit fooling with that electron microscope, Sam? I'm telling you, this smells like a bacterial illness to me and I don't think we need to waste our time looking for viruses."

Jakes grimaced while fiddling with dials and buttons on a large electron microscope built into a corner of the lab. "You think everything on earth is bacterial, Shirley, including men. You remind me of a carpenter whose only tool is a hammer, so he thinks every problem is a nail."

"And what is *that* supposed to imply, Mister Wizard?"

"Just that most cases of hemorrhagic fever, especially ones caused by organisms that are airborne and transmissible from person to person and having a one hundred percent mortality rate, are caused by viruses. I can't think of a single bacterium that has an onset of action as fast as this bug seems to have."

"Tell you what, Sam. I'll make you a bet this agent is a bacteria and not a virus."

"Precisely what are you willing to wager, Dr. Cole?" Jakes asked, wiggling his eyebrows suggestively.

"If it turns out to be a virus, I'll personally treat you and every friend you've got to a round of drinks at that male chauvinist pig hangout you frequent, the Recovery Room. I won't have much at stake since you have virtually no friends since you've driven them off with those damn cigars."

Jakes glared at her. Everyone knew the bar she mentioned near the Emory University Medical School campus, a favorite of his. He spent most nights there schmoozing with medical school professors and drinking while smoking his vile cigars.

"Okay, Shirley, and I'll bet it's a virus. If I'm wrong, you can bring all your friends to the bar, which will also probably only amount to one or two old maid femlibbers, and I'll buy all three of you as many drinks as you think you can metabolize without falling down."

Mason shook his head, attempting to concentrate on his work through all this banter. The Cytotec lab chamber, stuffed from floor to ceiling with every piece of scientific apparatus imaginable, was small to begin with. When three people, encased in bulky, cumbersome Racals, were all trying to work at once, each feeling his particular task was the most important, there was predictable conflict.

After a brief pause in the conversation, Jakes straightened in front of the large vacuum tube of an electron microscope where he'd been laboring for the past twenty minutes.

"Goddammit, Mason, this piece of crap is still not adjusted properly. I told you the aiming electron focusing beams were knocked out of alignment when those fools dropped it in Australia, and you told me it had been fixed!" He turned to glare at Mason, his hands on his hips and his expression sour.

Mason sighed deeply. He was in the middle of Gram staining tissue slides and didn't have time to argue at the moment. The delicate process, wherein slides were dipped in methylene blue dye, followed by iodine, scarlet red, and finally washed in acetone, was fairly simple, but if the correct sequence was not followed the tissue sections would be ruined.

Of course, Jakes never bothered to consider anyone else's duties could possibly be as important as his. Mason answered without raising his head. "The lab tech at CDC assured me it was repaired, Sam. What's wrong with it?'

"Hell, nothing's wrong with it except it won't focus the goddamn beam. Other than that, it's just fine. You understand my electron micrographs look like they were taken through frosted glass."

"That's probably because you've adjusted the focus and depth of field knobs incorrectly," Shirley mumbled snidely, just loud enough for Sam to hear.

Jakes glanced at her and just shook his head, as if such a possibility didn't bear consideration. "If we're dealing with a virus here it'd better be a big bastard, because I can't get my resolution below one hundred microns," he said. "That means if this bug is a filovirus like I suspect, we're gonna be shit outta luck finding it."

Mason was forming a reply when he was halted by an exclamation from Shirley. "Wait a minute, guys! I think I may have something here! Mason, come take a look at the slide of this lung section."

Mason took a few seconds to wash his slides with acetone, his hands shaking slightly from fatigue. They'd been working continuously without a break since arriving at the site.

He put the slides in a rack to dry, and then he moved over to the counter where Shirley was working. She made a slight adjustment to the focusing knobs on the Zeiss binocular microscope, bringing an image into sharper view on the computer VDT hooked to the Zeiss.

It was impossible to get close enough to the scope's double eyepieces while wearing a Racal hood, so the equipment was set up to send images to a thirteen-inch computer screen built into the wall of the lab.

On the screen, tiny air sacs of lung tissue appeared in the background like a large pink honeycomb. The air sacs themselves were filled with pink-stained proteinaceous debris, ruptured red blood cells, and clumped leukocytes, surrounded by literally thousands of tiny dark blue, almost violet cigar-shaped bacteria. The honeycomb shapes of the air sacs showed massive disruption with large areas where the lung tissue itself had been completely absorbed and destroyed by the bacteria.

"Jesus," Mason whispered, awed by the amount of tissue destruction and the large number of bacteria present in the specimen. "This is the most fulminant case of pneumonia I've ever seen."

"Yeah," Shirley replied. "This kid was one sick puppy all right. And unless I miss my guess, those bad boys there are our hot-bug."

"Sam, come over here," Mason said. "I don't think we need to worry about the electron microscope now. It looks like we're dealing with a bacterial etiology for the deaths, a Gram-positive rod of some sort." He stepped aside so Jakes could see the monitor.

"It does appear to be a bacillus," Jakes agreed, causing Shirley to roll her eyes, as if she couldn't believe he'd ever doubted her. "And look up there, in the upper left corner of the field—it looks like spores of some sort I don't recognize," Jakes muttered, pointing to a section of the screen containing what looked like tiny balls, some of which had ruptured, spilling out hordes of violet bacteria.

"Seems as if I was right, Sam," Shirley said, with poorly concealed enjoyment. "The only Gram-positive rod I know of that forms spores and can cause pneumonia this aggressive, along with hemorrhagic fever, is *Bacillus anthracis*."

Jakes turned to her. "But that doesn't make sense," he said in a bewildered voice, almost as if he spoke to himself. "We both know woolsorter's disease, respiratory or inhalation anthrax, has never been shown to be transmissible from person to person. It is inconceivable that so many people could have independently contracted respiratory anthrax in such a short time short of some sort of terrorist attack with powdered anthrax, such as we saw in the postal service back in the early 2000s."

"A terrorist attack out here in bug-fuck Mexico, that's your explanation?" Shirley asked incredulously.

Jakes shook his head, distractedly. "No, of course not, but besides that, the typical mortality rate of untreated anthrax pneumonia is only seventy to eighty percent, not one hundred percent like it appears to have been here."

Shirley shrugged, the shoulders of her Racal bunching with her movements. "I know you're right. But if tissues from the others show this pattern, I don't know what else it could be."

"What else do we need to do to be sure this bug is anthrax and that it did indeed cause the disease we see here?" Mason asked Shirley.

"Well, it's kinda hard to explain . . ."

"Trust us, Shirley," Jakes said sarcastically, "we're doctors too."

She shrugged within her Racal, "Okay, then, to be one hundred percent certain, we'll need to do pleural biopsies and subject them to immunohistochemical staining or IHC. Then we'll need to get some tissue samples from the bodies and check the levels of serum antibody or IgG to protective antigen or PA component of *Bacillus anthracis* using enzyme-linked immunosorbent assay or ELISA."

In spite of the seriousness of the situation, Mason had to smile. "Oh, is that all?"

Shirley smiled back. "Actually, no. To be absolutely certain, I'd also like to do a polymerase chain reaction or PCR on some tissue samples from different bodies, and we'll need to do specific staining for anthrax to make sure, but that'll only take a couple of hours. The rest of the tests, however, could take days to complete with the equipment I have here."

"Shirley," Jakes asked, his voice more reasonable now, "in light of what I said earlier about anthrax not being passed person to person, do you think it could be some mutant form of anthrax, one that jumped species or something, one we've never seen before?"

She hesitated. "Well, that would almost have to be the case if this is anthrax, since like you say, modern anthrax has never been shown to be transmissible from person to person or to be this aggressive or to have such a high mortality rate."

"Moreover," she continued, her forehead wrinkled in thought, "this bacterium is almost certainly four hundred or more years old, and has been isolated in an airtight, sealed burial chamber and has had to form spores and encapsulate itself in order to survive for so long without living tissue to replicate in, sort of like suspended animation. Anything's possible, I guess. The way bacteria mutate with exposure to antibiotics, viruses, and bacteriophages, it's certainly not outside the realm of possibility the strains we have today are totally different from those present in the early 1500s."

"I guess so," Jakes agreed, although he sounded doubtful.

"Don't you gentlemen remember your Bible?" Shirley asked, warming to her subject and looking back and forth between the two men.

"The Bible? What the hell's the Bible got to do with this bug, or anything else?" Jakes demanded, his irritation at having been proven wrong showing now.

Shirley grinned, her teeth flashing in the light from the monitor screen. "The book of Genesis talks about the fifth plague of Egypt in which hundreds of thousands of animals and people died over the course of a few years, and Moses mentions a disease with symptoms remarkably similar to anthrax in Exodus 9:9.

"It has always been suspected by biblical scholars that the hot-bug that caused the fifth Egyptian plague was anthrax, but the mortality rate and number of deaths was thought to be too high for anthrax as we know it today. Maybe an older species, or perhaps subspecies would be a better term for it, was this super virulent type that could be spread person to person."

"You're really reaching now, Shirley, quoting an obscure plague, described by people ignorant of the basic rudiments of environmental theory," Jakes replied, his tone thick with sarcasm.

Mason tried to end their argument. "Okay, people, let's calm down."

Shirley wasn't so easily stopped. She continued. "In the eighteenth and nineteenth centuries, a plague of anthrax swept over the southern part of Europe, taking a heavy toll in both human and animal life." She paused to remember details of the epidemic. "Make no mistake about it, gentlemen, and you too, Sam, we're dealing with a heavy hitter here. This bug is a real bad actor, and if you'd look at the evidence of history, it may have been around for a very long time." She glared at Dr. Jakes defiantly.

"Bullshit," Jakes snapped, making Mason wish he could turn down the volume of his earpiece. "I think it's good news, if it does turn out to be anthrax."

"How so?" Mason asked, curious how bacteria that had just wiped out an entire archaeological expedition could be classified as good news.

"It's simple," Jakes said, spreading his arms. "Anthrax is treatable by penicillin and ciprofloxacin, if my memory serves me, and we have a vaccine against it. In fact, it was the first infectious disease in which a vaccine was found to be effective. We can thank Louis Pasteur for that."

A quiet chuckle, clearly one of derision from Shirley came through Mason's headset. "*Au contraire,* my dear friend. You've been working with viruses so long you've forgotten your microbiology and your medical history, if you ever knew any to begin with."

"Oh?" Jakes sounded sure of himself. "And just where am I going wrong, Dr. Cole?"

"Almost everywhere, Sam. In the first place, the anthrax vaccine is ineffective against inhaled forms of anthrax, and in the second place, the treatment protocols for anthrax have undergone lots of changes since penicillin was used back in the dark ages when you were in medical school."

"What are the new treatment protocols, Shirley?" Mason asked.

"Antibiotics known to be effective in varying degrees are ciprofloxacin, amoxicillin/clavulanate or Augmentin, doxycycline or tetracycline, clindamycin, rifampin, vancomycin, and chloramphenicol."

"So what's our problem?" Jakes asked, smiling. "We just pump anyone who comes down with this bug full of antibiotics and go on our merry way."

"I have a feeling from the expression on Shirley's face that it's not going to be that simple, Sam," Mason said.

"You're right, Mason. In the first place, we've only had less than a hundred cases of anthrax in the antibiotic era, so only a handful of cases have actually been treated with these antibiotics, so the possible combinations and dosages haven't been fully worked out yet, and to make matters worse, *Bacillus anthracis* makes beta-lactamases, which often makes the bacteria resistant to antibiotics even while under treatment."

She hesitated, and then she continued in a grave voice, "Believe me, if this mutant form of anthrax gets out of the Mexican jungle we'll be looking at a plague that could make the influenza pendemic of 1918, which, by the way, killed fifty thousand people in the United States alone, look like the common cold."

Everyone remained silent while Mason and Jakes absorbed this latest news. Finally, Mason said, "Okay. Then it's our job to make certain this mutant strain, or subspecies, or whatever the hell it is, stops here and to make absolutely sure it is anthrax we're dealing with. I want those special stains done now, and I want some cultures set up to see if it'll grow on the normal anthrax medium, which it may not since it's either a mutated form or even a completely different subspecies.

"While you two do that, I'm going to start an IV on Dr. Matos and begin pumping all the antibiotics we have into him as soon as I can. With any luck and an early start, he might just beat the odds."

"There are two bits of good news," Shirley added.

"What are they?" Mason asked.

"One is we can get out of these damned Racals. If it is respiratory athrax we're dealing with, the only protection we need will be millipore-filter face masks and gloves when we're working with the bodies."

"What's the other good news?"

"Now we can make Dr. Jakes smoke those wolf-turds he calls cigars outside."

Mason wisely said nothing about Sam's cigars as he stepped through the heavy door at the end of the lab and into the so-called hospital chamber, where Dr. Matos was lying on one of the cots.

As he entered the next room, Mason could hear Shirley saying, "Sam, I prefer gin and Seven-up, and I'll let you know what my friends drink when we get to the Recovery Room."

Mason approached Dr. Matos, noting his nose was running and his eyes were already red-rimmed and bloodshot. Matos's skin was pale, and he was sweating profusely and shivering with chills.

Mason couldn't tell if these symptoms were due to early infection or merely a manifestation of fear and terror at what he was facing.

He glanced at a monitor suspended above the bed attached to Matos by means of numerous wires and probes. The temperature digital readout showed a fever of 99.7, and his blood pressure had dropped to one hundred over sixty with respirations of thirty per minute. His oxygen saturation, showing the concentration of oxygen in his blood, had fallen from its normal of ninety percent to seventy-five percent—all ominous signs pointing to a severe infection and possible incipient lung involvement.

Jesus, Mason thought, it has only been a few hours since his exposure and Matos is already showing symptoms of infection, serious infection. This was one hell of an aggressive strain, to be manifesting itself so quickly. He began to have doubts that antibiotics were going to be of much use against a bug this virulent.

"Eduardo, how are you feeling?"

"Like hell, Dr. Williams, like hell. I feel as if I am coming down with the flu." He turned watery eyes on Mason and grabbed him by the arm. "I must again protest this . . .

this incarceration. I need to go to a hospital where I can receive appropriate treatment."

Mason slowly removed Eduardo's fingers from his Racal sleeve. "Please, Dr. Matos, be assured we are making real progress here. We think we've identified the bacteria that's making you ill, and the good news is that it's usually treatable. I'm going to start an IV and begin treatment with a series of antibiotics right away."

"Oh, thank God!" Eduardo began mumbling to himself in Spanish with his eyes tightly closed.

As he swabbed Matos's arm with alcohol and started the IV solution, Mason didn't think it necessary or prudent to tell him his chances of survival were, at best, only fifty-fifty. A flip of a coin would determine whether he lived or died, and if it was to be death, it would be a terrifying, excruciating death with unimaginable suffering.

As he worked over the stricken man, Mason tried not to think about how many other people might end up facing the same kinds of suffering if the bug was allowed to escape the jungle and get loose among the teeming population of Mexico City, just a few hundred miles to the north.

He had a sneaking suspicion that with a bug like this, all the antibiotics in the world might not be enough.

Chapter 13

Mexico City

As the Wildfire Team worked feverishly to save Dr. Matos's life, Malcolm Fitzhugh waited in line before the Aero Mexico ticket counter in Mexico City.

He grinned to himself as he remembered how frightened he'd been when the big Mexican Army truck filled with soldiers had pulled him over on the road north and how relieved he'd been when he saw the sergeant in charge of the garrison was a man he'd done business with many times.

It was the matter of five minutes to cross the man's palm with more money than the soldier made in a month to get him back on his way to Mexico City.

He laughed out loud, and now here he was.

Neighboring ticket buyers shied away from the rough-looking and even worse smelling Fitzhugh, who still wore the sweat-stained khaki safari jacket and pants he had been wearing thirty-six hours previously in the jungle when he bought the collar.

Fitzhugh clasped his canvas duffle bag close to his chest as if afraid a thief might attempt to rob him of the treasure it contained. His red-rimmed, crusted eyes flicked nervously back and forth, searching the terminal for *policia* or customs agents who might be paying attention to him. He knew they would arrest him immediately if they discovered what he was carrying or even suspected he'd come from the jungle near Tlateloco.

The quarantine was all over the news, but Fitzhugh wasn't worried about catching whatever bug killed those American students. After all, he'd never gotten close to the village, having met the *Indio* boy a few miles north.

He patted the duffle bag that contained the artifact that was going to make him rich . . . lucky. Maybe fate was finally smiling down on him after all these years of a hard-scrabble existence.

An ex-commando in the British Army, Fitzhugh now eked out a meager living smuggling pre-Columbian artifacts and antiquities from Mexico to the United States. All that was about to change . . . he had finally hit the big score, a find that was going to reward him with riches beyond his wildest dreams.

He chuckled to himself, thinking fortune had finally repaid him for his years of wandering through bug- and snake-infested jungles searching for small statues and beaten-silver bracelets among the *Indios* of Mexico and Central America.

The man he had called in Houston was as excited as Fitzhugh about his find and was talking of a fee in the high six figures, an amount that would enable Fitzhugh to leave the jungle forever.

Fitzhugh chuckled again, then choked and covered his mouth as his chest tightened and a deep, phlegmy cough exploded from his lungs. His eyes itched and burned and mucus dribbled from his nose, matting and crusting in his three-day-old beard.

A woman standing in line ahead of him turned and glared at him as he coughed again, spraying her with droplets of phlegm. He held his hand up and attempted to apologize, but she had already turned to her companion, saying something about inconsiderate assholes loud enough for him to hear.

Fitzhugh shook his head and pulled a stained handkerchief from his pocket and held it against his mouth as another cough racked his body. He was mildly alarmed when he saw the bloodstains on it, but attributed his symptoms to the chronic malaria he suffered from, another memento of his years in the jungle.

When he finally got to the front of the line, a pretty young female ticket agent stared at him with a worried expression on her face. "Señor, are you all right? You appear to be ill."

Fitzhugh waved his handkerchief in the air, "I'm fine, just a touch of malaria." He coughed again, sending a spray of spittle over the counter in front of the agent who leaned back with a look of disgust on her face as Fitzhugh placed a wad of crumpled hundred-dollar bills in front of her.

"One-way ticket to Houston please," he rasped through a throat that felt as though it had been flayed with razor blades.

The agent straightened the bills and counted out the amount of the ticket, handing Fitzhugh his change and ticket folder. She brushed her hands against her dress to dry them from the dampness of the money.

"You'll have to hurry, señor, your plane leaves from Gate Five in ten minutes."

Fitzhugh swept up the ticket and bills in his hand and walked rapidly through the terminal thanking his lucky stars he was in Mexico City, where the security wasn't nearly as tight as it was in the United States. On the way to Gate 5, he ducked into a restroom, fearing he was about to throw up.

He leaned on a sink, looking into a mirror at his reflection. His face was flushed, almost scarlet in color, and perspiration beaded his forehead. He sleeved the sweat off with a forearm. He was burning up. Every muscle in his body ached and he felt as if he couldn't get enough air into his lungs. He knew from previous malarial attacks his fever had to be a hundred and two.

"Jesus, I haven't had an attack this bad since Costa Rica three years ago," he mumbled to himself. He bent to splash his face with water, not noticing its pink tint as it dripped into the sink.

He blew his nose in a wad of toilet tissue and dropped the bloodstained paper onto the floor as he hurried to catch his plane, dry swallowing a handful of aspirin to bring his fever down.

Twenty minutes later, he was airborne. He leaned his seat back and wrapped his arms around his duffle bag and tried to sleep, hoping he would feel better when he awoke in Houston.

Inside his body, the plague organisms multiplied by the millions, growing exponentially. With every breath, Fitzhugh exhaled the deadly bacteria, which were sucked up by the plane's air recycling system, passed through the ancient and inadequate air-filters, and blown out through the air returns to eventually infect every passenger on the airplane.

When the 230 passengers arrived at Houston International Airport and made their connecting flights, the plague would be on its way throughout the United States and into fifteen foreign countries less than two days after a lone man had breached the Mexican Army's quarantine perimeter in the jungles south of Mexico City.

Fort Detrick

Colonel Woodrow Blackman was awakened by his telephone at four a.m. He swung his feet off the bed and took the call while trying to clear his head of sleep fog.

"Hello?"

"A coded message just came through from Janus, Colonel. It is marked 'Eyes Only.'"

"How the hell did you know Janus's code, Lieutenant?"

"You gave it to me, sir, and told me to call you if anything from Janus came through."

"I suppose I did," he muttered, glancing over his shoulder to see if the call had disturbed his wife's slumber. "I'll get dressed and drive down in a minute. Make damn sure nobody else knows about this."

"Yes sir. I mean, no sir. No one else will know."

"Keep the fuckin' control room locked. Even if the president shows up, don't let him in. *Nobody* goes in there."

"I understand, sir."

He hung up and padded into the bathroom, deciding against a shower and shave . . . for now. If something had come through from Tlateloco at this hour it had to be important, damned important to USAMRIID.

He dressed as quietly as he could after brushing his teeth and slipped out of the house, climbing into his Buick Skylark for the short drive to Fort Detrick Headquarters Building.

Although a practical man, he refused to buy a Japanese or other foreign-made car even if they did get twice the gas mileage as American automobiles. While he was often the butt of jokes among his superiors at Fort Detrick for driving "gas guzzlers," his reply was always the same—

he'd be damned and French-fried before he'd support the industry of slant-eyed gooks who should have been bombed off the face of the earth during World War II.

He stubbornly held to the belief that America's economy was going to ruin because we let Japs and Chinks and commie Russkie bastards send television sets and stereos and cars to our shores while they refused to be pressured into allowing a single American-made item into their countries without exorbitant tariffs and taxes.

Blackie would only buy American-made TVs and electrical appliances. If a lone part was manufactured elsewhere, he refused to purchase it on patriotic grounds, nor would he allow his wife to buy imported wines or perfumes.

"Fuck 'em," he would say, his final word on any potentially foreign-made acquisition to the Blackman household. "Let the little yellow bastards starve."

He passed through two electronically operated security doors requiring his palm print before he reached the control room door, finding Lieutenant Jeremy Collins standing there with a deep flush in his cheeks.

"Why aren't you in there?" Blackie snapped.

"The security device won't let me back in, sir. It does not recognize my palm print now."

Blackie slapped his hand atop the metal plate and the door slid open. "Oh, yeah, I forgot. I changed the code last night 'cause I'm workin' on something supersensitive right now, Collins," he said. "As soon as I get what I need from one of our moles I'll put your prints back in the system. Now, stay in front of this door an' don't let anybody in."

"Not even General Cushing, sir?"

"Especially not the general. We don't need him mucking about in our business right now. Hell, he's home in bed now anyway. He told me his wife wakes him up every morning an' makes him 'cuddle' with her before he can come to work."

Blackie made a face and shivered elaborately. "God, but she's an ugly woman. I hate to think I'd have to cuddle the bitch."

He waited for Collins to chuckle at his joke, which the soldier did with a strained look on his face, and then he repeated, "You stand in front of the door, Lieutenant, until I get this coded message run off an' the chip's memory wiped clean."

"Yes sir, Colonel."

Blackie shut the door and pushed a button to secure the control room and went to his panel. A flashing light told him a message was stored in his "Top Secret" electronic mailbox. He sat down and punched in his access code, PATTON, watching the screen until the descrambler did its work.

A small LCD began passing a message in front of him.

Janus: This is it. Hot-bug is a bacteria, not a virus as we suspected . . . repeat, hot-bug is of bacterial origin. It is believed to be previously unknown form of airborne anthrax. Not recognizable under scope. Gram-positive and rod-shaped, but with anomalies. Human-to-human transmission confirmed. Send "Paco" to Mexican Army quarantine command post fifteen hundred hours for handoff. Sample is containerized, but must use all BL Four precautions. This baby is hotter than hot. Janus out.

"Anthrax," Blackie whispered. "It can't be. It shouldn't be human-to-human transmission if it's anthrax. Something's gotta be wrong."

They'd tested every known form of anthrax for years and not one variety of rod-shaped bacilli showed any promise. In cattle the transmission of anthrax among others in the same species was rampant, as well as in horses.

Humans only contracted respiratory anthrax from one type of anthrax bacillus, called woolsorter's disease because it was only found in sheep and in the early days of woolen manufacture the women who sorted the skins for manufacture were the only ones who'd ever caught the respiratory form of the disease. But the idea that a deadly respiratory anthrax affecting humans might exist, clearly in some mutant form found only in Mexico, was exciting, a revelation.

The offensive weapon they'd been looking for since biological warfare became a science might be respiratory anthrax, if this mutation could indeed be transmitted from human to human and if they could formulate an effective vaccine to protect our troops.

While an army wearing the proper protective gear would be immune, a rather simple breathing apparatus with a filter, mistakes would always happen, and pictures of our troops bleeding out and dying horrible deaths playing on twenty-four-hour news outlets would be disastrous.

Unsuspecting armies, on the other hand, would be devastated. Untreated anthrax in its respiratory form was almost eighty percent fatal, if he remembered the data on woolsorter's correctly. He made a mental note to call up all files they had on woolsorter's later to see what their data bank had on it.

"Bingo," Blackie said, rocking back in his swivel chair.

A formality lay before him, getting an agent for USAM-RIID code-named Paco to the quarantine perimeter set up by the Mexican Army around Tlateloco so Janus could hand over the all-important sample.

Within hours it would be at Fort Detrick under microscopes . . . if nothing went wrong.

He picked up a phone and auto-dialed Paco, glancing at the clock. He didn't care if Paco did not wish to be awakened this early. Paco had to be on the next flight to Mexico City, then to Tlateloco, to arrive by three o'clock.

Arturo Vela, code-named Paco, answered with a sleepy voice, "Hello?"

"This is Blackie. Get your Mexican ass out of bed and on the next plane to Mexico City. Use the *federale* credentials and uniform we gave you last year. You'll be in and out before anybody is the wiser.

"You're picking up a container from Janus at a quarantine command post outside a place called Tlateloco, a couple of hundred miles south of Mexico City."

Paco yawned and asked, "And how am I to get from Mexico City to this village in the jungle?"

"I don't give a shit how you get there . . . hell, rent a helicopter if you have to. Just get it back here as soon as possible."

Blackie hesitated, and then he said, "Oh, and Janus says to watch this motherfucker. It's really hot. Thirty dead in less than a week. CDC Wildfire is there, under Mason Williams. He and the other bug-chasers concur. They are calling it a mutant respiratory anthrax. Be real fuckin' careful how you handle it."

"Do you know what time it is, Colonel? I don't know if I can get to the airport in time to catch a flight to Mexico City that will get me there in time to do all this."

"I know what time I can have your court-martial scheduled for if you aren't on the next plane to Mexico."

Paco sighed and said wearily. "Yes, Colonel, I understand."

"I hope you do, Paco, 'cause a bullet to the brain is a lot easier than a court-martial if you fail me!"

After he hung up on Paco, Blackie sat thinking for a minute. Paco wasn't the sharpest tack in the box, he thought. Perhaps he'd better begin to arrange some insurance in case the stupid Mexican failed in his mission.

Blackie took out a key and opened the safe built into his desk. He took out a black book and opened it. There was a list of names of dishonorably discharged Navy SEALs and Army Rangers who he occasionally hired to do acquisitions from out of the country.

They were the meanest sons of bitches he'd ever worked with and had never failed him in all the years he'd been doing this dirty work.

He began to dial his encrypted phone. Might as well give them a heads-up in case he needed them later.

As he dialed, he made a mental note to have Lieutenant Collins get the BL4 lab up and running and ready for the specimens Janus was sending. He sure as hell didn't want to take a chance on letting a bug this hot escape their laboratory facilities into the Maryland countryside.

Chapter 14

Tlateloco

Dawn broke suddenly in the tropical jungle. One minute the sky was pitch black, the next a brilliant orange sun was burning morning mist away, raising temperatures. Mason came instantly awake in the dorm, a room at the end of the Cytotec BL4 in which the team members slept on small cots lined up adjacent to one another.

He rubbed his eyes, which were crusty and bloodshot after four hours of sleep. He'd made Shirley and Jakes go to bed at two a.m., fearing fatigue would cause an accident with these virulent samples and perhaps inadvertent infection of one of the team with a proven deadly pathogen.

He rolled on his cot, noting that Jakes was still snoring softly and everyone else in the dorm was also still asleep. He arose quietly, making as little noise as possible. His people had worked for almost twenty-four straight hours since their arrival in Mexico and he felt they deserved their rest.

After morning coffee jolted his system awake, he suited up in his Racal and entered the lab. The lab was the

one place in the Cytotec where absolute isolation procedures were practiced.

Prior to retiring the night before, Shirley had started
cultures of the hot-bug in both blood agar and nutrient
mediums, as well as chocolate agar and other more exotic
mixtures. Several slides were set up for fluorescent antibody staining and DNA probes and polymerase chain reaction tests and even the much more complicated ELISA
test.

The specimens had been "cooking" for four hours and
should be ready in about five hours. Meanwhile, Mason
intended to try specific toxin and antigen tests and a
monoclonal antibody experiment to see if the bacteria
had a capsule.

Before collapsing into his cot the previous night,
Mason pulled down a reference book on microbiology
and refreshed his memory about how the anthrax bacillus
was supposed to react to these tests. Today, he would determine if the organism in tissues from the archaeology
students was really anthrax or merely a closely related
imposter.

He had been working for three hours mixing reagents,
staining slides, inoculating tissues into growth mediums,
and putting drops of heavily contaminated serum in a
flame spectrometer to try to identify specific chemicals in
the bacteria when a loud knock on the glass of the lab
door caught his attention.

Jakes and Shirley pointed to the Racals in the adjacent
room and raised their eyebrows in question. Mason stepped
to a wall intercom and thumbed its transmit button. "No,
I'm doing okay for now. Why don't you guys have your
breakfast, then suit up the others and Dr. Sullivan and
form a search party. There's one student still unaccounted

for and I'd like to find him so we can send Lauren back to the States; also I want you to keep an eye out for the *Indio* boy Lauren and I saw yesterday. I still feel he might be the key to this entire mystery."

He started to turn away and then had another thought. "And could you take a look at Dr. Matos and see how he's doing this morning? I checked on him briefly when I got up but he was sleeping and I didn't want to wake him. He looked pretty ragged earlier and his temp was still elevated."

The two doctors nodded and moved off, Shirley rubbing her eyes while yawning. Mason watched them leave, worrying he was pushing everyone too hard, but he knew he had no choice. The first twenty-four to forty-eight hours of a Wildfire intervention were critical to the success of a mission. The disease had to be identified and local authorities, both medical and civil, needed to be apprised of whatever quarantine and medical precautions should be implemented. So very much to do, and so little time, he thought.

Leaning over the counter, Mason peered down at the culture plates, lined up in order of importance. Several petri dishes were growing small grayish-white bacterial colonies. On the blood agar, it was too soon to tell if colonies were nonhemolytic as anthrax was.

He broke open a box of commercial test strips and laid them on the counter. As soon as the cultures had grown enough, he would do sequential biochemical tests on the bacteria, as well as searches for presence or absence of a capsule, lack of motility, catalase positivity, lysis by gamma bacteriophage, penicillin susceptibility, and aerobic endospore production.

He rotated his head, trying to stretch tight, cramped

neck muscles inside his hood, thinking a massage would do wonders for his aching back. Unbidden, an image of Lauren intruded, breaking his concentration. There was no way he could keep his focus while thinking of a massage and of Lauren at the same time. He glanced around the lab.

Everything was in place waiting for the damned bacteria to grow enough in culture mediums to do required biochemical and genetic testing to determine what species they were dealing with. He figured he might as well break for coffee and breakfast while he waited. There was nothing else for him to do here until cultures were ready. And he could check on Lauren and see if she had been able to get some sleep in the crowded dorm. He noticed she'd looked exhausted by the time they were able to crawl into their cots last night.

He stepped into the shower room and washed his Racal with disinfecting solutions, hung it up, and then took his body shower, wrinkling his nose at the strong smell of chlorine in the water. Finally, he changed into his scrubs and went into the dining room. His staff and Lauren were finishing their morning meal when he arrived.

Joel Schumacher looked up from his powdered eggs and toast. "Hey Mason, how're you doin' this morning?"

"Good morning, Joel. Okay, I guess, other than feeling about ten years older than yesterday. How about you?"

"I'm cool. I got the Comsat link hooked up and we're tied into the mainframe at CDC. We're now officially on-line to Big Mamma."

"Good. How about downloading everything the computer has on anthrax, especially technical specifics for identification and differentiation of all known subspecies and other bacilli that look like anthrax? I've checked the reference books we have here, but the computer will be more up-to-date and may give us some hints on other tests we can run."

"Sure, boss. No problemo."

Suzanne Elliot wiped orange juice off her upper lip and said, "Joel, while you're doing that could you ask Mamma to give us all she has on incubation periods, infectivity, and modes of transmission of anthrax, as well as a printout of all previous outbreaks, especially ones that occurred in more modern times? I'd like to start a feasibility study of vector tracking and indexing of cases assuming a worst-case scenario if this bug happens to break our quarantine. Pretty soon I'll have to issue a CDC BOL bulletin to doctors in Mexico City listing symptoms of respiratory anthrax."

"You ought to know the symptoms of anthrax by heart, Suzanne. Didn't you work with that bug when you were at Fort Detrick, developing all those germ warfare killers?" Jakes asked with his typical sarcasm.

Suzanne fixed Jakes with a flat stare. "No, as a matter of fact we didn't. It didn't fit the protocol since it wasn't transmissible from person to person and there was no effective vaccine available to prevent infection of our own troops."

Lauren nodded good morning to Mason, and then she asked Suzanne, "What's a BOL bulletin?"

Suzanne glared at Jakes for a moment more and then she turned and smiled at Lauren, "Sorry about the jargon, Lauren, it's just verbal shorthand we use among ourselves. BOL means 'Be on the Lookout' for. It's a warning we send to local health departments and hospitals in areas where we fear an outbreak of a certain illness, especially a rare one like anthrax. The symptoms are rather general,

a flu-like illness that rapidly develops into a severe bron-
chitis or pneumonia, followed as you know by bleeding
problems. If this bug does escape the jungle and get into
the city, we want doctors there to be able to recognize it
and notify us of any new cases as early as possible so I
can assign an epidemiology team from CDC to start to
track them down and isolate any of their contacts. It's the
first step in stopping the spread of any infectious disease."

"I see," Lauren replied sleepily.

Mason poured himself a cup of coffee and heated an
MRE containing eggs in the microwave. "Lauren, you're
looking rested this morning. I hope Sam's snoring didn't
keep you awake last night."

Lauren started a smile, which degenerated into a yawn.
"A bomb could've gone off in the room last night and I
wouldn't have heard it. I can't remember ever being so
tired in my life. I don't know how you people do it."

Lionel Johnson chuckled and said in his deep voice,
"Don't think this is typical for us either, Lauren. Being a
CDC investigator is kinda like being an obstetrician,
ninety-five percent boredom and five percent terror."

When Lauren laughed, Mason said, "Lionel's right.
Most of our work consists of reading health department
reports and keeping statistics on routine disease outbreaks like flu and meningitis and AIDS. Only occasionally do we have a real Wildfire emergency and have to do
intensive fieldwork, like now."

"That reminds me, why do you call your group the Wildfire Team?" she asked.

Mason turned away as Shirley spoke up, "Mason's an in-
veterate reader, Lauren, and his taste runs to medical thrillers.
His secretary started using the term Wildfire Team from

Michael Crichton's book *The Andromeda Strain*, and it stuck. Our official title is CDC Special Pathogens Group, but that's a little pompous for us, so we use the Wildfire designation among ourselves."

Jakes poured himself a glass of tomato juice. "And it's a lot of foolishness if you ask me," he muttered.

Shirley couldn't resist an opening for a shot at Dr. Jakes. "I don't recall anyone asking you, Sam," she said, winking at Lauren.

"Still, naming ourselves after a fictional potboiler, it's undignified," Sam replied.

"No," Shirley said, giving Lauren another wink, "undignified is you wearing scrubs that droop in the rear showing your butt-crack every time you bend over like some redneck plumber."

"What?" Jakes yelped, looking back over his shoulder at his rear end.

"Just kidding," Shirley said sweetly, earning a scowl from Jakes.

"Now that you've heard from our resident experts on dignity," Mason said, "would you mind accompanying my team on a search for the last missing student? We need to get the list of casualties finalized as soon as we can, so you can get back home."

Lauren arched an eyebrow and her lip curled in a sly smile. "Trying to get rid of me? Is my company that bad, Dr. Williams?"

A few of the others grinned when Mason seemed embarrassed. "No, certainly not. It's just that . . . um . . . I don't want you to stay in a danger area any longer than necessary, that's all." As he finished talking the members of the team couldn't help but notice his face was flaming red all the way to his ears.

Suzanne stood up, brushing crumbs from her hands as she looked from Mason to Lauren, a speculative gleam in her eyes. "Come on everyone, the chief is hinting that we've wasted enough time sitting around here shooting the breeze. Time to get to work."

"While you're searching the area, Joel and I will download CDC data on anthrax from Mamma and I'll get the lab ready for tests on our cultures as soon as they've finished cooking," Mason said, trying to regain some semblance of authority.

"By the time you get back, I'll be ready to do specific tests to see if we're really dealing with anthrax."

Shirley asked, "Do you think we need to wear those damned Racals or just face masks?"

"I think we'd better err on the side of caution right now. Let's use the Racals until we're one hundred percent sure our bug is transmitted air to air only and not by contact. We should know for certain by this afternoon."

Guatemotzi watched the soldiers from deep shadows below the jungle canopy, wondering why they wore those curious masks. In heat so intense under a midafternoon sun he felt they must be suffering greatly, for he knew they were unaccustomed to the heavier air of summer.

When *soldados* came through Michoacán they continually sought shade, as if the sun burned their skins. Guatemotzi and his people often watched them drive trucks along jungle roads and it was said they were looking for revolutionaries, or traffickers in *las drogas*. Sometimes there was shooting, and Mexican soldiers had guns that fired many bullets in a single stream at a human target.

Thus Guatemotzi feared them, as did everyone in the village, and when they came to ask questions about *las drogas* or those who wanted to overthrow the government, no one spoke of the men hidden deep in the jungle who lived in small camps and turned leaves into white powder, or harvested a plant called marijuana, both taken to the cities at night in small trucks or on the backs of horses.

What was most puzzling were the actions of *los soldados* now as they formed this circle around Tlateloco. In his heart he felt he knew the soldiers were about to make war against *Los Oráculos*, and there were so many soldiers against so few of the ancient warriors with orange skins. Guatemotzi believed it was to be a test of strength, the power of these messengers from the ancient gods of the Aztecs pitted against the soldiers. And it did not appear *Los Oráculos* carried weapons, only small knives they used to cut up the dead *Americanos*. A test of magic powers and not guns, for surely the gods of the Aztecs would not send warriors without powerful magic that could defeat the weapons of the soldiers. Guatemotzi wondered when the battle would begin and if the orange skins *Los Oráculos* wore would turn aside bullets.

He had been dozing behind an escoba palm where he could see the winding path to Tlateloco when movement in the jungle brought him fully awake with his heart racing. One of the orange-skinned warriors was approaching a group of soldiers guarding the road.

"Only one?" he whispered, speaking his native tongue, which he preferred over the Spanish taught by the priests, for it was far easier to speak and think in Nahuatl. He could not make himself believe only one warrior had been sent to defeat so many *soldados*. The chief of *Los Oráculos* must believe very strongly in their magic powers.

A soldier wearing a mask came toward the Aztec warrior and they met where the road made a turn. Neither one appeared to be ready for battle. They stood before each other, doing nothing, until the warrior took a small pouch from his waist and gave it to the soldier.

An offering, Guatemotzi thought. *Los Oráculos* want peace, not war. Perhaps they are giving the soldiers parts of the dead *Americanos'* bodies as a gift to prevent a battle between them. It was a strange sight, to see a messenger from the Aztec gods give this *soldado* his pouch. The masked soldier turned around and went back to the others while the warrior disappeared into the jungle. What a curious meeting it was, the gift of a pouch halting a war between them.

He crept deeper into the forest when the soldier climbed in an automobile with no roof and drove back toward the city. Were the black pouch and its contents being offered to the *presidente* of Mexico so there could be peace between the new god, Jesus, and the gods of his ancestors? Guatemotzi's father and everyone else in the village would greet this news with great happiness. Now, perhaps the dreaded *soldados* would stop coming to Michoacán with guns to ask their questions of Guatemotzi's people.

Chapter 15

Lauren was at a point physically and emotionally where she believed she could go no further. One last body remained to be found according to the student manifest naming everyone on the expedition, and even with the help of several members of Mason's Wildfire Team, no one could find Jimmy Walker. James was one of Charlie's top doctoral candidates, perhaps the brightest of his teaching assistants, and as the search for him continued through the afternoon Lauren dared not hope that somehow he might have escaped in time before the illness entered his body.

Mason and the other doctors were now almost convinced they'd identified the "bug," as they called it, which Mason said spelled some hope for Eduardo Matos. But in her heart Lauren still harbored doubts, and even as briefly as she'd known Dr. Williams, she thought she detected a note of concern in his voice for Eduardo's chances of recovery.

Last night, when she tried to sleep, she continued to have vague feelings of a presence here in Tlateloco, as if some thing or some premonition haunted her innermost thoughts. She tried to dismiss them entirely, for she was a scientist trained in archaeology, not superstition or belief in ghosts or curses.

But at the same time she could not shake the memory of Eduardo's encounter with the sacrificial dagger. It was almost as if the accident was no accident at all but a further striking out by some malignant entity to punish the interlopers who dared to desecrate the emperor's tomb.

"I found a body," a woman's voice said over Lauren's headset and the sound startled her from her reverie. "It's southwest of the clearing, about three hundred yards into a palm grove. It's a male. Young, about twenty-five or so—it's hard to tell due to the destruction by scavengers. I'd venture a guess that a large cat of some kind has been feeding on the corpse. This boy is pretty badly chewed up. Dr. Sullivan, if you can hear me, come to the clearing and I'll take you to the body."

Lauren's voice caught in her throat. "It must be Jimmy. I really don't want to see him if he's . . ."

"Sorry, but it's necessary so we can link up with CDC and report all the names. Someone in Atlanta will notify the university, which can then notify his next of kin."

She turned around and trudged slowly back to the clearing, casting a quick glance in the direction of the temple. Sleeplessness muddled her thoughts and the heat inside her Racal was all but unbearable. She supposed she could force herself to see one last body before she asked for a helicopter to take her back to Mexico City.

She was, however, experiencing another set of feelings since last night, a curious attraction—if that was the right word—to Mason Williams. Of course, he was good-looking, brilliant, courageous, and sensitive, most of the time. What was there not to like? The trouble was thoughts like these made her very uncomfortable. Was she being disloyal to her friends and Charlie to feel attracted to a man she'd just met while in the midst of so much death and destruction? Oh well, there was little to no chance of consummating or even beginning a romantic attachment while they were living in the Cytotec lab. Privacy was not minimal, it was nonexistent.

She shook her head and pushed the unwelcome thoughts aside, chalking them off to fatigue, then joined Suzanne Elliot in the clearing, for the hundredth time making a futile attempt to wipe sweat off her face with her hand despite the Plexiglas mask.

"This way," Suzanne said gently. "I know how difficult this is for you, Dr. Sullivan, but according to your list, this will be the last one you'll have to identify."

"I suppose I can do it," she replied, following Suzanne into another section of the forest. "I guess I should be used to it by now."

Suzanne put a reassuring hand on her shoulder. "No, you never get used to it, dear. Trust me, I've been at this game of death for more years than I care to remember, and each new victim affects me just as much as the first ones I had to deal with."

Following a narrow jungle game trail, they came to a spot beneath a small tree named Black Poison Wood by local farmers, where Suzanne pointed to a badly mangled corpse, its chest cavity torn open, both upper legs chewed down to bare bone.

"That's Jimmy," Lauren whispered, recognizing James Walker's freckled cheeks and carrot-red hair. "What's left of him . . ."

Suzanne took Lauren by the arm. "That's all we needed, Dr. Sullivan. You can go home as soon as Joel can raise our chopper in Mexico City. It's our big Sikorsky Crane, the CH fifty-three that brought us the lab. Our backup group is standing by in case we need anything else. I'm sure Mason won't mind asking them to pick you up. It's noisy as hell and slower than Christmas, but it'll get you to the next commercial flight to the States."

Pushing brush and vines aside, Lauren followed Suzanne back toward the temple, feeling completely devoid of emotion. This had been the worst two days of her life and the thought of ending them sounded appealing, although she knew she would never escape the memories.

Getting out of this stupid orange space suit and going back to civilization held far more appeal, the way she felt now, than getting to know Mason better. Or did it? she wondered. She was becoming increasingly confused by her feelings toward him and even though nothing could ever come of it she still felt pangs of guilt over her feelings. It's a shame, she thought, that he couldn't be persuaded to ride back to Mexico City with her and perhaps spend a night or two decompressing from the stress of the search for the killer bug.

She shook her head. That would never happen, for she knew he was too dedicated to his job to even think of taking a day off until the bug was found and defeated.

A movement among the escoba trunks caught her eye and she stopped abruptly. "There he is again!" Lauren cried, pointing to a shirtless form running away from them into the jungle. "Do you see him? It's that same Indian boy. I *knew* I wasn't imagining it when I saw him last night!"

"I see him," Suzanne replied, her tone a mixture of curiosity and doubt. "How the hell can he be out here running around in a hot zone without protection? Remember what happened to your friend, Dr. Matos? That boy ought to be sick as hell or dead by now."

"Should we try to catch him?" Lauren asked.

"Hell no," Suzanne replied. "Did you see the way he moved through the brush, as if it weren't there? Plus, it'd be much too dangerous for us to go running through the jungle in our Racals, too easy to get a puncture and then we'd be laid up like poor Dr. Matos."

Lauren continued to follow Suzanne back to the clearing, where four Racal-suited forms stood outside the mobile laboratory.

Lauren heard Suzanne mutter, "Someone isn't here. We're missing a team member somewhere."

Lionel's voice replied, "Have any of you seen Shirley?"

Before anyone could reply, Shirley pushed her way out of thick brush and said, "I was just a short way up the trail, making sure the soldiers are doing their job and keeping sightseers and the press off our backs and out of the hot zone."

Mason, Shirley, and Jakes were in their Racals in the lab, printouts from the CDC mainframe computer known as Mamma spread before them. "These cultures have been growing for about twelve hours now and that should be enough," Mason remarked, glancing at a digital clock on a wall of the lab.

Shirley leaned over petri dishes arranged on the counter. "Mason, these colonies are very similar to what I would expect from anthrax, only they're slightly different."

"How so?" Jakes asked. "It's been twenty years since I looked at bacterial cultures. What are you looking for?"

"Anthrax is nonhemolytic, and that means colonies should grow on blood agar medium, and the grayish-white patches should have clean margins showing they're not hemolyzing or destroying blood in the medium. Here," she pointed to one of the culture dishes, filled with a dark reddish-brown jelly substance. "You can see these colonies have a small clear area around them, showing at least some hemolysis is taking place. That doesn't fit with classical anthrax."

Mason was across the room examining DNA probe test strips. "There are a couple of minor differences here, too. Not enough to show a different species, however there is a small but very distinct difference in the arrangement of amino acids in genetic coding for these bacteria."

Shirley glanced down at another test strip, "Uh-oh, here's another anomaly. The gamma-bacteriophage lysis test shows some differences."

Exasperated, Jakes asked, "Now just what the hell does that mean?"

Shirley explained without the usual impatience found in her voice when she spoke to Jakes, "Virulence in anthrax, its ability to produce disease, depends on three components: edema toxin, lethal toxin, and capsular material. Without any one of these, the anthrax bacillus is unable to cause significant illness. The production of the two toxic factors is regulated in anthrax by one plasmid and the capsular component by a second plasmid.

"As you know from viruses, plasmids are small bits of chromosomal material that interact with the bacteria's own chromosomes to determine its characteristics. In this bug, these appear a little different biochemically from the way classical anthrax plasmids should."

Jakes knitted his brow thoughtfully. "Hey, if that's

what's bothering you, maybe I can put one of these little bastards in my electron microscope and we can look inside the capsule and take a gander at its chromosomal makeup. Would that help?"

Shirley looked over at Mason and shrugged. "It may shed some light on what's going on with these little buggers."

While Shirley and Mason continued with their biochemical tests, Jakes took a specimen from one culture dish and prepared it for examination under his electron microscope. After roughly thirty minutes, he announced, "I'm ready over here."

Shirley and Mason stood behind him, peering over his shoulder at the monitor screen of the giant microscope.

As Jakes twisted dials and controls, the image of a single bacillus grew on the screen, appearing as if they were journeying deep inside the bacteria's capsule themselves.

Jakes pointed to the screen where a large, black circular object hovered in the meat of the bacteria. "Here's the nucleus, where all the chromosomal material is. Watch as I increase the magnification."

The picture slowly enlarged until it filled the screen, then enlarged further. "There are the bacteria's chromosomes, and over there," he pointed to one side of the nucleus, "near its outer edge are the plasmid components."

"Wait a minute," Shirley said, excitement raising her voice. "I see three plasmids, and anthrax is supposed to only have two!"

Mason stepped back, unconsciously attempting to rub his chin, instead stroking the hood of his Racal. "Shirley, if this is an ancient form of anthrax, do you suppose the third plasmid could be responsible for allowing it to be transmitted from person to person? We know present-day anthrax has only two plasmids, one for toxicity and one for capsular formation. What if the third was lost in some ancient mutation, causing anthrax to lose its ability to be spread in air-to-air transmission from one infected person to another?"

Shirley spread her palms. "Hell, chief, anything's possible. This bug has had four hundred years to change, and so far this is the only difference we've found between what may be an older version and the present forms of anthrax."

She pointed to the array of test strips and culture dishes on the counter behind them. "The extra plasmid could account for this bug's ability to lyse or destroy red blood cells, and its capability to be spread by aerosol or droplet transmission. Of course, it's going to take extensive DNA testing to determine exactly what chromosomes the extra plasmid contains and what its exact function is, and there is simply no way we're equipped to do it here. That's going to take all the facilities at the CDC lab in Georgia."

"You're right," Mason replied, after considering what Shirley said. "But can we safely assume we are dealing with respiratory anthrax, albeit in a slightly different, more virulent form?"

Shirley agreed quickly. "I think we can say that, at the very least."

"Let's let Suzanne know it's definitely anthrax and have her get those BOLs out to the authorities in Mexico. We'll need to make sure the military is notified of what we've got here, and we need to make some arrangements to dispose of those bodies so no one else is infected and to get transportation for Dr. Sullivan back to Mexico City."

"What about the site itself, Mason?" Jakes asked. "I think we should call in a fuel bomb and fry the *shit* out of this entire area before this son-of-a-bitch bug gets out to wreak more havoc."

Mason shook his head. "What we ought to do and what we're going to be allowed to do might be two different things. A lot will depend on what happens to Dr. Matos and if this bug makes an appearance anywhere else before we get a chance to really dispose of it."

He wagged his head. "If it does manage to escape the jungle and get to civilization, then there would be no need to burn this area as the cat would already be out of the bag."

Chapter 16

Mexico City

Arturo Vela, alias "Paco," did not worry about the contents of his briefcase as he found a vacant stool at a bar in the airport in Mexico City. He'd done this half a hundred times before and never with difficulty. Colonel Blackman said to handle this specimen carefully, but he always said that about any possibly active germ Arturo picked up from an operative of USAMRIID in foreign countries, as if Arturo might make a cocktail out of the stuff to see if it killed him first before he brought it to Fort Detrick to be tested.

Paco laughed as he hefted his cocktail and took a drink. Blackman was an idiot and a racist, but his money spent as well as anyone else's. And, Paco thought, raising the glass in a silent toast, he had to admit the bastard wasn't stingy with it. Another couple of missions and Paco thought he'd be able to retire and spend the rest of his days on a beach drinking and screwing brown-skinned babes day in and day out. He was in this game strictly for the money.

Blackie, on the other hand, was a blood-and-guts

soldier, a patriot from the "old school" who still believed in the big Communist threat and a world takeover by some lunatic dictator like Adolf Hitler or Joseph Stalin or Mussolini, or even worse, some heathen towel-head who killed in the name of his false god.

Blackman lived in a world of his own shrouded in secrecy, which he believed was necessary due to some poorly defined threat he insisted would come from Russia or Europe or China or Japan or the Middle East.

It mattered little to him that these threats were virtually impotent now—his crystal ball revealing the onset of world power struggles would not allow for any discounting of political realities in the twenty-first century.

And more than a few of his superiors lived in the same vacuum, permitting him to continue with biological offensive weapons experimentation despite a presidential order against it. General Cushing, a two-star and Blackie's titular boss, was every bit as radical as Blackie when it came to fears of germ warfare against the United States. Because of this, secret agents of USAMRIID were in place around the globe looking for "bugs" that had the potential to kill millions of people.

A pretty Mexican girl gave Paco the eye from a tiny table at the back of the club. He nodded, dispatching a waiter to her table to offer her a drink at his expense. She smiled and said something without taking her sultry gaze from Arturo's face as she placed her order.

He got up after an appropriate interval and sauntered across to the bar. *"Buenos días, señorita,"* he said in his best Castilian Spanish, hoping she might be well-bred despite her dyed blond hair and low-cut dress revealing a bit more of her bosom than a proper woman should—but then, if she were a proper woman, why was she sitting alone in an airport drinking establishment, giving a total stranger her best come-on look?

Paco placed his briefcase on the floor beside an empty chair when the woman replied, "*Buenos días, señor.* Your *Español* is accented. You are an American, *verdad*?"

"You are as insightful as you are beautiful, pretty lady," he said, switching to English. "I am indeed, *un Americano*, educated in the United States. May I sit down?"

"Si como no?" she answered, batting her false eyelashes, a hint of suggestion in her eyes and in the way she rested a nylon-clad leg over her knee, providing Arturo with a breathtaking view of her thighs.

"You were planning to sit down anyway, were you not?"

"I am so transparent," he said humbly, but with a gesture to the same waiter to bring him another drink.

"My name is Patricio Flores and I am working in co-operation with the Mexican Federal Police," he said, giving her his current alias. "I am in Mexico City on official business."

He reached into his coat pocket and showed her his credentials, a skillful counterfeit provided to USAMRIID by technicians at the CIA.

"May I ask your name, señorita?"

He was certain she would be impressed with his phony badge and the identification card bearing an official seal of Distrito Federal. Arturo found he could not keep from looking deeply into her eyes, though his gaze often drifted farther south to her ample bosom and then on down to her thighs.

"I am Rosa. Rosa Morales." She noticed his stare and made a move to lower the hem of her skirt, raising one leg slightly to tug her dress to a more modest level. With the same motion her foot touched Arturo's briefcase, the toe of her high-heeled shoe bumping his case ever so lightly. His briefcase fell over on its side and he scarcely noticed, with his full attention on Rosa's creamy skin where her breasts swelled above the deep slash at the top of her black, sleeveless gown.

"It is an honor to meet such a lovely woman," Arturo said as he dropped into an empty chair beside her.

Self-consciously, he adjusted his necktie and only then did he notice his briefcase lying flat on the floor beneath the table. He reached for it and placed it upright, thinking only of Rosa, her dark chocolate eyes and the way she stared at him without blinking.

She was a rare beauty, this one, and with two hours to spare before his direct flight to Maryland and the close proximity to the airport of several hotels, he saw distinct possibilities in their chance meeting, as if it were meant to happen.

He was in the airport restroom washing the heady scent of Rosa off his skin, when he first noticed a damp circle on the tile floor where his briefcase rested beside his foot as he washed his face and hands.

"Son of a bitch," he said under his breath, glancing around to see who might be watching before he bent down to open his lone piece of carry-on luggage.

What he saw did not disturb him—after several drinks and two hours spent with Rosa little short of a nuclear blast could disturb him.

An envelope surrounding the container from Janus was soaked and he felt sure it was only liquid protecting an inner capsule in which specimens were sent, a jellylike substance insulating the package's real cargo from a potentially dangerous accidental bump or a trip through airport security's X-ray and conveyor belt.

"I'll put it in another envelope," he said to himself, with little thought given to anything beyond delivering his package to Blackman and then getting the hell away from Fort Detrick in time to meet Diane, a young captain's wife who discovered her first orgasm when Arturo introduced her to the inherent skills of a Latin lover while her husband was overseas serving his country.

He tore open the ruined wrapping and tightened the capsule lid before placing it in another envelope, convincing himself the dampness clinging to his fingers was only insulating jelly and harmless. He heard his flight number being called. He tucked the newly wrapped package into his briefcase before hurrying from *el baño* to catch his plane to Baltimore, glad to be out of Mexico despite his enchanting rendezvous with lovely Rosa Morales.

Fort Detrick

Arturo flashed his ID badge to a guard sitting at a desk just inside the second security door to the USAMRIID laboratory building. The guard smiled in recognition as Arturo approached, then frowned as he came closer.

"Jesus, Arturo, you look like shit. You feelin' okay?"

Arturo sleeved sweat from his forehead and shivered with a sudden chill.

"Yeah, I guess so. I think I must be coming down with the flu. I've been on crowded planes for the past two days and in addition had to tramp through fifty miles of jungle so there's no telling what kind of crap I caught."

He held his briefcase up and tilted his head toward the inner laboratory down the hall. "I just gotta drop this off, then I'm home to bed."

The guard waved him through. "Take two aspirins and a hot blond and call me in the morning," he said with a smile and a wink.

Arturo Vela, code-named Paco, entered the final security door to deposit his deadly cargo on Colonel Blackman's desk in the lab, thus completing his latest task for the Colonel.

Though he did not realize it, it was to be his last delivery to USAMRIID.

Chapter 17

Houston, Texas

Malcolm Fitzhugh continued having symptoms of what he thought was malaria aboard Mexicana Flight 1151 from Mexico City to Houston. A sudden onset of a series of chills, cramps deep within his abdomen, and sweat flowing from his pores had him feeling terrible.

He ordered another drink from a stewardess, double bourbon and water and a twin pack of aspirin, waving away her concerns about his appearance.

There wasn't time to be sick. Not now. The jeweled artifact in his duffle bag was most certainly worth a fortune, a stroke of unexpected luck when he stumbled upon the wandering Indian boy who offered to sell it to him for a ridiculous sum, roughly the equivalent of two hundred dollars.

The boy had no idea how much the artifact was truly worth. Fitzhugh believed his story that it came from within Montezuma's tomb, since the tale coincided with what Fitzhugh had heard from the Mexican workers he had bribed to steal whatever they could and bring it to him on the road where he'd met the *Indio*.

Of course, the boy's story that all of the *Americanos* and even the Mexican laborers had died was patently false. Hell, he'd met with some of them only ten days before . . . they couldn't all have died in that length of time.

Malcolm chuckled to himself, thinking it was all a lie to cover up the fact that the boy didn't want him to go to the dig and tell them he had stolen the collar.

That the boy, who called himself Guatemotzi, was a thief did not matter in the least to Fitzhugh—hell, that was how he made his living, by dealing with thieves on a daily basis.

What *did* matter was what the artifact was worth to an antiquities dealer in Houston—hundreds of thousands of dollars if the artifact could be proven to be from Montezuma's tomb.

It was clearly from the Aztec period, which was not Fitzhugh's specialty, and the boy's story that it came from one of Montezuma's pets had made the dealer almost drool with anticipation as it fit perfectly with legends about how the Aztec emperor treated his pets.

Fitzhugh knew the dealer, Walter Simmons, was so anxious to obtain the artifact that he could probably be milked for something approaching its true value. Yes, he thought, the trinket hidden in the false compartment of his duffle bag was going to set him up for life, and he vowed then and there to never again set foot in a jungle of any kind.

An hour away from Houston he was sweating profusely. He left his seat to go to the bathroom at the rear of the Mexicana 737. When he passed a stewardess in the narrow aisle she gave him an odd look, paying particular attention to his eyes. His nose had begun to run and without a handkerchief or a tissue he could only sniffle back the discharge, noticing it had a peculiar coppery taste.

Clinging to his briefcase, he entered the bathroom and secured the door before he glanced in the mirror above the sink.

"Oh my God!" he exclaimed, reaching for a paper towel. His tear ducts were oozing blood and there was a trace of blood on his upper lip.

He quickly wiped the blood away just as a violent spasm hit his stomach. He retched, sounds hidden by the roar of twin jet turbines on either side of the tail section. But what he vomited into the sink horrified him. Raw blood and mucosa splattered into the stainless steel basin. He wiped his mouth with another towel, feeling strangely weak, a tremor in his legs and arms as he looked in the mirror again.

"What the hell is wrong with me?" he asked, speaking to his reflection, not entirely able to recognize the image he saw—pale gray skin beaded with sweat, bloody tears dribbling past his nose down his cheeks. This episode was far different from his other periodic bouts with malaria.

Had he contracted some rare jungle disease? he wondered. As one who traveled all over remote parts of Mexican jungles buying artifacts to smuggle into the United States, he'd been vaccinated for everything his doctor in Houston warned him about, and he'd been across these same jungle regions for years without mishap, only occasional bouts with dysentery when he was not careful enough about what he ate or where he ate it and his rare bouts of malaria.

He knew just enough about bodily functions to know he was hemorrhaging internally somehow, but that wouldn't explain the blood from his tear ducts or his nose. Had he contracted some rare blood disease?

His eyes widened and he gasped as the implications hit him—could the *Indio* have been telling the truth about all of the Americans dying . . . and could he somehow have gotten the same illness? "Oh Jesus!" he exclaimed out loud to the mirror. "Not now . . . not when I'm about to hit the jackpot."

He needed a doctor quickly. They were another hour from Houston International Airport. Surely he could endure this odd phenomenon for an hour, then a half-hour's drive to Walter's to leave his artifact, then a hurried taxi ride to a Houston hospital to find out what the hell was wrong with him. Surely, even if he had contracted the illness that killed the dig crew, modern medicine in a city as large as Houston could cure him.

But with his stomach muscles contracting so violently he might get sick in the customs inspection room and someone could then discover the piece of antiquity he was bringing into the country illegally.

A safer bet was to call Walter on the cell phone on the back of the seat in front of his and ask him to meet him at the airport, and of paramount importance was to have him take the briefcase if his copious bleeding alerted customs officers for a need to summon an ambulance or a doctor to the airport.

Walter would understand that the artifact would have to be protected at all costs, and he knew he could trust him for his payment later when he was feeling better. After all, he had been doing business with Walter for years.

He wiped his cheeks as best he could, taking another handful of paper towels and stuffing them into his jacket pockets to use to cover his face should the bleeding from his nose and eyes begin again. He left the bathroom on unsteady legs and made his way back to his seat to place a call to Walter.

He noticed the seats on either side of him were now vacant. He wrinkled his nose; even he could smell the sour smell of his sweat-soaked jacket. No wonder his neighbors had sought seats elsewhere.

A pretty Mexican stewardess, a worried look on her face, paused near his aisle seat to ask, "Are you all right, sir?"

He nodded as he was dialing Walter's number. "Just a bad case of the flu and this altitude may have ruptured my sinuses. I'll be okay. I have nosebleeds all the time on airplanes."

He wiped his eyes and nose, fighting back convulsions that were twisting his stomach into knots. An older Mexican woman in the seat across the aisle from him gave him a lingering stare as Walter's phone began to ring.

He didn't notice how she quickly crossed herself and began to murmur the Lord's Prayer in Spanish.

Walter Simmons opened Fitzhugh's briefcase in a basement room under the glare of a halogen lamp, peeling back a thin layer of a cardboard material to get at what was in the hidden chamber.

A shriveled piece of deerskin adorned with hammered silver and gemstones rested in the false bottom of the case. "Aztec all right," he said quickly, for there was no doubt. He peered closely at one silver filigree symbol. "Just as Fitzhugh had said, it was an animal collar, and I can clearly see that's the royal Aztec symbol for Montezuma. He was known to keep a menagerie of exotic pets at his side at all times."

Beatrice, Walter's wife, leaned over for a better look. "It is the royal symbol, the Thunderbird. If this thing is genuine and not a forgery, it's worth at least several hundred thousand, perhaps a bit more if we take careful photographs and if it is described in any of the writings of Díaz's letters home to Spain."

She touched one of the stones. "These are huge emeralds. There are six of them, and the silver work is so intricate. We'll ask four hundred and seventy-five thousand and see if we have any takers."

Simmons got off his stool. "I'd better call the hospital to see how Malcolm's doing. I've never seen anything like it. He was bleeding all over the place, from his nose and mouth, even his eyes and ears. He sounded worried over the phone, but I did not expect anything so serious.

"Everyone was so busy hovering over him when he collapsed in customs they never paid any attention to me or to the briefcase. There was blood all over the floor. It looked like he was going to bleed to death right there before the ambulance arrived. He couldn't talk and his eyes sort of glazed over. It was weird. I'd better call his sister in Dallas. For all I know he could be dying. I never saw so much blood in my life."

Beatrice put her hand on her husband's arm. "Walter, calm down, you're babbling. But just in case he doesn't make it, don't say anything to his sister about the artifact."

She grinned nastily. "One hundred percent of four hundred and seventy-five thousand is twice as good as fifty percent."

* * *

Maria Gomez embraced her son, then her daughter as soon as she put her suitcase on the sofa. "It is so good to see you, *mi hijo y mi hija*. It was a terrible ride on the plane. The man sitting in the seat across from me became very ill. He was bleeding. *Dios!* I think maybe so he has the cancer, like *Tío Roberto*. Blood was on my dress. See here?" She pointed to a dark brown stain on one side of her pale yellow skirt.

She took her children by the hand and led them into the back room, then the kitchen, where her husband Rodolfo was eating his lunch. Maria embraced him warmly and kissed his cheek.

He gave her a smile. "It is good to have you home, *mi esposa*. Both of the children have missed you very much," he said.

And then he stared into her eyes. "What is it, *mi amor*? You do not look well. Did you get sick while you were in Jalisco? Your skin feels hot like you have a fever."

Aboard Mexicana Airlines Flight 1151 a twenty-year-old stewardess named Carmen Villarreal collapsed in the bathroom at twenty thousand feet following a four-hour layover in Houston before taking off for its return trip to Mexico City. She had been serving drinks and sandwiches until she suddenly felt nauseous.

Another flight attendant found her, using a special tool to unlock the bathroom door when Carmen did not return to her duties after twenty minutes. Rosa Hernandez screamed when she saw blood all over the tiny bathroom floor coming from Carmen's nose and mouth.

The pilot was notified immediately and Flight 1151

made a looping turn toward the San Antonio Airport, radioing for an ambulance to meet the plane on the San Antonio tarmac instead of making its scheduled return flight to Mexico City with eighty-four passengers onboard, all but fourteen of them having eaten sandwiches or consumed drinks handled by Carmen Villarreal.

Houston

Dr. John Meeker, Chief of Internal Medicine at Houston Baptist Hospital, spoke to his head operating room nurse in a gravelly voice through his surgical mask. "Go ahead and remove the needle from his vein. He was bleeding faster than we could put blood in him anyway."

Meeker's eyebrows knitted, staring into the opening he made in Malcolm Fitzhugh's chest cavity. "He's gone past hemorrhagic shock and every clotting agent we've tried has failed. There's apparently nothing we could have done to stop his massive internal bleeding. Bring me his blood work numbers as soon as they're ready. For the life of me I can't imagine what this is. He's a healthy individual otherwise."

Suddenly the hairs on the back of his neck stirred and he had a terrible premonition. "Warn the lab to use every precaution in case this is Ebola or some other exotic virus. He must have been sick for days and I can't imagine why airport officials let him board a plane, bleeding from his tear ducts and nose and ears. Surely someone noticed the bleeding."

He looked down at his gloved hands covered in blood. "We may have been contaminated ourselves. I didn't think to wear the isolation suits. If it's a virus we have to notify the CDC immediately."

He looked into Nurse Hopkins's eyes. "We'd both better pray this is something else. Have someone find out what flight he was on and where it originated, where he got on the plane. We may have to consider the possibility that every passenger on that flight was contaminated."

He gazed down at Malcolm Fitzhugh again, remembering how he'd massaged the heart after numerous adrenaline injections failed. "What we may have here is a human time bomb that just went off on an airplane and in Houston International Airport, depending on what the blood tests show."

He sighed and backed away from the operating table a moment. "And it may have sunk its deadly teeth into us and everyone who came in contact with him, the ambulance attendants, emergency room staff, passengers at the airport, the works. I sure as hell hope I'm wrong, but just in case I'm not, you'd better notify hospital security. We've got to lock this place down *now*! No one else in or out until we've figured out what is going on."

He looked down at his bloody hands again and noticed they were shaking. He said in a quieter voice, "Nurse Hopkins, as soon as you've had security lock the hospital down, have the hospital operator call the CDC and transfer the call to my office. I have a pint of bourbon in my desk drawer and I think I'm gonna have a drink."

Kansas City, Missouri

Warren Adler, Sales Manager for World Software, walked off his plane at Kansas City Municipal Airport feeling faint, heading for the men's room as quickly as he could, feeling warning signs of diarrhea, knowing full well he shouldn't have eaten the plate of enchiladas at La Trinidad last night.

Too spicy, he thought, walking faster, carrying his garment bag and sample case, hoping he could make it to a free toilet since he had no change in his pocket at the moment. He almost ran across the tile floor of the bathroom to a toilet stall and dropped his pants, virtually collapsing on the commode seat before a rush of fluid came from his bowels. At the same time he sneezed, catching it with his hand, closing his eyes when a painful bowel spasm gripped him again.

When he opened his eyes he saw blood in his palm, and the sight of it caused his to gasp. "What the fuck?"

He took a handful of toilet paper to wipe blood off his nose and at the same time he tasted it on his tongue. A curious chill made him shiver. He wiped his hand and took more toilet paper to wipe his buttocks. From the corner of his eye he saw a wad of soggy, bright red paper between his fingers.

"Oh no," he whispered, experiencing the beginnings of terror. What could cause him to bleed from his nose and ass? How could the enchiladas at La Trinidad in Mexico City have been *that* bad?

Mexico City

Assistant Aduanales Inspector at Mexico City International Airport Gonzalo Fuentes was driving home, navigating through the impossible traffic in Mexico City toward Laguna Gloria, taking the rest of the day off because he didn't feel well. It scared him when he urinated in an airport bathroom an hour ago, for he did not pass yellow urine as he expected. First, there was a pinkish tint, then a brighter red, and finally nothing but blood filling the urinal. Fifteen minutes later blood was leaking from his rectum, flow he couldn't stop with tissue paper. Then he vomited, and now he was sure he was dying. He held his rosary in one hand, fingering each bead, saying prayers, wondering what was wrong with him. Should he stop at the church first to offer his confession?

Honking his car horn, he sped southeast with the Chevrolet's accelerator pressed to the floor, deciding it was better to go to the hospital. He felt dizzy and his underpants were soaking wet with blood, oozing out over the car's front seat cover, dribbling down his legs until his socks were damp.

Gonzalo was traveling at seventy miles per hour when he lost consciousness, slamming into the side of a delivery truck owned by Rosita's Tortilla Factory, sending the truck careening across Calle Los Petras through the front plate glass window of Miguel Vasquez's small grocery store, El Mercado. Miguel was crushed by the truck's front bumper, pinned against a side wall.

Gonzalo Fuentes's head struck his steering wheel first, driving the bony septum in his nose into his brain before his sternum cracked like green wood against the steering column, broken bone and slivers of metal passing through his heart and lungs, killing him almost instantly.

Within half an hour ambulance attendants removed the bloody remains of Assistant Aduanales Inspector Gonzalo Fuentes from the wreckage of his car to take him to a nearby funeral home, where dozens of his family members would pay their last respects, often by means of an old Mexican custom, kissing the dead man's hand.

Houston

At Houston Baptist Hospital, Dr. John Meeker pored over the lab results as glass slides were being prepared for a microscopic examination of Malcolm Fitzhugh's blood cells while he waited for a return call from the CDC in Atlanta. When he took his first look at the slides he saw nothing out of the ordinary. But there was one strangely shaped organism he couldn't identify. He had a vague feeling he should have been able to recognize it and yet for the moment, it escaped him.

"Get me Dr. Birdwell," he said, wanting the opinion of the chief of hematology before he did any more guessing. He looked into the microscope again, at a spore-like object that did not belong, not a virus but something else, more like a bacterium, although not a recognizable one. Could this be the mysterious killer? he wondered.

If it were transmittable by human contact, whatever it was, this could be the beginning of an epidemic far more deadly than Ebola or any of the similar resistant viruses. And what was the host? What had Malcolm Fitzhugh come in contact with that could kill him so quickly by means of hemorrhage beyond any form of chemical clotting control? In twenty-three years of internal medicine Meeker had never witnessed anything like the bleeding inside Fitzhugh, bleeding that nothing would stop.

A team from the city's Communicable Disease Agency was on the way, but Meeker had a sinking feeling they were going to be way too late—not only for him and the hospital staff, but for the city as well.

Kansas City

In Kansas City, Warren Adler collapsed waiting for a taxi in front of the main concourse at the airport. Blood pooled around him, spreading, drawing dozens, then hundreds of curious bystanders. Adler was dead by the time an ambulance arrived. Two young attendants placed Adler's body on a stretcher and loaded him into the ambulance. One man, David Starnes, had forgotten to wear his protective latex gloves.

A black janitor by the name of Billy Wells was summoned to mop up the blood on the sidewalk. The wringer on his mop bucket didn't work and he used his hands to wring blood and soapy water from his mop, wiping his palms dry on his pants when the job was finished.

Mexico City

Seventy-six passengers who had been aboard Mexicana Flight 1151 from Mexico City to Houston boarded other airplanes, or went home to their families and friends. Some began experiencing flu-like symptoms almost immediately.

A microscopic organism began moving across parts of the United States and Mexico, dividing, multiplying inside the host bodies of travelers, conquering immune systems with suddenness previously unknown to modern medical science, causing massive hemorrhaging and sudden death. Doctors did not recognize it when it was found in a victim's blood, although it was clearly not a virus, the tiny killers everyone in medicine feared. Lying dormant in a tomb for centuries, they reawakened in what was to be called "the summer of the plague."

Chapter 18

Houston

Maria Gomez lay in bed awaiting the arrival of her priest to perform extreme unction, the last rites to prepare her soul for life after death. She knew she was dying from the same cancer as her brother, Roberto, although he had not bled so heavily, only a small amount in the urine bag below his hospital bed, turning it red the last few days before he died.

Maria told her children to go down the street to stay with Aunt Esmeralda while she was sick as a way of keeping them from seeing her lying in a blood-soaked bed, nor did she want them there when the priest, Father Hidalgo, gave her the last rites.

When she called Father Hidalgo she had told him to come in without knocking, for she was too weak now to leave her bed to answer the door. Rodolfo was away driving the gasoline truck to Louisiana, thinking Maria only had a bad case of the flu . . . the bleeding had not started until the day he left and there was no way to reach him on the road when it became all too clear this was no ordinary illness.

And she did not want to worry him. When he left two days ago he was also complaining of feeling sick and that seemed odd. Rodolfo was never ill.

Maria knew now she should have gone to the doctor when the bleeding started, yet she feared being told she had the same cancer that killed her brother, preferring to wait and pray for a miracle, that this bleeding might be something else.

She heard the front door open.

"Mrs. Gomez?" a distant voice asked, a voice she knew well from attending Mass every Sunday.

"I am in here," she called out in a strangled reply, tasting blood, coughing when it thickened her throat.

Father Hidalgo entered the bedroom. He halted a few feet away from the bed, surprise and shock rounding his eyes. "Maria, what has happened to you?" he gasped. "Your sheets are drenched in blood, and your face . . ."

Tears flooded Maria's eyes. "I am dying, Father. Please, I beg you. Give me the last rites." She coughed again, spitting up a mouthful of blood. Please hurry." In her mind she saw a bright light when her eyelids fluttered.

"I'll call an ambulance," Father Hidalgo said, and his voice seemed farther away.

She heard him leave the bedroom. Moments later he spoke to someone, giving the address on Water Street. She closed her eyes and prayed for the safety of her children and husband, until she felt the priest touch her forehead, making the sign of the cross as he began reciting extreme unction in Latin, the same words he spoke to her brother when he came to the hospital last year to give Roberto last rites only a few hours before he died.

Maria kept her eyes tightly shut, gritting her teeth so she would not cry out from the pains in her chest while

Father Hidalgo prepared her soul for the journey to eternity.

Her mind wandered, back to the airplane ride from Mexico City to Houston, remembering the Anglo who sat across from her on the trip, bleeding from his nose and mouth, shivering with the same chills she felt when her fever started, wiping blood off his face with paper towels.

She saw the strange white light clearly now, and felt the sensation of moving toward it even though she was still lying on the bed. Father Hidalgo's voice became indistinct, and then there was silence and a feeling of peace as she was drawn ever closer to the circle of light.

Beaumont, Louisiana

Rodolfo Gomez was traveling west on Interstate 10 driving an eighteen-wheel tanker truck full of gasoline near Beaumont with a roll of paper towels between his legs. The floor of the cab of his White Freightliner was covered with blood.

Wiping his face and particularly his bleeding eyes, he knew he had to stop at a Beaumont hospital to find out what was wrong with him—he could not make it home to Houston as he planned when he first noticed the blood pouring from his nose, then his eyelids, and now from his rectum and ears.

Driving at seventy-five miles an hour, he pushed the Cummins diesel engine as hard as he could despite an increasing dizziness blurring everything in front of him. It was like being drunk, he decided, this odd feeling. But what would explain all the blood?

Rodolfo passed out three hundred yards from a convenience store at a bend in the highway where it entered the city limits of Beaumont. His tanker filled with eighty thousand gallons of gasoline plowed into a row of parked cars in front of the Stop and Go Drive-In, moving at sixty miles an hour until it rammed a blue Pontiac Grand Am, jackknifing truck and trailer at a ninety-degree angle only seconds before the tank trailer ruptured.

A ball of flame erupted, shooting exploding fuel hundreds of feet into the air that engulfed everything within a six-hundred-yard perimeter with heat so intense it melted automobiles, turning them into unrecognizable heaps of blackened metal.

Eleven customers of the East Side Stop and Go were incinerated. There were no survivors. Rodolfo Gomez was thrown through the windshield of his White Freightliner. His charred body was later found on what was left of the flat roof of the convenience store, identifiable only by means of dental records.

Houston

Walter Simmons died within two hours of entering the emergency room of Ben Taub Hospital in Houston. Emergency room staff handled his body with latex gloves and surgical masks.

Simmons's wife, Beatrice, was admitted directly from the ER and her room quarantined while the Chief of Pathology, Dr. Wilson Brewer, began a cautious autopsy of her husband, wearing a fully self-contained space suit in the hospital morgue, suspecting a rare and highly contagious virus, one of the African varieties. He found no viral evidence, only a strange bacterium-like organism in tissues and blood. He called for a staff meeting at two o'clock to show photographs of the microscope's findings, puzzled, unable to apply routine diagnostics to the evidence he prepared for the staff meeting.

Beatrice Simmons drifted in and out of consciousness, at times able to remember the sale of the jeweled Aztec artifact to a private collector in Miami who had flown into Houston within hours of being told about the royal symbols on it. He wrote a check for four hundred and seventy-five thousand dollars on the spot without even trying to bargain and took the collar with him back to Florida, delighted with his new acquisition, certain that it once belonged to the Aztec Chieftain Montezuma, an incredible find.

San Antonio, Texas

Mexicana Airlines flight attendant Carmen Villarreal died at Santa Rosa Hospital in San Antonio, Texas, after her flight to Mexico City had been diverted there due to her ill health.

She'd been taken directly to the hospital from the airport and the flight had continued on to Mexico City.

Four hours later the flight landed in Mexico City and three hours after that, Rosa Hernandez, the stewardess who found Carmen in the airplane's bathroom, went to see a *curandera* to purchase a special mix of garlic and herbs to quiet the bloody dysentery she'd been experiencing since she got home.

Her mother told her garlic powder and tincture of rosemary never failed to cure loose bowels. Rosa failed to mention the blood to her mother or the herbal healer since it was an embarrassing subject, and her boyfriend, Victor, had only last week introduced her to anal intercourse and this could be an explanation for the intermittent bleeding.

Mexico City

Jesus Contreras, an employee of Mexicana Airlines on the janitorial staff, collapsed at home in Colonia Santa Maria two days after cleaning blood from a bathroom of a 737. He had been coughing up blood for several hours and called in sick at work that day, wondering if he had contracted tuberculosis, for his lungs burned fiercely the night before and he'd been unable to sleep. His wife went screaming though the neighborhood asking for someone to call an ambulance, since she and Jesus were unable to afford a telephone.

Chapter 19

Tlateloco

Mason was conferring with Suzanne and Lauren in the dining area of the lab and had just checked Jimmy Walker's name off the list of students on the dig the university had given Lauren. It had been the last name without a checkmark.

He looked at her with warm, sympathetic eyes. "That's it, then, Lauren. All of the members of the expedition are accounted for. Now we've got to see about getting you off-site and back to Texas so you can get back to your life."

She smiled at him, her face a strange mixture of sadness and anticipation. "So many dead, and for what? To unearth some old bones and artifacts that no one except dried-up old museum curators will ever see."

He reached over and placed his hand on her arm. "They died doing what they loved, Lauren." He sighed and looked around at the cramped quarters of the laboratory. "And that's about all any of us can wish for."

He glanced over his shoulder. "I'll get Joel to see if he can schedule a chopper to come pick you up for the trip back to Mexico City."

"Are you in such a hurry to get rid of me, then?" she asked in a quiet voice, her eyes looking shyly down at her feet.

Mason glanced at Suzanne as his face flamed red in a deep blush. "Why . . . er . . . um . . . no, not at all," he said, wondering if she felt the same smoldering attraction for him that he felt for her.

He was saved from further embarrassment when the door to the communications room burst open and a wild-eyed Joel Schumacher rushed into the room, his yarmulke askew on his head for the first time in Mason's memory.

"Boss, you've got to see this!" he exclaimed, holding out his iPad.

The device was connected wirelessly to the Internet via Joel's satellite hookup and a newscast from Mexico City was playing. It was a cable news outlet and even though it originated in Mexico City, the newscaster was speaking in English.

The four of them watched as news of a major outbreak of an unknown illness was credited with killing over two hundred people and sickening thousands more in just the last twenty-four hours. Reports of hundreds of people staggering into emergency rooms and clinics showing massive hemorrhaging, high temperatures, and pneumonia-like symptoms filled the screen.

"Jesus!" Suzanne whispered, her hand to her mouth.

"Damn!" Mason said. "The damned bug has escaped the jungle into one of the most densely populated areas in this hemisphere."

Lauren put her hand on Mason's arm. "Are you sure this is our plague?"

"It has to be," Suzanne said grimly. "The symptoms are too close to our bug for it to be anything else."

Mason nodded grimly. "And if it's gotten to Mexico City, then it is probably well on its way across the entire world."

He handed the iPad back to Joel. "Get me the Battleship on the sat-phone . . . right now!"

"The Battleship?" Lauren asked Suzanne.

The corner of Suzanne's lip curled in a half-smile, but her eyes remained grim. "That would be Dr. Grant Battersee, the head of CDC and our boss of bosses."

Mason added almost as an afterthought, "We call him the Battleship 'cause once he gets started on a project he's as hard to stop as a battleship is under full steam."

"I'll gather all of the others here where we can make some contingency plans about what the spread of this pathogen is going to mean and how we're gonna deal with it," Suzanne said, pulling the handheld radio off her belt and moving over to a corner to alert the other team members of the new development.

Mason turned to Lauren, putting a hand on her shoulder. "I'm afraid you're going to have to endure our company for a while longer, Lauren."

"You mean I won't be able to return home?"

Mason shook his head. "If they haven't already done it, once I talk to Battersee, he'll make sure all international airports are shut down tight with no further travel between countries. Though I'm afraid it's much like locking the stall door after the horse has escaped, it's protocol in the event of a major outbreak like this is almost certainly going to be."

"Be careful what you wish for . . ." Lauren mumbled under her breath as she turned to look out the window of the lab.

"What's that?" Mason asked.

"Oh, nothing," she answered. "It's just that I'd been kinda hoping to get to see you again when . . . all this was over," she said, and now it was her face turning red.

Mason gently turned her back around to face him. "Lauren," he started, and then he glanced over his shoulder at Suzanne, who was standing with her back to them talking rapidly into her radio. He placed his palm against her cheek and pulled her to him for a gentle kiss on the lips, and then he leaned back and took a deep breath, as if he'd been deep underwater and had just surfaced. "Lauren, now is not the time to get into it, but believe me when I say I feel the same way, and I hope we get the chance to talk about it when, like you say, all this is over."

Before Lauren could suppress her surprise at his actions and reply, Suzanne turned around and headed toward them. "The others are on the way here for a C-O-W," she said.

Lauren looked from Suzanne to Mason with a puzzled expression until Mason said, "Council of War. It's what we call a conference where we all get together to decide how to handle various emergencies on our field trips."

Joel stuck his head out of the door and said, "I've got Dr. Battersee holding on the secure sat-phone that's encrypted. I figured you'd want some privacy for your talk."

"Good man," Mason said, looking back over his shoulder and giving Lauren a quick wink only she could see as he squeezed by Joel into the tiny communications room and shut the door behind him.

Lauren glanced over at Suzanne and found her staring back at her with a strange, unreadable expression on her face.

Fort Detrick

Colonel Blackman slammed his phone down into its cradle and swung his legs out of bed. "I'm gonna have me a security guard's balls for breakfast!" he muttered angrily as he marched into his kitchen to make a cup of coffee.

Paco was supposed to drop off the sample from Janus over four hours ago and Blackman had still not heard from the security guard on duty whether he'd arrived yet or not. And to make matters worse, now when Blackman called the guard post in the secure wing he got no answer. That post was supposed to be manned 24/7/365 and he was damn sure gonna make somebody pay for abandoning their post.

He'd just finished dressing and was pouring his second cup of coffee when his phone rang. "'Bout damn time!" he said, thinking it was the guard post calling to tell him Paco was finally here.

"Yeah?"

"Colonel Blackman, this is Sergeant James calling."

That's funny, Blackman thought. James was the perimeter guard, not the security wing guard. "What is it, James?"

"I've got a car out here in the parking lot with its engine running and a man in the driver's seat slumped over the wheel. He's got blood running from his eyes and ears and is unresponsive to me knocking on the window."

The hair on the back of Blackman's neck rose to attention as he asked hurriedly, "Did you open the car doors?"

"Uh . . . no, sir. The doors are locked and I was calling to see if you wanted me to bust open a window."

"Absolutely not, James. Form a cordon around that car of at least fifty feet and do not—I repeat, *do not* let anyone else get near it."

"Yes, sir! Is there anything else?"

"Yes, do not let anyone get closer than ten feet to you and as soon as you've got the car sealed off, report directly to the quarantine lab and I'll have someone waiting for you."

"Quarantine lab, sir?"

"James, remember your training. You may have been exposed to an unknown pathogen and we need to get you decontaminated as soon as possible."

"Yes, sir!" The man's voice had developed a definite quaver at Blackman's answer.

Blackman hung up the phone and ran his hands through his hair as he thought about what to do next. *If he is exposed to our new bug, he's a dead man walking, but we might be able to get some good intel from how he reacts to various treatments.*

It only took a moment for the other shoe to drop as he now thought he knew why the lab security guard was not answering his calls.

He picked up his phone and called the main security office to order an immediate lockdown of the entire facility. No one was going to be allowed to enter or leave the Fort until he discovered the extent of the contamination.

"Damn you, Paco," he said under his breath. "You may have killed us all."

When the security officer answered, Blackman said just two words to get the facility locked down, "Code Red!"

The guard hesitated, and then Blackman thought he could hear the fear in the man's words as he answered, "Code Red in effect, sir!"

"And I want everyone on base to get into contamination uniforms, with face masks and hats and booties ASAP!"

he added, causing a sharp intake of breath from the security guard.

He hung up the phone and walked slowly over to his closet. He opened the door and pulled an orange coverall off a hanger, unzipped it, and stepped into it.

As he zipped it up and took a paper hat and face mask off the shelf, he sighed deeply. He wondered how many people this bug was going to kill before he could gain control of it and whether he would be one of its victims.

Chapter 20

Tlateloco

As the team began to straggle into the lab dining room, fixing cups of coffee and sandwiches while they waited for Mason Williams to get off the phone with the head of the CDC, their eyes seemed dazed by the enormity of the news of the plague's spread to Mexico City.

The team members were discussing this in low tones as Suzanne sat next to Lauren on one of the benches.

"How you doin', girl?" she asked.

Lauren shrugged, glancing at her to try to make sense of the strange look she'd given her just a while ago. "Okay, all things considered . . . I guess. I keep seeing their faces in my mind—that is, their faces as they were the last time I saw them before they headed down here to the dig." She hesitated. "Of course, now that the plague has spread it means that many thousands or even millions of others are going to suffer the same fate as my friends did."

Suzanne nodded. "Yeah, that's for sure with a bug this deadly." She grunted and then asked, "Do you remember your history?"

"About?"

"The Black Plague back in the fourteenth century."

"I remember studying it vaguely but not any of the details."

Suzanne took a deep breath, staring off into space as she began to speak. "The Black Death as it was called started in China in 1333, and by 1347 had reached Constantinople, Alexandria, Cyprus, Sicily, and Italy. By 1348 it spread to France and Germany and then to England. In the next year it progressed to Scotland, Wales, and Ireland and within two years even to Russia."

"Why are you telling me this?" Lauren asked.

Suzanne's eyes focused and she turned to stare at Lauren. "By the time the Black Death burned itself out, it had killed an estimated one-third of the population of the entire world, and this was in a time when travel was much slower and less widespread and this plague was spread primarily by fleas and not person to person."

She paused, sighed, and continued, "Can you imagine in today's world of rapid transit the havoc a plague that is spread person to person will wreak on the world?"

Lauren was horrified. "It's almost unimaginable."

Suzanne nodded. "You're right, it is. This could be the virtual end of civilization as we know it if a cure or at least a vaccine isn't found quickly."

She turned to look at Lauren again. "It's got to be tough on a civilian to face this amount of death in all its ugly glory."

Lauren was thrown for a moment at the abrupt change of subject, and so she said the first thing that came to mind, "You say civilian like you're not one."

Suzanne snorted. "Well, I am now, but for a long time I wasn't."

"Oh?"

Suzanne turned to look at her. "Remember when I told you about my father and brother having been in the military?"

Lauren nodded. "Sure."

"Well, all that time I kinda considered myself in the army with them . . . you know how it is with family. One for all and all for one."

"I can understand that."

Suzanne looked down at the wedding ring on her finger. "This was my father's. My mom gave it to him when they married, and she took it off his dead body before his burial and then went home and killed herself."

"Jesus! Suzanne, I don't know what to say."

Suzanne smirked. "Nothing much to say," Suzanne muttered, patting Lauren's hand on her arm. "But you can see why I take tracking down bugs like this one so seriously. Bugs that can be used as germ warfare in the wrong hands must be controlled by a country that will only use them in self-defense, and the cures that we develop for them will help protect our country and our servicemen and servicewomen in the event of war."

"But this plague wasn't caused by a country using it as germ warfare," Lauren protested.

"Not this time," Suzanne said, her eyes burning with fervor.

Their conversation was brought to a halt when Mason stepped through the door. His hair was disheveled, and his face looked like he'd seen a ghost. It was plain that something had scared him half to death.

Lionel pointed to the coffeepot and Mason nodded. After he'd taken a drink from the cup Lionel handed him, he addressed the team.

"The situation is much worse than we thought. The

plague of what is almost certainly respiratory anthrax has already made an appearance in over twenty countries, and there are more than fifteen thousand dead at the last count a few hours ago."

"Holy mother of God," Sam Jakes exclaimed. "The damned bug couldn't have escaped from here more than one or two days ago at the most."

"Nevertheless, it's spreading like wildfire, and I use the term advisedly," he said, referring to the nickname for his team of experts. "It seems a few, and I emphasize a few, people have managed to survive contagion but only after massive doses of antibiotics and intensive hospital care with tracheotomies and assisted ventilation until they could get over the worst of their pneumonia symptoms."

He shook his head. "Clearly this is not something that is going to be available to a large population of those that have contracted the disease."

"Is there any particular antibiotic regimen that seems to be effective?" Shirley Cole asked.

Mason shrugged. "Who knows? The ones who survived had just about every antibiotic known to man poured haphazardly into their veins, so no one can tell which antibiotic was effective or what particular combination might have worked."

"Did the Battleship say what his plans for us are?" Jakes asked. "Are we supposed to fly to Mexico City and then home to help with the plague or what?"

"He said he's working through channels to try to get the Mexican government to allow a private CDC jet to land in Mexico City and then get a helicopter down here to shuttle us back so we can bring all our samples back to the United States for more detailed study."

"You said he's working through channels . . ." Joel said. "What does that mean?"

"It seems all international travel and most intranational travel has been suspended pending getting control of this plague," Mason answered.

He took a deep breath. "He says it's taking all the pressure he can apply to keep the Mexican authorities from fuel-bombing this site right now with us in it."

"What?" Jakes almost screamed.

Mason smirked. "Yeah, the geniuses in Mexico City think if the original source of the infection is eliminated the plague will magically disappear."

"Don't they realize the genie is out of the bottle?" Suzanne asked.

Mason spread his hands and sat down at the table. "You've got to realize what it's like out there in the world. People are dying by the thousands and soon to be hundreds of thousands and nothing they're doing is even slowing the infection rate," he said. "Hell, I wouldn't be surprised to see them call in witch doctors next."

Shirley Cole sat up straight, and as always she seemed the calmest one in the room. "Okay, boss. So we may be stuck here for the duration. What do you want us to do?"

"We do what we do best," he answered. "We continue to run samples against all known antibiotics with different dosages and combinations until we can find something that works on this beast."

Lauren cleared her throat, her face flushing red. "Can I ask a question?"

Mason smiled. "Sure, Lauren."

"I don't know a lot about medicine and plagues," she said, looking around at the team. "But it seems to me that

I remember from freshman biology that vaccines used to be made from the blood of persons who had acquired antibodies to a certain illness or something like that."

Mason's brows knit and he looked puzzled. "Yeah, so?"

"Well," she continued, "we have all seen the *Indio* boy running around the jungle as healthy as can be in spite of being exposed to the anthrax at the campsite. Might his blood not have the antibodies you need to make a vaccine or something else that might help treat the anthrax?"

"Jesus!" Jakes exclaimed, leaning over to kiss Lauren on the cheek. "Out of the mouths of babes . . ."

"She's right," Shirley Cole said, standing up in her excitement. "He's got to be immune to the bug, either through previous mild infection or through some genetic abnormality that helps to fight off further infection."

Suzanne also stood up, a thoughtful expression on her face. "And whatever it is that is protecting him might be able to be harnessed to help protect others."

"Damn, Lauren," Mason said, excitement on his face. "You've managed to look through the forest and see the one tree that might just be the answer we've been looking for."

Lauren smiled. "So I guess the next step is to try to find this boy and convince him to help us?"

"Yeah, but the problem is does anyone here speak *Indio*?" Joel asked, looking around the room.

Lauren held up her hand, hesitantly. "There is no *Indio* language, Joel. Other than Spanish, the only other language that might be spoken this far south is Nahuatl, a form of the ancient Aztecan language. However, I used to work at an outreach program in the Hispanic part of Austin. I speak pretty tolerable Spanish, and I think the boy would have to understand at least some Spanish to be up here this far north, so I can probably make myself understood . . . if we can get close enough to talk to him."

Mason jumped up. "Then let's do it! Everyone spread out through the jungle and look for the boy, and don't forget to take some of Shirley's sweet treats with you. A couple of cookies or one of her muffins might let you get close enough to him to get him to follow you back to the lab."

Jakes shook his head. "I don't know, Mason. Those damned Racals might just scare the poor little bastard off."

Mason shook his head. "No need to wear the Racal suits," he said. "Since we know now we're dealing with a respiratory bug, just wear the micropore masks and latex gloves and our scrubs that are contamination-proof and that should be enough protection." He hesitated, "Of course, we'll still use all decontamination protocols before reentering the lab."

"What about Dr. Matos?" Shirley Cole asked. "He's hanging on by a thread and I don't think it'd be a good idea to leave him all alone in the lab in case he takes a turn for the worse."

Mason sighed. "You're right, Shirley, as always. You'd better stay here and look after him."

She nodded. "And while I'm watching him, I'll try to cook up a good meal for the boy when you bring him back. A full stomach may make him more agreeable to letting us stick lots of needles into his arms."

"Needles?" Lauren asked.

"We're gonna need lots of his blood to run antibody titers and for DNA testing," Jakes said, "And we may even need to take some tissue samples before we're done with him."

Lauren cast a worried glance at Mason.

"Don't worry, Lauren," he said, patting her on the arm. "We'll do our best to make the tests as painless as possible, but remember, thousands and maybe millions of people's lives are at stake here."

"Yeah," she answered ruefully, "but I'm the one that's going to have to try to explain to a jungle boy who probably speaks no English why you're going to poke him with needles and take his blood."

Suzanne put her arm around Lauren's shoulders. "I'm sure you can do it, Lauren. Just tell him his gods need a blood sacrifice and it will assure him of a place in his heaven," she said, smiling.

Lauren laughed. "Yeah, right!"

Chapter 21

Colonel Blackman was in the middle of dealing with the first Code Red lockdown at Ft. Detrick since a vial of smallpox had gone missing back in the mid-70s. Both his phone and his cell phone were ringing continually, and he was having to deal with an amount of panic in the workers he hadn't really expected in a BL4 facility.

"These chicken-shit bastards knew what they were getting into when they hired on," he muttered to himself as he supervised men in Racal suits who were putting Paco's and the security guard's bodies in biohazard black body bags, which were double-sealed and then sprayed with a powerful disinfectant before being hauled off to the BL-4 morgue in the basement of the main laboratory.

Both the men in the Racals and the men in the body bags would then be subjected to additional multiple showers of bleach and other antimicrobial solutions until they were considered safe to be around.

The entry room to the lab was another question, as was the car in which Paco's body was discovered. Blackman thought he'd just have the fucking car burned until nothing was left of it but smoking ash. Of course, he thought, he couldn't very well do that to the room in the secure lab. The damned thing would just have to be repeatedly sprayed and irradiated and wiped down until nothing organic could live in the freaking place.

Just as he was about to decide to leave the scene for a quick cigar, the radio on his belt buzzed.

He grabbed it and pressed the send button. "Yeah?"

"Sir," his aide said, "Your computer is signaling a secure communication from the field."

Damn, he thought. It must be Janus checking in. He really didn't have time for this shit.

"I'll be right there," he growled, all thoughts of a calming cigar forgotten for the moment. He strode into his office and slammed the door before sitting at his computer and keying in his secret password to enable the satellite transmission of Janus's secure phone.

"What is it?" he almost shouted. "I'm up to my ass in alligators here, Janus."

Janus's voice, unlike his was calm. "I really don't give a shit what your ass is up to, Colonel."

In spite of himself, Blackman laughed. "Well, Janus, if you're gonna mention my ass, you might as well call me Blackie."

Janus laughed, too, for a second. "The good news, Blackie, is that I may have found a way to either control or even prevent the spread of this super anthrax."

"Uh-oh. What's the bad news?"

"I'm going to need an extraction team here at the site pronto. They're going to have to be prepared to bring a living specimen back to the States for tests, and they'll have to be prepared to bring him in while quarantined."

Blackman ran his hands through his hair. "You're not

asking for much, Janus. You do realize the whole world is in lockdown and nothing is flying anywhere right now?"

"Okay," Janus said, and Blackman could almost hear the shrug over the phone. "I guess I'll just let the CDC have him and let them get control of the vaccine and antidote to the anthrax then."

"You've got a vaccine?" he almost shouted.

"Calm down, Colonel," Janus said. "No vaccine yet, but I've got, or rather we're soon going to have, someone who is totally immune to the anthrax, and his blood and tissue are just as good as a vaccine." There was a slight hesitation, and then Janus continued, "In fact, there just may be an entire village of people immune to this bad boy, but I won't know that for a while yet."

"So, you want a medical extraction team to bring this person back to Fort Detrick?"

"Ummm," Janus muttered. "No, I think you'd better send the military boys, along with some heavy ordnance. Depending on the circumstances, they may have to do some wet work to gain control of the specimen."

"Wet work? On whom, or do I really want to know?"

"It could be the CDC team, or it might even be the entire fucking Mexican Army! What the hell do you care as long as we get control of this epidemic for ourselves?"

He chuckled. "You're right, of course. It really doesn't matter, but you'll have to forgive me for being a little rattled right now. That fucking Paco managed to contaminate the entire fort while killing himself in the bargain."

He could hear Janus sigh over the satellite connection. "I told you he wasn't right for a courier . . . too dumb and too unconcerned with security of the specimens I sent."

"Okay, okay. You were right. Now, tell me how I'm

gonna get a kill team from here to you without the entire world knowing about it."

"Check the satellite maps of Mexico. I seem to remember an abandoned airfield about ten klicks east of here. It should be okay for one of those twin-engine Air Kings to land, and they're big enough for your team and a couple of other passengers on the return trip."

"A couple of other passengers?"

"Yeah. If we have to waste the CDC team I'm going to have to disappear without a trace also, otherwise I'll spend the rest of my life looking over my shoulders for FBI trackers."

"You're right," he said thoughtfully. "I hadn't thought of that."

"That means this will be my last mission, but I might as well go out on a big one, right?"

"Right," he said, but he was thinking the team would only have to bring one passenger back. If Janus wasn't going to be of any further use to him, might as well have the extraction team kill the entire CDC team including his spy and leave no loose ends that might bite him in the ass.

"It'll take me a while to set this up, so hang loose and contact me again in a few hours and I'll give you the kill team's ETA."

"Don't dawdle, Blackie," Janus said, "I don't know how fast the CDC team will be able to get transportation for the specimen and I'd hate for you to come in second place in a race for a cure for this shit."

"Don't worry, Janus. I can act a lot faster than some dipshit government health service can. We'll get there first with the most, and I'll have you out of there before you know it."

Tlateloco

Mason, wearing long-sleeved scrubs, latex gloves, and a micropore mask, exited the lab and began to direct his team members down various paths through the jungle overgrowth to look for the *Indio* boy.

As he started to talk, he noticed Sam Jakes off by himself talking on a sat-phone. "Hey Sam," he said, after walking over to him so he could speak in private. "I didn't know you had a personal sat-phone."

Jakes's face colored and he stammered, "Er . . . uh . . . well, after the last mission to Australia where we were out of touch for almost a month, I decided to splurge on one to keep in touch with my family."

"Oh?"

"Yeah. I was just calling my sister. She lives in the Bronx, and I told her to take her husband and their two kids to my cabin in the Catskills until this plague blows over. I told her to have her food delivered and to get no closer than ten feet to anyone until this is over."

"What'd she say?"

Jakes chuckled. "She whined about her husband losing his job if they left on vacation without giving notice, so I asked her if she'd rather have a live unemployed husband or a dead one with a job."

"And?"

"She's packing."

Mason nodded. "You know, Sam, you might want to offer the sat-phone to the others so they can do the same thing for their relatives. I can't let them use the satellite uplink CDC provides us 'cause Joel's on it 24/7 giving the Battleship updates on our progress and checking on what's happening with the plague."

"Good idea, boss, I'll do that."

Mason turned and clapped his hands to get everyone's attention. "Okay, people, time to get moving."

He stood in the middle of the group and pointed out different directions for each of them to take to look for the boy, taking the one through the densest part of the jungle for himself.

Lauren had gone about three hundred yards, pushing her way through thick vines and bushy jungle plants, when she thought she smelled smoke.

She broke through into a small clearing and saw a brown-skinned boy sitting next to a tiny campfire. He was staring at her with wide, frightened eyes and had a child-size bow with an arrow notched and pointed at her chest.

She held her hands out in a nonthreatening way and said in Spanish, "I am a friend. I am not here to hurt you."

He replied in something that was close to Spanish but was not quite the same. "Are you one of *Los Oráculos*, messengers from the sun god, or are you a creature from the Spirit World sent to take me to the underworld?"

"I am neither, young one, but merely a person such as yourself."

"Did the warriors wearing costumes the color of *naranja* send you?"

Lauren had to bite her lip to keep from laughing, realizing how strange they must have seemed to this primitive young man. "Yes, I am one of the warriors who wore orange costumes, but they were to protect us from the sickness that killed the other Americans."

"You were friends with the *Americanos*?"

"Yes." Lauren pushed the lump in her throat down and said, "The older man was my . . . father."

Guatemotzi nodded. "He was a very nice man. He gave me money and food to help with the digging."

"Yes, he was," Lauren said, moving slowly closer to the boy as he lowered the bow and arrow. "My name is Lauren, what is yours?"

"I am called Guatemotzi," he answered, putting the bow down and moving an MRE pack around on the fire a bit.

Lauren grinned. "That is a very powerful name. You are named for the emperor who came to power after Montezuma?"

He sat up straighter and puffed out his chest a little. "Yes. My grandfather says he was killed when he would not tell the Spaniards the secret hiding place of *Los Aztecas'* gold. He was very brave." He pointed at the MRE. "Would you like some food, Lauren?"

She smiled, noticing his ribs showing through his skin. "No, thank you, Guatemotzi, but I think you need it far more than I do."

He expertly popped open the MRE and began to spoon out the steaming contents with his fingers and popped the food into his mouth.

Lauren squatted down across the fire from him. "Do you know what happened to the Americans?"

He nodded. "An illness came out of *Los Aztecas'* tomb and killed them."

"Do you know of this illness?"

"Yes. My grandfather told me of the bleeding sickness that killed *Los Aztecas* many, many years ago. He said the Aztecs that the sickness did not kill are the ancestors of our village and he prays to them every day."

Lauren felt her heartbeat quicken. If what this boy was saying was true, there could be an entire village of people immune to the plague. Surely Mason and the others could use them to help find a cure for the anthrax.

"Guatemotzi, where is your village?"

He pointed back over his shoulder. "It is in Chiapas, in the mountains to the south." He scrunched up his face for a moment, thinking, and then added, "It is not so far from the city of Tuxtla Gutierrez, but is on other side of very high mountain."

"Guatemotzi, would you mind coming back with me to our camp and meeting my friends? There is much good food there, and I know they would love to meet you and hear the stories your grandfather told you about the sickness."

He looked up from his food and stared intently at her. "Are they all like you . . . with no face?"

She laughed and realized she had forgotten she was still wearing her micropore mask. She reached up and pulled it down for a second so he could see her features. "No, we have faces. It is just that we have to wear these masks to keep from getting the sickness that killed the other Americans."

He grinned. "They make you look funny."

"I know. Will you come with me?"

He thought for a moment, and then he nodded. "Yes, I will come with you."

Lauren stood up and stretched. "Good, and I will see that you get some *pan dulce*."

His eyes lit up. "Sweet bread?"

"Yes, and we have lots and lots of cookies with pieces of chocolate in them."

He grinned widely. "Chocolate *es muy bueno*!"

Chapter 22

Mason Williams and the rest of the team, unsuccessful in their search for the *Indio* boy, returned to the lab just in time for Joel to tune the com-sat link to the latest news coming out of Mexico City.

Even as the female reporter spoke into the camera, scattered gunfire could be heard in the distance and she continually ran her hand through her hair, her frightened eyes lending credence to her terrible story.

"Many local citizens are now calling the widespread plague sweeping throughout Mexico into neighboring countries 'Montezuma's Curse,' thanks to rumors the illness originated in an archaeological dig in which the ancient emperor's tomb was opened. They say his spirit is seeking revenge for the desecration of his eternal resting place by a visiting team of American scientists."

She hesitated and looked over her shoulder as a much louder explosion seemed to come from just off camera. She pulled herself together and continued, "Still others are drawing analogies to the 'Fifth Plague of Egypt,' an ancient epidemic in which hundreds of thousands of animals and people died in 1491 BC, as was described in the

Book of Genesis. While many of these people believe this is a Biblical curse brought about by the disturbance of Montezuma's tomb, Catholic Church leaders are asking their parishioners to remain calm and to seek God's guidance in prayers and to not succumb to superstition or unproven rumors."

A man's dark head could be seen briefly on camera as he leaned in and handed the reporter a piece of paper.

She scanned it and then looked directly into the camera. "This is just in. There are reports of thousands of Mexican citizens rushing borders of neighboring countries to the north and south trying to escape the plague and even some reports of Central American countries' soldiers firing weapons indiscriminately into the fleeing masses, causing untold loss of life and escalation of international tensions and fear."

She lowered the paper. "The government has notified this station that the plague is virtually everywhere . . . it will do you no good to try to cross borders into other countries as the illness is there, too. According to the Mexican Institutes of Health, the best thing we can do is to stay in our homes and have as little contact with others as is possible."

She leaned in close to the camera, her eyes brimming with tears. "Stay home, gentle viewers, and pray for divine guidance. This is Veronica Gonzales signing off and heading home where I'm going to follow my own advice."

As the screen faded to black, Shirley Cole looked at the others. "She was spot on about the 'Fifth Plague of Egypt,'" she said. "Epidemiologists now think that was a plague of anthrax, just as this one is now."

"The only differences are that this particular bug

seems to spare animals, and this plague is spread person to person and that one was not, which makes this baby a magnitude worse than that one," Jakes said sourly.

"They also didn't have airplanes spreading the damn thing all over the world back then, either," Lionel Johnson said in his quiet voice.

"Well, look who's back, and look what she's brought with her," Suzanne Elliot said as Lauren and Guatemotzi walked out of the jungle and through the lab doorway into the decontamination chamber.

She spent some moments explaining to the boy what was about to happen and then they turned their heads as she removed her clothes and then his and went through the decontamination process. After they were dressed in scrubs and had entered the dining room, she addressed the group as casually as if she'd just invited a friend for tea.

"How about something sweet for Guatemotzi?" she asked, ushering him to a seat at the long dining table.

Shirley jumped up. "I've just taken some homemade cinnamon rolls out of the oven and I think we could all use some comfort food right about now."

She piled a few rolls on a plate, poured a soda into a plastic cup, and handed them to the boy.

She looked around at the group, arching an eyebrow. "The rest of you will just have to get your own."

Jakes cleared his throat and asked Mason, "Do you think we should don our masks in the presence of . . . what did you say his name was?"

"Guatemotzi," Lauren replied.

Mason shook his head. "I don't think so. The fact that he is immune should keep him from harboring any live bacteria organisms in his lungs and the shower should have killed any on his skin or in his hair."

While Guatemotzi hurriedly scarfed down the sweet rolls and the others availed themselves of like treats and coffee, Lauren repeated all that he had told her in the jungle.

Suzanne raised her eyebrows. "You mean there may be an entire village of people like him, people immune to this strain of anthrax?"

Lauren shrugged. "That's what he says. According to him, his village is populated by more or less direct descendants of the ancient Aztecs who survived the original plague hundreds of years ago."

"They must be so isolated that they've never integrated into Mexican society and therefore the immune strain of their blood has remained relatively pure."

"Or it could be due to a dominant gene, in which case even if they intermarried the offspring would still be immune," Lionel said. "Either way, those villagers could be a gold mine for us and may represent the best chance we have of producing a vaccine to prevent the spread of the illness."

Joel, who was rapidly typing on his laptop computer, spoke up, "It says here that the city of Tuxtla Gutierrez in the state of Chiapas was originally inhabited and founded by a tribe native to the region known as the Zoques who named the city Coyatoc, which means 'home of the rabbit' in their native tongue. Between 1486 and 1505, they were invaded by the Aztecs and the city was renamed 'Tochtlan,' which meant the same thing in Nahuatl. After the Spanish conquest, the name was changed to 'Tuxtla.'"

"So when the Aztecs invaded they could have brought the anthrax infection with them, and the survivors of that plague could be the ancestors of Guatemotzi's villagers and their blood could hold the secret to a vaccine against this bug," Mason said.

Jakes shook his head. "In spite of Joel's fascinating history lesson," he said sarcastically, "a vaccine is all well and good, but by the time we take their blood and transport it to CDC and a vaccine is made, mass produced, and then distributed across the world, hundreds of millions of people are going to die."

"Wait a minute," Lauren said. "You haven't heard the best part yet."

"Better than a vaccine?" Mason asked, a hopeful expression on his face.

Lauren nodded. "On the way here, I told him that many, many people were getting sick like the Americans he saw die at the dig site, and he said that his grandfather knows a *curandera* who lives near their village who uses certain plants and herbs to cure the illness in those who aren't immune and catch the 'bleeding' sickness as he calls it."

"What the hell is a *curandera*?" Jakes spit irritably.

"A Mexican herbal healer," Lauren answered.

"You mean she can cure the illness after the symptoms have already begun by using plants and herbs grown locally?" Shirley Cole asked.

Lauren shrugged. "That's what he says."

"He may just be right," Mason interjected. "Fully a fourth of all modern medicinal compounds have their origins in alkaloids derived from plants."

"Then we have no choice," Shirley said. "We must travel to this village and start taking blood samples and see what this herbal healer can teach us."

Mason glanced at Guatemotzi and shook his head. "I don't think the best idea is for a herd of strangers to descend on this village and try to get them to cooperate in a scientific exercise."

He stood up and poured himself another cup of coffee. "No, I think it best if just a couple of us go down there to see what we can find out. They'll be much less apprehensive with two of us instead of six, especially if we can convince Guatemotzi to lead us there."

"But there is so much to do," Suzanne said. "I think I should be the one to accompany you."

Again Mason shook his head. "No, I need someone who speaks the language. What I need from each of you is a list of what samples I need to obtain . . . what kind of tubes of blood, what tissue samples, and anything else you need me to get from the villagers. Meanwhile Lauren and I will talk to Guatemotzi and find out if the village is in walking distance or if we need to requisition a chopper from CDC."

While the others were making their lists and gathering their tubes and equipment and while Mason and Lauren were questioning Guatemotzi about the distance and direction to his village, Janus snuck away from the group and keyed in the sat-phone to Colonel Blackman's number.

He answered in a gruff whisper, "What part of I'm busy dealing with an emergency here don't you understand? I told you I'd call you when I had a schedule for the kill team nailed down."

"Listen up, asshole," Janus replied, also whispering so the other team members would not hear. "I'm trying to save your ass here, so don't give me any shit, okay?"

"I've got a bunch of soldiers sick and dying, my main lab is off-limits due to contagion with a deadly pathogen, and my superiors are crawling up my butt asking why a civilian was allowed in the lab in the first place, so please, be my guest and save my ass."

"Okay, you can thank me later. The *Indio* boy now says there is a medicine woman in his village who has a mixture of herbs and shit that can cure the 'bleeding sickness' in those who are not naturally immune. Blackie, this is even better than the chance to make a vaccine, but we've got to act immediately or we're gonna lose the cure to the CDC, who will naturally give it to the entire world free of charge and without any political leverage."

"Damn, that's great news, Janus. With a cure in hand we can blackmail the Saudis for cheap oil forever, not to mention what other countries will give us to keep all of their citizens from dying a horrible death. The United States will again be king of the world."

"Yeah, well don't count your chickens just yet, esteemed leader. Even as we speak, Mason Williams is on the phone with the CDC to see if he can get a helicopter from Mexico City to take him to the boy's village to get the samples and the cure that will blow us outta the water."

"Those helicopters from Mexico City are army choppers, aren't they?"

"Yeah, so?"

Blackman chuckled again. "I happen to have a general in the Mexican Army who owes me big-time for pulling his ass out of a sling. I'll drop a bug in his ear to make sure no choppers are flying to your neck of the woods for the foreseeable future."

"Good, that's a start. I'm thinking it'll take Williams several days at least to hike through the jungle to the boy's village. Now what about that team I need to take control of the samples? When can I expect them to arrive on the scene?"

"I'm fixin' to interview the leader right now. They can be wheels up in a few hours and should arrive at your camp midday tomorrow."

"That long?"

"Remember, Janus, there is a worldwide airport shutdown so these dudes are gonna have to fly a propeller aircraft to stay under radar, which means they fly low and slow."

"Okay, I'll do my best to stall Williams until your guys get here."

"Good, and while you're at it, see if you can get the precise location of the boy's village from him so there won't be any delay in our acquiring the cure."

Janus laughed. Blackman was a complete idiot. "Sure, boss, I'll just ask him the GPS coordinates and that should do it."

"What?"

"He's an uneducated Indian boy, Blackie. When we asked him where his village was he just shrugged and pointed south, which in case you've forgotten your geography, encompasses a hell of a lot of jungle. He did say it was somewhat near a city called Tuxtla, but I don't know just what he considers 'somewhat close,' so the best bet is for your guys to follow them to the village."

"And just how the hell are they going to trail them through the jungle without giving themselves away?" he asked gruffly.

"I'll try to plant a GPS bug on one of them and I'll let you know if I succeed."

Pausing for a moment, Janus then added, "And Blackie,

now that Williams and the American archaeologist are going to be off in the jungle by themselves, you won't need to kill the CDC team, and I'll be able to stay onboard with them to help you out in the future. No need for me to disappear now."

Blackie considered his choices before he asked, "But, what about Williams and the archaeologist? They'll still have to be . . . umm . . . eliminated."

"I would rather you didn't," Janus said. "Williams is a good man doing good work, and since I have a good working relationship with him, I won't have to try to get close to whomever the CDC would pick to take his place . . . so hands off. After all, their interception will take place in a remote jungle location many days' journey from civilization, so they won't be able to warn anyone until well after you have your samples."

"That may not be enough time," Blackie replied.

"Well then, take them prisoner and hold them until you've processed the samples, but I'm serious. I don't want Williams harmed."

"Okay, okay, stay calm. I'll tell the team to treat them with kid gloves, all right?"

"You'd better, or I swear I'll make you pay."

Janus clicked the phone off, hearing him swear just before the call ended.

Oh, well, Janus thought. Some days you just can't please anyone.

Chapter 23

Congressman Michael O'Donnell's aide knocked on his door once and entered, carefully closing the door behind him.

O'Donnell looked up from the position paper he was reading and his heart beat a little faster. He knew something was up, for Jimmy Palmer never bothered to shut the door for routine matters.

He leaned back in his chair and raised his eyebrows. "What's going on, Jimmy?"

Jimmy looked over his shoulder, a light gleam of sweat on his forehead. "You were right, boss," he said in a low voice as if afraid he might be overheard. "Something really serious is going on over at USAMRIID."

Now O'Donnell's heart really began to beat hard and his stomach did a nervous flip. He'd been suspicious of Colonel Blackman for some time. He had always felt the man was a devious bastard who would do anything to advance his career, including putting the State of Maryland at risk if necessary. Though only a congressional freshman and low man on the totem pole of the House National Security Committee, Military Research and Development Subcommittee, O'Donnell was a rarity in Washington circles. He was still naive enough to be both patriotic and not afraid to risk his career if he thought the country was in danger.

Some months back he'd tasked Jimmy with keeping a close eye on USAMRIID in general and Colonel Blackman in particular. Now it seemed his suspicions were about to bear fruit.

He sighed. "What have you found out, Jimmy?"

Still speaking in a low voice, Jimmy said, "You know I've been kinda dating that secretary to the army member of the Joint Chiefs of Staff?"

O'Donnell nodded. Jimmy's dating habits were both profuse and something of a legend around the capitol.

"Well, she let slip last night over dinner that there'd been a Code Red lockdown at USAMRIID a couple of days ago. Said her boss had got his knickers in a knot over it and had looked like he was going to have a stroke when he found out."

"Did she say what had caused the Code Red?"

"No, and in fact when I seemed more than a little interested in it, she backed off and mumbled something about it was probably just a drill and then she changed the subject abruptly, as if she knew she'd said too much."

Damn! O'Donnell thought. *I knew that bastard was going to unleash something terrible on my state, and I'll bet it has something to do with the plague that's ravaging the country.*

"You did good, Jimmy. Best not rock the boat by asking any more questions of your girlfriend—we don't want her carrying tales back to her boss."

"What are you going to do, Chief?"

"I'll work it from my end. There are some men on the subcommittee I still trust, so I'll make some calls and see what I can find out."

Fort Detrick

At that very moment, the army representative on the Joint Chiefs of Staff, four-star General Mac McGuire, was on the phone with Colonel Blackman.

"Goddamn it, Blackie, I told you to be careful with those samples of the plague!"

Blackman sighed. He knew he'd stepped in the shit and now he was going to have to crawl a little bit or he'd lose his most valuable ally on Capitol Hill. McGuire had covered his ass on several occasions, getting him men and equipment when it meant going through back channels so no one else would know what he was working on.

"I know, Mac, but how was I to know one of my couriers would get careless and contaminate the whole damned laboratory?"

"Hell, Blackie, I told you it was risky using those damned Mexicans for transporting dangerous samples."

Blackman sighed. "Well, Mac, who do you think I should've used—a chink or a black? The man had to go into Mexico for Christ's sake, so him being a Mexican was kinda necessary, don't you think?"

"Don't make excuses, Blackie," McGuire growled. "It's a sign of weakness. Just get this shit cleaned up and do it pronto. My secretary tells me O'Donnell's man, Palmer, is already sniffing around about the Code Red."

This information scared the shit out of Blackman. He had most of the members of the Military Research and Development Subcommittee in his pocket, but O'Donnell was a wildcard who couldn't be reasoned with. He was a naive little do-gooder who just didn't understand the way the world worked and knew even less about the things men of vision needed to do to protect the country.

"Uh, you want me to have one of the boys talk some sense into Palmer?" he asked. "Maybe teach him not to stick his nose where it doesn't belong?"

"For Christ's sake, no, you asshole!" the general exploded. "We're talking about a sitting member of Congress, not some nobody we can muscle without consequences. O'Donnell may be a junior member but the *New York 'Slimes'* loves the liberal bastard. Just get the lab cleaned up and see if you can put a security blanket on the deaths that occurred. Maybe you can use the outbreak of the plague in other parts of the country as an excuse for the blackout of information."

"I'll handle it, General," Blackman said, though he had no idea how at the moment.

"You'd better, Blackie, or I might just have to have a couple of *my* boys have a talk with you."

In spite of his many years in combat, Blackman felt his testicles shrivel at the tone in the old man's voice. He's seen some men who'd had a talk with the general's boys and it wasn't a sight he wanted to remember. They'd ended up looking like they'd been through a meat grinder.

He hung the phone up and turned to his Rolodex. He flipped the pages until he came to the name Bear. He called the number and when it was answered, he said, "Get your A-team together and meet me at the safe house as soon as possible."

The man hung up without answering, having an aversion to having his voice heard over any electronic instruments.

Fort Detrick

Blackman kept an apartment not far from his office at Fort Detrick for just such secret meetings. The lease was under an old friend's name and the bill was paid in cash for six months at a time. He wanted no trail leading back to him on this assignment.

He entered the apartment and found six men sitting around the room, talking quietly and drinking beers they'd gotten from his refrigerator. They were all hard-looking men, and they were all ex–special forces who'd been dishonorably discharged from their various branches of the armed forces.

The man Blackman knew only as Bear held up a small black box and pointed it at the colonel. It hummed for a moment and then a green light appeared, showing Blackman wasn't wired or transmitting any electronic signals. Bear was a very careful man.

Even the colonel didn't know his real identity. His full name was Robert Eddleman, but he'd gotten the nickname Bear while in the Navy SEALs because he had a habit of roaring in a loud voice while on the attack in combat and because he was the approximate size and shape of a grizzly bear and had the same nasty temper when crossed.

"Hello, Colonel," Bear said, holding his hand out.

Blackman knew the drill and handed Bear his cell phone. Bear opened the back of the phone and removed the battery so the GPS tracking of the phone was disabled and then he handed both back to Blackman.

He sat down, picked up a beer, and took a deep swig and then he asked, "What've you got for us this time?"

Of all the men present, the only one whose name Blackman knew was Bear, and he was sure it was a pseudonym. Back in the day when General McGuire had introduced the two, Blackman had asked what the rest of his name was and Bear had just smiled and had not answered. Blackman had gotten the hint and had felt a frisson of fear at the soulless black eyes that stared back at him.

He handed a sealed manila envelope to Bear.

"The details are in there, along with photos of the relevant players. I have a plane waiting for you in the usual place and speed is of the essence. You're to fly below radar to an airfield in Mexico—the coordinates, along with your instructions, are in the envelope," he said, knowing Bear was an accomplished pilot.

"Mexico, huh?" Bear asked. "That's where the plague started, right?"

Blackman frowned and nodded. "Yes, but you'll be flying to the safest place in the country. The people you'll be dealing with are immune to the plague, so you won't be exposed, especially if you're careful and wear millipore masks and gloves."

Bear nodded. "Sounds good to me. Anything else I need to know?"

Blackman, too, was cautious. He knew the NSA had ears everywhere and so he would give no precise verbal instructions for his own protection. Just because you were paranoid didn't mean the bastards weren't out to get you was his motto. He just wagged his head in answer to Bear's question.

"And our fee?" Bear asked.

"As per our usual arrangement for umm . . . dangerous work, one-half has already been wired to your account in the Caymans, and the other half will be paid upon satisfactory conclusion of the assignment."

Bear smiled and nodded, his snake eyes glittering. He and his team got to their feet. He winked at Blackman as they filed out of the apartment, all of them taking their beers with them so as to leave no fingerprints behind.

Blackman took a deep breath and wiped sweat from his forehead as he locked the door behind them. No matter how many times he dealt with Bear and his team, he had to admit they scared the living shit out of him.

He moved to the window and watched as the team got into a black Suburban with mud-smeared license plates and motored off. What a cliché, he thought, just like the Secret Service vehicles.

As he stood there, he thought again about General McGuire's warnings about O'Donnell and his staff looking into his affairs. Maybe when he had the cure and the blood to make a vaccine, he'd think about letting Bear and his team loose on the congressman.

By then he'd be so powerful he could tell the general to fuck himself and there was nothing the old man could do about it. Hell, by then he'd be the most powerful man in the world!

Chapter 24

Tlateloco

While Mason and Lauren were working with Guate-motzi, trying to get him to understand the idea of a map or satellite photo, Shirley Cole was busy washing Guatemotzi's clothes in a strong bleach solution to get rid of any anthrax bacteria still clinging to them from his days around the campsite and in the nearby jungle.

Finally, after Lauren had tried for the tenth time to get the boy to point toward his village on a map, he just shook his head and pointed over his shoulder at some distant mountains to the south and west of the camp.

When Lauren asked him how many days to walk to his village, Guatemotzi thought for a moment, looked at her and then at Mason and grinned as he held up five fingers.

Mason laughed. "Something tells me he doesn't think too much of our ability to travel at speed through the jungle. He probably doesn't think we'll be able to keep up with him."

Lauren raised her eyebrows. "I don't know about you, Doctor, but I play tennis three days a week, jog at least five miles a week, and can swim a quarter-mile in just ten seconds off the current college record."

He shook his head and grinned. "Gosh, that leaves me in the dust. I can't run anymore 'cause of a knee injury I got while serving in the Navy, but I do bicycle to and from work every day—about five miles each way."

"A bicycle?" she asked. "What are you, a sissy-boy? Does the bike have training wheels on it?"

"Hey," he protested. "I'll have you know I take my life in my hands every day to do battle in Atlanta traffic."

She started to smile and then frowned. "Hey, what about weapons? I don't want to be a worrywart, but if we're gonna trek through the jungle for five days, there is no telling what kind of critters we might run into along the way, and I'd just as soon not try to fend off a cougar with my nail file."

"Not to worry," Mason said. "I got proficient with a .45 while in the Navy, and we have a cabinet in the lab with a few Armalite AR-15 rifles and plenty of ammunition."

And then he frowned. "But I think our worries should be more on running into drug cartel members rather than wild animals. The animals will try to give us a wide berth if we let them, but the drug dealers with try to kill us if we stumble upon a marijuana field or a plot of poppies they are cultivating to turn into heroin."

Lauren smirked and looked at her watch. "Jeez, Doc, I just realized I'm late for an appointment in Mexico City—not that I don't want to come on this trip with you since you make it sound so romantic and all."

He waved a dismissive hand. "Oh, don't be such a cry-baby," he joked. "I'm sure Guatemotzi knows trails that are both safe from wild animals and will keep us away from the drug lords who might be in the area."

She glanced at the *Indio* boy. "Great, I'm putting my life in the hands of a teenage boy who can't even read a map, cannot speak much English, and who is most probably friends with all the drug kingpins in the area."

She smiled feebly and spread her arms out. "You are right, Dr. Feelgood, what do I have to be worried about?"

Mason laughed again and put his hand on her shoulder. He was momentarily surprised at how right it felt to touch her and how good it made him feel. "Come on, let's get packed . . . but keep it light. Remember we're gonna be slogging through five days of jungle heat and humidity, not to mention the many small mountains we may have to climb, and those AR-15s are not exactly light-weight."

She shook her head as they walked toward the lab. "Man, you sure know how to show a girl a good time, Mason. First a worldwide plague, then a five-day jaunt through jungles filled with drug lords and wild animals looking to eat us, and all while trying to keep up with a teenage Tarzan of the Jungle."

"And don't forget," he added with a sly smile, "after we're done in the village, we get to walk back through the jungle for five more days."

She glanced sideways at him. "I think your momma misnamed you. Shoulda called you Simon Legree or Marquis de Sade."

After they were packed and ready to leave the camp, Shirley Cole walked over to Guatemotzi and turned him around and began to fiddle with the snaps on the small backpack Mason had provided for him. "Here you go, Guatemotzi," she said, "I'm putting a couple of extra Hershey's bars and even a chocolate chip muffin from Shirley into your pack in case you get hungry on the trip."

The boy grinned, understanding most of what she'd said, especially the part about the Hershey's bars.

Suzanne walked up and patted Guatemotzi on the back, and then she looked over his shoulder and said to Mason, "I still think I should come with you, in case you need help with the samples or the blood drawing."

He shrugged his shoulders. "I think you'll be much more valuable here, Suzanne. After all, this may all be a wild goose chase and the Battleship is going to need your advice on measures that can be taken to slow or stop the spread of the plague until a vaccine or cure can be found."

"Okay, okay, I know when I'm licked," she said, smiling sadly. "But you guys be careful," she added, looking into Mason's eyes. "I'd hate to never see you again."

"Not to worry," he said, hoisting his pack on his shoulders. "I'm like a bad penny . . . I just keep on turning up."

"Until you do, we'll keep on working on that nasty little bug and see if we can't find a combination of antibiotics that will kill the little fuckers," Shirley said, surprising everyone with the profanity. "Hopefully in time to save Dr. Matos's life."

None of them had ever heard her say anything much harsher than dadgummit. It was a measure of just how worried each of them was about the slim possibility of stopping the plague before it depopulated most of the civilized world.

Mason gave her a hug and said he knew she'd find a

way to kill the bug, and then he followed Guatemotzi and Lauren into the brush.

A half-hour later, Bear felt the sat-phone in his jacket pocket vibrate. He was riding copilot to Jinx, who was the team's designated pilot for touchy low-altitude flying, though all members could fly the plane in an emergency.

Bear pushed a button on the side of the phone and put it to his ear. "Yeah?"

"The *Indio* boy and Mason and the woman from the college just headed into the jungle toward the boy's village," a static-filled voice said. "They are heading south-southwest from the dig site, and I managed to plant a GPS signaler on the boy. It will signal on four hundred and forty megahertz and you should be able to pick it up within about two to three miles, depending on the terrain."

"Thanks, Janus."

"Bear?"

"Yeah?"

"Try to get the boy and the samples without killing Mason, okay? I don't give a shit one way or another about the woman, but I'd like Mason to make it through this if it's possible."

Bear's gunmetal gray eyes widened. He'd never heard Janus be sentimental about anyone before. "I'll see what I can do," he said, without promising anything. After all, the boss had as much as ordered him to kill Janus, too, which kinda pissed him off since the spy had always been straight with him and his men.

He clicked off the phone and put it back in his pocket.

"What was that about?" Jinx asked, glancing sideways at him in the darkening gloom of the late afternoon.

"Nothing," Bear grunted irritably, looking out the airplane's windows and wondering for the first time if he was on the right side. He and his team had intercepted plenty of possible germ warfare agents before in the years they'd been working for Blackman, but this time it was different. Half the fucking world was dying and their orders were to take a possible cure and hand it over to the megalomaniac who employed them and hope he did the right thing with it.

He and his team had killed many times in the past, and their victims probably numbered in the dozens if not hundreds, but never before had the stakes been in the hundreds of millions, and Bear found himself in strange territory. He was suddenly thinking about things like morality and if being responsible for the deaths of hundreds of millions of innocents would wither his soul beyond redemption. Not that he necessarily believed in a soul, but still . . .

He shook his head and sighed deeply. He'd always been a man of action and was unused to indecision. Indecision and hesitation could get a man in his line of work killed faster than a speeding bullet.

He glanced over his shoulder into the rear seats of the plane and saw his men with their heads back against the seats dozing, and he envied them their lack of imagination.

They had no thought for the millions of people who may die in agony because of their actions. To them, this job was just another paycheck and another chance to kick some ass and take some names.

He turned back around and stared out the window at

the dying embers of the sun off to their right and wondered what his final decision would be and whether he would ever be the same after this mission was over.

Hell, after this job maybe it was time to stake out a place on the beach in the Caymans and drown his memories in liquor and babes.

Chapter 25

At first, Lauren thought the trip through the jungle wasn't so bad. Guatemotzi was in the lead with her behind him and Mason bringing up the rear.

The old growth forest trees were pretty well spaced out and the underbrush was manageable. The trees even provided shade, which kept the tropical heat at a bearable level, though the almost one hundred percent humidity made breathing feel like sucking air through a wet woolen blanket.

After a while, as the land became hillier and the mild breeze died down, Lauren knew it was time for a break.

"Hey, Guatemotzi, how about we stop for a water break?"

The young *Indio* smiled back over his shoulder at her. The little shit wasn't even breathing hard and was barely sweating, she noticed.

"I'll second that," Mason called in a somewhat breathless voice from a few paces back.

As Lauren and Mason dropped their packs and he unslung the Armalite rifle from over his shoulder, Guatemotzi ambled a few feet off the animal trail they were following and fished around in a dry bush until he found a relatively straight branch and then he broke it off and returned to the group.

He slipped his pack off and sat on a large boulder and pulled a small pocketknife from his pack and began to whittle on the branch, making it into a small arrow for his tiny bow.

Between sips from her canteen, Lauren said, "I recognize that knife. It belonged to Professor Adams."

Guatemotzi grinned and nodded. "*Sí*. The professor gave me this very fine knife for helping him around the camp." After a moment his smile faded and he lowered his eyes. "He said my name was a very fine name but was too long for everyday use, so he used to call me 'Motzi.'"

He raised his eyes to stare at Lauren. "When the other young ones began to get the bleeding sickness, he told me to run into the jungle and to not come back or I would die, too."

"But you didn't run . . . you stayed," Lauren said.

"*Sí*. The old one was very good to Guatemotzi. I stayed and tried to make him better by giving him some of the plants that the *curandera* in our village uses to cure outsiders who come there and get the bleeding sickness."

"Do you know of these plants?" Mason asked.

Guatemotzi shrugged. "Some of them only. They made the old one a little better, but soon he got sick again and finally he died."

Tears formed in his eyes. "I should have listened better to the old woman when she showed me what to pick and the old one would still be alive."

Lauren glanced at Mason. "That must be why Charles was the last one to die, even though the others were younger and stronger."

He nodded. "Of course. The herbs Guatemotzi gave him must have slowed the progression of the disease significantly, but they weren't strong enough for a complete cure."

"Do you have any of those plants with you now?" Lauren asked.

"*Sí.*" He reached into his pack and pulled out a small deerskin pouch and removed five shriveled plants, two of them with flowers still attached. He handed them to Lauren, who passed them to Mason.

Mason quickly took the sat-phone off his belt and dialed Joel's number at the camp.

When he answered, Mason said, "Joel, find Suzanne and put her on the phone, quickly."

While he waited, he asked Guatemotzi, "How do you give these to a person with the sickness?"

Guatemotzi pulled a small round rock and a slightly larger flat rock from his pouch. He made a grinding motion using the round rock against the flat rock. "After this, put in hot water and make him drink it, once in morning and once at night."

Mason nodded, and then he turned back to the phone. "Suzanne, the boy has told us about some of the plants the *curandera* uses to cure the illness. He only knows a few, not enough to cure the plague but enough to slow the progression of the disease significantly."

He described the five plants Guatemotzi had given him, and then he said, "I'll text you pictures of the plants from the sat-phone. As soon as you can, have the team spread out and try to locate as much of these as you can, then grind up one of each into a fine powder, mix them with hot water, and give the tea to Dr. Matos twice a day, approximately every twelve hours."

He listened to the phone for a moment, and then he spoke. "I know it's dangerous and unscientific, but from what I saw the last time I looked in on Matos, he doesn't have much to lose, and if we can slow the progression of the disease it may give the antibiotics time to cure the disease."

He listened again. "I know it's a long shot, but I vote we give it a try. If it works, you can go to work trying to identify the alkaloids in each plant that are the active ingredients and we'll have gone a long way to gaining control of the bug."

After another moment of listening, he said, "Okay, I'll get back in touch when we've reached the village and gotten a description of the other plants and herbs the *curandera* uses. I'll give those to you by sat-phone and you can be working on those until we get back to camp with the blood and tissue specimens from the immune villagers."

He turned off the sat-phone and put it back on his belt. Handing the plants back to the boy, he said, "Thank you, Motzi. You may have helped save a man's life with these plants."

"*De nada, Señor Mason.*" His eyes shined with pride.

Lauren pointed at the small arrow the boy was shaping. "Motzi, that arrow doesn't look strong enough to do much damage to an animal. It looks much too small and flimsy."

Guatemotzi's eyes wrinkled at the word flimsy, but he said, "Is not size of arrow, but what on it that make animal go to sleep."

He again reached into his deerskin pouch and pulled out a large green leaf rolled into a tube. He unrolled the leaf and inside it was a bright orange tree frog's body.

He smiled and pointed at the two rocks and said, "Like with plant, after use rocks, put in water and put on tip of arrow. When dry, arrow will make animal go to sleep if I aim good."

"Those frogs must have a form of curare in their skin toxins," Mason said.

"I noticed some pictographs of such frogs carved into the walls of Montezuma's tomb when Dr. Matos and I went in there," Lauren said. "They must have been recipes for the poison the Indians left for the gods to use when they came for Emperor Montezuma."

Mason nodded and glanced at the sky. "Well, we're burning daylight so we better get a move on or we'll never get to Motzi's village."

As they were gathering their packs and things together, a small plane flew overhead, its wheels almost touching the tops of the trees.

"Jesus!" Mason said, involuntarily ducking at the closeness of the sound. "He can't be more than a hundred feet off the ground."

"I thought all planes were grounded because of the plague," Lauren said.

Mason shrugged. "I did, too."

He slung the AR-15 and his pack over his shoulder and said, "Come on, time to hit the trail."

As their plane flew over Mason's group, Bear saw the light on his GPS locator go from red to green and a set of coordinates flashed on the screen.

"Got 'em," he said, calling out the coordinates to one of his men who was looking at a map.

"They're on a course of south by southwest from the camp," he said.

"Good," Bear said. "Let's land at the field Janus told us about before it gets too dark, and we'll head in the same direction on foot. We should be able to catch up with them by morning, assuming they stop to sleep."

"And if they don't?" the man with the map said.

Bear shrugged. "Then we'll catch them by noon anyway. If you guys can't move through the jungle faster than two academics and a small boy, then I'm paying you way too much."

The map man smiled evilly, the scar on his black cheek turning white and making the corner of his mouth turn down. "Oh, we'll catch them, you can count on that, boss."

Bear grinned back. "Jinx, head for the landing site Janus gave us and hurry it up."

"You got it, boss man," Jinx replied, putting the small plane in a steep bank and pulling up to gain some altitude so he could find the field in the dense jungle all around them.

One of the others asked, "We gonna take them as soon as we catch up with them, Bear?"

"No, we've got to let them lead us to the village they're heading for, and we've got to let them take their blood samples and all that crap before we take them down."

He hesitated, "Unless you jokers want to draw a bunch of blood samples from the Indian villagers?"

The black man with the scar on his face pulled out a wicked-looking KA-BAR knife and held it up. "Naw, this is what I use to draw blood, boss. Ain't never had much use for needles and syringes."

"Good, then we'll get within range of the GPS locator Janus planted on the Indian and then we'll just quietly follow them until they get us what we need." Bear grinned, but the smile didn't seem to reach his eyes, "And then I'll turn you loose on them to do what you do best."

Chapter 26

Jinx looked over at Bear in the copilot's seat. "Hey boss, we're coming up on the GPS coordinates Janus gave us for the landing field in the jungle. Tell the guys in back to keep a sharp lookout, would'ya?"

Bear turned in his seat and pointed two fingers at his eyes and then at the windows. His men understood the signal and all turned to stare out of the windows at the dense carpet of jungle below.

After a few moments, Blade raised a fist and then pointed out of the window next to his seat on the right side of the plane.

Bear glanced out of his window and saw a ribbon of dirt extending in a straight line in the greenery below.

He tapped Jinx on the shoulder and pointed to the right.

Jinx glanced that way, nodded once, and then began to spiral the plane in a slow turn to the right.

Five minutes later they were bouncing along a rutted, rough patch of dirt that was more road than landing field.

"Goddamn!" one of the men in the back shouted. "Take

it easy, Jinx, I just had a filling replaced and you're about
to jar it loose."

Jinx laughed, his head bobbing back and forth with the
roughness of the landing. "Roger that, Psycho!" he called,
and then he leaned toward Bear and spoke in a low voice.
"Can you imagine wasting good silver fillings in teeth
like Psycho's?"

Bear smirked, looking over his shoulder to make sure
Psycho didn't hear the exchange. Even Bear was a little
spooked by Psycho and didn't want to test who would
come out alive if they ever had a serious disagreement.

Finally, the plane slowed and came to a halt fifty yards
from the end of the runway.

"Turn it around and have it ready for a quick takeoff,"
Bear ordered. "We may be in a hurry when we come
back."

"Ten-four, boss," Jinx replied, gunning the engine and
turning the plane in a tight circle until it was pointed back
the way it'd come.

"Load up your packs and check your weapons," Bear
said to the men in the rear of the plane. "We're gonna be
on the trail in ten minutes, and throw that camo-net over
the plane. No need to leave it out here in the open to be
seen and stolen by the first narco-trafficker that passes by."

As he finished speaking, his sat-phone buzzed and he
saw that he was receiving an email. He keyed it in and
saw an announcement from his old gunnery sergeant in
the Marines. The email said that his ex–commanding officer, Johnny Walker, had recently died and gave directions about the whereabouts and timing of the funeral.

Bear smiled sadly in remembrance of his old friend, a
man the entire unit had called Scotch due to his name.

He'd been the straightest and most honorable man Bear had ever known, and he remembered how the unit had followed the man into hell and back several times over the course of Bear's fifteen-year hitch in the Marines.

He'd heard through the Marine grapevine that Scotch had developed brain cancer and so he'd known the end was near for this brave man, but that did little to alleviate the sadness he felt at the news.

He turned blurry eyes on his men in the rear of the plane, wondering what Scotch would think of his current five-man team.

Hoss, a six-foot-six-inch cowboy, with shoulders as wide as an ax handle, a drooping moustache, and sun- and wind-leathered skin; Blade, a dangerous-looking black man with a scar on his cheek that turned parchment white when he smiled or grimaced. He carried no fewer than five knives of various designs and lengths, and he could play them like musical instruments. Fittingly, he was also totally devoid of compassion or conscience; Psycho, a thin, wiry man with bushy, wild hair and electric blue eyes that were always darting around in paranoia. He looked and acted so crazy that even his teammates were a little afraid of him, and these were men who would look Death himself in the face and spit in his eye; Babe, who was movie-star handsome and clean cut and innocent-looking and who got his name from his legendary successes with women of all stripes. A man who looked good enough to bring home to your mother, but if you did he'd probably end up raping her and cutting her throat for no reason at all; Jinx, also wiry and quick as a cobra and just as deadly, who was a master of all things that flew and all machines that shot bullets meant to kill.

Bear shook his head, feeling a little ashamed for the

first time since he'd been court-martialed out of the Marines for using excessive force against civilians in Afghanistan, though he knew there were really no civilians in that godforsaken country, just combatants, either enemy or friend, and damn few of them were friendlies.

He realized the men he'd handpicked to be his team would never have been accepted by his old friend, Scotch. Walker would have shit-canned the entire group, knowing they were psychopaths and unworthy of his command.

Oh well, Bear thought, getting to his feet to gather his own equipment together. In the mercenary business, you took what was available and what would get the job done, no matter how flawed or unworthy. In fact, flawed and unworthy was synonymous with the term mercenary.

He wiped his eyes with the back of his hand and put the sat-phone back on his belt. Time to get down to business and to get on the trail of the doctors and the Indian boy, he thought, wondering if he'd have the guts to pull the trigger on people he knew to be totally innocent of any wrongdoing.

In all his years as a merc he'd never before stooped to killing innocents. In fact, most of his victims had been men even worse than those he served with now. Oh well, he guessed he'd find out if he had the stomach for the job when the time came.

Mason's knees were aching and his clothes were soaked through with sweat from trying to keep up with Guatemotzi, who moved through the jungle like a cat through fog and just as silently.

"Hey, Motzi," he called, "slow down a little, will ya?

Guatemotzi grinned over his shoulder. "*Sí*, Señor Mason."

"I thought you were in great shape from all your bicycling, Doctor boss man," Lauren said playfully from behind him.

He half turned to give her an argument and his foot caught on a root and he went down, sprawling on his face in the thick humus on the jungle floor.

"Oh Jesus," she said, rushing to kneel by his side. "I'm sorry. I didn't mean to make you fall."

His face flushing bright red, Mason said, "You didn't make me fall. My own clumsiness made me fall."

He stopped and stared at her flushed, sweaty face and then he grinned. "Aha, I see that you're a bit out of shape, too, Doctor Sarcastic Lady."

She smiled. "Yeah, I'll admit it. I was just about to ask Motzi to take a break when you beat me to it."

She wiped her brow with her shirtsleeve. "I can't believe this heat and humidity. I thought Austin was bad, but this is ridiculous."

Mason nodded and smirked. "Yeah, I keep expecting to see fish swimming in the air it's so thick with moisture."

He glanced at his watch and then at the sun sinking low over the treetops to the west. "In fact, I think that it is about time to make camp and see if we can get some food and some rest before we continue tomorrow."

"If you're asking for a vote, I vote yes," Lauren said. "What about you, Motzi?"

Guatemotzi shrugged. "Is okay."

Mason struggled to his feet and they moved off the trail until Guatemotzi found a small clearing in the jungle large enough for them to pitch their tents and build a fire.

While Lauren and Mason put the tents together, Guatemotzi gathered up dead-drop wood and made a small pile in the center of the clearing. Gathering rocks of assorted sizes, he built a circle around the fire and carefully scraped away the inches-thick humus down to bare earth so the fire wouldn't spread and get out of control.

Thirty minutes later, beef stew was heating in a small pot over the fire and the three were lying nearby, sipping boiled coffee from tin mugs.

Lauren slapped at her neck, glanced at her palm to see a mosquito as big as a bumblebee, and said, "Ah, the great outdoors. I just love camping out in a prehistoric jungle."

Mason glanced at her. "Hey girl, I thought you did this for a living."

She shook her head. "Very few archaeological dig sites are in the middle of a jungle, and if they are, I've always had plenty of students to get the camp set up with tents and showers and civilized stuff like that before I got on-site."

She pointed at him and said sternly, "Remember, in all of my previous digs I was the boss!"

Mason grunted and moved to spoon all of them some steaming stew onto tin plates. "Well, try this Mulligan Stew and see if it's civilized enough for you, Professor Spoiled Girl."

Lauren blew on it and then took a tentative bite. Her eyebrows went up and she grinned widely. "Hey Doc, this is the best thing I've eaten since I came to this god-forsaken jungle."

He laughed. "Now that is a testament to just how hungry you are."

"No, really. It's great. Don't you think so, Motzi?"

With a full mouth, Guatemotzi nodded. "Is much better than MREs," he said.

"Wow, what a glowing compliment," Mason said. "My Mulligan Stew is better than months-old mass-produced army food."

Lauren held out her empty plate. "Quit your grousing and spoon out some more of that wonderful stuff. About the only thing that'd make it better would be some nice hot cornbread slathered with butter."

He shook his head as he handed her a plateful of stew. "Don't push your luck, lady, or it's back to MREs for you."

After they'd finished eating, they cleaned up the campsite and put enough wood on the fire so it would last most of the night, both for warmth and to help keep the bugs at bay.

Guatemotzi yawned and said good night and crawled into his small pup tent, glancing around at the walls like it was the first time he'd ever used a tent while in the jungle.

Lauren wrapped her arms around her shoulders and shivered. "It still amazes me how the jungle that is so blazingly hot during the day can get so cold at night."

Mason arched an eyebrow. "Uh, Lauren, if you're really cold, you know these two sleeping bags can be zippered together into one large one?"

"Oh?"

He shrugged, he face flaming red with embarrassment. "I'm just saying, we could . . . um . . . keep each other warm."

Lauren smiled and moved over toward him. "I'm flattered, Doc," and she leaned in and kissed him gently on the cheek. "And any other time I would gladly accept your offer."

He grimaced, "I sense a but in there."

She nodded. "But tonight, after slogging in tropical heat all day, and without a handy shower to use to wash the sweat and grime off, I'm gonna have to decline."

"But . . ." he started to say.

"No, Mason," she said, putting her hand on his arm. "If we ever do get to the point where I share your bed . . . or sleeping bag, I don't want to do it smelling like a draft horse . . . ," and she lowered her voice to a whisper, "Or with a teenage boy sleeping ten feet away."

He glanced at the nearby tent, and then he grinned and whispered, "Because you might make some noise?"

As she turned away toward her tent, she looked back over her shoulder and winked. "Of course, 'cause if you're not going to make me get loud, then it won't be worth it, will it?"

Before he could reply, she was inside her tent with the flap snapped shut.

He stood there for a moment, watching her silhouette on the tent wall as she undressed for bed, and then he made himself turn away. He knew if he didn't get into his tent quickly he'd soon be testing the strength of the snaps on her tent door.

As he crawled into his sleeping bag, he heard a low giggle coming from Guatemotzi's tent next to his.

"Motzi, did you hear all of that?" he asked quietly.

"Sí, señor," Guatemotzi answered with a low chuckle. "I think the señorita is *muy bueno*."

"Me, too, Motzi, *muy bueno* indeed!"

Chapter 27

Lauren startled awake as a hand holding a steaming cup of coffee slipped through her tent door. The hand slowly waved the cup back and forth, sending the tantalizing aroma of fresh-brewed coffee spreading throughout the small space.

She rubbed her eyes and sat up. "Oh my God, can it be my Prince Charming bringing me coffee in bed?" she said groggily.

"Wake up, sleepyhead," Mason said, "We're burnin' daylight."

She sat up, grabbed the cup, and took a deep drink, sighing at the wonderful flavor. She leaned forward, squinted her eyes to peek out the tent door, and then she snorted. "Burning daylight my ass! The sun isn't even up yet."

Mason stuck his head into the tent, his eyes widening slightly at the sight of her wearing only a T-shirt with nothing on under it. He coughed and then croaked, "Nevertheless, breakfast is served in five minutes. You snooze . . . you lose!"

She blushed momentarily when she saw where his eyes were glued, and then she grinned slightly until she opened her compact and saw that her hair was as tangled and messy as a bird's nest.

Got to find a stream or waterfall to wash up in, she thought. Another day sweating in the jungle heat and humidity and even the wild animals wouldn't want to eat her.

It took her seven minutes to get dressed, fight her hair into some semblance of order, and crawl out of the tent.

She stood and stretched the kinks out and then looked around. "Ummm," she said diffidently, "any suggestions on where I might . . . ummm?"

Mason and Motzi both grinned, and Mason pointed off to the left of the trail. "The restroom facilities are over that way. I left a roll of toilet paper hanging on a stub of a branch and a collapsible shovel to bury the . . . leavings with."

She blushed again and made her way into the brush. Damn, she thought, another couple of days like this and they would have no secrets from one another left.

When she returned, she found sliced bananas and powdered eggs were cooking in the skillet.

"Not exactly Cordon Bleu," Mason said, stirring the eggs, "but it's guaranteed to fill you up."

"It smells wonderful," she said, grabbing a tin plate and scooping a banana and some eggs onto it.

Motzi grinned and took her cup and refilled it with fresh coffee. "I find bananas," he said proudly.

She grinned around a mouthful. "Thanks, Motzi, you did good."

After they'd finished eating and had cleaned and packed

the dishes away, Mason spread a map out on the ground. He oriented it with a compass, and then he asked Motzi to point in the direction of the *curandera*'s village.

After fussing with the map and lining up a line of sight of distant mountain peaks, he turned to Lauren. "As best I can tell from Motzi's directions and the map, it looks like the village is somewhere in the middle of the Tuxtla mountain range, probably near Santiago Tuxtla or even Tuxtla Gutierrez.

"Are we equipped to climb mountains?" Lauren asked.

"Well, the Tuxtla mountains are only about six hundred meters high," he said, shrugging. "Still, climbing six hundred meters through thick jungle isn't going to be a picnic."

"Motzi find many good trails through mountains. Make it easy for you," Motzi said, puffing out his chest a little.

Lauren grinned and ruffled his hair. "I'm sure you will, Motzi."

It was late on the third day of their journey when Lauren noticed Motzi acting strangely.

The young man kept glancing from side to side as he led them through the jungle, and even occasionally stopping to peer back down the trail the way they had come.

Finally, Lauren asked, "Motzi, what's wrong?"

Motzi blushed and shrugged, but his eyes had a worried look in them.

Mason could feel the boy's fear and he slipped his rifle off his shoulder and held it in his hands, ready to fire. He followed Motzi's gaze back down the trail and asked, "Is someone following us, Motzi?"

Again the boy shrugged. "I not know, Señor Williams.

But I see birds fly after we pass, and I no hear big cats growling like usual. Something back there make them not right."

Mason looked at Lauren. "Perhaps it is some narco-traffickers moving on the same trails as us."

Lauren glanced at Motzi. "Do you know of these men, Motzi? The ones who carry drugs through the jungle?"

He nodded. "*Sí,* but this not them. They no use this trail . . . is why I come this way."

"How far until we reach your village, Motzi?" Mason asked.

The boy looked ahead, glancing from one mountain range in the distance to another. After a moment, he answered, "I think maybe tomorrow if we not sleep too much."

"Mason, I think the best thing to do is to have a cold meal tonight without a fire and to get a really early start in the morning," Lauren said, her eyes reflecting the worry in Motzi's.

Motzi nodded, murmuring, *"Sí . . ."*

Mason glanced at the darkening sky. "I think we can get another couple of hours in before we make camp, so let's try to get as close to Motzi's village as we can before we set up camp."

After they'd eaten cold sandwiches and washed them down with tepid water from canteens, they pitched their tents and each climbed inside and flopped down exhausted from the long day's march.

Lauren was startled when Mason eased his way into her tent, his finger to his lips.

"What's going on, Mason?" she whispered, pulling her sleeping bag up to cover her chest.

"I'm going to backtrack down our trail and see if I can find out what or who is back there," he answered in a low voice.

"Are you crazy?" she asked, her eyes wide. "It could be anything from a cougar tracking us to some other wild critter that's liable to jump you in the dark."

He shook his head. "Uh-uh. Just a while ago I back-tracked about a mile and I'll swear I could smell wood smoke on the wind." He smirked in the low light from Lauren's lantern. "And last I heard wild animals don't cook their meat before they eat it."

"Did you see any glow from a fire?"

"No, and that means they're taking great care to hide their presence from us, which means they are probably up to no good."

She reached out and put her hand on his arm. "Mason, I don't like this. How about I go along with you? After all, two guns are better than one."

"Two guns also make twice as much noise," he said, shaking his head."

"But what if something happens to you?"

He reached into his coat pocket and handed her his sat-phone. "If you hear anything . . . gunshots, shouting, any-thing at all, then you grab Motzi and beat feet as fast as you can to his village. Once you're there, call the camp and have them send the cavalry as fast as they can."

She reluctantly took the phone. "Okay, boss man. I'll do this your way, but only because the stakes for the rest of the world are so high and they are counting on us to get a cure for this plague."

"But," she added, arching a brow, "That doesn't mean I have to like it."

He smiled and leaned forward, kissing her tenderly on the lips. "Good, that means you'll be so glad to see me when I get back that you'll jump into my arms and cover me with kisses."

She leaned back and punched him in the arm. "In your dreams, Buster. But if you don't come back, I promise I will kick your bony ass next time I see you."

"Bony?" he asked, wrinkling his forehead. "I always thought my ass was one of my better features," he mumbled as he eased back out of her tent."

Bear had not survived fifteen years in the Marine Corps and another seven as a hired gun by being unobservant or stupid. He'd sent Jinx up ahead of their team to keep an eye on the camp of their prey. Jinx, being the smallest of the group, was the only man Bear trusted to be able to slip through the dense jungle undergrowth without sounding like a bull in the brush.

About two hours later Jinx signaled Bear on their handheld radios. "Hey, boss man," came the whispered voice.

Bear keyed his own radio. "Yeah?"

"Something's wrong here."

"Elaborate."

"You know how every night so far they've made their tents, built a fire to cook on, and then kept the fire going to keep bugs and animals at bay?"

"Uh-huh."

"Well, tonight there was no fire. They ate cold sandwiches and then went to their tents without lighting a fire at all."

Bear thought for a moment and then cursed softly to himself. "Damn, they're on to us," he murmured into the radio.

"How?" Jinx asked. "We've been damn careful to stay well back and keep our noise to a minimum."

Bear was perplexed. He had no idea how the group ahead had sensed they were being followed. He stood up, scratching his head, looking around the camp for some clue as to how they'd betrayed their position.

Then he saw it. A small plume of smoke from their low campfire was curling up into the night air and bending toward the trail that led to the group ahead of them.

He keyed his radio. "Jinx, can you smell anything?"

"What . . . ?" Jinx asked, and then he paused, sniffing. "Damn, Boss. I can smell our fire. It smells like a damn barbeque."

Bear nodded, trying to think what the group would do now. He doubted they'd try to come back after them. Hell, even though they were carrying Armalites, they were doctors and academics, not soldiers. They'd probably just huddle in their tents, terrified of what the smoke might mean. Most likely they'd think they were dealing with narco-traffickers or other *Indio* natives.

"Hey Boss," Jinx whispered again.

"Yeah?"

"The main man is slipping out of the lady's tent with his rifle and he's sneaking back down the trail right at you."

Bear chuckled. So much for assumptions. Evidently the doctor had more balls than he'd given him credit for.

"Stay put, Jinx, and make sure nothing else goes wrong."

Bear whirled around and gave a low whistle, their signal for immediate battle stations. His men came immediately awake, their hands on their weapons. "Hustle up!" Bear urged in a low voice. "We've been compromised. We've got to clear camp fast and make it like we were never here."

"How long've we got?" Hoss asked as he scrambled to his feet.

"Probably about twenty minutes," Bear answered. He figured they were about three miles back of the group ahead, and he didn't think the doc could cover that in less than half an hour without using a flashlight.

"Soon as we've packed up and policed the camp, melt into the brush and hunker down. I don't think the man will search very far off the trail."

Blade pulled his long knife out of his scabbard. "Why don't you let me take the bastard out?" he asked with a wicked grin.

Bear sighed. "Why don't you shut up and follow my orders . . . unless you think you're ready to assume command of the unit?" Bear snarled menacingly.

The smile faded from Blade's lips. "Someday you're gonna go too far, boss," he growled.

"Yeah? Well, until then, or until you think you can take me, get your ass in gear and get this place scrubbed down tight."

Mason inched his way down the trail, making as little noise as he could. There was a half moon, which gave off just enough light for him to keep from wandering off the trail into the jungle and getting lost.

He backtracked for over an hour and found nothing to indicate anyone was following them. At one point he thought he could pick up a faint whiff of wood smoke, but he found no evidence of a campfire or of any disturbance in the surrounding bush to show a camp had been made.

Finally he sighed and straightened up, easing the cramped muscles in his back from walking crouched over for the past hour and a half. He looked around, shaking his head. "Guess I was just being paranoid," he mumbled to himself.

He put the rifle strap over his shoulder, snapped on his flashlight, and walked back up the trail toward their camp. As he whistled softly in the darkness, he was unaware of the eyes that watched him from nearby bushes and of fingers on triggers in case he saw them.

Chapter 28

By the time they reached the outskirts of Motzi's village, Mason and Lauren were exhausted, while Motzi looked as fresh as if he'd just stepped out for a short hike in the woods.

As soon as he saw some of his young friends up ahead, Motzi began to yell and wave and run toward them.

The boys gathered around him, slapping him on the back and asking questions about what it was like working with the *Americanos* up north.

They quickly became silent when they noticed Mason and Lauren straggling up the path to the village, looking as if they'd been dragged through the jungle instead of walking through it.

As Mason and Lauren approached, a small, dark man waved the children aside and stooped to embrace Motzi, grinning from ear to ear.

Motzi looked toward Mason and Lauren and began speaking rapid-fire Nahuatl, explaining who the man and woman were.

After a moment, the man looked up at them and smiled. In broken English, he said, "My son say you friends. He

say you help him many time. I am Fernando . . . his father."

Lauren smiled back as she pulled twigs and leaves out
of her tangled hair. "Yes, Guatemotzi is our friend, Fernando. He brought us here to meet a *curandera* to see if
she could help us."

Fernando's forehead wrinkled and he glanced at his
son, who quickly began to explain to him in Nahuatl about
the plague that was killing millions of people across the
world and how it was caused by the "bleeding sickness"
that used to kill newcomers to their village.

Fernando nodded gravely and motioned for Mason and
Lauren to follow him. He turned and walked toward the
far end of the village where a grass-roofed shack stood
off by itself. The front of the shack had colorful designs
and pictographs painted on the walls in different colored
clays.

There was a post stuck in the ground in front of the
shack. It had a small, black cast-iron bell affixed to the
top.

Fernando stepped up to the post and rang the bell one
time, and then he stepped back and stood with his hands
clasped in front of him.

After a moment, a woolen blanket that served as the
shack's front door was pulled aside and a very pretty
woman of indeterminate age stepped through. She was of a
slim build and had hair that was an almost iridescent white
color that hung down to her shoulders. Her eyes were so
dark a brown as to almost be black and gleamed with intel-
ligence.

Fernando began to speak rapidly in Nahuatl but she
stopped him with a raised hand as she stared first at Mason
and then at Lauren.

"Hello," Mason said, inclining his head in a gesture of respect. "I am Dr. Mason Williams and this is Doctor Lauren Sullivan."

In surprisingly unaccented English, the woman said, "I am Maria. I, too, am a doctor . . ." she smiled slightly and continued, "at least, I am the closest thing to a doctor that this poor village has."

Mason grinned. "You speak beautiful English, Maria."

She smiled again, and it was as if a light shined from within as she said, "I was birthed by missionaries many years ago and they gave me the name of the Blessed Virgin and then they schooled me in English for several years as they ministered to the natives in this region."

Not wanting to waste a minute, Lauren stepped forward, "We have come seeking your help, Maria."

Her eyebrows rose. "Oh? And how can a poor woman deep in the jungles of Mexico help highly trained physicians such as yourselves?"

Lauren shook her head. "I am not a physician, Maria. I am a doctor of archaeology."

Maria nodded and glanced at Mason.

"I am a physician, Maria," he said. "And right now there is a terrible sickness spreading across the entire world killing millions and millions of people." He hesitated for a moment. "Guatemotzi tells us you know of this illness and you call it the 'bleeding sickness.'"

She shook her head. "That is a very bad illness. Over the years it has taken very many of my people."

"But Guatemotzi tells us you know of a cure for the bleeding sickness," Lauren said.

"It is true that I know of some herbs and plants that can help if given soon enough, before the illness has progressed too far."

"Maria," Mason said earnestly, "There is a great need for you to show us what you know. It could mean saving millions of lives."

She nodded. "I will gather some of the boys who help me find the herbs and plants and we will go into the forest and begin to get as many of them for you as we can."

She hesitated and looked back and forth at them, grinning. "Meanwhile, there is a stream running behind the village that has clear, clean water in it and if you wish you may wash up while I see if Fernando can provide you with nourishment while you wait."

Lauren laughed, running her hands through her hair. "Do we look that bad?" she asked.

Maria blushed. "No, not at all. But you have come a long way and the journey must have been hard on you. A nice, refreshing swim will make you feel much better."

"Come on, Lauren," Mason said, wrinkling his nose. "Don't look a gift horse in the mouth. I can't wait to get out of these clothes and into some freshwater. I feel like I'm gonna have to scrape the grime off with a knife."

Maria pointed to a small trail into the jungle that ran behind her shack. "At this time of day you will have complete privacy if you follow that trail to the river. There is a small sandy area where you can enter the water and several boulders where you can place your clothes in the sun to dry after washing them."

"Uh, what about critters?" Lauren asked. "Are there any snakes or alligators or such in the river?"

Maria smiled. "No. This stream runs too fast for snakes or other animals to be a danger to you. You might feel a fish against your legs but they are of no consequence."

Lauren grabbed her backpack and headed up the trail without a backward glance.

Mason hesitated, not knowing whether to follow her or to give her some privacy for her bath.

After about ten yards, Lauren stopped and looked back over her shoulder, a wide grin on her face. "You'd better come on, Mason, unless you're planning on staying downwind of our hosts for the rest of the visit."

He raised his eyebrows. "That bad, huh?"

"No worse than a wet goat, I suppose," Lauren answered as she turned and began to jog up the trail.

"Well you're not exactly roses, Missy," he called back as he trotted after her.

Maria gave Motzi a puzzled glance and he shrugged, spreading his hands and grinning said, *"Amor."*

"Ah," Maria said, smiling as she watched the couple disappear into the jungle.

Then she clapped her hands and told Motzi to get his friends together and to begin to gather the herbs and plants she would need.

Mason slowed to a walk, letting Lauren get ahead of him as she disappeared into the jungle. "Slow down, Mason," he said to himself. "No need to run after her like a horny schoolboy."

When he finally sauntered into the sandy beach area of the river, he saw all of Lauren's clothes washed and spread out on several large boulders baking in the tropical sun. He could almost see the steam rising from the clothes in the humid heat of late afternoon.

He peered around the edges of the river, but overhanging tree limbs caused much of the river to be in deep shade and he did not see Lauren anywhere.

Oh well, he thought, she probably swam around a nearby

bend in the river so she could bathe without me staring at her.

With a sigh of relief, he slipped out of his clothes, taking off his underwear, shirt, and pants and scrubbing them in the rapidly moving water and then placing them on boulders next to Lauren's clothes to dry.

He eased into the water up to his neck, surprised at how cool the temperature was. He shivered a little as he scrubbed his hands up and down his grimy skin, trying as best he could without soap or a washcloth to get himself clean.

"Jesus!" he screamed as a pair of hands slid around his stomach and up to his chest from behind him.

"Holy smoke, boss man. I thought you were going to jump right out of your skin," she gasped around peals of laughter.

He finally had to smile back at her, though his heart was still pounding like a jackhammer.

"What did you expect, silly woman? I'm out here in a jungle river in the middle of southern Mexico, surrounded by who knows what manner of beasts, when something grabs me from the depths."

She continued to smile as she arched an eyebrow. "What did you think it was . . . a river nymph?"

He noticed for the first time that she still had her arms around him and that there were two warm, soft breasts pressed against his chest, while her legs slowly hooked around his thighs.

He blushed at this realization, and at the inevitable biological response this was causing in his nether regions.

"Ummm . . ." he mumbled, feeling like his face was on fire.

"What's the matter, Doc?" she asked coyly, staring deep into his eyes. "Cat got your tongue?"

As he felt her pelvis push against his beneath the water, he slipped his arms around her and did what he'd wanted to do ever since he first laid eyes on her. He pulled her tight against him and kissed her as hard and as deeply as he had ever kissed anyone in his life.

As they kissed, standing chest deep in water, he felt her hand reach down between them and adjust their bodies so that his erection was between her thighs.

His hand went to her breast as she slowly undulated her hips, rubbing her inner thighs against him in a most provocative way.

"Jesus," he whispered against her lips as her nipple hardened and rose to meet his caress.

"Ummm," she whispered back, "Was this worth waiting for or not?"

He leaned his head back so that he could look into her green eyes. He put his other hand on her hips and pulled her pelvis tight against his straining penis. "What do you think?"

She laughed again, shaking water out of her hair and planting her full, throbbing lips against his and spreading her thighs, allowing him to enter her as she arched against him, shuddering.

Then he shuddered too, exploding inside her as he climaxed, throbbing again and again in wondrous release.

She quickly followed, gasping and jerking as she came with him, her fingers digging into his back and her thighs squeezing him as if she would never let go.

Breathing heavily, he inched his way toward the bank and into shallower water and sat back down, with her still on his thighs and their bodies still locked together.

He laid his head back onto the sandy shore and took deep breaths, waiting for his heart to slow.

After a moment, she eased off him and lay on her back beside him in the shallow water, her breasts heaving up and down as her breathing slowed.

He turned on his side and leaned over to capture a nipple between his lips, gently nipping it with his teeth. Again it hardened and rose into his mouth as she gasped in delight at the feeling.

She looked down and put her hands on his cheeks and slowly raised his head so she could kiss him again, her tongue darting between his lips.

After a moment, her hand drifted down under the water and between his legs to discover that he was hard again. She groaned happily and leaned back to look at him, smiling. "Wow, that was a quick recovery."

He grinned proudly. "I'm not as old as I look."

"It's either that or you've been out in the field and away from female company for much too long," she said, caressing him for a moment before finally letting him go.

"Oh, don't stop," he begged, reaching for her as she moved out of his reach and toward their clothes on the rocks nearby.

She glanced back at him, shaking her head. "As much as I'd like to lay here making love to you all day," she said, "we've got important work to do. Millions of people are counting on us, Mason."

"Just my luck," he groused as he rose from the beach and waded toward the boulders. "Falling for a woman with a sense of moral responsibility."

"Oh," she said mischievously, "and have you 'fallen' for me?"

He grinned, spreading his arms. "What? You think I let just any old girl have her way with me on our first date?"

She laughed again and shook her head. "Mason, men are notoriously easy to bed, and you are most definitely a man."

He took her by the shoulders and turned her so that she was facing him, standing waist deep in the water, her breasts pressing against his chest. "Lauren, I know you're teasing, but don't make light of this. I've wanted you since the first day I saw you."

She reached up to caress his cheek. "I know, Mason. I've felt the same way, but I need to take it a little bit slower. It's been a long time for me since . . . since I've felt like this about anyone and I want to make sure of my feelings before going off the deep end."

He nodded. "All right, we'll take it slow. But don't expect my feelings to change. I know the real thing when I feel it."

"That's a deal."

When they got back at the village, they entered Maria's shack and found six handwoven baskets full of herbs and flowering plants. Each basket had only one kind of plant in it and they were arranged along a shelf against a back wall of the one large room in the house.

On the floor, six boys were squatting in front of stone mortar and pestles, busily grinding the various plants and flowers into green paste.

Maria moved back and forth between them, supervising the boys and offering suggestions and advice here and there.

She looked up when they entered the room. "I am having the boys prepare the herbs for you to carry with you back to your camp. Guatemotzi told me that is where you

have your laboratory and where you will use these plants
to make medicine to cure the bleeding sickness."

While Mason began to take pictures of the various
plants with his sat-phone, Lauren moved closer to Maria.
"Maria, this is wonderful, and it will go a long way toward
curing the bleeding sickness, but I'm afraid we're going to
have to impose on you and the villagers even more."

"Oh?"

"Yes. Motzi told us that many in your village have a
natural resistance to the bleeding sickness and do not get
ill even when outsiders come into the village carrying the
illness."

Maria nodded. "Yes, that is true. The missionaries told
me that is because we carry the blood of our Aztec ancestors and that protects us from the illness."

Lauren nodded. "That is true, Maria. And if you and
the villagers will permit us to take samples of your blood
that may make an even better medicine to not only cure the
sickness but to prevent it from ever infecting anyone again."

"This taking of the blood . . . is it painful?"

Lauren smiled, shaking her head. "No worse than the
sting of an ant, or a small bee."

"Then I will explain to my people the need for this and
I am sure they will agree."

Chapter 29

Bear lay on his stomach, observing the village through high-power binoculars. He was on the crest of a small hill a couple of hundred yards from the village, hidden by a clump of thorny bushes.

Blade sat about ten yards behind Bear. He slowly moved the blade of one of his knives over a sharpening stone, while his eyes glared at Bear's back. He was thinking it wasn't going to take many more smart-mouthed comments from Bear before he was going to slit him from crotch to gullet.

Bear felt Blade's eyes on him and he had already loosened his 9mm Glock semiautomatic pistol in his shoulder holster, just in case the idiot finally got the courage to act on what Bear knew he was thinking.

Bear knew that being the leader of a group of men as dangerous as his crew was like walking a tightrope. On one hand, you had to be tough and not take any shit from anyone, or soon discipline would be lost and all of their lives wouldn't be worth spit. On the other hand, you had to rule with a little bit of flexibility because these men

needed to cut loose occasionally. By definition, as mercenaries they weren't real good at following orders. That's
why they'd all been kicked out of the military—an orga-
nization that valued following orders above all else.

Bear knew that Blade thought he could run the crew as
well as or better than he could. But what Bear knew was
that Blade, while tough as skull-steak, was dumb as a pole.
Tough wasn't enough in this new world of electronic surveillance. You had to be smart as well, and that's where
Blade fell far short of leadership material.

Bear also knew that after this mission, he was going to
have to do something about Blade. Either cut him loose
or kill him, and it didn't make much difference to Bear
which it would be.

Mason finished taking pictures of the plants and flowers in Maria's baskets and stepped outside the shack to
use his sat-phone to message the pictures back to their
camp. While none of his team were experts in botany as
such, he felt that Suzanne Elliot would be best to send the
flower pictures to. With her experience in epidemiology,
she'd probably spent the most time of any of the team
checking out indigenous species of plant life in previous
cases she'd handled.

He added a text message:

Suzanne, here are the plants the *curandera* says will
cure the plague if given soon enough in the course of the
disease. Will check with her about specific order of use
and different dosages if there is such. Will get back with
you shortly. Mason.

He turned the phone off to save its battery and went back into the shack.

"Maria," he said, "Do you know which of the plants is the most important one in curing the sickness and are they all given in the same way?"

She shook her head. "I am sorry, Dr. Williams, but I always give all of the plants at the same time. They are ground up as I showed you and the pulp is mixed with boiling water to make a 'tea,' which is then given two times a day until the sickness is cured or the patient dies."

Mason nodded. "That's okay, Maria. When the samples arrive back at our lab we can do an analysis of them to see which of them has the active ingredients that will fight the infection."

Lauren picked up her backpack and motioned toward the door. "Mason, Maria has spoken to the villagers and they have all agreed to have their blood drawn so we can take samples back to the lab."

He rubbed his hands together. "Good, then let's get started. I'd like to be able to head back toward the lab early tomorrow morning."

"Regarding that," Lauren said, a hopeful look on her face. "How about checking by phone to see if we might be able to get the Mexican Army to allow a helicopter to pick us up? It would save us several days in getting to work on the samples."

"That's a great idea, Lauren. I'll get right on it while you set up the blood-drawing equipment in the center of the village."

He stepped aside to send another text to Suzanne:

The curandera says all of the plants are used equally,
plants ground into a paste, boiled in water to make "tea,"

and the dosage is twice a day. Also check with Mexican
authorities to see if helicopter is available to pick us
up and get us back to the lab sooner.

As soon as Suzanne got the pictures on her phone, she
forwarded them to a botanist she knew back in the CDC
and asked if he could identify the plants and send her a
list of their names and all of the places where they might
be found.

Just as she finished sending the message, Shirley Cole
stuck her head into the room. "Suzanne, come in here
right away. There's something I want you to see."

Suzanne followed Shirley back through the corridors
of the Bio-Lab building until they came to the intensive
care unit room that housed Dr. Matos.

Shirley stepped to the side and ushered Suzanne
through the door with a "Voilà!"

A much thinner but clear-eyed Dr. Matos smiled up at
her from his bed.

"I can't believe it!" Suzanne said. "You were as close
to death as anyone I've ever seen."

In heavily accented English, Matos said, "Like your
Mark Twain, the rumors of my death were much exag-
gerated . . . not to mention premature."

"Isn't it wonderful," Shirley said. "The magical tea
that Guatemotzi provided enabled him to fully recover.
There is absolutely no trace of the infection in his blood
whatsoever."

"But, the *curandera* said that the tea had to be given
early in the course of the sickness for it to work."

Shirley nodded. "Yes, but that is in people who are receiving no other treatment. Evidently, the tea worked in

conjunction with the antibiotics we were pouring into Eduardo's blood and either enhanced their effect or worked with them somehow to completely defeat the bacterial infection."

"That's . . . that's wonderful, Eduardo. I am so happy for you," Suzanne said, though her eyes were focused far away as if she were thinking about something else.

"Have you heard from Mason recently?" Shirley asked. "I can't wait to tell him the good news."

"Yes, but he's been keeping his sat-phone turned off to conserve the battery life, since there is no way to recharge it out in the jungle. I'll be sure to let him know if he calls me back."

"Well, I wish he'd hurry up and get us some more of those magical plants. The world is waiting."

"Yeah," Suzanne said absently, "me too. I guess he'll let us know as soon as he has something to report."

Bear felt his phone buzzing in his pocket. He rolled to the side to check on Blade's position before he lowered his right hand and pulled it from his pocket.

"Yeah?"

Janus said, "What is your situation?"

"They've got the plants and are now in the process of drawing blood from all the villagers. It's getting late here now and it doesn't look like they'll be able to break trail until tomorrow morning."

"Okay, tonight I want you to break into wherever they are keeping the plant samples and blood specimens and bring them back here as fast as you can."

"What about the doc and the lady? If we leave them

alive they'll just collect more samples and beat feet back to the lab, and we'll only have delayed them by a few days at most."

"Like I said, I don't care what happens to the lady, but I don't want Williams killed. You can steal his phone and break his leg or something so he can't travel, but don't do anything permanent to him. Once you have his phone, let me know and I'll make up some story to the others on the team about him traveling on foot back to the camp, that way it'll be five or six days before they realize he's late. By then our mutual boss should be way ahead of anything the CDC can do as far as a cure is concerned."

Bear chuckled. "You got a soft spot for the doc, Janus?"

"That is none of your concern. But he is a hero who has risked his life many times to help protect people from many different diseases, and he doesn't deserve to die for no reason."

"Okay, okay," Bear replied, feeling relieved for some reason that he was not going to be forced to choose whether to kill the doctor or not. He was still undecided about the lady, but he was sure he would figure something out when it was decision-making time.

"By the way, Janus, how do you feel about all the people who are going to die because we interfered with the doc and held up the world getting a cure for this plague?" he asked.

There was a pause of almost thirty seconds, and then Janus replied, "People die every day, Bear, for all sorts of reasons. I can't think of a better reason than giving my country a leg up on all of the other countries in the world, most of whom would just as soon kill us as look at us. So forget the cheap moralizing and do your fuckin' job!"

Bear grinned ruefully. So, he thought, Janus was having trouble dealing with what they were doing, too, in spite of the rationalization he'd just heard.

He checked on Blade one more time and then he rolled back over and continued his surveillance of the village below.

Mason was in the midst of drawing samples of blood from the villagers when Motzi's father Fernando pushed his way through the line to gesture to Lauren.

She handed her rack of blood-filled tubes to Maria and eased her way through the crowd and followed him back to the small house he shared with Motzi and his younger brothers and sisters.

"What is it, Fernando?" she asked, stepping through the door.

He moved to a small handmade table and picked up a black, circular device with a pin affixed to the back of it. "You know what is this?" he asked, holding it out to her.

She took it and shrugged. "No. Where did you get it?"

He held up the shirt Motzi had been wearing on their journey, which was still wet from being washed in a basin next to a window in the room used as a kitchen. "It was here," he said, pointing to a small hole in the upper back of the shirt.

Lauren turned the thing over and over and still could not figure out what it was or what its purpose was. Still, she thought, the very fact it was pinned to Motzi's shirt was highly suspicious. The only way she could imagine it got there was for someone on Mason's team back at the dig site to have put it there.

"I will ask Dr. Williams what this is, Fernando, and we will let you know as soon as we figure it out."

Putting the device in her pocket, she walked back out to the table where Mason sat drawing blood.

"Hey, boss," she called. "How about taking a short break and drinking some water?" She glanced up at the burning tropical sun. "You don't want to get dehydrated since we have a long trip tomorrow."

Mason sighed and wiped his sweating brow with a small towel on the table. "You're right, Lauren." He turned to Maria, "Maria, if you would continue to label these tubes with the person's name I'll be back in a few minutes."

"Of course, Doctor," she said.

Lauren led Mason to the shade of a large banyan tree and handed him bottled water.

As he tipped it up and began to drain it, Lauren whispered, "Look what Fernando found pinned to Motzi's shirt when he took it off to wash it."

Blocking the view from the village, she slipped the small device into his hand. As he replaced the cap on the bottle of water, he glanced down at the device and gave a low whistle.

"What is it?" she asked.

"I think it's a state-of-the-art GPS transmitter."

"You know it could only have been put on him by someone at the lab."

"Yeah," he nodded. "That's what bothers me." He pocketed the device and looked around the village. "Why would a member of my team want to do that? They knew where we were going, and they knew I'd stay in touch with them by sat-phone."

"They knew generally where we were headed, but we and they didn't know exactly where Motzi's village was. Maybe they were afraid we'd get lost and they could use this thing to help us find our way out of the jungle."

He wagged his head. "That doesn't make sense, Lauren. My sat-phone has a GPS finder function in it so this thing is superfluous."

He thought for a moment. "Unless one of them is working at cross-purposes to the rest of us, perhaps for someone else, and they wanted to be able to track us without the other members of the team knowing about it."

"Wait a minute," she said, snapping her fingers. "Remember that wood smoke we smelled the other night? What if the GPS unit was used so that someone else could track us? That way they could follow us without having to stay so close that we would notice them behind us."

"Of course, that must be it," he said. He used the motion of taking another drink of water to mask his glance at the surrounding jungle.

He started and immediately looked down at the ground. "Holy shit, Lauren! I just saw the glint of sunlight off of a glass in the jungle on that ridge over there," he said, casting his eyes toward a ridge a couple of hundred yards from the edge of the village.

Resisting the urge to glance in that direction, Lauren asked, "Do you think someone has us under surveillance?"

"I hope so," he said. "It's either binoculars the sun reflected off of or it's a rifle scope."

"It's got to be binoculars," she said. "Whoever it is has had plenty of opportunities to kill us if that's what they had in mind."

"What do you think they want?" he asked, trying his best not to look up at the jungle again.

"Are you kidding?" she asked. "Do you have any idea what a cure of the anthrax plague would be worth? Heck, it'd have to be worth billions at least."

He shook his head. "I just can't believe any member of my team would become a traitor for money."

She shrugged, "Okay then, maybe it's not for money. Maybe it's political, or to settle a grudge against America, or hell, I don't know. It could be anything, and without more data to go on we could guess all day and still might not get it right."

"You're right, the reason doesn't matter right now. What matters is what are we going to do about it?"

"They've got to be following us hoping to get their hands on the plague cure, for whatever reason. So what we have to do is figure out how to get back to the lab and get our results to the right people without being stopped."

He glanced around at the jungle-covered mountains surrounding the village and frowned. "Any ideas on just how we might be able to do that?"

She smiled grimly. "I just might have, but I'm going to have to talk to Motzi first. Now, you get back to drawing blood as if nothing has happened and let's continue to play dumb and try not to look up at that ridge anymore. Whoever they are they've got to be thinking that we're not going to leave until morning, and they've got to believe that we'll be heading back the way we came. If I'm right, I think we'll be able to use those beliefs against them."

Chapter 30

While Mason went back to his blood drawing, Lauren searched out and found Motzi surrounded by a group of smaller boys. He was in the midst of regaling them with stories of his heroic journey back from the dangerous *El Norte* and how he'd outwitted the treacherous *soldados*.

"Motzi," she called, beckoning him to join her as she ambled down the path toward the river.

"Sí, señorita?" he asked, scrambling to keep up with her as she wound her way through the jungle that rimmed the river.

She turned to face him and waved her hand at the river. "Motzi, do you know the river well?"

He glanced at the rapidly flowing water and shrugged. *"Sí,* I think so."

She knelt before him and took his shoulders in her hands. "Motzi, I need to tell you something, but it is a very important secret, and you must promise not to tell anyone else in the village . . . not even your father. Okay?"

"Sí," and Motzi solemnly crossed his heart as she'd seen American kids do when they made a serious promise.

"Good. Dr. Williams and I have discovered that some

very bad men have been following us and are going to try to take the medicine and the blood samples from us when we head back down the trail tomorrow."

Motzi's eyes grew large and he hit a fist into his palm. "I knew it!" he exclaimed. "I . . . I felt like when big cat in jungle is watching Motzi hunt, but I no tell you 'cause I feel you make fun of Motzi."

"Your feelings were right, Motzi. We think they followed us all the way from the lab to your village."

He frowned. "*Bastardos!*" And then he winced and said, "I sorry, señorita. Not mean to say bad word."

Lauren laughed. "That's okay, Motzi. I agree with you. They are bastards, and Dr. Williams and I are counting on you to help us escape them."

Motzi stuck out his chest and grinned. "Hokay."

Lauren stood and looked up and down the banks of the river. Every so often, small skiff-like flat-bottomed boats were pulled up on the sandy shores. Most were pretty ragged but there were a few that looked to be well-cared-for and in good shape for what she had in mind.

"Do you know where the river goes?"

Motzi thought for a moment, and then he nodded uncertainly. "Motzi never go all the way downriver, but I been told goes around big mountain and comes out in big water near village of Tehuantepec." He frowned, "But Señorita Lauren, that many, many miles away."

"That's okay, Motzi." She smiled, "We'll be riding, not walking."

She began to move back up the trail toward the village. "Now, here's what I want you to do. Go to Maria and see if she will make us some food that we can carry with us, and it'll have to last us for at least a week. Also, you'll need to gather up all of our empty water bottles and fill them with clean water so we won't get dehydrated on our journey. Do you think you can do that without the bad men who are watching us from the jungle seeing you?"

He nodded eagerly. *"Si."*

"After you've done that, bring the food and water down to the river and find the best boat and put the supplies in the boat."

"Hokay."

She stopped walking and again knelt in front of the boy. "Now, Motzi, here is the hardest part, and you are going to have to trust me."

He gave her a puzzled look.

"After our boat is all ready, I want you to take an ax and put holes in the bottoms of all the other boats."

Now he stared at her aghast. "But, my people need boats to catch the fish for us to eat."

"I know, but if you don't do that the bad men will follow us when they discover where we've gone and if they catch us they will kill us and steal our samples. You're going to have to trust me when I say Dr. Williams and I will make sure our government replaces all the boats with even better, newer boats as soon as we get back to our lab."

He continued to look unsure but he finally nodded.

She stood up. "Now, let's get to work and try not to let the bad men know what we are planning."

The sun was just disappearing behind the jungle canopy when Mason finally drew the last blood sample and packed it in the padded case with the others. He now had two small suitcase-sized bags by his side, one holding the plants and flowers and the medicinal "tea" Maria and the village boys had gathered and prepared, and the other with the blood samples from virtually everyone in the village.

"What did you do with Maria?" he asked Lauren when they approached the table. "I could have used her to help pack up the last of the samples."

"She's doing something for me that is much more important than that," Lauren said, giving him a wink.

When he stood and stretched, trying to ease his cramped muscles from having sat hunched over all day drawing blood, Lauren looked around the village and grinned.

"What's with all the kids in the village running around with sticks poking out of their mouths?" she asked.

He chuckled. "Leave it to Shirley Cole," he said. "She packed a large sack of suckers in the bag with the blood-drawing equipment. I guess she thought if the kids were going to have to endure the pain of a needle, they should get some reward."

"Probably the first suckers they've ever seen," Lauren commented.

He nodded. "You are right. I had to show the first couple of children how to eat them, but the rest caught on real quick."

"The State Department could learn something from your candy diplomacy," Lauren said.

He gave her a mock serious look. "Hey, giving a child candy is the surest way to get him on your side."

He moved around the table and got close to her. "Have you figured out a solution to our problem?"

"Uh-huh. But first we've got to get something to eat and drink and figure out where we're gonna bed down tonight."

His eyebrows rose. "Did I hear you say we're going to bed down . . . as in the two of us together?"

She laughed. "Down boy, don't get your hopes up. If my plan works out, neither of us is going to get much sleep for the next few days."

They began to amble over to where a group of the village women had spread a large amount of food out onto some blankets in the center of the village square, along with pitchers of fruit juice, sliced coconuts, various fruits, and other tropical delicacies.

Lauren leaned over to whisper in his ear. "Eat hearty, Mason. It might be the last chance we get to eat for many hours."

He glanced at her with a quizzical expression on his face, but he didn't have to be told twice to eat, having had nothing but water since breakfast.

After stuffing themselves until they couldn't force another bite of food into their mouths, they glanced toward Maria.

"Is there a vacant house where we might sleep?" Lauren asked. She already knew the answer, having earlier told Maria they needed a house with a back door facing the river and away from the area where they knew the men watching them were camped.

"Yes, please follow me."

Maria led them to a small house sitting right next to the trail that led down to the river and showed them inside.

Once they were inside, Lauren pulled Maria aside. "Did Motzi tell you of our plan to use the river to escape?"

Maria nodded, but put her hand on Lauren's arm. "Yes, but is *muy peligroso* . . . ummm, dangerous. The river runs very fast and there are many rapids on the way around the mountain where the land falls quickly toward the ocean."

Lauren shrugged. "I know, but we don't have any other choice, Maria. If we go back the way we came, we'll be ambushed and probably killed, and the medicinal plants and blood samples will be stolen."

Mason moved closer. "Did I hear someone say 'river'?"

Just then Motzi slipped silently into the back door. Without saying a word, he picked up the two sample bags and both Lauren's and Mason's backpacks. He grinned at Lauren and moved just as quietly out the back door and into the jungle beyond.

"Maria," Lauren said seriously, "Once we're gone and the men who are following us realize they've been tricked, they may come down into the village to find out where we've gone. I want you to tell them everything you know, okay?"

Maria looked alarmed. "But . . ."

"No, listen to me," Lauren entreated. "These are very bad men and my guess is if you try to stall them, they may start hurting people in the village to make you talk. Perhaps even the children." She shook her head. "Mason and I do not want to have to worry about your people, Maria. Once we get a good head start down the river, even if they know where we've gone it will be very hard for them to catch us."

"Wait a minute," Mason said, pulling the small GPS unit that had been fastened to Motzi's shirt out of his pocket, "I've got a better idea."

He handed the unit to Maria. "About an hour after we leave, pin this to the fastest, most agile boy in the village and have him run as fast as he can back up some trails through the jungle in the general direction from where we came, okay?"

Maria looked unsure but she nodded. "Tell him to stay just off the trails and to be very careful not to let the bad men catch him. Do you have someone who can do that?"

Maria nodded. "Jesus Garcia. He runs like the deer and he is very quick in the jungle. But why do you want this done?"

Lauren smiled and said, "The bad men have a machine that will allow them to follow this thing. It will make them think we have left the village in the night and have headed back the way we came. If they follow Jesus, even for a little while, it will help us get farther ahead of them, maybe far enough ahead so they won't be able to catch us."

Maria clasped both of her hands in hers. "As you wish, Señorita Lauren, but I will pray for you and will only say, *vaya con Dios*."

"Going with God sounds pretty good to me," Mason said, and he leaned down and kissed Maria gently on the cheek. "Thank you so much for all you've done, Maria. The world will owe you a great debt that can never be repaid."

Maria blushed, smiled, and then quietly left the room.

After she left, Lauren took Mason by the shoulders and pushed him toward a small bed in the corner of the room. "Come on, boss man. We need to get a couple of hours of sleep before we begin our journey. It may be a long time before we get another chance."

He gave her a leer. "Both of us in that tiny bed?"

She shook her head. "Don't get any ideas, mister. We need the sleep worse than what you're thinking of."

"Speak for yourself," he said resignedly.

* * *

Blade crawled up next to Bear on the ridge and watched the doctor finish his meal and then take the two suitcases with the samples in them into a small house on the edge of the village, followed by the Mexican lady and the white woman.

He licked his lips and turned to stare at Bear. "How about we go down there and take them right now? We could be in and out with the samples in less than thirty minutes and on our way back to the real world in an hour."

Bear stared back at him, his eyes narrowed. "And I guess they'll just put down their Armalites and hand over the cure for the worldwide plague to us if we ask them nicely?"

Blade whipped out his knife. "Who says we're gonna ask them anything? I say we take what we need and to hell with the doctor or the babe."

Bear nodded. "I see, and the hundred or so villagers . . . or should I say witnesses, what do you propose we do about them?"

Blade grinned evilly, showing yellowed teeth. "Simple, like my biker friends always say, we kill 'em all and let God sort 'em out."

Bear took a deep breath and rolled on his side looking at Blade. "I'm going to try to make this so simple even an imbecile like you can understand, Blade. Wouldn't it be much easier, and a whole lot safer, if we just ambushed them along the trail back home . . . or even better yet wait until they make camp tomorrow night and take them while they're asleep? That way there're no pesky witnesses that have to be killed and we run almost no risk of them getting off a lucky shot with those Armalites and maybe killing one or two of us in the process."

Blade's face flared red at the word "imbecile" and his lips compressed into a tight white line. "I don't know!" he growled.

"Jesus," Bear said, "you're even stupider than I thought."

Blade grabbed Bear by the front of his shirt and stuck the point of his knife against Bear's throat. "I've had about enough of . . ."

He stopped when he felt the barrel of Bear's Glock push up against his groin. "Enough of what?" Bear asked quietly as he thumbed back the hammer on the 9mm. "Enough of living with your dick attached to your body . . . enough of lying there breathing instead of writhing in the dirt covered with your own shit . . . enough of taking orders from me? Well let's ask the others if they want to follow my orders and get a huge paycheck, or listen to you and spend the rest of their lives looking over their shoulders after killing an entire village of one of the United States' best and nearest allies?"

He ground the barrel against Blade's balls until Blade was groaning and sweat was pouring off his face. "What do you think their answer will be, Blade?"

"Uh . . . uh . . ." he mumbled and lowered the knife to his side.

"I thought so," Bear said derisively, "now get the hell out of my sight before I make you buzzard bait and blow your stinking brains all over my new fatigues."

Blade backed up a foot and then he stuck the knife up to its hilt in the dirt in front of Bear. "This ain't over yet, Bear."

Bear sneered. "Yes it is, 'cause if you had the balls to challenge me you'd already have done it. You're finished with this team, Blade, and after I get through telling our clients that you proposed killing an entire village, I don't think you will be getting many calls for work in the future."

Blade took a deep breath to respond, and then he noticed that standing behind him with weapons drawn and pointed at his back were Jinx, Hoss, and Psycho, while Babe was just standing with his arms crossed in front of him smiling as if he hadn't a worry in the world.

"Man makes a lot of sense to me, Blade," Jinx drawled, letting the barrel of his pistol drop just a little. "Perhaps it would be best if you go back to camp and hunker down and think about your options before you go off half-cocked, and we'll see if we can't get Bear to give you another chance to stay with the team."

"Or you can pull that other pigsticker you have in that scabbard on your belt and we can finish this right now," Psycho said with a wild look in his eyes.

Blade forced himself to chuckle and he held up his hands palms out. "Hey, guys, just a little disagreement between friends. Ever'thin' is cool now, okay?"

"Yeah, cool," Hoss whispered. "Now you go on an' do like Jinx said an' git yoreself all calmed down back at camp. We'uns will watch the village till it gits dark."

After Blade had slunk off toward their camp hidden a hundred yards back in the jungle, Bear told Jinx to take the first watch and said the others would relieve him every four hours until dawn, when they would all be up and ready to shadow the doctor and his companion back toward the lab.

"What about Blade?" Jinx asked quietly.

Bear shrugged. "Keep one eye on him. If he behaves himself, I might let this slide. Otherwise," he drew a finger across his neck.

"You want him to stand a watch tonight?" Babe asked, his eyebrows raised.

Bear grinned and shook his head. "Not unless you want to stay up with him. We'd probably all wind up with a knife in our gizzards."

Chapter 31

Two hours after they'd laid down, the alarm on Mason's wristwatch gave a series of small beeps.

He and Lauren came instantly awake. His left arm was under her neck and his right arm was curled around her cupping her breast while he spooned her from behind.

She yawned and said, "As nice as this is, maybe we'd better get up before we both get other ideas and fall behind schedule."

He moaned in disappointment. "You are a hard taskmaster, lady." He pulled his arm out, rolled over, and sat up to put on his shoes.

Moments later, they slipped out of the small bed they'd shared and began to get ready for their upcoming journey. They'd laid everything out so it would be easily found in the darkness, as they didn't dare turn on a light for fear the watchers would see it and get suspicious.

Several small blankets were rolled up and put under the bedcovers to simulate two bodies still sleeping in the bed just in case someone decided to check up on them.

Finally, everything they were carrying with them was packed and ready to go. As Lauren moved toward the back door, Mason stopped her with a hand on her shoulder.

As she turned to face him in the dark, he leaned down. "How about a kiss for luck?"

"You got it, boss man," and she pressed her lips to his, wishing they had time for more than a quick kiss.

Mason eased the back door open and slipped out, moving in a crouch so he couldn't be seen from more than a few yards away. Lauren followed close behind him, shutting the door behind her as she moved through the darkness.

The moon was obscured by a canopy of clouds, but they had no trouble following the path to the river as it was the only cleared ground through the jungle.

When they arrived at the river's edge, they found Motzi sleeping in the boat he'd chosen for their journey.

Even their almost silent footfalls in the soft dirt of the trail were enough to bring the *Indio* boy instantly awake.

"Buenos noches," he called softly to them as he stretched and jumped to the shore to help them load their cargo.

"Good evening to you, too, Motzi," Lauren whispered, handing him a couple of blankets they'd use to cover themselves in the cool evenings on the water.

Mason grunted as he passed over the two Armalite rifles and a small bag containing extra clips and ammunition.

"Did Maria give you the other supplies?" Mason asked, looking in the boat to make sure the blood and plant samples had been packed securely under the bow.

"Sí, she give me food and water," he answered, holding up a burlap sack filled with food and a five-gallon jug of water.

"You think this boat will handle all of us and our gear and food?" Lauren asked.

As always, Motzi gave her his shrug, as if like all things this was in the hands of the gods. "Perhaps," he said, grinning and winking at Mason at the look of horror on Lauren's face.

"I do believe the boy is teasing you, silly lady," Mason said, returning Motzi's wink.

She assumed a fierce glare and whispered, pointing at him, "There is an old American saying you need to learn, Motzi . . . paybacks are hell!"

He assumed an innocent look and spread his hands, "*Que?*"

She took Mason's hand and let him help her into the boat. "Oh, I think you understood me, Motzi. So you better watch your back from now on . . . and you, too, mister boss man," she added with a look at Mason that should have frozen his testicles.

He pushed the boat off from the shore and jumped aboard, picking up one of the oars as Motzi did the same thing on the other side of the wide, flat-bottomed craft.

"How about the other boats?" Mason asked Motzi as they paddled out into the middle of the rapidly moving current.

Motzi pointed to a small hatchet in the bottom of the boat. "They no float no more," he said, quietly, as if the sabotage he'd carried out on his friends and neighbors' boats caused him some shame.

"Don't worry, Motzi," Lauren assured him, "we will make sure the village gets many boats, newer and better boats so that they can catch many fish."

Since the current was moving so fast, they didn't have

to row at all, just use the oars as rudders to keep the boat heading straight down the middle of the river.

Mason leaned back against his backpack and smiled. "Man, this is much easier than I thought it was going to be. If we keep this pace up we should be at the coast by dawn."

Just then they rounded a wide bend in the river and a loud crashing noise could be heard from up ahead of them.

Lauren leaned forward and peered into the semidarkness ahead and saw a white, frothy phosphorescence as the rapidly flowing river seemed to fall off a small cliff and crash into and around large boulders scattered throughout the water.

"Uh-oh, Captain Ahab, I think you're about to earn your captain's bars. Rapids ahead!" Lauren called over the increasingly loud noise.

"Oh, shit!" Mason cried, sitting up and gripping his oar so tight he was afraid he was going to leave gouges in the rough wood.

Motzi glanced over at him. "When I say left, you paddle fast, when I say right, you dig oar in and hold tight."

"What about me? Is there anything I can do?" Lauren shouted, looking over her shoulder at them.

"Hang on and try not to get thrown out of the boat!" Mason shouted back at her.

Lauren shook her head and turned back around and grabbed the sides of the boat with death grips, mumbling to herself, "Great advice, I never would have thought of that."

*   *   *

The Navy SEAL watch on Psycho's wrist beeped softly twice, signaling him that it was midnight and time for him to relieve Jinx, who was keeping watch on the house in case the doctor and his woman decided to leave early.

As he rolled out of his sleeping bag, Bear whispered to him, "Hey, Psycho, if you think you can do it without raising an alarm, take a peek in the window of the house and make sure everything is copacetic."

"No problem, boss. As hard as those two worked today, I'll bet I could go in there and shake the bed without waking them up."

Bear grinned around a yawn. "That won't be necessary, just a quick and dirty recon should do the trick."

"You got it."

Fifteen minutes later, a sleepy-eyed Jinx slipped silently into the camp and over to his sleeping bag. "Hey Bear," he whispered.

"Yeah?"

"Psycho wanted me to tell you he peeked in the window and both our targets are sleeping like babies."

Bear raised an eyebrow. "In the same bed?"

"Yeah, why?"

Bear smiled. "If they're getting friendly, then that might just give us an edge if we have to question the doctor. If he cares about the lady, my guess is he'll tell us whatever we want to know to keep her from getting hurt."

Jinx smiled as he pulled the sleeping bag up over his head. "You're right. Never hurts to have an edge."

Due to extensive combat training, both men were asleep within thirty seconds of laying their heads down.

* * *

Blade lay in his sleeping bag unable to sleep. He just lay there, getting more and more furious with Bear for the way he'd been treated.

"I'll make that son of a bitch pay if it's the last thing I ever do," he told himself.

As he lay there, he ran various scenarios through his mind, trying to come up with some way to make Bear sorry he'd dissed him, and at the same time to earn his respect again.

Finally, just before dawn, it came to him. The perfect plan. Bear had objected to Blade's plan to kill the doctor and the bitch now and take the samples because he said there would be too many witnesses in the village, and they'd have to kill a bunch of people and that would piss off the man who hired them.

Well, Blade reasoned, what if I sneak into their house before the sun comes up, silently slit their throats, steal the plants and blood samples, and get back here before dawn with none of the villagers the wiser? Hell, Bear can't object to that. We'd get the goodies, and we'd be on our way before the natives even found the bodies and nobody would ever know who killed the two Americans.

He chuckled to himself. Sounds like a perfect plan to me, he thought. And since Psycho is the man on guard until sunup, he will probably be willing to go along with my plan, since the only thing Psycho likes better than killing a man is killing a woman.

Blade eased out of his sleeping bag and crept out of camp and toward where Psycho was standing guard. He made sure to make enough noise so that Psycho wouldn't think he was trying to sneak up on him.

When he got to within ten yards of Psycho's location, he whispered hoarsely, "Hey, Psycho, it's me, Blade."

Suddenly there was a KA-BAR knife pressed against the back of Blade's neck. "Whatchu want, Blade? Didn't Bear tell you to stay in camp?"

Blade swallowed around a lump in his throat. Good thing he hadn't tried to sneak up on Psycho or he'd be lying on the ground with his spine severed.

"Well, uh, that's what I wanted to talk to you about, Psycho."

"So, go on, talk," Psycho answered lowering the knife but keeping it in his hand and his hand ready to strike a killing blow if Blade made the wrong move.

"Okay. You know how Bear practically tore my head off for suggesting we kill those two now and head on back to the plane right away?"

Psycho laughed low in his throat. "Yeah, thought you was gonna turn white you was so scared."

Blade bristled. "I wasn't . . . oh, never mind. Anyway, I've been thinking that maybe we could kill those two now, while everyone in the village is still asleep, get the stuff, and get back on the trail toward home and our paycheck before anyone even discovers the bodies."

Psycho pursed his lips and used the blade of his knife to scratch the whiskers on his cheek. "Uh-huh, an' did you run this brilliant idea by the boss?"

"Uh, not really. I thought we might surprise him with the goods and the job already done."

Psycho laughed again, tapping Blade's chest with the point of his knife. "You just don't get it, do you, Blade? That's why the man is called boss, an' why he gets the big bucks . . . 'cause he gets to do the thinkin' for all of us so's we don't have to bother."

"But I thought . . ."

The knife dug in just enough to draw a small drop of

blood that spread through Blade's shirt. "That's yore problem, Blade. You tryin' to do somethin' you ain't bein' paid to do . . . think!"

They both heard the click of a pistol being cocked behind them and they turned to see Bear standing there holding his Glock by his side. "Did you really think you could sneak out of camp without me hearing you?" He grunted, "If it wouldn't wake everyone up within five miles I'd put a bullet in your spine and leave you to die in the dirt," he said in a mild tone.

Blade slowly raised his hands. "Bear . . . I didn't mean . . ."

"You are truly dumber than dog shit, Blade. Do you really think I didn't consider doing just what you just thought of? The problem with that plan, you ignorant piece of shit, is that as soon as the villagers found the bodies or the blood or even found the doctor and the lady missing, they would eventually tell someone and the shit would hit the fan."

"But . . ."

"But nothing, just shut the fuck up before I have Psycho make you into a shish kebab. My way, the doc and the lady disappear into the jungle and no one will ever know if it was foul play or if some narco-traffickers or wild animals killed them. All they'll know is they didn't make it back to civilization with the samples."

Blade nodded slowly. "Oh, I see."

Bear looked at Psycho and shook his head. "Now he gets it." He sighed. "Do you think he's too dumb to salvage, Psycho, or should we just gut him and forget him?"

Sweat began to pour off Blade's head. "Now boss, don't do nothin' you'll regret."

Psycho glared at Blade for a minute, and then he

smiled. "Well, he is pretty good with a knife, boss. Shame to waste a talent like that, 'specially if you think he's learned his lesson 'bout not thinkin' too much."

"I have, I have, I promise," Blade pleaded, sweat running off his forehead to hang in a large drop on his nose.

Bear shook his head again. "Oh, just get the fuck out of my sight before I change my mind and kill you right now."

As Blade jogged silently off into the jungle, Bear released the hammer on his Glock and put it in his shoulder holster.

"Whattaya think, Psycho?" Bear asked.

"I think long as yore up anyway, why don't you take the rest of my watch an' I'll get me some shut-eye."

Bear laughed. "Go on, you slacker, I'll take over till dawn, but you got to fix breakfast."

"Deal," Psycho said and he disappeared silently into the jungle.

Chapter 32

Janus walked by the window into the intensive care unit at the Cytotec lab and marveled at the sight of Eduardo Matos laughing and enjoying his first solid meal in a couple of weeks. It was truly amazing how fast the plants that the *Indio* boy, Guatemotzi, had given them had cured his infection. Now all they had to do was go back through the records of his treatment to find out which antibiotics had been given at the same time as the plants and they would be halfway home to a cure.

Jesus, Janus thought, General Blackman is going to cream his pants when I tell him we've already got a potential cure for the anthrax plague even without the additional plants and blood samples that his team of mercenaries is going to get for him.

Janus even thought for a moment of having the general call off the hit team so that there would be no chance of Mason Williams getting seriously hurt or killed. Janus had grown seriously fond of Dr. Williams in the years they'd worked together, and even though their goals in this case were diametrically opposed, Janus did not want the doctor harmed.

No, Janus realized not for the first time that the general could not be trusted. Even though Janus had warned him in the strongest possible terms not to harm Mason, there was still a better than even chance the son of a bitch would have him killed anyway. Mason's fate was truly in the hands of the gods now and there was nothing anyone could do about it.

What did trouble Janus almost as much was the fact that now that the Wildfire Team knew about the plants and how they had cured Matos and how valuable they were as a potential cure for the plague, they would all almost certainly have to die.

Before Matos's cure, if Mason and Sullivan had "been lost in the jungle," the team would have probably forgotten all about the plants and figured they were not worth the trouble of risking someone else's life to obtain them. But that was all changed now . . . they knew the plants were invaluable, not to mention the potential value of the blood samples for a vaccine.

In an ironic way, Matos's salvation meant death for the Wildfire Team, for the only way the plants and the blood samples were of any use to General Blackman was if no one else knew about them. He had to have a complete monopoly on the cure for his blackmail of the world to be effective in securing for him what he wanted.

Janus liked the Wildfire Team and hated to see them all die, but sometimes the few had to be sacrificed for the good of the many. Janus had learned this lesson well from bitter personal experience.

Stepping outside, Janus once again used the sat-phone the general had provided.

"Blackman here," the general answered on the first ring.

"Janus, General. I have some important news about the plants the *Indio* boy provided."

"What about them?"

"They were a complete success. The patient Matos was completely cured less than twenty-four hours after the dosages were started."

"Goddamn, that's great news!"

"Yes, and remember, the boy only gave us a few of the plants that the *curandera* uses. Presumably there are more plants to be tested that might be even more potent against the infection than these are. Once I have all the data, I will text you the antibiotics that were used in conjunction with the plants so you'll have all the info you need to begin testing in Fort Detrick's lab."

Janus paused to let that sink in and then added, "And we're not even talking about the possibilities the blood specimens will give us as far as concocting a possible vaccine against ever becoming infected with the virus in the first place."

"Janus, you've done great work for me and for your country. I am going to make sure that you get your just rewards for your loyalty when all this is over."

"General," Janus continued, in a low voice, "there is something else you need to consider."

"Yeah?"

"The Wildfire Team here on-site knows of the plants and of their miraculous ability to cure this plague. I've managed to temporarily sabotage our communications systems so that no one here can send a report about the plants back to the CDC, but that won't stop them for long."

"Uh-huh, I see."

"So, you'll take care of keeping them from telling anyone of our success?"

"Yeah, I'll have Bear's team make a detour down there as soon as he delivers the specimens to my men who are waiting at the Mexico City airport."

"You'll also have to make sure that none of the Mexican soldiers or doctors are allowed to fly down here before Bear has . . . uh . . . taken care of things on this end."

"Don't worry, Janus, I've already given Bear instructions to make sure there are no loose ends down there."

Janus disconnected the call and took a few steps before the implications of what the general had said hit home. How had he known to tell Bear to "make sure there are no loose ends" before I told him about the success of the plants? What loose ends were there before we knew we had the cure?

Son of a bitch, the bastard was talking about me! Janus realized. That asshole is planning to kill me after all I've done and all I've risked, just to make sure I never talk about what he's done. That bastard!

Janus pounded a fist into the side of the lab wall. Well, I've still got a few tricks up my sleeve and I intend to use them all before this is over. Two can play at the betrayal game.

Janus opened the sat-phone and dialed 411. When the operator answered, Janus asked for the office number of a congressman named Michael O'Donnell. He'd been a thorn in Blackman's side for over a year now and Janus intended to make sure he became even more so in the not too distant future.

In fact, if Janus had anything to say about it, Blackman just might come down with a fatal dose of the congressman.

*　　*　　*

Whether it was the stress of the dangerous game he was playing with Blade, or whether it was the long journey through the jungle with very little sleep, he never knew, but Bear did something he'd never before done in all his years in service and as a mercenary—he fell asleep while on guard duty.

In his dreams, Bear, or Bobby Eddleman as he was known back in the real world, was standing before the casket containing his older brother, Virgil Eddleman, called Virg by his friends. Bobby had his arm around his nephew, Virgil's son, who was named Victor.

His brother, a veteran of Vietnam as well as Afghanistan, had been killed in a firefight with rebels in the mountains on the Pakistani border. For his heroism, he'd been awarded the Silver and Bronze Stars but they'd done little to lessen the grief felt by Virgil's wife, Patricia, and his son Johnny.

God, Bobby thought in his dream, is there anything more sad than a military funeral?

After the funeral, he walked with Pat and Victor to the long, black Cadillac limousine for the ride back to the funeral home.

Pat ushered Victor into the backseat and then stepped back, saying, "I've got to talk to Uncle Bobby for a minute, sweetie. I'll just be a second."

She shut the door and turned to face Bobby. "I heard from your commanding officer about the dishonorable discharge, Bobby."

Bobby felt his face flare red. How the hell had she found out so soon? The discharge papers had come through less than a week ago. "Uh, I can explain that, Pat . . ."

She put her hand on his chest to stop him. "Bob, don't bother." She took a deep breath and continued, her eyes cast down at the pavement at her feet. "I know you loved Virgil more than life itself, and I suspect you feel the same way about little Victor . . ."

He nodded his head, his throat too choked up to talk, for he feared he knew what was coming.

"But, I'm afraid I'm going to have to ask you not to see or contact Victor again. I won't have a man with a dishonorable discharge in his life, not after the sacrifice his father made for all of us."

"But . . ."

"I'm sorry, Bob, but maybe when he's older . . . when he can better understand the circumstances . . ."

Bobby didn't let her finish. He just turned on his heel and walked away, toward the setting sun . . .

"Agghhh!" Bear cried, waking up from the dream to the steamy humidity of a southern Mexico dawn.

Though Bear hadn't seen or talked to his nephew Victor or his sister-in-law Patricia since that day, one third of everything he'd earned as a mercenary had gone into a trust account to be used for Victor's education or for whatever the boy wanted when he came of age.

Sometimes, when the going got rough, he gauged his actions on what he thought would make his brother Virgil or his nephew Victor proud of him, trying to do right in a world where the principles of right and wrong were subjective at best.

He rubbed sleep out of his eyes and peered down at the house through his binoculars. That's strange, he thought. It's almost dawn and there are no lights in the house and no sign of anyone moving around. Up to now, the two doctors had always been up just before dawn and on the trail at first light.

He doubted they'd been able to get up and get packed

and not wake him up, because his years of combat had taught him to sleep very lightly and to awaken at the least sound out of the ordinary.

Still, his gut was telling him something about this just wasn't right. He eased to his feet, drew his Glock, and made his way through the lightening sky down the hill to the house.

He moved around the corner to the rear and peeked in the window, seeing the same two sleeping forms in the bed that Jinx had.

He eased the door open and tiptoed over to the bed and put the barrel against one of the rounded lumps under the covers.

"Goddammit," he exclaimed, throwing the covers back and revealing the two rolled-up blankets that had been used to trick them.

He whirled around and ran at full speed back up the trail to his camp. While shouting at the team to get their asses up, he rummaged in his pack until he found the GPS tracker and turned it on. He'd made another serious mistake, gotten complacent, and turned the damn thing off when they tracked the couple to the village.

While the tracker warmed up, he told the men how he'd gotten suspicious when the couple didn't show up at dawn and how he'd discovered they weren't in their house.

As the tracker finally came to life, he saw immediately that the device showed a faint blip almost five miles away moving through the jungle back toward the camp at the dig site.

Jinx yawned and looked over his shoulder. "Well, that was close, boss. Good thing you thought to check on them or they'd of been out of range 'fore we could track them."

Psycho grinned around yellow, blackened teeth. "Yeah, won't be no time at all 'fore we can catch up to 'em in the brush and take care of business."

"Wait a minute. This doesn't make sense."

"What, boss?" Blade asked, trying his best to get back in Bear's good graces.

"No man alive could sneak past me when I'm on sentry duty and especially not two civilians with no military training."

"But what about the tracker, boss?" Jinx asked.

"It's got to be a trick," Bear said. He looked around and added, "Get geared up and get the camp broken down fast. I'm gonna take another look at the village and see what I can find out before we go off half-cocked running through the jungle."

He turned and trotted back down the trail while his men hustled to get ready to go wherever they had to in order to catch the two doctors.

Bear circled the village and came up to the rear of the house the couple had slept in. He eased through the door and made sure none of their gear was still there. The cabin was bare as Mother Hubbard's cupboard.

He slipped out of the rear door and saw the trail heading down to the river. He decided to follow it.

When he got to the riverbank where the village boats were docked, he found every boat had been sabotaged. They all had gaping holes in their hulls.

"Son of a bitch!" he yelled, not caring if every person in the village heard him.

Chapter 33

The trip down through the rapids was so harrowing that Lauren screamed several times when huge boulders rushed at the prow of the boat only to slip just off the side at the last moment—usually more from luck than skill as Motzi and Mason paddled frantically, trying their best to control a craft that acted more like a wild beast than a riverboat.

Finally, when they reached calmer water, Mason called to Motzi, "Pull over there to the bank. I've got to rest and make a call."

They eased the prow of the boat up onto the grassy shore and Lauren climbed out, shivering from the dowsing with river water she'd endured. Luckily, the sun was so hot that within minutes the water in her clothes was steaming as it evaporated off her.

Mason and Motzi followed her, pulling the boat far enough up on shore so the current wouldn't rip it away from them.

Motzi grinned at Lauren, looking about five years old in his enthusiasm. "*Mucho* fun, eh, Doctor Lady?"

Lauren just laughed and threw herself down on the mossy grass, too exhausted to reply.

Mason moved inland until he was in a small clearing with a clear view of the lightening sky. He pulled out his sat-phone, wishing he'd thought to wrap it in waterproof plastic. He dried it off as best he could and with a silent prayer turned it on.

He was relieved when the screen lit up. Quickly, not wishing to test his luck, he dialed the main number for the CDC in Atlanta.

Interminable moments later, he was put through to Dr. Grant Battersee, the man the team affectionately referred to as the Battleship.

"Hey, Mason, I didn't expect to hear from you . . ."

"Grant, this is an emergency call. There are a group of men who've followed us into the interior of Mexico and I think they're after the plants and blood samples that we've collected."

"What plants and blood samples?" Battersee asked in a puzzled voice.

How could he not know about the plants and blood samples that Lauren and he'd come looking for? He'd left strict instructions for the staff at the lab to relay the news to Atlanta about a possible cure.

"Grant, there is no time to go into that just now, but we may have a cure for the plague, one that works immediately, as well as blood samples that may lead to a vaccine against the plague."

"That's wonderful news, Mason, but why wasn't I told?"

Mason sighed. "I'm afraid that's part of the problem, Grant. We may have a traitor on the Wildfire Team who is working at cross-purposes to us."

"What? I can't believe that one of our people . . ."

"I'm having trouble believing it myself, but that seems to be the only explanation for several things that have happened down here lately. Now, to make a long story short, Dr. Sullivan and I are trying to escape the men chasing after us by traveling down a river toward the ocean. I'm told the river comes out near a coastal village called Tehuantepec on the west coast of Mexico."

"What do you need me to do, Mason?"

"See if you can get a military vessel to meet us there and take the plants and blood samples into custody. Grant, this could mean an end to the plague, so do your damnedest and don't take no for an answer. I have no idea what these men want with these samples, but whatever it is it can't be good for the United States or the world."

"I'll get right on it."

"And Grant . . ."

"Yeah?"

"Tell them to bring a company of Marines with them and to come armed. I have a feeling these men following us mean business and won't take kindly to their prey being taken from them." He hesitated a moment, and then he added, "Also, I'd keep this under your hat and don't share any of it with the authorities in Mexico City or with the Wildfire Team until we know who our friends are and who's been working against us."

Atlanta

Grant Battersee hung up the phone, wondering for a moment if his old friend and employee was losing it. Had the chronic overwork and stress of his job, not to mention the isolation and deprivation of his current assignment, finally gotten to him? Well, he thought, I don't care what he says, I do not believe there is a traitor on the Wildfire Team. Hell, they're some of my best and brightest people, all of whom have sacrificed more than the world will ever know to keep America safe and healthy.

Well, I guess the least I can do is give Mason the benefit of the doubt. For now, I'll work around the group in Mexico and not alert them to this latest development.

He shook his head, but for the workers in the lab to have a possible cure for this worldwide plague and to not let me know about it? I just don't believe it, and what could some men who are supposedly following Mason and Dr. Sullivan possibly want with the cure? Of what use could it be other than to cure the ill and dying?

He picked up his phone and thought for a moment. He didn't know or have any significant contacts with anyone in the Department of the Navy, so who could he call to have a ship sent to the western coast of Mexico, and who would listen to him with all that the Navy and other military services had on their shoulders right now. Hell, the Navy alone was being tasked with evacuating hundreds of thousands of U.S. citizens from foreign countries where the plague was even more advanced than in America and bringing them back to our superior medical facilities.

Suddenly he snapped his fingers. "I know," he said to himself, "I'll call General Mac McGuire. He's head of the Army Chiefs of Staff and he is Colonel Blackman's immediate superior at USAMRIID, and both are men we've worked with on many occasions."

He checked his Rolodex and pulled out the card with General McGuire's contact information on it. He'll know who to call at Navy to get a ship to the location Mason mentioned, and then maybe we'll be able to get to the bottom of this mess.

Washington, D.C.

Less than fifteen minutes later, General Mac McGuire was on the phone and chewing great big chunks out of Colonel Blackman's ass. "Goddammit Blackie, I give you a simple job and you manage to fuck it up beyond all recognition!"

Sweat popped out on Blackie's forehead as he stammered, "What . . . what do you mean, Mac? I've got everything under control just like I told you yesterday."

"Oh, so you've got everything under control, huh?" Mac asked sarcastically.

Uh-oh, Blackie thought. What does he know that I don't? "I'm telling you, Mac, I don't know what you're talking about."

"Well, if you've got everything under control, how come I just got off the phone with Battersee, the fucking head of CDC, who says his man Dr. Williams is on the run from a bunch of men who are trying to steal a cure for the fucking plague?"

Oh, shit! Blackie thought. That goddamned Bear has fucked up again! He took a deep breath and figured his only chance was to brazen it out and pretend he knew what was going on. "Oh, that," Blackie answered, trying his best to sound confident. "I told you that Bear and his team were following the doctor but that they had to wait until he had procured the cure before they moved on him or else they'd risk losing it."

McGuire laughed harshly. "Nice try, Blackie, but

you're not fooling me for a minute. I know for a fact that your man and his team have failed miserably and that the doctor has managed to elude them and is even now on the verge of getting away with the cure and the blood samples that might mean a vaccine for our troops."

Blackie pulled a handkerchief out of his back pocket and wiped his sopping forehead with it. Bear must have really screwed the pooch for the doctor to be on the loose with the samples and able to contact the CDC for help. That wasn't supposed to happen. "Okay, Mac, I'll admit it. I haven't heard from my team since yesterday, but at that time they said they had everything under control. The doctor was about to pick up the plants that cure the disease and to take blood samples from natives that our mole Janus said could lead to a vaccine, and after that Bear was all set to take them out."

"Well, since then your team has managed to not only lose track of the samples, but to lose track of the doctor and his lady friend, too."

"Shit!"

McGuire finally calmed down enough to chuckle. "Never fear, Blackie. Your Uncle Mac has everything under control. As we speak, the good doctor is headed down a river in southern Mexico that comes out into the ocean near a town named Tehuantepec on the western coast."

Blackie grabbed a pen and notepad. "Slow down a minute, Mac. Spell that town for me . . ."

After he'd done so, Mac asked, "Are you still in contact with your man and his team?"

"I damn sure can be," Blackie answered.

"Then give him this information, and tell him for me this is his last chance. If they fuck this up, there is no place on earth remote enough for them to hide from what I will do to them . . . and you, too, Blackie."

Blackie swallowed around a sudden lump in his throat. "Yes, sir, I'll make sure he understands what's at stake here."

"Good."

"But Mac, what are you going to do about Battersee? Won't he know that you double-crossed him?"

"Naw, I'll just tell him I passed his information on to someone at Navy, and that by the time the ship arrived at that location, there was no sign of his people. He'll never check far enough to know there never was any ship sent there."

"Okay, then we're good to go."

"Oh, speaking of good to go, have you taken care of that little matter of Janus at the CDC lab site?"

"That's due to be taken care of by Bear as soon as he's passed on the samples and blood specimens to my men in Mexico City."

"Huh, well I hope he handles that little task better than he did the doctor."

"He's never failed me before, sir."

"Good, 'cause it's not only his ass on the line here, Blackie. Do you understand what I'm telling you?"

"Yes, sir."

"Okay then, as long as we understand one another, I guess I can sleep easy tonight knowing you've got things under control."

"Absolutely, sir," Blackie said with far more certainty than he felt.

Chapter 34

Tlateloco

"Hello, Congressman O'Donnell's office, Jimmy Palmer speaking," the young voice said into the phone.

Damn, Janus thought. The congressman's aide sounds like he's still in high school. "Hello, Mr. Palmer. This is Janus speaking and I need to talk to the congressman right now."

Janus heard a deep sigh. "I'm sorry, uh . . . Janus was it? But all calls to the congressman must go through me. So if you'd like to state your business . . ."

"Listen, junior, what I have to say is way above your pay grade. So if your congressman is still trying to get the goods on Colonel Blackman, I'd suggest you put him on the line right now or I'll take my information to the *New York Times* and let them get all the credit for bringing that bastard down." Janus said bitterly.

"Wait . . . wait just a minute," Palmer said hurriedly. "Who did you say . . . ?"

"Cut the shit, Junior. You've got ten seconds to connect me or I take my story elsewhere. One . . . two . . . three . . ."

"Okay, okay! Hold on and I'll get him!" Palmer almost screamed into the phone.

Five seconds later there was a click and Congressman Michael O'Donnell was speaking. "What can I do for you, Janus?"

"I hear you're looking for dirt on Colonel Blackie Blackman."

"I don't know where . . ."

"Oh, for Christ's sake!" Janus exclaimed. "Can't you Washington assholes ever give a straight answer? I know what you've been doing, congressman, 'cause I happen to work for Blackman and he is very well aware of your . . . uh . . . interest in him and his activities."

There was a pause, and then O'Donnell continued, "Well, Janus, if you're so well informed, perhaps you can tell me what I need to know."

"I know that Colonel Blackman has been working for years to subvert the will of Congress, and that he has committed countless acts of treason, murder, and other various felonies too numerous to count."

Another pause. "I see, and I suppose you have proof of these . . . ah . . . nefarious acts?"

Janus said, "You bet . . . ," and began to talk rapidly.

"Slow down, Janus," O'Donnell said as the words poured from Janus's mouth.

"Look, Congressman, don't try to bullshit me while you trace this call. I know you're recording every word so if I speak too fast just rewind the tape later, okay?"

"Uh . . . sure."

"And don't waste your time with the trace; this is a black sat-phone provided to me by our mutual friend Colonel Blackman, completely off any lists and its GPS coordinates are untraceable, just like the ones issued to the CIA."

Janus laughed. "Maybe my having one of those very special phones will give my accusations a tad more credibility, huh?"

"Since even I don't rate one of those, it most certainly will," O'Donnell answered, glancing up at Jimmy Palmer standing in his doorway listening to the voice coming over the speakerphone.

Palmer shook his head no, indicating the trace was unsuccessful.

"Let me start with the most serious and most recent of Blackman's criminal acts," Janus continued, the voice becoming less strident and more reasonable. "As I'm sure you are aware, there is a very serious plague of a type of mutated anthrax sweeping the entire world. Current estimates are that unless something is done and done soon, up to one-third of all the people alive today will succumb to this infection."

"What?" O'Donnell started to say.

"Most of that hasn't been made public yet, but if you doubt me, just put in a call to Dr. Battersee at the CDC and he will confirm what I've just told you."

"Okay . . . okay . . . I'm having a hard time swallowing this, but even if this is true, what does this have to do with Colonel Blackman? Are you intimating that he started this plague . . . that this is one of his experimental bugs gone rogue?"

Janus laughed. "No, but the son of a bitch has found out that there is an imminent cure for this plague, as well as a possibility of a vaccine against future outbreaks, and he is doing everything in his power to gain control of both the cure and the vaccine so that he can extort the world to do his bidding."

"But . . . but that would be monstrous!"

Janus chuckled at the congressman's naiveté. "Don't tell me you've been investigating Blackman for this long and don't yet realize that he is just that sort of monster."

When O'Donnell didn't speak, Janus continued, "At this very moment, there is a team of CDC investigators down in southern Mexico who are very close to finding a cure for the plague, and Blackman has sent a team of hit men and mercenaries to hijack the ingredients for the cure and vaccine and to bring them back to Fort Detrick so that he can use them for his own purposes."

"Now," O'Donnell continued, "tell me more about this cure for the plague sweeping the world and Blackman's attempt to steal it. I'm still a little unclear as to just how the colonel could benefit from possessing this cure."

"Well, to begin with, Congressman, you're going to have to add General Mac McGuire to your list of coconspirators in the theft of the plague cure. In fact, Blackman is operating under direct orders from the general in this particular instance."

"Holy shit!" O'Donnell exclaimed.

Janus grinned into the phone. "This little revelation getting too rich for your blood, Congressman? Does the general have a little too much juice for you to take him on?" Janus asked mockingly.

O'Donnell took a deep breath, trying to calm the sinking feeling in his stomach. "No one committing treason has too much juice for me to take them on, Janus. So go on with your story."

And so Janus did . . . detailing just how Colonel Black-

man and General McGuire planned to extort the world
with the cure.

When Janus was finished, O'Donnell said, "I have just
one more question for you, Janus . . . why are you telling
me all this?"

Janus grinned into the phone, "'Cause the son of a
bitch made the mistake of planning to kill me!"

Bear ran as fast as he could back to his men's camp
and gathered them around him. "Okay men, the doctor
and the lady have fucked us up but good."

"How the hell?" Jinx asked. "When I checked on them
a few hours ago they were sleepin' like babies."

Bear snorted. "Not hardly, Jinx. What you saw were
two blankets rolled up and made to look like they were in
bed asleep. Evidently our doctor is smarter than we gave
him credit for and they have flown the coop and have at
least several hours' head start on us."

He chuckled and shook his head, a wry grin on his
face. "In addition, the good doctor and his lady friend are
not slogging it through the jungle like our GPS monitor
says, but they commandeered a village boat, sabotaged
all the other boats, and are even now sailing downriver
toward the coast."

He looked around at his men, "Like I said, the doc
isn't as dumb as we thought he was."

Blade gave a nasty laugh and snarled, "Well, our high
and mighty leader has made the classic and unforgivable
tactical mistake of underestimating the enemy."

Bear glanced at him, smirked, and with a motion so
quick the eye could not follow it, drew his KA-BAR as-

sault knife and made a lightning-fast backhand motion across Blade's throat.

The man dropped like a stone, with only a slight gurgling noise as blood gushed from his severed carotid arteries.

Bear calmly leaned over and wiped the blade clean on Blade's jacket and replaced it in his scabbard.

"Now," Bear asked, his eyes searching his teammates', "any other questions?"

Jinx grinned and shrugged. "Just the one, boss. What the hell do we do now?"

"First thing we do is get on the horn to our leader and see about getting a chopper out here to pick us up and then to see if we can catch the good doctor before he gets back to civilization."

Bear had no sooner spoken than the sat-phone on his belt vibrated, signaling an incoming call.

Bear glanced at the screen. "Well, speak of the devil."

He flipped the phone open. "Bear here."

He listened to angry squawking for a few seconds and then cut it off. "Shut the fuck up, Colonel! I know the doc is on the run and that we're significantly behind him. What I want to know is what can you do about fixing the situation instead of whining like a little baby?"

There was silence on the phone for a moment and then a lower, more reasonable tone asked a question.

"What do I need?" Bear asked, raising his eyebrows and glancing at his teammates as if to say, "can you believe this asshole?" "The first thing is I want you to get a chopper headed this way from Mexico City, unless you've got one closer on a ship offshore somewhere?"

Bear listened again. "I know we're out of range of a

helicopter, but just do what I tell you and everything will be okay. Have that Mexican general you have in your pocket pull out one of the old Huey skids he has stored there and have him take all the armament off it and load it full of gasoline cans and a Zodiac riverboat. They should be able to get enough gas on there for them to make the trip here all right. Just send them to these coordinates," and he read the GPS settings from the phone's screen.

He listened again. "No, I don't know if they'll have enough fuel to make it back and I don't give a shit, as long as they have enough to take me and my men down the river to the outskirts of that town the doc is heading for. They can drop us there on the bank and we'll take it from there."

The voice on the phone raised in volume and again Bear cut it off with an angry retort, "Colonel, I'm only going to tell you once more to shut the fuck up about the past or I'm going to come up there to Maryland and shove this phone up your ass!"

When there was silence, Bear said in a more concilia-tory tone, "Once we have the specimens, we'll contact you and by then you should have figured out some way to get us from the coast of Mexico back to Mexico City and then on to you with the specimens."

With that, he hung up the phone without waiting for a reply. He turned to his men, "We've got a couple or three hours until the chopper will arrive, so let's grab some shut-eye, 'cause I have a feeling once it gets here we're gonna be balls to the wall until this clusterfuck is over."

Houston

Dr. John Meeker stopped in the middle of the hallway of Houston Baptist Hospital and took a deep breath. He'd been going nonstop for close to thirty-six hours and there was no end in sight.

He glanced around at the dozens of stretchers that lined the halls, each occupied by a coughing, hacking patient except for those that had patients on them that had already expired, covered with sheets that more often than not had copious bloodstains on them. The nurses and attendants were so overworked that they hadn't had time to even remove the bodies, the living sick that needed care being their first priority.

He shook his head. While in medical school he had an interest in medical history and had read Dr. Samuel Pepys's diary of the Black Plague that swept the world in 1665 where it caused the death of a third of the entire world's population. Though caused by a different organism, the results were markedly similar, with over ten thousand deaths per week being described in the city of London, England, alone during that hellish summer of horror.

As he stared around the hospital, Meeker thought that number would be paltry compared to what he was seeing today, and he knew that losing a third of the world's population to this particular plague was entirely possible if no cure were found and found quickly.

He was startled from his reverie when a nurse leaning over a nearby stretcher groaned and fell to the floor.

He rushed to her side and was saddened to see her flushed face and feel her fevered brow. She had obviously come down with the illness she had been so gallantly treating.

He knelt and picked her up and began to carry her

toward the nearby triage rooms, though he knew he'd not find any space for her there.

Just outside one of the rooms, he paused and rolled an obviously dead body off the stretcher onto the floor and placed the nurse gently down upon it. He'd be damned if he wasn't going to give this selfless servant of medicine his full attention right now.

"Nurse," he bellowed over his shoulder.

A breathless young woman moved quickly to his side. "Yes, sir?"

"Get me an IV setup and some antibiotics for this patient stat!"

"Uh, I'll try, sir, but I must warn you we are running dangerously low on both IV fluids and antibiotics."

He stared down at her. "Then go up and down the hall and take them from anyone who is already dead or looks to be near death, and get someone to help you. It does no good to be giving IVs and antibiotics to dead patients."

He whirled away from his patient and took out his cell phone. He dialed the number of the hospital administrator's office. When he answered, Meeker practically yelled, "Mr. Sampson, where are my IV fluids and antibiotics? I told you this morning we were going to be running short, and now I'm told that we are completely out of both."

Sampson answered, "Good Lord, man. I'm doing all that I can. I've called everybody in the book and there are just none of those supplies left in the city."

Meeker's shoulders slumped. "Then God help us," he groaned, "'Cause the rider on the white horse named Death is galloping down these corridors and there is no one to stop him now."

Chapter 35

Tlateloco

After he'd made his phone call arranging for a transport ship to pick them up at the harbor at Tehuantepec, Mason and Motzi pushed the boat back out into the river current.

The river was wider here and the current slower and much less rough. Lauren turned around and leaned her back against the bow of the boat as she watched Mason paddling and guiding the craft into the center of the river.

She noticed, not for the first time, how his tall, rangy body was lean and muscular without being overdeveloped. It was the mountain biking that kept him so fit, she supposed, doubting that a man such as he would spend a lot of time lifting iron in a gym.

His face, while not classically handsome, was well-proportioned and pleasant to gaze upon. You could almost see his compassionate nature in his ice-blue eyes, while his unruly black hair gave him an almost impish appearance.

She smiled. All in all, not too shabby, she thought, feeling a tingling warmth begin to spread in the pit of her stomach.

Then she sobered as she began to wonder just what this . . . what . . . this connection that seemed to have grown between them over the past weeks would lead to. After all, he lived and worked in Atlanta, Georgia, half a country away from her Austin, Texas, home. There was simply no place else in the world where he could do the work that he obviously loved with all his heart.

She pursed her lips. Could she . . . would she be willing to leave Austin and move to Atlanta if he asked? Shaking her head, she realized that she just didn't know.

On one hand, there were several top-notch universities in or near Atlanta. Emory University, for example, had a very well-known archaeology and anthropology department, as well as a medical school that was one of the best in the country. She knew she would have no trouble getting a job there if she wanted it, especially if their present expedition resulted in a cure for the plague sweeping the country.

On the other hand, she had a life and friends and a very satisfying career already set up in Austin, and she loved the city with its eclectic nightlife and many activities centered around young professionals such as her.

Girl, she told herself firmly, turning her gaze from the mesmerizing good looks of Mason to focus on the jungle around them, you are getting way ahead of yourself. One romp in the hay, or rather in the river, and you're already making plans and picking out china and drapes for your love nest with a man who may not have the slightest interest in anything other than a fling with the only available woman in a thousand miles.

Better to wait and see what develops, if anything, and

not to get her hopes up too much. There would be plenty of time later to figure out just what they might or might not mean to each other.

She closed her eyes, leaned her head back, and let the gentle swaying of the boat lull her to sleep, to dream of blue eyes, coal-black hair, and muscles like iron.

It took several hours for the chopper from Mexico City to finally arrive at the clearing where Bear and his team were anxiously awaiting it.

They'd had time to take a much-needed three-hour nap, bury Blade, and pack up all of their equipment in waterproof duffle bags in case they had to jump into the river at their destination.

Their weapons were locked and cocked, they were fed and rested, and they were all ready to "kick some ass and take some names" as the saying went.

The chopper barely had time to settle before the team was aboard and Bear was signaling the pilot to take off by whirling his finger in a circle over his head.

He slipped a pair of earphones on so he could talk to the pilot over the roar of the blades. "How long until our destination?" he asked.

The chopper leaned to the right and the nose dipped as the pilot applied full throttle. "About an hour and a half if we cut across country and don't follow the river," the man replied in heavily accented English.

Bear considered his options. It would be far smarter to follow the river so that they might come upon their quarry in an isolated area where there would be no witnesses to the interception. However, the doctor had at least an eight-hour head start on them and he had no idea how long it would take the party to reach Tehuantepec by boat. He also didn't know if they had a motor on the boat or were relying on the current alone to propel them downriver.

He doubted there was a motor, as he'd seen no signs of any storage of gasoline or oil in the village that would be needed to keep it running. Plus, all of the other boats had contained only oars and primitive paddles with no sign of any mechanical aids to navigation.

Still, to be on the safe side, it would be better to head straight for Tehuantepec, deplane there with their Zodiac, and then head upriver to catch the doctor and his party unawares if there was no sign they'd already reached the city.

He leaned forward and tapped the pilot on the shoulder. "Head across country on the most direct route to Tehuantepec and kick this pig! We need to be there yesterday!"

The pilot turned his head and raised his eyebrows. *"Qué?"*

Bear had forgotten about the language differences. "Go as fast as you can," he said.

The pilot nodded and grinned, *"Sí,* I will kick the pig as you *Americanos* say."

Back at the lab at the excavation site, Shirley Cole had called a meeting of all hands. When they'd gathered around the table in the dining room and had all gotten settled with their cups of coffee or soft drinks, she stood and addressed them.

"First of all, I'd like Joel to give us an update on our communication problems."

Joel adjusted his yarmulke and stood, nervously twisting his hands together. One-on-one, he was perfectly able to carry on an intelligent conversation, but his inner geek really manifested itself when he had to address a group, even a group of people as close to him as the Wildfire Team was. "I don't know what to say. I've run diagnostic protocols on all of the computer communication gear, and they all say the computers are working perfectly."

"But it can't be the computers alone, Joel," Sam Jakes interjected crossly. "None of our smartphones or sat-phones are working either. How do you account for that?"

Joel spread his hands and shrugged. "I don't know. The only thing I can think of that would cause all of our devices to malfunction at once is either a major weather phenomenon, such as massive sunspot activity or a violent electrical storm in the area, neither of which is occurring, or a deliberate blocking of our signals by a jamming device of some sort."

"Bullshit!" Jakes growled. "We're a thousand miles from the nearest outpost of civilization, and even the Mexican military units have all pulled back to Mexico City, so who in the hell could have a jamming unit out here in the boondocks—a freaking Indian?"

Joel shrugged again. "It would have to be one of us, I guess." He glanced around as their eyes widened in shock. Spreading his arms, he added, "It's the only thing I can think of that makes sense."

"Are you insinuating that one of us is deliberately blocking all communication with the outside world?" Lionel Johnson asked incredulously, his voice so low that they had to strain to hear it. "Why would anyone here want to do that?"

Shirley Cole stood up and said, "Thank you, Joel." As he sat down she asked gently, "And I suppose that there is nothing you can do to overcome this 'jamming'?"

He shook his head. "Not unless I could find the unit itself and disable it." He hesitated, and then he added, "And I don't have the faintest idea where to start looking for it. With the newer units, it could be located anywhere within half a mile and still keep our devices from working."

"But no one has answered my question," Lionel exclaimed, his eyes downcast on his feet. "Why would one of us want to do such a thing?"

Shirley Cole looked around the room, from one face to another. "I can only think of one reason," she said. "The jamming didn't start until we realized we had a potential cure for the anthrax infection that is sweeping the world. For some unknown reason, one of us does not want that information to be relayed back to the CDC, to Dr. Williams, or to the Mexican authorities."

"But what good will keeping us silent about the cure do?" Suzanne Elliot asked. "As soon as the Mexican authorities realize we have lost touch, they'll send someone to come check on us and the word will get out then."

"Not if we're all dead by the time that happens," Shirley answered, her voice grim. "The only scenario I can think of where silencing us for a short while makes sense is if whoever is doing this knows we won't be around to spread the word about the cure later."

"But, that's crazy," Suzanne said. "Why would anyone in their right mind want to keep the existence of a cure a secret? What would they have to gain?"

"I didn't say they weren't crazy," Shirley said. "But it could be as simple as money."

"Money?" Sam asked.

Shirley smiled grimly. "I know we're not used to thinking in terms of monetary gain," she said, "especially considering the slave wages the CDC pays us. But do you have any idea how much money a cure would be worth to the world? Whoever controls the cure could literally ask for billions of dollars and every country in the world would be lining up to pay the ransom to save their people."

"What if it's not money the person wants?" Joel asked quietly. "What if the cause is ideological? Suppose a person wanted just one country or one regime to have the cure so that all of their enemies would be killed off by the plague?"

Shirley shook her head. "Whatever the reason, monetary gain, ideology, or some misguided sense of patriotism, it doesn't matter much in the end. What matters is that for the person to succeed with their plan we all have to die."

"But . . . but that's monstrous!" Sam said forcefully.

"So is condemning millions upon millions of innocent people to a horrible death by anthrax," said Shirley. "Once you get by that, the death of a half-dozen or so scientists doesn't count for much."

"But, we're all friends here," Lionel said. "We've worked and practically lived together for years. I can't believe one of us could do such a thing."

"Me either, but unless you want to postulate some third party hiding out somewhere close by in the jungle and spying on us, I'm afraid that's the only thing that makes sense."

Suzanne stood up. "Well, I for one don't believe it for a minute. None of us could stand by and let such a thing happen to our friends." She turned to stare at Joel. "Joel, you must be wrong. There simply has to be another reason our communications gear isn't working right . . . maybe the jungle humidity has rusted the inner circuits, or the heat has fried the diodes, or something equally simple."

Joel shrugged and turned toward his communications cubicle. "I doubt it, but I'll run all the diagnostics again to make sure there was nothing I overlooked."

Chapter 36

Atlanta

Grant Battersee was busy shuffling papers and taking phone call after phone call from doctors all over the country pleading for help in dealing with the plague. Unfortunately, there wasn't much he could tell them except that the CDC was working as fast as it could to develop either a cure or at the very least a vaccine to prevent further infections and that in addition the CDC was releasing its stockpiles of antibiotics and other pharmaceutical supplies to help to ease the shortages that seemed to be cropping up everywhere.

His phone rang again almost as soon as he'd hung it up from the previous call.

"Hello!" he said, somewhat more stridently than he'd intended.

"Hello, Dr. Battersee," a pleasant male voice said. "I have Congressman Michael O'Donnell holding for you."

A moment later a somewhat deeper voice asked, "Dr. Battersee?"

"Yes."

"This is Congressman Michael O'Donnell, and I am a

member of the House Select Committee on National Security and also on the House Military Research and Development Subcommittee."

"Hello, Congressman," Battersee said in a more reasonable tone. "Of course, I know who you are and how important the work your committees do is to the nation's welfare. However, if you are calling me to try and get CDC to work harder or to do more about the current anthrax outbreak, I'm afraid I'm going to have to disappoint you. We are working double and triple shifts and are . . ."

"No, no," O'Donnell interrupted. "You misunderstand the reason for my call."

"Oh?"

"I've just gotten off the phone with a person who claims to be a spy working on one of your Wildfire Teams, and this person, code-named Janus, informed me that Colonel Woodrow Blackman along with General Mac McGuire have concocted a plot to steal some plants and blood samples from one of your doctors and to use these samples for their own nefarious purposes."

"What? You've got to be kidding . . ."

O'Donnell gravely answered, "No, Doctor, I assure you I am not, and furthermore this information backs up a line of inquiry my office has been pursuing for some time into the activities of USAMRIID and Colonel Blackman. However, I have to admit this is the first time General McGuire's name has come to my attention."

The congressman went on to tell Battersee everything that Janus had told him about the operation and the mercenaries involved.

"Oh my God!" Battersee exclaimed. "Just a short while ago my doctor in the field in Mexico called to tell me he had specimens that he was sure would lead to a cure for the plague and that he was being pursued by a group of armed men. He asked me to arrange for a ship with a contingent of Marines aboard to meet him on the coast of Mexico to save him and the samples from the mercenaries."

"Good," O'Donnell said. "Then maybe we're not too late to foil Blackman's plan."

"No, you don't understand. The man I asked to arrange the pickup was General McGuire."

"Shit!" O'Donnell exclaimed, though he very rarely cursed. "Quick, give me the details of the pickup location and what your man needs and I'll get the admiral in charge of Naval Operations to intercede as fast as we can. Maybe we can still get those Marines there in time to save your man."

Tehuantepec, Mexico

As the chopper neared the place on his map labeled Tehuantepec, Bear could see that it was more of a large village than a city. The roads were dirt or gravel and none were paved, and there were no buildings over two stories high and damn few of them.

He tapped the pilot on the shoulder. "Circle around to where the river merges with the ocean and let's take a look."

The pilot nodded and banked the chopper in a wide turn, buzzing low over the small harbor where the river entered at one end and the ocean opened up at the other side. There were numerous boats on the river and in the harbor but they were all small and all seemed to be occupied by natives with no white people around.

Bear nodded. Good, they'd gotten here in time and before the doctor could make it to the open ocean. He snorted.

Not that it mattered since the ship the doctor was planning on meeting was not going to be showing up.

"Okay, take us down to that beach just where the river begins to curve into the harbor."

As soon as the helicopter's wheels touched down, Bear's team had grabbed the Zodiac boat and thrown it to the sand, followed quickly by their duffle bags. The men jumped to the ground and within seconds had the boat floating in the water.

Bear made a slicing motion horizontally in front of his throat and the pilot cut the engines.

"Refuel the chopper and keep it shut down until I return."

"But, señor, I was ordered to return to Mexico City as soon as I let you off."

Bear rested his hand on the butt of his Glock .45. "Give me the keys," he said, holding out his other hand.

The pilot frowned but quickly complied. "And don't even think of hot-wiring the engine, or I will hunt you down and shoot you in the face," Bear growled.

The pilot had no idea what "hot-wire" meant, but he got the idea Bear was conveying and shook his head. "*Sí*, I will wait here."

Bear smiled and turned to run and jump aboard the Zodiac. He pulled an MP5 machine gun from his duffle bag, inserted a thirty-round magazine, jerked back the lever to load a shell, and yelled, "Fire it up, boys, and let's go fishin'!"

Jinx grinned and pulled the starter cord on the forty-horsepower outboard engine.

When the engine roared to life, he twisted the handle and the Zodiac leapt forward as if it'd been shot out of a cannon, Hoss and Psycho hollering "hoo-hah" as they held onto their hats with one hand and the boat's gunwale with the other.

Mason noted that the river was slowly narrowing and thus the current was quickening. "Motzi, do you know about how far until we reach Tehuantepec?"

Motzi glanced around and then behind him toward the mountain the river had wound around and then he gave his usual shrug. "Maybe one . . . two hours."

Lauren began to awaken, yawning and stretching as she gazed around at the thick jungle on both sides of the river.

"Did Sleeping Beauty have a nice nap?" Mason asked with a grin.

She yawned again, trying to cover it with a palm. "Yes, as a matter of fact, I did. Since you macho men left nothing for me to do I decided a nap was in order."

"And did you have pleasant dreams?"

He was surprised when Lauren blushed a deep crimson. "Why . . . uh . . . yes, I did in fact," she answered.

Mason smiled and shrugged. "Well, I would have let you paddle with Motzi, but you know what they say about women drivers."

She laughed. "Yeah, and I know all about men drivers who would rather get lost than ask anyone for directions. If we were anywhere but on a river with but one destination, five will get you ten you would've gotten us lost."

Mason laughed with her. "I plead guilty to rarely asking for directions, since it is unmanly and since it is infinitely more fun to get lost if you have the right company."

"I'll have to take your word for it, since in my business, getting lost often means you don't find your way back."

He frowned and held up his hand, "Listen," he said urgently.

She cocked her head and could hear the high-pitched whine of an outboard motor from up ahead of them around the next bend.

"What do you think?" she asked, a worried look on her face.

"Since that is the first outboard motor we've heard on the entire river, and since I doubt very seriously if there are any gas stations in this part of the jungle, I don't think it is good news. In fact, I think the best thing we can do is get to the shore as fast as possible and try to make ourselves scarce."

He and Motzi put their backs into it and began to paddle toward the right bank of the river as fast as they could, but the current was so strong it was several moments before they could get the nose of the boat pointed in the correct direction.

Suddenly, it was too late. A bright orange Zodiac came careening around the bend just as they nosed into the bank.

Mason could hear shouts as the men on the boat saw them, and seconds later the Zodiac was headed straight toward them.

Mason and Lauren grabbed their bags and rifles and ran into the jungle, following Motzi as he led them up a narrow, ill-defined trail away from the river.

Jinx shouldered his M-16 and took aim, but Bear forced the barrel of his rifle down. "No, don't shoot. We might hit the blood samples and that would really piss our boss off."

Jinx snarled. "But . . ."

"What?" Bear shouted. "You afraid we can't run down a couple of civilians and an *Indio* boy in jungle terrain?"

Jinx relaxed. "Well, when you put it like that . . ."

He put his rifle down and twisted the throttle of the outboard motor and ran the nose of the Zodiac up on the grassy bank.

Bear jumped to the ground and turned. "Hoss, you stay with the Zodiac and keep an eye out in case they try to circle back around and get to their boat."

"Why do I have to stay behind and miss all the fun?" Hoss groused.

Bear smiled and shook his head. "Because a three-hundred-pound behemoth wearing size-fourteen boots isn't the most agile creature to go chasing through a jungle on a trail barely two feet wide. Hell, they'd hear us coming from a mile off."

Hoss smirked. "Guess yore right, boss."

Bear pointed at him. "Keep your guard up, though. This doctor has already proven to be plenty smart, and I wouldn't put it past him to try to sneak up on you to get the Zodiac and leave us stranded here." He looked toward the jungle and shook his head, "And I'll swear I saw them carrying what looked like rifles when they lit out."

"No worries, boss. I'll smash a hole in their boat and then I'll take the Zodiac over to the other side of the river and wait for your signal. If they appear back here, I'll fire a volley of three shots in the air."

Bear nodded. "Good thinking." And then he punched Hoss in the shoulder. "I guess you're not just a pretty face after all. We'll see you soon."

* * *

Running as fast as they could through uncleared jungle trails soon tired Mason and Lauren out. Motzi looked as if he could run forever, but Mason could see sweat pouring off Lauren's face and could hear her panting like a steam engine.

"Hold on," he gasped, stopping and leaning over with his hands on his knees. "We can't keep this pace up much longer, and we're making way too much noise."

Lauren did likewise, her chest heaving as she looked around. "You're right, but I don't see any place to hide where they won't spot us instantly."

Motzi dropped his backpack and quick as a fox shinnied up a nearby tree. When he got to the top he looked around in a complete circle.

Seconds later, grinning, he dropped to the ground. "Follow Motzi," he said and grabbing up his backpack took off at a slant through the jungle.

After a couple of hundred yards Mason noticed the ground began to rise and it felt as if they were moving uphill.

Sure enough, after another hundred yards the jungle thinned and they could see a hillock rising out of the jungle ahead of them. As they climbed it, Mason noticed the jungle gave way to knee-high grass for the last hundred yards up to the top of the hill.

When they reached the top, they found several small boulders and fallen trees that made a natural fortress of the height.

Motzi grinned and shrugged. "If cannot outrun bad men, can maybe stay here until help come from ship."

Mason nodded. "Great idea, Motzi. I'll get on the phone and see if Battersee can contact the ship and have them send reinforcements. Meanwhile, you two get down behind cover and get ready to hold off a charge if the men decide to try to take the hill."

They were moving so fast up the trail that they almost missed the signs, but Psycho noticed a bent and broken limb just off the trail to the left.

"Hold on, guys. I think they went this way."

Bear stopped and looked around. "Why in the hell would they leave the trail and head off into thick jungle where they won't be able to move as fast?"

Babe moved over next to Psycho and took a look. "I don't know, boss, but they sure as hell went this way."

"Okay, let's get after them, but be careful. This thick jungle is an ideal place for an ambush."

Psycho snorted. "You think this civilian doctor has got the balls to try and ambush a superior force?"

Bear shook his head. "I don't know, but I've already underestimated this man once. I don't intend to do it again."

He hesitated, "But since you don't think it's possible, why don't you take point, Psycho?"

"But . . ."

Bear's hand fell to his Glock. "I said take point. I won't say it again."

"Yes, sir," Psycho said and he turned and began to follow the trail through the jungle, but Bear smiled to himself as he noticed Psycho was moving at a much slower pace and his head was swiveling back and forth as he checked the jungle ahead for a possible trap.

*   *   *

In less than twenty minutes they came to the edge of the jungle where a grassy embankment rose to the apex of a hillock up ahead.

A clear trail of trampled grass led up the sides of the hill to the top where an outcropping of boulders and fallen trees blocked their view of what lay waiting for them up there.

"Shit!" Bear growled. "They've taken the high ground."

"But boss," Babe said, "There's only two of them and one of them's a woman. We can surround the hill and rush it all at once and it's damn sure they can't get all of us."

Bear looked at Babe as if he were crazy. "Yeah, you're right, Babe. We do know however that they have at least two rifles up there. What we don't know, however, is what kind of rifles they have, if they're single shot or semi-automatic, how much ammunition they have, or how well trained they are. For all we know that 'woman,' as you put it, can shoot the balls off a gnat at fifty yards."

He looked around at the others. "Now I don't know about you boys, but I personally am not inclined to rush a fortified position, uphill, through at least a hundred yards of open ground."

He shrugged. "I don't know where you boys got your combat training, but my old instructor would kick my ass up to my ears if I suggested a harebrained battle plan like that."

Babe's face flushed bright red. "You're right, boss. I wasn't thinking."

Bear put his hand on Babe's shoulders. "That's all right, Babe. You are correct that we are up against amateurs, but even amateurs can get lucky, especially with modern long guns in their hands." He shook his head,

"Trouble is nowadays everyone goes to the gun clubs and they all think they're Buffalo Bill."

"So, what do you want to do, boss?" Psycho asked. "Wait until dark and then try to sneak up the hill?"

"Maybe eventually, but not just yet. Why don't we see what a little reasoning might accomplish, especially after they lay up there in the sun without any shade for a couple of hours? The way they took off from their boat I'll bet they didn't take a whole lot of water with them."

"Reasoning?" Jinx asked skeptically.

"Sure," Bear said, and then he pulled them all together. "Now here's what we're gonna do . . ."

Chapter 37

Mason turned on his phone and called Grant Battersee. "Hello."

"Grant, this is Mason. What the hell happened to the ship and our reinforcements?"

"Oh, thank God it's you, Mason. I've been trying to call you but I keep getting voicemail."

Mason took a deep breath, puzzled by Battersee's greeting. Dealing with bureaucrats almost always gave him a headache. Most of them had their heads up their asses, but none of them had ever thanked God when he called. "I've had the phone turned off to conserve battery power, Grant, but just answer my question, where in the hell is the ship with Marines on it I told you I needed?"

"I screwed up, Mason. I don't know anyone in the Department of the Navy so I called General Mac McGuire instead since we worked with him before."

"You mean you dealt with the General McGuire who is Colonel Blackman's boss?" Mason interrupted. "The man who has tried to hijack every bug we've ever found and use it as some sort of biological warfare agent?"

"You don't have to yell, Mason. I know now that it

was a mistake. Congressman Michael O'Donnell just called and said that McGuire and Blackman have inserted a mole named Janus in our Wildfire Team and that they are the ones who sent a team of mercenaries after you to steal the specimens. I'm sorry I didn't believe you when you said you suspected a traitor on the team, Mason. It might have made a big difference in how all this turned out."

"Why did this Janus decide to change sides?" Mason asked.

"Janus found out Blackman planned to tie up all the loose ends, including killing Janus as well as the rest of the Wildfire Team."

Jesus, what a clusterfuck, Mason thought. "What else did this congressman say?"

"He said his committee had been investigating Blackman and USAMRIID for some time, and that he would use his influence to see if he could get a ship with some Marines on it to your location as fast as possible but that it might take some time."

Mason's shoulders slumped as he looked around the small area on top of the hill where they were surrounded. "Well, we just might not have much time, Grant." He hesitated, another idea popping into his head. "Did O'Donnell tell you who the spy in the Wildfire Team was?"

"No, he just said he got a tip from someone calling themselves Janus, and the phone had a voice distorter on it so he couldn't even tell if it was a male or female."

"Okay, never mind, I'll try and figure it out. Now, get out your cell phone, I'm going to send you some pictures of the plants we think might be a cure for the plague. Get someone on the horticultural team at the CDC to try to identify them and if they grow anywhere else get some samples and begin work on them on your end just in case our samples don't make it back."

Battersee gulped, knowing that Mason meant in case he didn't survive the mission. "Mason," he said, his voice choking, "I'm . . . I'm sorry I messed up so terribly."

Mason chuckled grimly. It wouldn't be the first time a deskbound bureaucrat had messed up his life, but it might well be the last. "That's okay, Grant. You take care, and God willing we'll see you soon. Oh, by the way, I'll also text you the coordinates of the village in southern Mexico that's filled with Indians immune to the plague. They might be useful to formulate a vaccine in case our blood samples also don't make it."

Mason turned and saw that Lauren had already pulled the plant samples out of their bags and laid them out on a small blanket in the sunlight so the colors of the blossoms would show up the best. He snapped several pictures of them and forwarded them to Battersee's cell number along with a text of the coordinates of Motzi's village.

"I'm guessing by the tone of your conversation that it didn't go exactly as you expected it to?" Lauren asked, a grin on her lips.

Mason turned to her as they packed the specimens back into their bags. "I don't know what you find so funny," he growled. "It seems we've been hung out to dry and to fend for ourselves. We can't expect any help from the United States to get here in time to make a difference."

"Hey," she said, punching him lightly on the shoulder. "You're superdoc, boss man. Just do what Indiana Jones would do and we'll be all right."

He glared at her for a moment, and then he gave a crooked smile. "Yeah, but I left my bullwhip and fedora back at home, and pretending to be Indiana Jones might just get us killed."

She shook her head and leaned over a fallen log, her Armalite at the ready. "Don't count your chickens, Mason. We're not dead yet. You may not be Indiana Jones, but I'm as good with a rifle as Annie Oakley. I'll bet I can part that bastard's hair down there at a hundred yards with this scope."

He shook his head. This woman never ceased to amaze him with her grit, determination, and courage. She was very special. Then, shaking off such thoughts, he grabbed his rifle and peeked around a boulder on his side of the small flat area on top of the hillock. "What've we got, Motzi?" he called softly.

Motzi, who had been watching the jungle below from the middle of a thick bush next to a boulder, said, "I think three, maybe four men below. Two moving around to other side of hill behind us."

"So, what's the plan, boss man, since it seems from your phone call the cavalry isn't going to be riding to the rescue any time soon?"

His face was serious as he answered, "I think we have only one shot, Lauren. If we can hold out until dark, then we can send Motzi with the samples down the hill and into the jungle. From there he can hopefully make it to our lab at the excavation site. At least then the cure and possibly the vaccine will get out to the world."

"You think Motzi can sneak through four armed men who have us surrounded?" Lauren asked over her shoulder.

Mason grinned, glancing at the small boy almost hidden in the bush nearby. "I think the jungle is Motzi's home, and no matter how good those mercenaries are down there, it is not their home. Yes, I think he has a fair chance to make it through them."

She stared at him for a moment. "From what I could hear of your conversation, there is a spy in the Wildfire Team? What makes you think they'll let the samples get tested and sent back to the CDC?"

He shrugged. "I just don't think someone who's worked on the team for several years could simply kill the rest of the team in cold blood just to steal some plant samples. I don't know of anyone on the team who could be that cold-blooded."

She marveled at his naiveté and faith in others' innate goodness, but then she realized that was probably one of the things that drew her to him like a bee to nectar. "And us?" she asked.

He hesitated. "I think we need to stay here and keep the men at bay for as long as possible so that Motzi can get a good head start."

She gave a low, sad laugh. "Like I said, boss man, this is a helluva first date. First we traipse through miles and miles of tropical jungle, and then we get to be sacrificial lambs in order to save the world."

"Ummm, maybe I can make a bargain with them to let you go . . . plead that you're a woman who has nothing to do with all this."

"Not on your life, Mason," she said, raising her rifle and snapping a shell into the firing chamber. "I'm in this for the long haul."

She aimed and fired, eliciting a shout of "Shit!" from below as her bullet clipped a tree trunk inches from a man's face.

"Whoo-hoo!" Lauren hollered. "Why don't you come on up here and get us, tough guy?

* * *

Jinx put his hand to his cheek and it came away streaked with blood. "Goddamn, the bitch almost blew a hole in my fuckin' head," he exclaimed.

Bear chuckled to himself. It was a good lesson to his men not to underestimate their enemy as he had done.

He took out his radio and keyed the mike, "Hoss, come in," he said in a low voice.

"Yeah, boss?"

"We've got the group surrounded so you can bring the boat back to this side of the river and join us. Just follow the trail and you'll find us."

"Roger that, boss."

Bear cupped his hands and put them to his mouth. "Ahoy, the hill!" he shouted. Time to do some bargaining. Maybe they'd be able to get out of this without losing any more men or having to kill any more innocent people.

Mason kept his eyes glued to the jungle at the base of the hill in case the shout was a distraction for an attack. "Yeah, whattaya want?"

Bear smiled. As if they didn't know what he wanted. "You know what we want. Give us the plant samples and the blood specimens and we'll be on our way and let you go free."

"Yeah, right," Mason yelled back sarcastically. "And I suppose you'll even give us a ride back to Mexico City in your helicopter and maybe buy us a couple of beers?"

Bear had to laugh. This guy had stones the size of basketballs. In any other situation he felt he would probably like the doc. "Yeah, I guess you have a right not to trust us."

"Ya think?" Mason called back, chuckling himself now.

"I'm getting tired of yelling. How about meeting me

halfway up the hill under a flag of truce? Your people can keep me covered and mine will keep their sights on you."

Mason glanced over at Lauren. "What do you think? Do we trust him?"

She shrugged. "Sure, 'cause he's seen me shoot. If he so much as blinks I'll put one right through his eye."

"Okay, I'm coming down. You come up without a weapon," Mason hollered, and then he bent down and gave Lauren some instructions, which caused her to smile widely.

Jinx whispered hoarsely from behind a nearby tree. "Are you crazy, boss? That broad almost took my ear off at a hundred yards. She might just take you out to even up the odds."

Bear put his MP5 down and stepped out from his cover. "Naw, Jinx. These guys are civilians. They'd never kill anyone in cold blood, especially under a truce agreement."

"You want me to take him out when he steps out?" Jinx asked. "That would cut them down to just the woman and the boy."

Bear glanced at Jinx. "Yeah, and what about me?"

Jinx scoffed, "You could be ready and duck down into the grass when you hear me shoot."

Bear glanced at the grass and realized even lying flat parts of his body would be exposed. "How far did she miss you, Jinx?"

"Uh . . . I see what you mean."

"No, stand down for now. Let's see what they've got to offer to keep us from just rushing them and killing them and taking the samples."

But in spite of his brave words, he knew a tactic like that would be suicide and that two experienced shooters with rifles that they obviously knew how to use could hold that hill against many more men than he had. No, it'd be much better if he could let them know how hopeless their situation was and try to get them to trust him to let them go if they gave him what he wanted. Right now, his greatest ally was the scorching tropical sun overhead. They'd be lucky to last until dark in this temperature.

He held his hands above his head and began to climb up the hill through the knee-deep grass as the doctor did the same thing and headed down toward him.

They met halfway down the hill and Bear stuck his hand out. "Hello, Dr. Williams. My name's Bear."

Mason just stared into his eyes. "Forgive me if I don't shake hands with the devil."

Bear laughed and spread his arms. "Devil? Me? I'm not the devil, Doc, just a man trying to make a buck."

Mason noted Bear's high and tight haircut and glanced at a tattoo of a globe and anchor on Bear's right forearm with the words *Semper Fi* on a banner underneath. It was the symbol of the Marine Corps.

He inclined his head at Bear's arm. "Marines?"

Bear's eyes narrowed and he held his arm out to stare for a moment at the tat. "Yeah. You?"

"No, I was a Navy doc. The Marines used our doctors and corpsmen, as you know."

Bear nodded. He'd always been impressed with the medical care the Navy docs provided to the Marines. While the Marines and Navy had a fierce rivalry among themselves, it'd never extended to the Navy doctors or corpsmen who provided both services with excellent care.

"So I guess you've forgotten what that means?" he asked, again inclining his head at Bear's tattoo.

Bear sneered as he looked at the words. "Naw, I know what *Semper Fi* means . . . always faithful." He gave a short laugh. "But I don't believe in that shit anymore. I was dishonorably discharged for striking an asshole officer who got a bunch of my friends killed."

He took a deep breath as if to calm himself down at the memory. "And what do you think happened to the man who fucked up and got them killed? Nothing!"

Mason shook his head. "And punching out the officer is how you honored the memories of your dead comrades? I guess your family's really proud of you now, huh?"

Bear had a brief vision of the disappointment in little Victor's eyes when he'd turned and walked away from him at his brother's funeral.

"My family's none of your fucking business!"

Mason raised his eyebrows. "No? Have you ever seen anyone die from anthrax, Marine?"

Bear opened his mouth, but before he could answer, Mason added, "Be sure to think about your family while you're doing this, 'cause you're subjecting them to a one-in-three chance of dying a very miserable death from the very disease I'm trying to cure."

"Bullshit!" Bear almost shouted. "The man I'm getting this for is trying to do the same thing you are and that's to develop a cure for the plague."

Mason laughed contemptuously. "You mean that asshole Colonel Blackman? Sure he is. And after he has the cure I'm sure he's going to make sure everyone in the world has access to it, right?"

Bear nodded, surprised that the doctor knew his boss was Blackman. He wondered briefly how much else he knew about their mission. "At least, he'll get it to everyone in the United States."

"You don't look that dumb, Marine. Once he gives anyone else access to the cure he's lost control of it, so what good would all this intrigue do him then? No, Blackman's gonna use this for his own purposes and the rest of the world, including the United States, be damned."

"Quit calling me Marine! I told you I was busted out."

Mason shrugged. "My friends in the Corps always told me 'once a Marine, always a Marine.'"

"Well they were wrong. Now let's cut the bullshit. Are you going to give us what we came for or are we going to have to take it?"

Mason looked over his shoulder at the hilltop and was pleased to see a plume of smoke rising from behind the boulders and brush.

"Oh, I think not, Mr. Bear."

Bear shook his head, "Not Mr. Bear, just Bear. You know you're just delaying the inevitable? Come nightfall we'll sneak up the hill in the dark, kill you all, and still wind up with the goods."

"I don't think it'll be that easy for you, Bear. Take a look at the sky."

Bear glanced up and saw a clear, blue sky with a huge faint full moon visible just above the horizon.

"The hill will be lit up like a parking lot with that moon," Mason said calmly, and then he shrugged. "Oh, I'm sure you'll eventually overwhelm us and kill us, but it will do you no good, and you'll lose at least some of your men trying."

Bear looked puzzled. "So? At least we'll have accomplished our mission."

Mason shook his head again. "Oh dear, I thought all Marines were good tacticians. Why do you suppose my companions are building a large fire in the heat of the day?"

Bear glanced up the hill with a sinking feeling in his chest. Goddamn, this was one clever son of a bitch. "So, if we attack you'll burn all the plants and the blood specimens?"

Mason nodded. " 'Fraid so."

"But then no one will have them."

Mason shrugged again. "Oh, that's not true. The plants and the blood donors are all still out there and our people know who and where they are," and he held up his satphone and scrolled through the pictures he'd sent Battersee. "But just to make sure, I sent pictures of the plants back to the CDC in Atlanta along with the coordinates to the village where we got the blood samples. Experts are even now working to identify them. It might delay their acquisition a few days, but right now other teams are headed to the region we just left to gather the same specimens we did. Of course, it'll mean a few million more dead due to the delay, but at least the world will eventually get the cure and your man won't."

Bear put his hands on his hips and stared around at the surrounding jungle. There was simply no way he could get back to the chopper and back to the village where the plants were gathered before the teams Mason had summoned could get there. And if they had pictures of the plants at the CDC they were truly fucked.

Finally, after working it back and forth in his mind, he glanced up at Mason and grinned. "Man, I knew you had some gigantic stones, but I never thought you'd be this good. You've thought this all out really well."

"Someone, I forget who, once said that nothing focuses the mind like the prospect of imminent death. Whoever he was, he was correct."

"So, I guess I have no reason to follow this through and kill you."

"Not unless it's for spite."

"I told you I was in this for the bucks, not for spite."

"Let me ask you something, Bear."

Bear shrugged. "Sure, go ahead."

"Would you really have let a billion or more people die just for money?"

Bear laughed. "Hell no, Doc. I know you have no reason to believe me, but the plan all along was to give Blackman his plants and specimens, just not the entire batch. As soon as he'd paid me and my team, I was going to make a side trip to the CDC and make an anonymous donation of the rest of the specimens to your lab. So," he spread his arms again, "the world would still get the cure it needs, me and my men would get amply rewarded, and Blackman would get royally fucked, as he so richly deserves."

Mason grinned and stuck out his hand. "Bear, now I'll shake your hand."

As they shook, Mason whispered, "You know, Bear, as far as I know, Blackman has no idea what the plants look like, and all blood looks the same. Since it's going to take me a while longer to get back to my team than it does for you to get to Mexico City, why not give the asshole what he wants: a basketful of pretty plants and some tubes of blood?"

"And we'll get paid and that asshole will still get fucked! Damn, Doc, you are not only smart, you're a devious bastard, too."

"Now, Bear," Mason added, putting his arm around Bear's shoulders. "As one old sailor to another, the feds are onto Blackman, so don't take too long to make your deal or you'll have to do your negotiating through iron bars in Leavenworth." He hesitated, "And I wouldn't let the money sit in one place too long after tomorrow, 'cause the feds have a long reach and I have a feeling Black-man's gonna be giving up anybody he can to save his skin."

Bear looked into Mason's eyes. "Thanks for the heads-up, Doc. I'll make sure not to let any grass grow under our feet when we make the deal." He took a couple of steps and then he asked, "Do you guys need a lift back to your lab?"

Mason shook his head, knowing as nice as his talk with Bear had been, he still couldn't trust him with the samples. "I talked to my boss and he's sending in the Marines, literally. They're gonna pick us up at Tehuante-pec . . . probably tomorrow." He smiled. "That should give you time to get your samples to Blackman, get his money transferred, and to disappear."

Bear laughed and pointed his finger at Mason, "Once that money's been wired, we're gonna be like smoke in the wind . . . poof."

Mason edged closer and lowered his voice, "Bear, there's one more thing I want to talk to you about . . ." He talked quietly for several moments, and Bear nodded his head once and they shook hands again.

As Bear turned to go back down the hill and give the news to his men, he wondered briefly if Victor would be proud of what his uncle had done today.

"Yeah, I think he would," he said to himself, grabbing Jinx by the shoulder.

"Change in plans, Jinx, an' I think you're gonna like it 'cause it means your skinny ass won't get shot at and we'll all still end up rich as hell."

Chapter 38

When Mason sauntered back up the hill like he didn't have a care in the world, Lauren grabbed him by the front of his shirt and shook him like a rag doll. "What the hell did you do down there? You guys looked like you were going to tear each other's throats out and then suddenly you're best buds."

When Mason just grinned and hesitated, she shook him again back and forth yelling, "Tell me . . . tell me . . . tell me . . . !"

Mason glanced back down the hill and saw Bear explaining the change in circumstances to his men. "There, Lauren, is at least a partially honorable man."

She stepped back aghast. "What the hell is that supposed to mean? The bastards chase us all over God's creation trying to kill us and steal a cure for the world's worst plague in history and all you can say is he's a partially honorable man?"

"Come on, help me get our things together and I'll tell you the damnedest story."

When he'd finished, she just shook her head. "Men!" was all she'd say as she finished packing up the specimens and blood samples. "Do you really think we can trust them to keep their word and allow us to leave with the specimens?"

He stared down the hill, watching Bear and his men pack up their gear and head off into the jungle. "I think so, as long as our interests and theirs coincide."

He smirked, "But I would hate to be on the other side from Bear . . . he is one tough son of a bitch."

He turned from staring at the jungle to look at her. "You know," he said, pulling out his phone. "Battersee said Congressman O'Donnell told him Blackman had turned one of the Wildfire Team's members into a spy for him . . . one code-named Janus."

Lauren laughed sourly. "Imagine that! A spy on the team, just like you suspected, Mason." After a moment, she added, "Janus, well that's an appropriate name for a spy anyway."

Mason raised his eyebrows. "How so?"

"Not up much on your Roman mythology, huh?" Lauren teased. "Janus was a god with two faces, one pointing to the front and one to the rear."

"Two faces, huh?" Mason asked, nodding. "You're right; it is an appropriate name for a traitor."

"Did Battersee say why this spy had suddenly had a change of heart and decided to work on the side of the angels?" Lauren asked.

"Evidently Janus had suddenly figured out Blackman was going to tie up all the loose ends by killing the Wildfire Team . . . along with his spy Janus."

"Why in the world would he do that?"

Mason shrugged. "Think about it. If Blackman's mercenaries had succeeded in getting the plants and blood specimens from us and eliminating us, the only other people who knew about the existence of a possible cure would be the Wildfire Team. There's no way he could leave either us or any members of the team alive to talk, otherwise every law enforcement agency in the world would be after him . . . he'd have no place to hide."

After a few minutes of dialing and then redialing, he gave Lauren a puzzled look. "I can't get through to the team. I keep getting a busy signal."

She shrugged. "Maybe one of them is on the phone."

He shook his head. "Nope, if the line is busy, I'm supposed to get a voicemail where I can leave a message."

"Then something's wrong with the satellite hookup."

"Maybe," he said doubtfully. "Or maybe this Janus had sabotaged the lab's communications gear before he or she decided to change sides."

"Why, what would that accomplish?" Lauren asked.

"Well, for one thing, it would keep the team from alerting the CDC that we had a lead to a possible cure, and that would give Janus's mercenaries a chance to kill us and get the plants before anyone in the States knew anything about them. But since Janus has now changed sides, it might just be to keep Blackman from suspecting his spy has turned until the congressman has a chance to nail his ass."

"So, what do we do now?"

He shrugged. "We meet the boat that the congressman has hopefully sent for us and arrange for transportation back to the lab."

"What about Janus?" Lauren asked.

"Our one big advantage is that Janus doesn't have any idea that we know there is a spy among us. For all Janus knows, the only person aware of his/her existence is Congressman O'Donnell and Colonel Blackman, and Janus will have no idea that O'Donnell will have called Battersee and alerted him to the existence of a spy on the team."

"Especially since Janus has presumably made the team incommunicado," Lauren said.

"That might just give us enough of an edge to smoke this Janus out before he/she can escape."

"So we're going to go back into the jungle and join up with the Wildfire Team, a team that we know Colonel Blackman has targeted for elimination?" Lauren questioned.

"Uh, when you put it that way . . ." Mason responded.

"And not only that, we don't have any idea who he has hired to do the killing or when they are scheduled to attack?"

"Ah . . . again, no we don't."

"Any chance we can get a squad of Marines to go back to the lab with us?" she asked.

"That might not be such a bad idea. Let me think about it."

Lauren gave him a sideways glance. "And since the sleeping arrangements are already tight, if any of those young, muscular Marines need a place to bunk . . ."

"Hey lady, Marines are used to roughing it. They can sleep in their pup tents, or sleeping bags, or whatever!"

She leaned over to put her hand on his shoulder. "Does that green look in your eyes mean you wouldn't want me sharing my bed with a Marine?"

"No, 'cause then I'd have to kill him, and Marines are notoriously difficult to kill."

They heard a laugh from behind them and turned to see Motzi, his face flaming red, laughing at them. "Señor Williams is . . . how you say . . . jealous!" he said, grinning at Mason.

"*Sí,* Motzi," Mason said, returning the grin, "*mucho* jealous!"

With that, they gathered up the rest of their gear and headed down the hill toward the river to see if the mercenaries had left their boat intact.

When they got there, they found a note attached to the bow of the boat. "Doc, I'm leaving your boat intact with the understanding that you will delay contacting the CDC or your team in the jungle until I've had a chance to sting Blackman. I should have our fees collected by midnight tonight since he can release money from his Cayman bank account into ours at most any time. After that, you're free to do with him what you will."

Bear had scrawled his name at the bottom of the note.

Mason let Lauren read it. "Are you going to give him the time he asked for?"

Mason shrugged. "Sure, we had an agreement. And besides, I don't mind seeing some of Colonel Blackman's ill-gotten gains going to a good cause."

"A good cause?"

"Yeah, Bear said this was his retirement money, so he's going to be out of the mercenary game, which is better for all concerned in my mind."

Lauren laughed. "I can't disagree with that."

They loaded their packs into the boat and Mason and Motzi pushed the boat out into the current, where it lazily headed toward the village of Tehuantepec a couple of miles downriver.

On the way, they heard the staccato roar of a large military helicopter taking off in the distance. Bear was on his way, Mason thought.

After about thirty minutes, they began to see dwellings and small buildings and shacks on both sides of the river, along with dozens of natives up to their knees in the river water washing out clothes and utensils and generally doing what they did every day of their lives.

Motzi called out in either rapid Spanish or Nahuatl to a couple of the ladies nearby and they laughed and called back something in the same language, which made Motzi blush a deep red color.

Lauren caught his look and couldn't resist teasing him. "Oh-ho, Motzi. What's going on? You got a new girlfriend?"

If possible, Motzi turned an even darker shade of red. "No, not that."

"So, what was that all about?" Lauren continued, not about to let him off the hook.

"Motzi ask how water was, and lady called back for me to take my clothes off and jump in and she would do same and join me in a swim."

Mason laughed. "Well, we've got a few minutes to spare; want to take her up on it, Motzi?"

Motzi shook his head rapidly. "No! Motzi just . . . how you say . . . teasing."

Lauren suddenly stood up in the bow of the boat and pointed. "Look, I think that's our transportation up ahead."

Mason turned and looked downriver and his mouth dropped open at the sight of one of the strangest watercraft he'd ever seen. It looked like a huge Zodiac-style boat with two fan-looking propellers on the rear and various and sundry other smaller structures on each side. The boat appeared to be some sort of hovercraft as it was floating a couple of feet off the surface of the river and moving in slow circles just inside the river's opening into the ocean.

There was what looked to be a fifty-caliber machine gun affixed to the bow with two Marines manning it, and the barrel was pointed directly at them.

Lauren looked worriedly at Mason. "They are expecting us, aren't they?"

"I certainly hope so."

He stood up and waved his arms. "Ahoy, the boat," he called. "I'm Dr. Mason Williams and these are my associates."

The engines on the boat stilled and the boat sunk down until it floated on the river current, until one of the large anchors on the starboard side was lowered into the river.

A naval officer with lieutenant commander bars on his collars stepped to the front of the boat. He said a couple of words to the men manning the machine gun and they relaxed, letting the barrel rise to point at the sky.

He waved at Mason, beckoning them onward. "Come aboard, Dr. Williams and crew," he added, smiling widely. "Glad to see you survived until we arrived."

Thirty minutes later they were aboard, their gear had been stored, and they were in the galley being treated to the first decent meal they'd had since they left the Cytotec lab.

The naval officer walked into the room and said, "Good evening and welcome to our LCAC. I am Lieutenant Commander Steven Piner."

Mason stood up and held out his hand. "Hello, Commander. I'm Dr. Mason Williams, and this is Dr. Lauren Sullivan, and our native guide and friend, Guatemotzi."

Piner shook hands with Lauren, but when he turned to

shake hands with Motzi he was surprised to see the boy snap to attention and give him a first-class salute, his face dead serious.

"I am named for the last and greatest Aztec emperor," Motzi intoned.

Piner grinned and returned the salute, "And I can see why your father gave you this honor, for you are surely a great warrior, also."

As Motzi beamed with pride, Piner gestured for them all to sit down. "Please, continue with your meal."

He took a cup of coffee from the steward and joined them, sitting at the head of the table so he could watch all of them as they talked.

"Commander," Mason said around a mouthful of roast beef. "You said this boat is called an LCAC?"

"Yes, it's a little easier than saying welcome to our Landing Craft Air Cushion, otherwise known as a hover-craft."

"Commander Piner," Lauren said, "would you mind telling us a little about the boat, as it is quite the strangest-looking craft I've ever seen."

Piner beamed, "Sure, ma'am, I'd be pleased to. The LCAC is used primarily as a landing craft by the United States Navy's Assault Craft Units. In addition to up to a full payload of helicopters, tanks, and sixty tons of cargo, we can transport twenty-four fully loaded, geared-up, and battle-ready Marines. Our top speed is seventy knots or about seventy-five mph and our range at that speed is about one hundred and forty miles, depending on how heavily loaded we are."

"Jesus," Mason said, eyebrows raised in surprise. "This thing really moves."

"Yeah, and since it's a hovercraft, over eighty percent

of the world's coastline is accessible to us. She's quite an asset."

"So, do you cross the ocean in this or are you carried by another ship?" Lauren asked.

"We're transported aboard the USS *Makin Island* out of San Diego, California. We were the closest asset to your position when you called for help."

"The USS *Makin Island*?" Mason asked, holding up his cup for a refill.

"All of the LCACs are carried aboard what is called the Wasp Class of Landing Helicopter Dock amphibious assault ships, or LHDs." Piner grinned, "You can see why the military loves their acronyms, since the official names of these things are quite cumbersome."

Lauren reached over and patted Mason's shoulder while grinning at Piner. "Mason, I think we're in very good hands indeed."

She held up her coffee cup in a toast to the commander, "Thank you for rescuing us, fair sir."

Piner nodded, blushing a slight bit. "You are quite welcome, ma'am."

"So what now?" Mason asked.

Piner shrugged. "That's up to you, Doctor. My orders, and they come from very high up, are to take you wherever you want to go and to give you any assistance you need—apparently up to and including going to war with Mexico if we need to."

He paused and looked intently at Mason. "If you don't mind my asking, just what the hell are you two up to?"

Mason glanced at Lauren, who nodded for him to go on. "Well, we might just have the beginnings of a cure for this plague that is sweeping the world, and there are a group of bad guys, including some in the Mexican military, who are trying to prevent us from getting the cure to the rest of the world."

Piner's face flushed red. "You mean you might have the answer to all these millions of people dying and some sons of bitches are trying to stop you?" he growled.

Mason nodded. "That's about the size of it, Commander."

Piner stood up. "Well, hell, then, my men and I will deliver you to the very gates of hell if need be to stop this plague."

"That won't be necessary, Commander." Mason took a pen and paper from the middle of the table and wrote on it and then handed it to Piner. "If you can deliver us and a squad of armed Marines to those coordinates, we should be able to take it from there."

"You got it, Doc. I'll take these to our navigator and we'll get you within helicopter range and then we'll get you delivered safe and sound as soon as we can."

Chapter 39

Houston

The United States was in the midst of the largest and most intensive airlift since the days of the Berlin Airlift in 1948 and 1949. Hospitals, clinics, and doctors' offices that had a surplus of antibiotics and IV fluids were donating their extras to places that were experiencing acute shortages.

Typically more rural areas were less hard hit by the plague than places with a more densely compacted population. It was the same with countries, but most of the less densely populated countries were also the poorest and their supplies were never very copious to begin with.

Under the auspices of the U.S. Air Force, practically every plane that could fly, as well as every pilot that was not sick with the plague, was being conscripted to fly medical supplies from one location to another, and it was starting to make a difference, as the number of new plague victims was starting to level out a bit.

People were hunkering down in their houses and staying away from crowds and other people and that also was making a difference. Only people with essential jobs were going to work, so the economy was taking an enormous hit, but compared to the loss of life, no one cared.

Dr. John Meeker at the Houston Baptist Hospital had long since been reduced to sending nurses and orderlies out to nearby supermarkets to buy as much sugar and salt and purified water as they could find, and he was directing the pharmacy staff and all available interns in the arcane art of making saline and glucose solutions from scratch since they were out of the manufactured supplies.

He looked up from a patient he was ministering to when a nurse called excitedly, "Dr. Meeker, you've got to come see this!"

He sighed, gave the nurse at his side some quick orders on what to do for the patient, and then he followed the other nurse down the hall and out to the loading bay at the rear of the hospital.

There was a large truck with green canvas over the top of the rear compartment being unloaded. There were cases and cases of IV fluids along with cardboard boxes labeled cephalexin, ciprofloxen, ampicillin, minocycline, and other assorted antibiotics, some of which he hadn't used in years but which he was delighted to have. They were trying many different combinations of antibiotics on the plague, hoping to hit some fortuitous combination of drugs that would either cure or at least slow down the progression of the illness.

So far they hadn't had much luck with the cure part but there was some evidence the massive onslaught of antibiotics was slowing the progression of some patients' disease.

He quietly clasped his hands, looked heavenward, and said softly, "Thank you, Lord."

And then he rolled up his sleeves and began to help unload the truck.

"Is there anything I can do?" the nurse asked.

He looked over his shoulder. "Yes, get every nurse and intern and orderly who is not directly caring for a patient down here to cart this stuff to the pharmacy so we can begin to use it."

Coast of Mexico

While they rested in the ward room as the LCAC raced up the coast of Mexico to get them within helicopter range of their Wildfire camp, Mason, Lauren, and Motzi watched TV news about the worldwide plague and its horrors.

After a while, Lauren glanced at Mason, "Why do you suppose this anthrax bacillus doesn't infect animals as the normal type of anthrax does?"

Mason shook his head. "I don't know for sure since we've been too busy looking for a cure to do a complete DNA sequencing on this particular hot-bug, but I would guess that the same mutation that caused this species to be transmissible from person to person also caused it to be unable to infect animals."

She wagged her head. "Thank God," she said. "Can you imagine how much more horrible the plague would be if it was also killing all warm-blooded mammals like the old anthrax did? We would be awash in dead animal bodies and then we'd have other plagues caused by illnesses related to that."

"I truly doubt mankind could have survived such a plague," Mason said seriously. "If we can extract a cure for the infection from these plants and even better a vaccine to prevent future infections in the next few days and get the results to the CDC within the week, I think we may be able to keep the worldwide death toll down to fifteen to twenty percent of the population rather than the thirty to forty percent if it is allowed to run its course unhindered by medicine."

Lauren shuddered. "Fifteen to twenty percent of almost four billion people is still horrendous."

"You're right, of course, but right now we must focus on the almost one billion people our cure will save rather than the billion already lost." He sighed and wiped a hand across his face. "God, the responsibility of what we have in those bags is almost too much for one man to bear."

"You're not alone, Mason. You've got me and Motzi and a whole lot of Marines who are going to help you get the needed cure, not to mention the support and help from members of your Wildfire Team."

Just then Commander Piner stuck his head in the door. "I'm told we'll be in range for your transfer for your flight to your coordinates in Mexico in about six hours, just before sunrise. So, if you're gonna arrive there bright-eyed and bushy-tailed, you'd better get some shut-eye. Dr. Sullivan, since we're not yet coed on this vessel, I'm giving you my stateroom to sleep in." He glanced at Mason, "Doc, you and Motzi can bunk down here in the wardroom."

"What about the Marines?" Mason asked.

"Those guys could sleep standing up if they had to, but we've fixed up a tarp on the rear deck to keep the sea-spray off of them so they'll be fine in their sleeping bags."

Aware of Piner's eyes on them, Mason walked over to

Lauren and gave her a brotherly hug and then he and Motzi dove into their packs to get their sleeping bags ready while she followed Piner out the door toward his cabin.

Mexico City

It was almost midnight before Bear and his team landed at the Mexico City airport. As they piled out of the chopper, they unloaded two duffle bags of assorted plants and flowering bushes, each different type bound together by twine into bunches. They'd spent about an hour roaming around the jungle and picking up anything that looked the least bit exotic or special before they climbed aboard the helicopter for the trip to Mexico City.

"What about the blood samples we don't have?" Jinx asked Bear quietly as they unloaded their gear.

"Leave that to me," Bear said. He turned to their pilot and said, "A couple of my men have come down with jungle fever, but I want to make sure they don't have the plague. Can you direct us to the airport doctor's office?"

At the mention of the word plague, the pilot blanched almost white, adjusted the white cloth mask that virtually everyone was wearing nowadays, and pointed toward the left wing of the airport terminal. "What do I tell General Mendez? He is waiting to talk to you about your mission."

"Tell him we'll meet him in the airport manager's office as soon as I'm sure my men don't have the plague . . . unless he'd like to meet us before we know for sure?"

The pilot held up his hands palms out. "No, no, I am sure the general will be happy to wait until your men have been tested. I will tell him myself."

"Thank you," Bear said with a smirk, and then he and his men took off at a jog toward the airport doctor's office.

Thirty minutes later, they were outside the airport manager's office with a briefcase containing thirty vials of blood and twenty spit-soaked Q-tips in vials labeled for DNA testing.

"You don't think we took too much of that doctor's blood, do you?" Babe asked, a concerned look on his face.

"Nah," Bear replied. "He'll heal up fine as soon as he wakes up from that shot of phenobarbital you gave him."

He knocked once and entered the door without waiting for a reply. Behind a desk at the far end of the room sat a corpulent, sweating, mustachioed Mexican in a Mexican Army general's uniform.

"You must be General Mendez?" Bear asked, striding forward to shake the man's hand.

"*Sí*, and you are Señor Bear?"

"That's right, General. I assume you can contact Colonel Blackman so we can conclude our business?"

Mendez nodded, his eyes narrow as he glared at Bear's men standing behind him. "Your men, they are all right?"

"Yeah, just a touch of jungle fever, no sign of anthrax, the doctor said."

"And the specimens? You have them?"

"Yep. Here they are," and Bear handed the duffle bags and briefcase over the desk. "Be careful with that case, it contains the blood and DNA samples Dr. Williams took from the villagers."

Mendez unzipped the duffle bags and bent to look inside them. "And this Dr. Williams?"

"He is swimming with the fishes in the river, along with his bitch friend and the native boy," Jinx piped up from behind Bear, a snarl on his lips.

Mendez pursed his lips and smiled. "Colonel Blackman will be most happy to hear that." He stood up and put his general's cap on his head. "I will leave immediately by jet airplane to take these samples to the colonel."

He stopped suddenly, his mouth agape when three MP5 machine guns were suddenly pointed at his midsection.

"Uh, I'm afraid that is not going to happen until I talk with Colonel Blackman, General."

Mendez's lips tightened, but he stepped back behind the desk, dialed the phone, and handed it to Bear.

A moment later, Blackman answered, "Hello, General. Did everything go all right?"

"It's not the general, Blackman. It's Bear."

"Oh . . ." there was a pause. "So, Bear, is everything on track?"

"Yep, the general has all the plant specimens as well as the blood and DNA samples Dr. Williams took. Now all that has to happen for him to be on his way to you with them is for you to pay me and my men our fee."

"But, that wasn't our deal!" Blackman bellowed. "You were to be paid when I got the samples and made sure they were legitimate."

"That deal was made before you assigned us to terminate your spy, Janus, in order to tie up loose ends. Now my men and me are figuring we might just qualify as loose ends, too, so we'd just as soon be paid now and then we'll be glad to finish your dirty work for you, Colonel."

"I will not be blackmailed like this!" Blackman shouted. "I'll have you and your men hunted down and . . ."

"Hold this phone, General," Bear said and handed the phone to Mendez while Blackman was in midshout.

"Jinx," Bear said.

"Yes, sir," Jinx replied and he took the duffle bags and briefcase from Mendez and stepped over and sat them in the corner of the office.

Hoss then pulled a small bottle of alcohol from his coat pocket and began to pour it over the duffle bags and briefcase while Bear took out a Zippo lighter and snapped its flame to life.

As he bent over to hold it next to the alcohol-soaked duffels, Mendez shouted, "Wait!"

He began to speak rapidly into the phone, describing what Bear and his men were up to.

After a few seconds, his face pale, he handed the phone back to Bear.

"You were saying, Colonel?" Bear asked sarcastically.

"Okay, you win. I'll have the money transferred to the account numbers in the Caymans you gave me. But . . ."

Bear cut him off. "You've got fifteen minutes, Colonel, and then we have ourselves a wienie roast." He hung up the phone and looked at his watch.

Glancing at Mendez, he stepped over behind the desk, pulled Mendez to his feet, and pushed him aside. He sat down and put his iPhone on the desk and keyed in the Internet function and logged onto the Cayman bank's website where they did business.

A moment later he smiled, keyed in his account number, and transferred all of the money Blackman had just deposited into another account that Blackman knew nothing about.

He stood up, and Jinx sat down and did the same with his accounts, as did Hoss and Psycho after him.

When they had all moved their money out of Blackman's reach, Bear shook Mendez's hand. "General, we're gonna borrow your helicopter for a short ride to where we have our plane stashed. We'll radio you the coordinates of where it can be picked up in a couple of hours. It was nice doing business with you."

Jinx gave a mock salute as they left the office. "Tell your friend Blackman we'll be in touch . . . and to keep looking over his shoulder."

Hoss touched his forehead. "A pleasure, General."

Psycho just pursed his lips and gave a smacking kiss good-bye.

Babe just nodded, and then smiled a smile that made the hair on the back of Mendez's neck rise.

Suddenly he felt a rumbling in his stomach and then a horrible stench arose from his chair. He realized he'd soiled his pants and ran quickly toward the nearest restroom.

Tlateloco

Mason and Motzi were awoken at five o'clock in the morning to the aroma of freshly brewed coffee, scrambled eggs, crisp bacon, and what looked to be homemade biscuits.

Just as they were digging in, Lauren appeared in the doorway looking fresh as a daisy.

As she helped herself to coffee and breakfast and sat down to join the men, the commander walked in, a sheepish grin on his face.

"Uh-oh," Mason said. "What's up?"

"In a clear violation of all standards of political correctness, the men made me promise to give you this, Dr. Sullivan."

He handed her a rolled-up piece of thick paper.

She unrolled it, read it, and then burst out laughing, her face flaming red.

Mason raised his eyebrows and she showed it to him. It read, "Dr. Lauren Sullivan" in an elaborate handwritten calligraphy script across the top of the page. Below it read, "Voted the doctor most Marines would love to be lost in the jungle with."

Mason also laughed and showed the paper to Motzi, who raised his eyebrows in question, obviously unable to read the fancy script. "I'll bet the vote was one hundred percent," Mason said.

The commander blushed again and he said, "Actually there was one dissenter. The cook voted for you, Dr. Williams."

"You're kidding," Mason said, with a puzzled look on his face.

The commander shrugged, "It's a new Marine Corps. We don't ask and they don't tell."

Now both Lauren and Mason laughed out loud, with Piner joining in.

Mason glanced at a still puzzled Motzi and between guffaws he said, "I'll explain to you later."

"Enough fun and games," Piner said when he'd finally managed to quit laughing. "Get geared up, you guys. We'll be in range in fifteen minutes and we need to get you on the chopper."

As Mason rose, he said, "I didn't see any helicopters on deck when you picked us up."

"You're right, Doc. The *Makin Island* has steamed on an intercept course with us all night and is now only a few miles away. She's sending over one of her CH-53 Sea Stallion helicopters."

"Sea Stallion?" Lauren asked.

"You've probably seen earlier versions on old films of the evacuation of Saigon at the end of the Vietnam War," Piner said. "They're the ones you saw picking up people from the embassies and military camps. They've been updated quite a bit, and now they're great for transporting personnel and are just right for jungle overflight and letting you guys down in small areas surrounded by trees and jungle bush."

"Can they land on the deck to pick us up?" Mason asked.

Piner shook his head. "No, but they'll hover just a few feet above the deck and we'll make sure you are all lifted aboard."

"What about the Marines?" Mason asked.

"Who do you think will be standing in line to help lift Dr. Sullivan aboard?" Piner replied with a wink.

Then he smiled. "But you and Motzi just might have to get aboard on your own."

Chapter 40

Just before Mason left the ward room on the way to the helicopter pickup, his sat-phone buzzed and he took the call.

He turned his back to Lauren and Motzi and spoke in low tones for several moments, and then he nodded and hung up the phone.

Lauren gazed at him through squinted eyes. "You got that cat-that-ate-the-canary look on your face, boss man. You're up to something . . . I know you."

As Motzi followed Piner out onto the deck, Mason pulled Lauren aside. "That was Bear. His team concluded their business with Blackman last night, and they are in their plane on the way to disappearing forever."

She raised her eyebrows. "So? What're you guys now . . . best buds? He call you to say bye-bye?"

Mason put his hand on her shoulder. "Right before we split up yesterday, I asked him to tell me about Janus since he was leaving Blackman's employ anyway."

"And?"

"He said he didn't know Janus's real name, but that his best guess was that Janus was a female on the Wildfire

Team and that she must've had some feelings for me 'cause she tried to get Blackman to guarantee that I wouldn't be killed by Bear and his men when they stole the specimens."

"Then it's got to be either Shirley Cole or Suzanne Elliot, right?"

He nodded. "Yeah, and what's more, Bear said that he told Blackman that they'd killed all three of us while stealing the specimens so if Blackman tells Janus that, then the one of the two women who is most surprised to see us alive will probably be Janus."

As they walked toward the waiting helicopter, Mason hung back and motioned for Piner to join him.

"What's up, Doc?" Piner said with a grin. "I've always wanted to say that," he added.

Mason smiled, having heard the old joke a million times. "Here, Commander," he said, handing the man a small duffle bag.

"What's this?"

"These are most of the specimens we retrieved from the natives in Mexico. I need you to get these to the CDC in Atlanta as soon as possible so they can start working on a cure for the plague."

"But, I thought that's what you're gonna be doing down at your lab in the jungle."

Mason nodded. "We are, but the CDC has much better equipment and lots of really, really smart doctors who can probably do a better job there than we can in the jungle. I am taking a few of the plants and blood samples with us, but the world is counting on you getting the rest of these to Atlanta as fast as humanly possible, Commander."

Piner nodded, a serious look on his face. "I'll get this duffle over to the *Makin Island* and have one of their helicopters rendezvous with the nearest ship with a jet onboard, and I'll tell them to have the pilot use the afterburner the entire way, Doctor."

Mason clapped Piner on the shoulder. "Good man!" He glanced over to where several Marines were jostling to see who would be the one to "help" Lauren up onto the deck of the hovering helicopter.

"Do you think they'll fight like that over me?" Mason asked, smiling.

Piner shook his head. "Doubtful, Doc, doubtful."

And he was right. Mason had to fight his own way up onto the chopper with no help from the Marines, who just stood there smiling, all their eyes on Lauren.

As they settled into their jump seats, Mason cast a suspicious eye on Lauren. "By the way," he said, "Motzi and I had to shower in the ship's crew showers last night."

She cut her eyes toward him and with an impish grin, said, "Uh-huh?"

"You're looking very clean this morning . . . just where did you shower?"

"In the crew's shower," she said.

"What?"

"Yes, but two very nice young Marines volunteered to stand watch to guard my modesty." She smiled, "They said the entire crew had drawn lots to see who got to stand guard and that they'd won."

In spite of himself, Mason laughed as he took her hand in his and squeezed it as they lifted off from the ship.

Janus spat into the sat-phone, "You bastard! I told you not to let your dogs hurt him!"

Blackman replied. "I already told you, Janus. Those

were my instructions, but when dealing with the kind of men we use to do this kind of job, accidents will happen."

"You'll pay for this, Blackie."

"Oh, don't be so melodramatic. This is as much your fault as it is mine, Janus. After all, it was you who came to me asking to work with me against your masters at the CDC."

"Don't remind me."

"Anyhow, now that the samples are on their way here, you can be of more use up here in Maryland than you can down there in Mexico. When Bear and his men arrive to . . . uh . . . take care of the rest of the Wildfire Team, why don't you return with them and come to work for me full time? I can always use someone with your . . . special skill set."

"How would we explain my survival when the rest of the team ends up dead?"

"Oh, we can say you were out gathering samples of plant life when the lab must have been attacked by a band of narco-traffickers looking for drugs. I can have Bear drop you off a few miles from the perimeter guards and you can approach them with a horrible story about the deaths of your friends and the destruction of the lab."

"I'll think about it," Janus said hanging up the phone and thinking "in a pig's eye." She knew Blackman was just offering her the job with him to put her at ease until he could have his hit men take her out with the rest of the Wildfire Team. She shook her head, thinking if Blackman ever came within her reach he was a dead man. Janus owed him for what he'd done to Mason Williams, a man Janus had loved for many years.

Janus put the phone away and stared off into the jungle, wondering if Mason had felt any pain when the mercenaries had killed him. Finally, wiping tears from her eyes, she entered the Bio-Lab to continue pretending to work on a cure for the plague while she figured out a way to disappear into the jungle just before Bear and his men arrived to execute the team.

Mexico City

Jinx looked over at Bear in the copilot's seat as their small airplane lifted into the air and banked over the jungle on a northward course. "Okay, where to, boss?"

Bear stared out the window for a moment before answering. "You can drop me off in Baltimore. After that, you and the men can go anywhere in the world you'd like."

Jinx's eyebrows rose. "Baltimore? Why there?"

Bear shrugged. "I've got some unfinished business with Blackie."

"Oh?"

"Yeah. Now that I've got enough money to retire and sit on a beach somewhere drinking umbrella drinks, I don't want to have to spend my time looking over my shoulder."

He looked over at Jinx. "Blackie is a fool, but he's a hard man with a lot of resources at his command, and he's not going to take it lightly that we double-crossed him. Remember, he's still expecting us to take out the Wildfire Team in the jungle, and I expect he'll be a mite pissed when he discovers the samples we gave him are bogus and that we ignored his orders to kill the scientists at the lab."

"You think he'll send some hard-dicks to come looking for us?"

"I think we can count on it. After all, that's what we'd do . . . right?"

Jinx nodded thoughtfully. "I think you're right." He looked over his shoulder at the other men in the rear of the airplane. "But boss, the man lives on a fuckin' army base. You might just need some help to get to him."

Bear shrugged. "I'll admit the thought had crossed my mind."

Jinx grinned. "Good. Then that's settled. We'll all come with you and we'll take that bastard down as our last official job together."

Bear showed his teeth. "I can't think of a better way to end our association."

Chapter 41

Suzanne Elliot entered the Bio-Lab and almost ran into Eduardo Matos. She stepped back and gave a low whistle. "Boy, Eduardo, lookin' good, my man," she said with a lascivious leer, trying to cover her grief with the casual banter she was known for.

The short and previously very pudgy man beamed and preened. "Do you really think so, Señorita Elliot?"

"Yeah, I do. You must have lost fifty pounds, Eduardo," she said, thinking anthrax had been particularly good for this pig of a man. Hell, he could probably see his prick for the first time in twenty years.

"Fifty-three," he said proudly, patting his stomach. "There is nothing like nearly dying of a prehistoric illness to make *un hombre* lose weight."

Suzanne poked him in his now flat belly. "Now, you stay away from the enchiladas and beans and eat more healthy and I'll bet the lovely, young, señoritas will be following you around like starving puppies."

Now he blushed. "I am very afraid my wife would not take kindly to such activities," he said with feigned pomposity.

Suzanne laughed and elbowed him with a wink, "What the little lady doesn't know won't hurt her, will it Eduardo?"

He gave a hearty laugh. "No, but it very well may hurt me."

Shirley Cole and Joel Schumacher walked up in the narrow corridor. "Are you teasing our guest?" Shirley asked with a mock frown.

"No, just telling him how good he looks since the illness caused him to lose so much weight," Suzanne answered.

"Well, don't embarrass him too much, 'cause he's on his way back to Mexico City today. The INAH is sending a helicopter to pick him up and take him home," Joel said.

"Good for you, Eduardo," Suzanne said, holding up a fist.

Matos glanced down at her fist, a puzzled look on his face.

Joel took his hand, made it into a fist, and bumped Suzanne's fist with his. "A new American custom, Eduardo," Joel said, grinning.

"Ah, I will have to remember that to show my children. They are always interested in anything having to do with America and your strange customs."

Shirley put a hand to her ear. "I do believe I hear your helicopter coming in for a landing, Eduardo."

She eased around them and went to the door. "It should land in the clearing about fifty yards to the north."

"Come on," Suzanne said, taking his arm. "We'll all walk you out to your ride, after all, you are our first plague cure and we wouldn't want you to get lost in the jungle."

* * *

In the descending helicopter, Mason spoke into his helmet microphone. "Let me be the first to exit the helicopter. I want to give whichever person is Janus a real surprise."

"That is strange," Matos said, using his palm to shield his eyes from the ever bright tropical sun. "That is an American Navy helicopter. I thought the INAH was going to send a Mexican military helicopter for me."

The entire staff of the Bio-Lab had turned out to see Matos off, and they all stood there with hands up for shade looking at the chopper as it settled into the clearing in a wall of dust.

As the rotors slowed and the dust began to settle, a man strode out of the cloud and walked rapidly toward them.

Suzanne Elliot gave a strangled cry and fainted dead away, sinking to the ground before anyone could catch her.

Mason Williams walked up and spread his arms to the group. "Daddy's home, children," he cried with a wide grin.

Following close behind him, Lauren gave a narrow-eyed glance at Suzanne lying on the ground and then smiled up at the group. "I'm not Mommy," she said laughing, "but I'm home, too."

"And me!" Guatemotzi hollered as he ran out of the dust cloud carrying their duffle bags and backpacks in his sinewy arms.

The group didn't know whether to hug Mason or to see to Elliot, who lay on the ground moaning, "It can't be . . . it can't be . . ."

Matos knelt next to her and began to gently pat her cheeks. "Señorita Elliot . . . Señorita Elliott, are you all right?"

"She'll be just fine," Mason said cavalierly, picking her up and slinging her over his shoulder like a side of beef. He strode to the lab, entered, and went into the ICU cubicle and flopped her down on the bed there.

The rest of the crew followed him, puzzled expressions on their faces.

"What in the name of all that is holy is going on, Mason?" Sam Jakes asked, anger in his voice at the way Mason was manhandling Suzanne.

"Yes," Shirley asked, moving to stand beside Suzanne. "Why are you being so rough?"

As Suzanne began to come around, Mason stepped to the head of the bed and addressed the group. "I believe Suzanne is a spy, code-named Janus, who has been working undercover for Colonel Blackman at USAMRIID to thwart our finding a cure for the plague, or to steal it for him if we found one before the army did."

Everyone except Lauren gasped and seemed to step back from Suzanne, as if her treachery might be contagious.

She moaned and moved her head back and forth as she began to come to. Upon hearing Mason's words, her eyes filled and she wiped at her tears as she stared at Mason with anguished eyes. "How did you find out?"

"The mercenaries your boss hired to kill us and steal the specimens told me."

Suzanne laid her head back down on the pillow with her arm draped over her face and began to cry softly.

Mason stepped to her side and searched her white clinic jacket, pulling a sat-phone from her left pocket. "Come on," Mason said to the others, walking out of the room.

When the room was empty except for Suzanne, he locked the door from the outside and walked to the dining room so they could tell the others the tale of their trip and all that had happened to them since they'd been gone.

"Shirley, would you make a large pot of coffee?" he asked. "We've got a helluva story to tell and it's going to take quite a while."

She stared at him through slitted eyes. "Would some chocolate cookies go good with that? I just happen to have a fresh batch cooling in the galley."

"Damn right," he said.

Baltimore, Maryland

Colonel Woodrow Blackman entered his office three days later at 0630 with a cup of coffee in one hand and a sheaf of papers in the other. He hadn't slept for the past two nights waiting for word from Bear that he had taken Janus out, but he'd heard nothing.

He did not look happy and had a deep scowl on his face as he read what was written on the top sheet of paper. "That son of a bitch is a dead man," he muttered as he reached over and flipped on the lights.

When he looked up from the paper, his hand jerked, spilling scalding hot coffee all over the front of his uniform.

"Goddamn!" he exclaimed, shaking his hand and glaring with wide eyes at the group of men sitting scattered around his office.

"What the fuck . . . ," he started to bellow until he looked into the barrel of the ACP .45 caliber semiautomatic handgun Bear was pointing at his chest. The hole looked big enough to get lost in.

He swallowed whatever it was he was about to say and glanced around at the other men with Bear. Evidently he didn't like what he saw in their eyes, as his hand began to shake and sweat popped out on his forehead.

Bear smiled. "Have a seat, Colonel."

Blackie eased around his desk and sat down slowly. He placed the empty coffee cup on his blotter and the sheaf of papers on his desk in front of him.

A sickly smile appeared on his face and he slowly reached for his phone. "Hey, Bear . . . guys . . . let me order us all some coffee . . ."

Bear wagged his head side to side and said in a low voice, "Put the phone down, Colonel. Let's keep this meeting just between us for now."

"S . . . s . . . sure, Bear," Blackie stuttered. "What can I do for you?"

Bear's forehead creased, and he asked, "What were you cursing about when you came in just now?"

"Oh, nothing."

Jinx stood up from his chair in the corner and crossed to lean over and read the sheet of paper Blackie had been holding in his hand. "Boss, this here paper Blackie was readin' says all the DNA samples are from the same person, as were all of the blood samples."

He reached down and turned the paper over. "And this next one says that all of the plants rendered for examination are common variety jungle plants with no medicinal value at all, whatever the hell that means."

"It means you fucked me, you bastards!" Blackie exclaimed, leaning forward and slapping his palm down on his desk, trying to assert some of the authority he was used to carrying.

Jinx put a puzzled look on his face. "Did we fuck the Colonel, boss?" he asked Bear.

Bear grinned. "Yep. An' we didn't even kiss him first."

Blackie looked from one to the other of the men and his

face paled. "Uh, just why are you here, Bear? You got your money and you screwed me, so what do you want now?"

"Who else is in this with you, Blackie? I know you don't have the balls or the brains to put all this together without some high-powered help."

Blackie shook his head. "I'm not going to tell you that, Bear. As long as you don't know who else knows about your involvement, you can't afford to kill me or they'll make sure you never live to spend the money you stole from us."

Bear cut his eyes to Psycho who was sitting across the room. "Psycho, see if you can convince Blackie to give us the information we need."

Psycho was on his feet in an instant and before Blackie could move, the point of Psycho's KA-BAR knife was almost touching his right eyeball.

Psycho leaned in close to Blackie's ear and whispered, "I'm not near as good with one of these as Blade was, but I bet I can figure it out, Colonel."

Bear smiled, but there was no humor in it. "Do you know how Psycho got his nickname, Blackie?"

Blackie opened his mouth to speak, but nothing came out but a strangled gurgle.

"Nod your head if you don't want to find out," Bear added after a moment.

Blackie glanced up into Psycho's red-rimmed, crazy eyes and he slowly nodded his head.

"Shit," Psycho muttered and he slid his KA-BAR back into its scabbard and he sat back down.

Bear raised his eyebrows and looked at Blackie. "We're all ears, boss," he said in a low voice dripping with sarcasm.

Blackie sighed and leaned back in his chair, frantically trying to think of some way out of this situation. After a moment, he figured if he couldn't bargain his way out of this, about the only thing he could hope for was a quick and relatively painless death.

"The only other man who knows about you and your team is General Mac McGuire."

"The same McGuire who sent us to you?" Babe asked.

Blackie looked at him and nodded. "One and the same."

"Does he know our real identities or just our nick-names?" Bear asked.

"Hell, I don't even know your real identities," Blackie pleaded. "You have nothing to fear from either one of us."

"Pick up the phone and tell your Adjutant Lieutenant Collins that you'd like him to go over to the canteen and pick you up some breakfast," Bear said.

Blackie shook his head, his eyes wide. "If I do that you'll kill me!"

Bear sighed. "We can kill you anyway, Blackie. All it takes is for me to let Psycho loose on you with that KA-BAR and Collins wouldn't hear a thing. I just need you to get rid of him so we can sneak out of here without being seen."

He grinned amiably. "After all, as you just said, we don't have anything to fear from you or McGuire."

Blackie thought about it for a moment and then he picked up his phone and pushed a button.

"Yes, sir?" Collins said.

"Jeremy, I'm kinda hungry this mornin'. How about going over to the canteen and pickin' us both up some breakfast? I'll pay you for it when you get back."

"Yes, sir!" Collins answered and hung up the phone.

"Give him a minute and then peek out the door and let us know when the coast is clear," Bear ordered.

When they heard the outer door open and shut, Blackie stood up and peeked out of his door. "Okay, he's gone. You can leave now."

As he sat back down at his desk, Bear moved over and held out his hand as if to shake. "Pleasure doing business with you, Colonel."

Blackie scowled, but he held out his right hand, "Sorry I can't say the same thing."

As they took hands, Bear came out from behind his back with his left hand and put a silencer against Blackie's right temple and pulled the trigger.

The automatic coughed once and the side of Blackie's head exploded all over the opposite wall.

Bear unscrewed the silencer and put the gun in Blackie's limp right hand, which was hanging down at his side.

He looked over his shoulder at Jinx. "You got the paperwork?" he asked.

"Right here, boss," Jinx said, and he took the forged registration papers for the pistol out of his pocket and stashed them in the colonel's bottom desk drawer.

Bear then took a tissue out of his pocket and wiped his left hand with the tissue and then transferred some of the gunpowder residue to Blackie's right hand, just in case the crime scene guys thought to check for it.

As the men started to leave, Jinx asked, "We goin' after McGuire next?"

Bear grinned. "Whatta you think?"

"Cool," Jinx said as he moved through the empty outer office. "I ain't never killed a general before."

Chapter 42

Mason took his time telling the Wildfire Team of their adventures in the Mexican jungle, and by the time he'd finished all of the cookies and most of the coffee had been consumed.

The team was flabbergasted and dismayed when he came to how he'd learned of the spy named Janus and how she'd conspired to undo all of the good works the team had accomplished, not to mention her complicity in the plan to have the Wildfire Team exterminated.

Jakes shook his head, "I just can't believe Suzanne would do that. Just think of all the people she would've consigned to an early grave if she'd managed to derail our finding of a cure to this deadly disease."

"Believe it, Sam," Mason said. "Evidently, she is a true believer in what USAMRIID is doing and there is nothing as dangerous as a true believer."

"I can almost see a true ideologue conspiring for US-AMRIID to have control of the cure for this plague, but to agree with its leader to kill all of us . . . her friends who have been more like family than coworkers for more than five years? That is beyond the pale," Shirley Cole said, shaking her head in disgust.

When no one had anything to add, Mason stood up and parceled out the specimens and plants to the various team members. "Now, I want you all to get to work and don't spare the horsepower. The Battleship and his team back at the CDC are also working on these samples and I would like our team to be the one to come up with a reliable cure first." He spread his arms and grinned. "After all, aren't we the world-famous Wildfire Team?"

Everyone laughed, got up from the table, and went to work on the samples.

Joel Schumacher said, "I'll get on the net and run down everything I can about all of these plants and see if anyone has already done any in-depth chemical analyses of their composition. It might just save us some time."

Shirley Cole took a few of the plant samples and said, "I'll grind up a sample of each of the plants and test them against the anthrax colonies I've got growing in the lab. The ones that show promise in killing the bacteria will be the first to go under the electron microscope for further analysis."

Lionel Johnson picked up the tubes of blood samples. "I'll run these through the blood analyzer and see if any unusual antibody formations show up. Those that look different or strange I'll flag for further, more in-depth analysis."

Mason nodded. "Good. While you guys are getting started on that, I think I'll go have a talk with Suzanne and see if I can't find out more about why she decided to betray us and everything that we stand for."

Lauren asked, "Is there anything a professor of archaeology who knows next to nothing about chemistry or medicine can do to help?"

Shirley took her arm. "Come with me dear, and I'll show you how to grind up plants like an expert."

When Mason got to the ICU cubicle, he saw that Suzanne had recovered from her faint and was busily pacing back and forth in the small room.

He unlocked the door and entered the room, holding out a cup of Shirley's steaming coffee. "Here," he said. "It looks like you could use this."

She glanced at him with a bleak expression and sat on the hospital bed in the center of the room. He handed her the coffee and she took a sip, and then her eyes watered.

"Cream with two sugars, just like I like it. You remembered."

He sat on a stool in the corner of the room. "Of course I remember, Suzanne. We've been teammates for almost five years." He hesitated, and then he added, "And I thought friends for at least that long."

She stared at him with a strange expression on her face. "Friends . . . yeah, I guess you could say that." She had no intention of further humiliating herself by letting on how much and for how long she had loved him over the years.

He pursed his lips. "Suzanne, the team and I are having a hard time understanding why you did what you did. Would you care to tell me about it?"

She took a long swig of the coffee and then let out a sigh. "You wouldn't understand."

"Try me."

She glanced down at the wedding ring on the third finger of her right hand. "You never asked me why I wear this ring."

"I figured you'd tell me when you were ready."

"It belongs to my brother." She looked up at him. "His wife left him when he came home from the Gulf War suffering from Gulf War syndrome. He threw it in the trash the day she left, but I saved it so that I would never forget."

"Forget what?" he asked, puzzled.

She took a deep breath. "Okay, I guess you deserve the full story. I'm an army brat, Mason. My father was a distinguished army physician who served in the Vietnam War. When he came home several cancers ate the flesh right off his bones. The army blamed it on Agent Orange, but I never believed that."

She paused to finish her coffee. "I read up on it and found that Agent Orange was studied up one side and down the other and there was never any sign that it would be carcinogenic."

She shook her head. "Hell no, it wasn't Agent Orange that killed my dad. I believe the Vietcong must have used some sort of chemical or biologic agent against our troops over there. One that we never found out about . . . or at least, one that we were never told about."

He stared at her, beginning to see where her obsession with biological and chemical warfare must have come from.

She glanced at him and gave a sad smile. "And that's not all. The army brass has always tried to say that Gulf War syndrome is due to the pollutants in the air from the burning oil wells of Kuwait."

She wagged her head. "I don't believe it for a minute."

He took a deep breath, realizing she was on the verge of being a paranoid psychotic. "So, it is your contention that your brother's illness was also caused by biologic or chemical weapons unleashed by Saddam Hussein?"

"Of course. Don't you see, Mason. If all the other countries arrayed against the United States have already or will in the future unleash these weapons, then we must stay in the game ourselves and develop our own biologic and chemical weapons to combat theirs."

"So, you were willing to let a third of the world's population die, almost a billion and a half people, just so Colonel Blackman could get a cure and a vaccine against this anthrax so he could use it as a weapon?"

Her eyes widened and she looked like he had slapped her in the face. "Of course not! He promised me that once we had the formula for the vaccine and the cure he would make all of it the world needed and would stop the plague in its tracks."

"And you believed him? An evil megalomaniac who thought nothing of having anyone who stood in his way murdered?"

She paled. "He . . . he gave me his word."

He stood up and took the coffee cup from her limp hands. "Oh, Suzanne, you are so naive and so, so misguided."

Without looking back, he exited the room and locked the door behind him.

He took out his sat-phone and called the CDC. When he was connected with Dr. Battersee, he said, "Have the samples and specimens arrived yet?"

"Yes, they just got here. I've already put them in the pipeline for full analysis."

"Grant, I need you to call your contacts at the army and tell them that Colonel Woodrow Blackman has installed a spy onto our team and has been working against us to delay us from finding a cure or vaccine for the plague."

"I know, Mason," Battersee said, surprising Mason. "Congressman O'Donnell called me while you were on your jaunt down the Mexican river and filled me in. He got his information from the spy, Janus, who evidently feared for her own life from Blackman." He chuckled, "In fact, it was O'Donnell who managed to get the Navy to come to your rescue, not me."

"So, you probably also know he was responsible for the black-ops team sent into the Mexican jungle to kill us and steal our specimens before we could get back to civilization."

"Yes, O'Donnell filled me in on that, too, and he has instituted a full congressional investigation into both Blackman and General McGuire." He hesitated, and then he added, "But Mason, I guess you haven't heard. Colonel Blackman was just found dead in his office. Preliminary indications are he took his own life."

Mason smiled and shook his head. Bear, he thought. The man certainly didn't let any grass grow beneath his feet.

"Well, Blackman certainly didn't do this on his own, and it sounds like this McGuire might have been in on it, too. If you don't mind, Grant, keep me informed of what O'Donnell finds out. I don't want to have to keep looking over my shoulders until this is finished."

"Okay, Mason, if you think it's necessary."

"And Grant, be extremely careful who you talk to from now on. We have no idea how far up the chain of command the rot extends—McGuire might not be the end of it and whomever else is involved might try to

cover his tracks by getting rid of those of us directly involved in searching for the cure to the plague."

Baltimore

At that moment, General Mac McGuire was in his ar-
mored staff car on the way to check out Colonel Blackman's office. He'd ordered the entire office sealed off as
a possible crime scene so that he would have time to get
there and sterilize anything in the office that might impli-
cate him in the plot to steal the cure for the plague. He
had no idea Janus had already given his name to Congressman O'Donnell, or that the congressman had already
launched an investigation in which his name figured
prominently.

About two miles from the army base, they rounded a
corner and his driver slammed on the brakes to avoid a
car that was crosswise blocking the road.

When they'd come to a full stop, General McGuire
leaned over the seat and told his driver to get out and see
what the problem was.

Alone in the car he heard a roaring like an approaching
freight train.

He whirled in his seat and looked out the rear window
of the staff car and saw a driverless eighteen-wheeler
bearing down on him at forty miles an hour. He just had
time to scream before the gasoline tanker plowed into his
car, exploding and engulfing both the auto and General
McGuire in a horrendous wall of flames.

His driver was blown off his feet and knocked unconscious by the blast but was otherwise unharmed.

Bear and his team shielded their faces from the heat as

they emerged from the forest alongside the road and got into the car blocking the highway and pulled away, another job completed.

Jinx leaned his head out of the driver's side window and whistled softly. "Good thing this is a stolen car, boss. All the paint on this side has been melted plumb off."

"You didn't hurt yourself when you jumped out of that eighteen-wheeler, did you, Babe?" Bear asked over his shoulder.

Babe answered from the rear seat. "Naw, boss. Piece of cake."

Bear leaned back in the front seat, pulled out a cigar, and lit it, thinking that by this time next week he'd be on a beach drinking mai tais with his money earning ten percent.

He grinned around the cigar, realizing his nephew Victor could now go to any college he wished since cost was no object. Hell, maybe Patricia would even let him come visit them once in a while now that he was a retired man of leisure.

Chapter 43

Tlateloco

For the next several hours, Mason moved from one member of his team to another, checking on their progress and in some cases offering suggestions on additional steps to take to find a cure.

Finally, he took a break and went in search of Lauren. He had some unfinished business with her that needed clearing up; the thought of her and their time in the jungle river kept intruding on his mind and screwing up his concentration.

He stood in the doorway to Shirley's lab and watched as the two women worked quietly and efficiently side by side. Lauren was busily grinding up plants while Shirley was examining the slurry under her various microscopes.

Lauren's hair was bound up in a ponytail, and as she turned her face to wipe off a drop of sweat, she noticed him standing there staring at her.

"Uh-oh," she said in a stage whisper to Shirley, "watch it girlfriend, the boss is checking up on us."

Shirley turned around and shook her hair out of her eyes and glared at Mason. "So, if you don't have anything better to do than to skulk around and check up on the worker bees, I've got some samples that need staining."

Mason blushed and stammered, "Uh . . . I need . . . that is . . . I'd like . . ."

Shirley glanced at Lauren and then back at Mason, a slow grin curling up the corners of her mouth. "Oh . . . I see. Well," she said, taking off her lab apron, "I think I'll go brew up some fresh coffee for the troops."

She grinned again and glanced at her wristwatch. "I'll probably also make some chocolate chip cookies so it'll probably take me a good fifteen or twenty minutes, if you'd like to keep Lauren company until I get back."

Mason nodded, returning the smile. "I think I can spare a few minutes for such an agreeable task."

As Shirley squeezed by him in the doorway, she whispered, "Go get 'em, tiger."

Lauren crossed her arms across her chest and leaned back against the counter, looking at him from under raised eyebrows. "Did you need to see me about something, Dr. Williams?"

He walked over to her and put his hands on her shoulders, moving into her personal space. "Yeah, I need to remind you of something."

"What?" she asked quizzically.

"This," he said, and he bent his head down and covered her lips with his.

Hesitantly at first, and then with more vigor, she put her arms around him and pulled him to her, feeling the hardness between them as she pressed against him.

After a moment, she broke free and leaned back, staring into his eyes. "Oh, that," she said, smiling. "And you thought you needed to remind me because . . . what . . . you thought I'd forgotten?"

"No," he said, bending to kiss the side of her neck, "because I wanted more of the same."

She shuddered at his touch and then she took a deep breath and pushed him away. "Mason, as much as I'd like to keep doing this for the rest of the day, this is neither the time nor the place for kissy-face. We've got serious, life-saving work to do."

His face reddened and he nodded. "Yes, of course you're right." He turned to go, but he stopped in the door-way and pointed at her, "But as soon as we've gotten the cure, you and I are going to have a long, serious talk."

"What about?" she asked coquettishly.

"About the future," he said, and then he was gone.

Ten minutes later, when Shirley returned, Lauren was still flushed.

Shirley grinned. "The man does have quite an impact, doesn't he?"

"Man, you can say that again."

Shirley sighed. "Yeah, I've worked with him since he was a pup, and frankly, if I was a dozen years younger, I'd be giving you a run for your money for him."

"Wow, does everyone love him?"

"I wouldn't say that, but he's the kinda guy that men want to be his friend, and women want to either mother him or bed him, depending on their ages."

Lauren laughed. "Can you guess which one it is with me?"

Shirley joined in. "The answer to that, my dear, is perfectly obvious."

* * *

It took the team the better part of two weeks to come up with an answer to the anthrax plague. Shirley Cole had noticed some anomalies in the electron microscope images of the roots of a particular plant with a yellow flower, species unknown. She took the images to Lionel Johnson, the team specialist in fungi and mycobacteria, and asked his opinion.

After some digging and some complex chemical analysis, Lionel came up with the answer. "Shirley, I'm damned if this chemical structure doesn't resemble tigecycline."

"Tigecycline? You mean the latest generation of tetracycline?"

He nodded, still examining the complex chemical structure they'd mapped out.

"But that doesn't occur naturally," Shirley said. "It's made by tweaking the original tetracycline molecules."

He sighed. "I didn't say it was exactly the same, Shirley. I merely said it was similar."

She shook her head. "Well, no matter. Tigecycline only works on cutaneous anthrax, so even if this is similar, it probably won't do us any good."

He shrugged. "Hey, you never know until you try. Remember, this plague isn't being caused by typical anthrax but a mutated form. Just maybe a mutated form of tigecycline will work on it."

"You're dreaming, pal, but what the hell. I'll throw some of it on the cultures in the lab and see what happens."

What happened was the drug distilled from the yellow-flowered plant killed the anthrax bacterial colonies at an amazing rate.

When they showed Mason the results, he got on the sat-phone and discussed the discovery with Dr. Battersee. Less than four days later the drug was being manufactured in quantity and within two weeks was being shipped to every country in the world.

Additional good news came less than a month later when the scientists at the CDC were able to concoct a preventative vaccine from the blood samples of the villagers that Mason and Lauren had brought out of the jungle.

With the twin discoveries, the worst plague in the history of the world was essentially over.

Their work accomplished, the team was in the process of dismantling the Bio-Lab when Mason was finally able to break away from his administrative duties long enough to find Lauren and hustle her outside for a private conversation.

As they strolled through the jungle adjacent to the lab, he took her hand in his.

"So," he began, "about that talk we need to have about our future . . ."

Lauren took a deep breath and glanced over at him. "I'm afraid a future for us is going to be problematic."

He stopped walking and turned to her. "What do you mean . . . problematic?"

She stepped to the side of the path and sat on a boulder. "Well, you have your work in Atlanta—work that takes you all over the world for weeks at a time—and I have my work in Austin, Texas, that frequently takes me to remote areas of the world for weeks at a time."

She smiled sadly and spread her arms. "Just how do you propose we reconcile those two disparate lifestyles?"

He frowned. "I don't know, but there's got to be a way. Maybe you could move to Atlanta. Emory University has a great archaeology department."

She raised her eyebrows. "Yeah, and maybe you could

move to Austin. The University of Texas has a great communicable disease department."

"But . . . that's different."

She wagged her head. "No, Mason, no it isn't."

"Well, then we can take turns flying back and forth for visits."

She shrugged. "We could, but we both know long-distance relationships never work. Not that I would mind a few lust-filled weekend encounters, but we shouldn't fool ourselves into thinking it could ever be anything more."

"Dammit, Lauren. You're just being too damned logical."

She smiled. "Sorry, it's just the scientist in me, I'm afraid."

He grabbed her and pulled her to her feet, kissing her as if he'd never get another chance. As he pulled back he looked into her eyes and said, "Believe me when I tell you that I'm going to find some way for us to be together."

She leaned her head on his shoulder. "Believe me when I tell you that I hope you do."

Chapter 44

Two months later, Lauren was busy overseeing a team of twenty undergraduate and graduate students as they pored over the hundreds of specimens in Montezuma's tomb and the surrounding area.

Guatemotzi, whom Lauren had hired as a native guide and all-around assistant, came up to her holding out a small, jewel-encrusted dagger.

Her eyes widened as she took the dagger from him. "Oh my God, Motzi, where did you find this?"

He grinned, his teeth white against the dark cocoa color of his face. "Motzi find it next to big, flat rock over there," he said, pointing toward an area of the nearby jungle that hadn't been explored yet.

"Jesus," she exclaimed. "That might be a sacrificial rock where the Aztecs cut the hearts out of their enemies, and this might be one of the ceremonial daggers they used."

She grabbed the small boy and squeezed him tight in a hug. "Motzi, you just might have made the biggest discovery of the site."

As she stepped back from him, she heard a distant

whup-whup and glanced up to see a helicopter weaving its way toward them from the direction of Mexico City, tropical sun glinting sharply off the Plexiglas windshield.

"Huh, I wonder what that chopper is doing coming here today? We're not due for supplies for another week," she said.

Motzi shrugged, as if to say such things were beyond his pay grade.

She handed him the dagger, told him to take it to the tent holding the specimens, and to be sure to document when and where he found it for their records, and then she walked down the path toward the helicopter landing area in the jungle.

By the time she got there, the helicopter had landed and though the rotor blades were slowing, the air was filled with a dense cloud of dust.

Out of the cloud walked a man wearing a snap-brimmed hat that she swore she'd seen in the Indiana Jones movies.

As he drew nearer, the man looked up, and she saw that it was Dr. Mason Williams grinning at her from under the brim.

"Oh, Mason," she cried and she ran into his arms and held him as tight as she could.

After a moment, he leaned down and kissed her until she finally had to come up for breath.

"What are you doing here?" she asked as he put his arm around her and led her back down the path toward her dig site.

He smiled and gave her a wink. "It seems there's a significant outbreak of dengue fever in the jungle around here," he said. "And I convinced the CDC that an expedition was necessary to see if we could get it under control before it spread all the way to Mexico City."

She stopped and turned to face him, grinning widely. "Then . . . then you're going to be here for a while?"

"Several weeks at least. We'll be setting up the Bio-Lab in the same spot we did last time we were here."

"You mean the same Bio-Lab with air-conditioning and Shirley's famous cookies and muffins and cakes and the glorious hot showers?"

He nodded. "And it's the same Bio-Lab with the private quarters for the leader of the team, which just happens to be me."

"Well, then, come on down and I'll show you my camp. We have a dozen tents for the students and one slightly larger tent for the leader of the expedition, which just happens to be me."

She hesitated, and then she added, "Of course, it doesn't have air-conditioning or hot showers, or any privacy whatsoever, but it is my home away from home."

As they neared the camp, she pursed her lips and looked at him with raised eyebrows. "Just how serious is this dengue fever outbreak, anyway?"

He shrugged. "Not very, but when I found out from your dean that you were down here for a couple of months, I called in some chips and arranged for an in-depth study of the outbreak."

She narrowed her eyes, "Why do I feel you're going to spend the entire time trying to convince me to move to Atlanta?"

"Well, not the entire time," he said with a lascivious smirk. "I plan to spend a significant amount of time making love to you, too."

"Good," she said, with a flip of her head as she turned toward her tent. " 'Cause that'll give me a lot of time to talk you into moving to Austin. You won't believe what goes on down on Sixth Street."

As she took his hand and led him toward her camp, she looked back over her shoulder, "And I warn you, Mason, I can be very persuasive when I put my mind to it."

He sighed and shook his head. "It's not your mind I'm worried about."

As he followed her down the path, he patted his breast pocket that contained his brand-new Texas driver's license and his faculty card showing he was now a professor of Communicable Diseases at the University of Texas Institute of Health Sciences in Austin, Texas.

His life without her for the past two months had been miserable and so he'd flown to Austin and interviewed for the position he now held. The dean had been tickled to death to have someone with his practical field experience agree to come teach at the medical school as soon as his present assignment for the CDC was over.

As he watched Lauren's ponytail bobbing in front of him down the path, he planned to give her a few days of trying to convince him to move to Texas before he revealed the truth to her that he already had.

This was going to be fun.